OTHER ...

Jamison Valley Series

The Coppersmith Farmhouse

The Clover Chapel

The Lucky Heart

The Outpost

The Bitterroot Inn

The Candle Palace

Maysen Jar Series

The Birthday List

Letters to Molly

Lark Cove Series

Tattered

Timid

Tragic

Tinsel

Clifton Forge Series

Steel King

Riven Knight

Stone Princess

Noble Prince

Fallen Jester

Tin Queen

Runaway Series

Runaway Road

Wild Highway

Quarter Miles

Forsaken Trail

Dotted Lines

The Edens Series

Christmas in Quincy - Prequel

Indigo Ridge

Juniper Hill

Garnet Flats

Standalones

Rifts and Refrains

A Little Too Wild

CONTENTS

PROLOGUE

"Poppy!" Jamie came rushing out of the office and into the kitchen.

The grin on his face made my heart flutter, just like it always did, which meant I'd been a mess of flutters since the day I'd met him five years ago.

We'd run into each other on the first day of our sophomore year at Montana State. Literally. I'd been rushing out of an economics lecture, my arms overloaded with books, notepads and a syllabus. Jamie had been rushing in, too busy looking over his shoulder at a buxom blond to see me in the classroom's doorway.

After the two of us had recovered from the crash, Jamie had helped me off the floor. The moment my hand had slipped into his, the buxom blond had been all but forgotten.

That was the day I'd met the man of my dreams.

My husband.

James Sawyer Maysen.

"Guess what?"

"What?" I giggled when he picked me up and set me on the

1

counter, fitting himself between my open legs. Excitement radiated from his body and I couldn't help but smile at the light shining in his eyes.

"I just added a couple things to my birthday list." He pumped his fist. "Best ideas yet."

"Oh." My smile faltered. "Please tell me these ones aren't illegal."

"Nope. And I told you, the fire alarm one might not be illegal. I might *legitimately* need to pull a fire alarm before I turn forty-five."

"You'd better hope so. I have no desire to bail you out of jail just because you're determined to mark an item off your crazy list."

Jamie's "birthday list" had become his latest obsession. He'd started it a couple of weeks ago after he'd gotten the idea from a sitcom, and ever since, he'd been dreaming up these grand ideas —though some were more ridiculous than grand.

This list was Jamie's version of a bucket list. Except, rather than one long list to work through in retirement, Jamie had been assigning himself things to do before each of his birthdays. He didn't want to tackle some daunting list when he had all but lived his life. Instead, he wanted to tick things off the list every year before his birthday. So far, he'd filled in nearly every birthday until he turned fifty.

We had our own "couples" bucket list—places we wanted to travel and things we wanted to do together. This birthday list wasn't for that. It was just for Jamie. It was filled with things *he* wanted to do, just for him.

And though I may have grumbled about some of the riskier and crazier items, I supported it wholeheartedly.

"So what did you add today?"

He grinned. "My best idea yet. Here goes." He raised his arms, drawing them out wide and framing an invisible marquee. "Before I turn thirty-four, I want to swim in a pool of green Jell-O."

"Okay." I smiled, far from convinced it was his best idea yet, but it was Jamie. "But why Jell-O? And why green?"

"Don't you think it would be cool?" He wiggled between my legs, smiling even wider as he dropped his arms. "It's one of those things every kid wants to do but no parent will let them. Think of how fun it would be. I can squirm around in it. Squish it between my fingers and toes. And I picked green—"

"Because it's your favorite color," I finished, surprised I'd even asked the question in the first place.

"What do you think?"

"Honestly? It sounds like a mess. Besides that, Jell-O stains. You'll be a walking alien for a week."

He shrugged. "I'm cool with that. My students will think it's awesome, and I have you to help me clean it up."

"Yes, you do."

I'd help him scrub his skin back to its normal tan and dispose of a pool filled with green Jell-O because I loved him. Some items on Jamie's list seemed strange to me, but if they made him happy, I'd do what I could to help. For the next twenty-five years—or for however long he wanted—I'd be by his side as he crossed things out.

"What else did you add today?"

He slipped his hands around my waist and moved in a little closer. "I actually added one and crossed it off at the same time. It was for my twenty-fifth birthday. I wrote a letter to myself in ten years."

"That's cute." If I had a birthday list, I'd steal that idea for myself. "Can I read the letter?"

"Sure." He grinned. "As soon as I turn thirty-five."

I frowned but Jamie erased it with a soft kiss.

"I need to go run some errands. Do you need anything while I'm out?"

Errands. Riiight. Tomorrow was our one-year wedding anniversary and I'd bet good money his "errands" were to find me a last-minute gift. Unlike me, who had bought his present two months ago and stashed it in the laundry room, Jamie was always shopping on Christmas Eve or the day before my birthday.

But instead of teasing him about his tendency to procrastinate, I just nodded. "Yes, please. Would you mind going to the liquor store for me?" We were hosting a spring barbeque tomorrow to celebrate our anniversary and the only booze we had in the house was Jamie's favorite tequila.

"Babe, I told you. We don't need to have fancy cocktails. Just pick up some beer at the grocery store tomorrow and we'll drink my stuff."

"And, honey, I've told you. Not everyone likes to do tequila shots."

"Sure they do. Tequila shots are a classic party drink."

I rolled my eyes and laughed. "We're not having a frat party tomorrow. We're adults now and can afford some variety. At the very least, we could get some margarita mix."

"Fine," he grumbled. "Do you have a list?"

I nodded, but when I tried to move off the counter, he kept me trapped.

"Can I ask you something?" His eyebrows came together as his grin disappeared.

"Of course."

"We've been married for almost a year. What's your favorite thing about being married to me?"

My hands came up to his face, brushing the blond hair away from where it had fallen into his blue eyes. I didn't even have to think about my answer. "I love that I get to say I'm your wife. It fills me with pride every time. Like whenever we're at your school and parents come up to tell me how much their kids love your class, I'm so proud that I get to call you mine."

The tension in his face washed away.

I wasn't sure where his question had come from, but it was a good one. Especially today, the eve of our anniversary.

Jamie backed away but I grabbed the collar of his shirt and yanked him back into my space. "Hold up. It's your turn. What's your favorite thing about being married to me?"

He smirked. "That you have sex with me every day."

"Jamie!" I swatted his chest as he laughed. "Be serious."

"I am serious. Oh, and I love that you do all the cooking and my laundry. Seriously, babe. Thanks for that."

"Are you kidding me right now?"

He nodded and smiled wider. "I love that I get to be the one to watch you grow more beautiful with each and every day."

My heart fluttered again. "I love you, Jamie Maysen."

"I love you too, Poppy Maysen."

He leaned forward and brushed his lips against mine, teasing me for the briefest moment with his tongue before he stepped back and let me go.

"I'll get your list for the liquor store." I hopped off the counter and got the sticky note I'd made earlier.

"Okay. Be back soon." Jamie tucked the list in his pocket and kissed my hair before he walked out the door.

Three hours later, Jamie still hadn't returned. Every time I called his phone, it rang and rang and rang until his voicemail kicked in. I was doing my best to ignore the knot in my stomach. He was probably just shopping. Any minute, he'd be home and we could go out to dinner. Knowing Jamie, he'd just lost track of time or bumped into a friend and they'd gone out for a beer.

5

He's fine.

An hour later, he still wasn't home. "Jamie," I told his voice-mail. "Where are you? It's getting late and I thought we were going to dinner. Did you lose your phone or something? You need to come home or call me back. I'm getting worried."

I hung up and paced the kitchen. *He's fine. He's fine.*

One hour later, I'd left him five more voicemails and bitten off all my fingernails.

One hour after that, I'd left fifteen voicemails and started calling hospitals.

I was looking up the number for the police department when the doorbell rang. Tossing my phone on the living room couch, I ran toward the door, but my feet stuttered at the sight of a uniform through the door's glass pane.

Oh, god. My stomach rolled. *Please let him be okay.*

I opened the door and stepped out onto the porch. "Officer."

The cop stood tall, his posture perfect, but his green eyes betrayed him. He didn't want to be knocking on my door any more than I wanted him on my porch.

"Ma'am. Are you Poppy Maysen?"

I choked out a yes before the bile rose up in my throat.

The cop's posture slackened an inch. "Mrs. Maysen, I'm afraid I have some bad news. Would you like to go inside and sit down?"

I shook my head. "Is it Jamie?"

He nodded and the pressure in my chest squeezed so tight, I couldn't breathe. My heart was pounding so hard in my chest that my ribs hurt.

"Just . . . just tell me," I whispered.

"Are you here alone? Can I call someone?"

I shook my head again. "Tell me. Please."

He took a deep breath. "I'm sorry to inform you, Mrs. Maysen, but your husband was killed earlier today."

Jamie wasn't fine.

The cop kept talking but his words were drowned out by the sound of my shattering heart.

I don't remember much else from that night. I remember my brother coming over. I remember him calling Jamie's parents to tell them that their son was no longer in this world— that he had been killed in a robbery at a liquor store.

I remember wishing that I were dead too.

And I remember that cop sitting by my side the entire time.

CHAPTER ONE

30TH BIRTHDAY: BUY POPPY HER RESTAURANT

POPPY

Five years later . . .

"Are you ready for this?" Molly asked.

I looked around the open room and smiled. "Yeah. I think so."

My restaurant, The Maysen Jar, was opening tomorrow.

The dream I'd had since I was a kid—the dream Jamie had shared with me—was actually coming true.

Once an old mechanic's garage, The Maysen Jar was now Bozeman, Montana's newest café. I'd taken a run-down, abandoned building and turned it into my future.

Gone were the cement floors spotted with oil. In their place was a hickory herringbone wood floor. The dingy garage doors had been replaced. Now visitors would pull up to a row of floor-to-ceiling black-paned windows. And decades of gunk, grime and grease had been scrubbed away. The original red brick walls had been cleaned to their former glory, and the tall, industrial ceilings had been painted a fresh white.

Good-bye, sockets and wrenches. Hello, spoons and forks.

"I was thinking." Molly straightened the menu cards for the fourth time. "We should probably call the radio station and see if they'd do a spotlight or something to announce that you're open. We've got that ad in the paper but radio might be good too."

I rearranged the jar of pens by the register. "Okay. I'll call them tomorrow."

We were standing shoulder to shoulder behind the counter at the back of the room. Both of us were fidgeting—touching things that didn't need to be touched and organizing things that had been organized plenty—until I admitted what we were both thinking. "I'm nervous."

Molly's hand slid across the counter and took mine. "You'll be great. This place is a dream, and I'll be here with you every step of the way."

I leaned my shoulder into hers. "Thanks. For everything. For helping me get this going. For agreeing to be my manager. I wouldn't have come this far without you."

"Yes, you would have, but I'm glad to be a part of this." She squeezed my hand before letting go and running her fingers across the black marble counter. "I was—"

The front door opened and an elderly man with a cane came shuffling inside. He paused inside the doorway, his gaze running over the black tables and chairs that filled the open space, until he saw Molly and me at the back of the room.

"Hello," I called. "Can I help you?"

He slipped off his gray driving cap and tucked it under his arm. "Just looking."

"I'm sorry, sir," Molly said, "but we don't open for business until tomorrow."

He ignored Molly and started shuffling down the center aisle. My restaurant wasn't huge. The garage itself had only been two stalls, and to cross from the front door to the counter took me exactly seventeen steps. This man made the trip seem like he was crossing the Sahara. Every step was small and he stopped repeatedly to look around. But eventually, he reached the counter and took a wooden stool across from Molly.

When her wide, brown eyes met mine, I just shrugged. I'd poured everything I had into this restaurant—heart and soul and wallet—and I couldn't afford to turn away potential customers, even if we hadn't opened for business yet.

"What can I do for you, sir?"

He reached past Molly, grabbing a menu card from her stack and rifling the entire bunch as he slid it over.

I stifled a laugh at Molly's frown. She wanted to fix those cards so badly her fingers were itching, but she held back, deciding to leave instead. "I think I'll go finish up in the back."

"Okay."

She turned and disappeared through the swinging door into the kitchen. When it swung closed behind her, I focused on the man memorizing my menu.

"Jars?" he asked.

I grinned. "Yes, jars. Most everything here is made in mason jars." Other than some sandwiches and breakfast pastries, I'd compiled a menu centered around mason jars.

It had actually been Jamie's idea to use jars. Not long after we'd gotten married, I'd been experimenting with recipes. Though it had always been my dream to open a restaurant, I'd never known exactly what I wanted to try. That was, until one night when I'd been experimenting with ideas I'd found on Pinterest. I'd made these dainty apple pies in tiny jars and Jamie had gone crazy over them. We'd spent the rest of the night brainstorming ideas for a jar-themed restaurant.

Jamie, you'd be so proud to see this place. An all-too-familiar sting hit my nose but I rubbed it away, focusing on my first customer instead of dwelling on the past.

"Would you like to try something?"

He didn't answer. He just set down the menu and stared, inspecting the chalkboard and display racks at my back. "You spelled it wrong."

"Actually, my last name is Maysen, spelled the same way as the restaurant."

"Huh," he muttered, clearly not as impressed with my cleverness.

"We don't open until tomorrow, but how about a sample? On the house?"

He shrugged.

Not letting his lack of enthusiasm and overall grouchy demeanor pull me down, I walked to the refrigerated display case next to the register and picked Jamie's favorite. I popped it in the toaster oven and then set out a spoon and napkin in front of the man while he kept scrutinizing the space.

Ignoring the frown on his face, I waited for the oven and let my eyes wander. As they did, my chest swelled with pride. Just this morning, I'd applied the finishing touches. I'd hung the last of the artwork and put a fresh flower on each table. It was hard to believe this was the same garage I'd walked into a year ago. That I'd finally been able to wipe out the smell of gasoline in exchange for sugar and spice.

No matter what happened with The Maysen Jar—whether it failed miserably or succeeded beyond my wildest dreams—I would always be proud of what I'd accomplished here.

Proud and grateful.

It had taken me almost four years to crawl out from underneath the weight of Jamie's death. Four years for the black fog of grief and loss to fade to gray. The Maysen Jar had given me a purpose this past year. Here, I wasn't just a twenty-nine-year-old widow struggling to make it through each day. Here, I was a business owner and entrepreneur. I was in control of my life and my own destiny.

The oven's chime snapped me out of my reverie. I pulled on a mitt and slid out the small jar, letting the smell of apples and butter and cinnamon waft to my nose. Then I went to the freezer, getting out my favorite vanilla-bean ice cream and placing a dollop atop the pie's lattice crust. Wrapping the hot jar in a black cloth napkin, I slid the pie in front of the grumpy old man.

"Enjoy." I held back a smug smile. Once he dug into that pie, I'd win him over.

He eyed it for a long minute, leaning around to inspect all sides of the dish before picking up his spoon. But with that first bite, an involuntary hum of pleasure escaped from his throat.

"I heard that," I teased.

He grumbled something under his breath before taking another steaming bite. Then another. The pie didn't last long; he devoured it while I pretended to clean.

"Thanks," he said quietly.

"You're welcome." I took his empty dishes and set them in a plastic bussing tub. "Would you like to take one to go? Maybe have it after dinner?"

He shrugged.

I took that as a yes and prepared a to-go bag with a blueberry crumble instead of the apple pie. Tucking a menu card and reheating instructions inside, I set the brown craft bag next to him on the counter.

"How much?" He reached for his wallet.

I waved him off. "It's on the house. A gift from me to you as my first customer, Mister . . ."

"James. Randall James."

I tensed at the name—just like I always did when I heard

Jamie or a similar version—but let it roll off, glad things were improving. Five years ago, I would have burst into tears. Now, the bite was manageable.

Randall opened the bag and looked inside. "You send to-go stuff in a jar?"

"Yes, the jar goes too. If you bring it back, I give you a discount on your next purchase."

He closed the bag and muttered, "Huh."

We stared at each other in silence for a few beats, every ticking second getting more and more awkward, but I didn't break my smile.

"Are you from here?" he finally asked.

"I've lived in Bozeman since college, but no, I grew up in Alaska."

"Do they have these fancy *jar* restaurants up north?"

I laughed. "Not that I know of, but I haven't been home in a while."

"Huh."

Huh. I made a mental note never to answer questions with "huh" ever again. Up until I'd met Randall James, I'd never realized just how annoying it was.

The silence between us returned. Molly was banging around in the kitchen, probably unloading the clean dishes from the dishwasher, but as much as I wanted to be in there to help, I couldn't leave Randall out here alone.

I glanced at my watch. I had plans tonight and needed to get the breakfast quiches prepped before I left. Standing here while Randall pondered my restaurant was not something I'd figured into my plans.

"I, um—"

"I built this place."

His interruption surprised me. "The garage?"

14

He nodded. "Worked for the construction company that built it back in the sixties."

Now his inspection made sense. "What do you think?"

I normally didn't care much for the opinions of others—especially from a crotchety stranger—but for some reason, I wanted Randall's approval. He was the first person to enter this place who wasn't a family member or a part of my construction crew. A favorable opinion from an outsider would give my spirits a boost as I went into opening day.

But my spirits fell when, without a word, Randall pulled on his cap and slid off the stool. He looped the takeout bag over one wrist while grabbing his cane with his other hand. Then he began his slow journey toward the door.

Maybe my apple pie wasn't as magical as Jamie had thought.

When Randall paused at the door, I perked up, waiting for any sign that he'd enjoyed his time here.

He looked over his shoulder and winked. "Good luck, Ms. Maysen."

"Thank you, Mr. James." I kept my arms pinned at my sides until he turned back around and pushed through the door. As soon as he was out of sight, I threw my arms in the air, mouthing, *Yes!*

I wasn't sure if I'd ever see Randall James again, but I was taking his parting farewell as the blessing I'd been craving.

This was going to work. The Maysen Jar was going to be a success.

I could feel it down to my bones.

Not thirty seconds after Randall disappeared down the sidewalk, the door flew open again. This time, a little girl barreled down the center aisle. "Auntie Poppy!"

I hurried around the counter and knelt, ready for impact. "Kali bug! Where's my hug?"

DEVNEY PERRY

Kali, my four-year-old niece, giggled. Her pink summer dress swished behind her as she raced toward me. Her brown curls—curls that matched Molly's—bounced down her shoulders as she flew into my arms. I kissed her cheek and tickled her sides but quickly let her go, knowing she wasn't here for me.

"Where's Mommy?"

I nodded toward the back. "In the kitchen."

"Mommy!" she yelled as she ran in search of Molly.

I stood just as the door jingled again and my brother, Finn, stepped inside with two-year-old Max in his arms.

"Hi." He crossed the room and tucked me into his side for a hug. "How are you?"

"Good." I squeezed his waist, then stood on my tiptoes to kiss my nephew's cheek. "How are you?"

"Fine."

Finn was far from fine but I didn't comment. "Do you want something to drink? I'll make you your favorite caramel latte."

"Sure." He nodded and set down Max when Molly and Kali came out of the kitchen.

"Mama!" Max's entire face lit up as he toddled toward his mother.

"Max!" She scooped him up, kissing his chubby cheeks and hugging him tight. "Oh, I missed you, sweetheart. Did you have a fun time at Daddy's?"

Max just hugged her back while Kali clung to her leg.

Finn and Molly's divorce had been rough on the kids. Seeing their parents miserable and splitting time between homes had taken its toll.

"Hi, Finn. How are you?" Molly's voice was full of hope that he'd give her just a little something nice.

"Fine," he clipped.

The smile on her face fell when he refused to look at her but she recovered fast, focusing on her kids. "Let's go grab my stuff from the office and then we can go home and play before dinner."

I waved. "See you tomorrow."

She nodded and gave me her biggest smile. "I can't wait. This is going to be wonderful, Poppy. I just know it."

"Thanks." I smiled good-bye to my best friend and ex-sister-in-law.

Molly looked back at Finn, waiting for him to acknowledge her, but he didn't. He kissed his children good-bye and then turned his back on his ex-wife, taking the stool Randall had vacated.

"Bye, Finn," Molly whispered, then led the kids back through the kitchen to the small office.

The minute we heard the back door close, Finn groaned and rubbed his hands over his face. "This fucking sucks."

"Sorry." I patted his arm and then went behind the counter to make his coffee.

The divorce was only four months old and both were struggling to adjust to the new normal of different houses, custody schedules and awkward encounters. The worst part of it all was that they still loved each other. Molly was doing everything she could to get just a fraction of Finn's forgiveness. Finn was doing everything he could to make her pay.

And as Molly's best friend and Finn's sister, I was caught in between, attempting to give them both equal love and support.

"Is everything set for tomorrow?" Finn propped his elbows on the counter and watched me make his latte.

"Yes. I need to do a couple of things for the breakfast menu, but then I'm all set."

"Want to grab dinner with me tonight? I can wait around for you to finish up."

My shoulders stiffened and I didn't turn away from the espresso drip. "Um, I actually have plans tonight."

"Plans? What plans?"

The surprise in his voice wasn't a shock. In the five years since Jamie had died, I'd rarely made plans that hadn't included him or Molly. I'd all but lost touch with the friends Jamie and I'd had from college. The only girlfriend I still talked to was Molly. And the closest I'd come to making a *new* friend lately had been my conversation earlier with Randall.

Finn was probably excited, thinking I was doing something social and branching out, which wasn't entirely untrue. But my brother wasn't going to like the plans I'd made.

"I'm going to a karate class," I blurted and started steaming his milk. I could feel his frown on my back, and sure enough, it was still there when I delivered his finished latte.

"Poppy, no. I thought we talked about giving up this list thing."

"We talked about it, but I don't remember agreeing with you."

Finn thought my desire to complete Jamie's birthday list was unhealthy.

I thought it was necessary.

Because maybe if I finished Jamie's list, I could find a way to let him go.

Finn huffed and dove right into our usual argument. "It could take you years to get through that list."

"So what if it does?"

"Finishing his list isn't going to bring him back. It's just your way of holding on to the past. You're never going to move on if you can't let him go. He's gone, Poppy."

"I know he's gone," I snapped, the threat of tears burning my throat. "I'm well aware that Jamie isn't coming back, but this is my choice. I want to finish his list and the least you can do is be supportive. Besides, you're one to talk about moving on."

"That's different," he countered.

"Is it?"

We went into a stare-down, my chest heaving as I refused to blink.

Finn broke first and slumped forward. "I'm sorry. I just want you to be happy."

I stepped to the counter and placed my hand on top of his. "I know, but please, try and understand why I need to do this."

He shook his head. "I don't get it. I don't know why you'd put yourself through all that. But you're my sister and I love you, so I'll try."

"Thank you." I squeezed his hand. "I want you to be happy too. Maybe instead of dinner with me, you should go to Molly's? You could try and talk after the kids go to bed."

He shook his head, a lock of his rust-colored hair falling out of place as he spoke to the countertop. "I love her. I always will, but I can't forgive what she did. I just . . . can't."

I wished he'd try harder. I hated to see my brother so heart-broken. Molly too. I'd jump at the chance to get Jamie back, no matter what mistakes he might have made.

"So, karate?" Finn asked, changing subjects. He might disapprove of my choice to finish Jamie's list, but he'd rather talk about it than his failed marriage.

"Karate. I made an appointment to try a class tonight." It was probably a mistake, doing strenuous physical exercise the night before the grand opening, but I wanted to get it done before the restaurant opened and I got too busy—or chickened out.

"Then, I guess, tomorrow you'll get to cross two things off the list. Opening this restaurant and going to a karate class."

"Actually." I held up a finger, then went to the register for my purse. I pulled out my oversized bag and rifled around until my fingers hit Jamie's leather journal. "I'm going to cross off the restaurant one today."

I hadn't completed many items on Jamie's list, but every time I did, waterworks followed. The restaurant's opening tomorrow was going to be one of my proudest moments and I didn't want it flooded with tears.

"Would you do it with me?" I asked.

He smiled. "You know I'll always be here for whatever you need."

I knew.

Finn had held me together these last five years. Without him, I don't think I would have survived Jamie's death.

"Okay." I sucked in a shaky breath, then grabbed a pen from the jar by the register. Flipping to the thirtieth-birthday page, I carefully checked the little box in the upper right corner.

Jamie had given each birthday a page in the journal. He'd wanted some space to make notes about his experience or tape in pictures. He'd never get to fill in these pages, and even though I was doing his list, I couldn't bring myself to do it either. So after I finished one of his items, I simply checked the box and ignored the lines that would always remain empty.

As expected, the moment I closed the journal, a sob escaped. Before the first tear fell, Finn had rounded the corner and pulled me into his arms.

I miss you, Jamie. I missed him so much it hurt. It wasn't fair that he couldn't do his own list. It wasn't fair that his life had been cut short because I'd asked him to run a stupid errand. It wasn't fair that the person responsible for his death was still living free.

It wasn't fair.

The flood of emotion consumed me and I let it all go into my brother's navy shirt.

"Please, Poppy," Finn whispered into my hair. "Please think about stopping this list thing. I hate that it makes you cry."

I sniffled and wiped my eyes, fighting with all my strength to stop crying. "I have to," I hiccupped. "I have to do this. Even if it takes me years."

Finn didn't reply; he just squeezed me tighter.

We hugged each other for a few minutes until I got myself together and stepped back. Not wanting to see the empathy in his eyes, I looked around the restaurant. The restaurant I'd only been able to buy because of Jamie's life insurance money.

"Do you think he'd have liked it?"

Finn threw his arm over my shoulders. "He'd have loved it. And he'd be so proud of you."

"This was the one item on his list that wasn't just for him."

"I think you're wrong about that. I think this *was* for him. Making your dreams come true was Jamie's greatest joy."

I smiled. Finn was right. Jamie would have been so excited about this place. Yes, it was my dream, but it would have been his too.

Wiping my eyes one last time, I put the journal away. "I'd better get my stuff done so I can get to that class."

"Call me afterward if you need to. I'll just be home. Alone."

"Like I said, you could always go eat dinner with your family." He shot me a glare and I held up my hands. "Just an idea."

Finn kissed my cheek and took another long drink of his coffee. "I'm going to go."

"But you're coming by tomorrow?"

"I wouldn't miss it for the world. Proud of you, sis."

I was proud of me too. "Thanks."

We walked together to the door, then I locked it behind him before rushing back to the kitchen. I dove into my cooking, making a tray of quiches that would sit overnight in the refrigerator and bake fresh in the morning. When my watch dinged the minute after I'd slid the tray into the fridge, I took a deep breath.

Karate.

I was going to karate tonight. I had no desire to try martial arts, but I would. For Jamie.

So I hurried to the bathroom, trading my jeans and white top for black leggings and a maroon sports tank. I tied my long red hair into a ponytail that hung past my sports bra before stepping into my charcoal tennis shoes and heading out the back.

It didn't take me long to drive my green sedan to the karate school. Bozeman was the fastest-growing town in Montana and it had changed a lot since I'd moved here for college, but it still didn't take more than twenty minutes to get from one end to the other—especially in June, when college was out for the summer.

By the time I parked in the lot, my stomach was in a knot. With shaking hands, I got out of my car and went inside the gray brick building.

"Hi!" A blond teenager greeted me from behind the reception counter. She couldn't have been more than sixteen and she had a black belt tied around her white uniform.

"Hi," I breathed.

"Are you here to try a class?"

I nodded and found my voice. "Yes, I called earlier this week. I can't remember who I talked to but he told me I could just come over tonight and give it a shot."

"Awesome! Let me get you a waiver. One sec." She disappeared into the office behind the reception counter.

I took the free moment to look around. Trophies filled the shelves behind the counter. Framed certificates written in both English and Japanese hung on the walls in neat columns.

Pictures of happy students were scattered around the rest of the lobby.

Past the reception area was a wide platform filled with parents sitting on folding chairs. Proud moms and dads were facing a long glass window that overlooked a classroom of kids. Beyond the glass, little ones in white uniforms and yellow belts were practicing punches and kicks—some more coordinated than others but all quite adorable.

"Here you go." The blond teenager returned with a small stack of papers and a pen.

"Thanks." I got to work, filling out my name and signing the necessary waivers, then handed them back. "Do I need to, um, change?" I glanced down at my gym clothes, feeling out of place next to all the white uniforms.

"You're fine for tonight. You can just wear that, and if you decide to sign up for more classes, we can get you a gi." She tugged on the lapel of her uniform. "Let me give you a quick tour."

I took a deep breath, smiling at some of the parents as they turned and noticed me. Then I met the girl on the other side of the reception counter and followed her through an archway to a waiting room. She walked straight past the open area and directly through the door marked *Ladies*.

"You can use any of the hooks and hangers. We don't wear shoes in the dojo, so you can leave those in a cubby with your keys. There aren't any lockers, as you can see," she laughed, "but no one will steal anything from you. Not here."

"Okay." I toed off my shoes and put them in a free cubby with my car keys.

Damn it. I should have painted my toenails. The red I'd chosen weeks ago was now chipped and dull.

"I'm Olivia, by the way." She leaned closer to whisper. "When we're in here, you can just call me Olivia, but when we're in the waiting area or dojo, you should always call me Olivia Sensei."

"Got it. Thanks."

"It'll just be a few more minutes until the kids' class is done." Olivia led me back out to a waiting area. "You can just hang out here and then we'll get started."

"Okay. Thank you again."

She smiled and disappeared back to the reception area.

I stood quietly in the waiting room, trying to blend into the white walls as I peeked into the dojo.

The class was over and the kids were all lining up to bow to their teachers. *Senseis.* One little boy was wiggling his toes on the blue mats covering the floor. Two little girls were whispering and giggling. An instructor called for attention and the kids' backs all snapped straight. Then they bent at the waist, bowing to the senseis and a row of mirrors spanning the back of the room.

The room erupted in laughter and cheers as the kids were dismissed from their line and funneled out the door. Most passed me without a glance as they went to find their parents or change in the locker rooms.

My nerves spiked as the kids cleared the exercise room, knowing it was almost time for me to go in there. Other adult students were coming in and out of the locker rooms, and I was now even more aware that I would be the only person tonight not wearing white.

I hated being new. Some people enjoyed the rush of the first day of school or a new job, but not me. I didn't like the nervous energy in my fingers. And I really didn't want to make a fool of myself tonight.

Just don't fall on your face.

That was one of two goals for tonight: survive, and stay upright.

I smiled at another female student as she emerged from the locker room. She waved but joined a group of men huddled on the opposite wall.

Not wanting to eavesdrop on the adults, I studied the children as they buzzed around until a commotion sounded in the lobby.

Determined not to show fear to whoever came my way, I forced the corners of my mouth up. They fell when a man stepped into the waiting area.

A man I hadn't seen in five years, one month and three days appeared in the room.

The cop who'd told me my husband had been murdered.

CHAPTER TWO

26TH BIRTHDAY: TAKE A KARATE CLASS

COLE

P*oppy Maysen.*
Holy fuck.

Poppy Maysen was standing in my dojo.

"Hi, Sensei."

"Hey," I replied automatically, turning from Poppy to acknowledge a student as he walked past.

It didn't take long for my gaze to wander back to Poppy. She was standing frozen against the wall, staring at me like she'd seen a ghost.

How long had it been? Five years? The last time I'd seen her, she'd been asleep on her living room couch, trembling from the nightmare I'd delivered to her doorstep.

And now she was here, dressed in gym clothes and waiting to take a karate class. To take *my* karate class.

"Hey, Cole." Danny, a teenaged black belt, slapped my arm as he walked by.

I was standing right in the way of people coming and going to the locker rooms, staring at Poppy like a fool. "Hi, Danny."

I tore my eyes away from her again and shuffled aside. When I glanced back over, she hadn't moved.

What was going on in her head? Was she about to bolt? My face had probably triggered an onslaught of bad memories. And me standing here, gawking at her, probably wasn't helping.

Shit. I forced one foot in front of the other, giving her a slight nod as I disappeared into the men's locker room. If she was still in the waiting room by the time I got out, I'd be shocked, but I'd say hello. Maybe a few minutes would give her—and me—a chance to get over the surprise of being in the same room once again.

"Hi, Cole Sensei."

"Hey, boys." I greeted a couple of the younger kids in the dressing room as they tied on their shoes. "Did you learn anything new today?"

The kids started yammering on about the new punches they'd learned in class tonight, though neither could remember the Japanese names. I tuned them out, dropping my duffel bag on a bench and raking a hand through my hair.

Poppy Maysen.

What had she been doing these last five years? What had become of her life? I hadn't kept tabs on her after that awful night, but now I wished I had.

She was just as stunning now as she had been years ago.

Loose waves of long, ginger hair. Skin as flawless and creamy as melted ice cream. For a redhead, Poppy didn't have the typical smattering of freckles—just a few on the bridge of her nose. And those cornflower-blue eyes. Still hauntingly beautiful, just like they'd been on her porch. I'd never forget the moment the fire behind them had smoldered out.

"Bye, Sensei!"

"Bye," I called as the boys walked out the door. Hopefully they hadn't said anything important because I hadn't registered a word they'd said.

Fuck. Poppy Maysen.

I ran into people all the time from the past, but none of them had shocked me this much. And if I didn't get a handle on it, I'd be falling all over myself in class.

Rubbing my hands over my face, I slid the sunglasses out of my collar and tossed them on the bench. Then I zipped open my bag and hurried to change from jeans and a black polo into my white gi. With my black belt tied around my hips, I sucked in another long breath. A few other guys were changing, but I kept my back to them, needing just a minute to get my head on right.

Had she found a way to spark that fire behind her eyes again? I really wanted to find out. That was, if she wasn't already miles away from the dojo, never to return again.

"See you out there." I nodded to the other guys and pushed the locker room door open.

Poppy was still standing in her spot against the wall. Her eyes darted between the people crowded in the waiting area. It was loud as everyone visited before class, and she hadn't noticed me slip out of the locker room. And despite her obvious nerves, she kept a small smile on her stoic face.

Graceful strength.

Poppy had a graceful strength. I'd thought the same all those years ago. I'd never seen a person so devastated, yet collected. She hadn't screamed or cried or lashed out. She'd just . . . kept it together. In all my time with the Bozeman Police Department, I'd never met anyone—cop or civilian—who had handled a trauma like she had.

Poppy hadn't noticed me yet so I took my opening and slid

into the empty wall space at her side. I leaned down and spoke softly. "Hi."

Her face whipped to mine, then she swallowed and blinked. While I'd been in the dressing room, she had apparently steeled herself for our next encounter. "Hello."

Hello. Even her voice affected me. Five years ago, the words she'd spoken had all been full of pain. But now? Her voice was so clear. There was nothing soft or timid about it. Nothing jaded or raspy. It was the purest voice I'd ever heard.

Nonchalantly wiping the sweat from my palm, I held out my hand. "I'm Cole Goodman."

"Poppy Maysen."

I nodded. "I remember."

Poppy's eyes darted to my hand still outstretched between us and back up to my face. Then, slowly, her delicate fingers fit themselves into mine. The minute her soft skin brushed my calloused palm, a zing of electricity traveled up my arm.

While I froze, Poppy's breath hitched.

We stared at each other, still holding hands, and probably looking like crazy people to the other students standing around, but I didn't care. Not when Poppy's hand was still in mine and she hadn't made a move to take it back.

"Cole. Got a sec?" Robert called out from his office.

"Yeah." I kept Poppy's hand for another second before letting it go and walking to the office. I resented every step away from her side.

Robert, my instructor and the owner of the dojo, was sitting at his desk with a pair of reading glasses perched precariously on his nose as he flipped through a stack of messages. His hair had started to thin last year so he'd shocked us all this week by coming to the dojo with a freshly shaven scalp. I'd been taking karate from Robert for nearly two decades, ever since I'd been in high school, and his new look was still throwing me off.

"What's up?" I took the chair in front of his desk.

"Can you take that new gal tonight? She called to try the intro class but I kind of spaced it. I'd teach her but I need to spend some time working with the brown belts tonight to see who might be ready to advance."

"You got it." I hoped it wouldn't be too uncomfortable for her because I wanted some extra time with Poppy, a chance to learn what she'd been up to in the last five years. To see how she'd recovered from that night. Maybe figure out why I'd reacted so strongly to her after only thirty seconds.

"How's work?" Robert asked, taking my thoughts away from Poppy.

"Busy. We kicked off the new drug task force today."

"Good. It's about time."

Overdue, really. As a former cop, Robert knew the drug problem in the area was becoming unmanageable. He'd retired from the county sheriff's department years ago, making karate his full-time job, but the drug trade had been escalating even when he'd been on the force.

"Did that idiot chief of police at least put you in charge of the task force?"

I grinned. "He did."

Robert grinned back. "Maybe your dad's not so stupid after all."

I chuckled. Robert and Dad never missed a chance to jest with one another, even if the other wasn't in the room. Their friendship was the reason I'd started karate at the age of seven— Dad liked to bring me along when he met up with Robert to practice.

"Robert Sensei? Can I—" Olivia came into the office from the lobby but stopped short. "Oh, um, hey, Cole Sensei." She tucked a stray lock of hair behind her ear and studied the floor, trying to hide her red cheeks.

"Whatcha need, Olivia?" Robert asked.

"I'm, uh . . ." She fidgeted for a moment, looking between the floor and the door. When her eyes came back to mine, she spun around and left.

"Jeez," Robert muttered. "Not another one."

I held up my hands. "Hey, it's not my fault."

I couldn't help that Olivia had developed a bit of a crush on me this past year. Her and her seventeen-year-old friends. Not only was it fucking weird—I'd taught some of them since they were little kids—it was pissing Robert off because they'd all huddle in the back of the dojo and giggle.

"You could help me out here." Robert stood from his chair.

"How? Stop coming here?" I couldn't help the face I was born with and I damn sure wasn't going to let my body go just because of some twitterpated teenagers. "I basically ignore them already. Do you want me to be a dick to them and scar them for life?"

"No," he muttered. "At least bring Aly in every once in a while so these girls can see you're taken."

Not happening.

Now wasn't the time to give Robert an update, but Aly wouldn't be at the dojo anytime soon, at least not on my arm.

I stood and followed Robert back into the waiting area. He kept walking into the dojo, bowing in the doorway before he entered, but I stopped in front of Poppy. "We're going to get started."

She nodded and forced a nervous smile. "Sounds good."

"You'll be with me tonight."

Her eyes got a bit wider. "Okay."

Was she scared to be around me or just anxious about the class? Probably both, but I didn't want to make her even more uncomfortable, so I jumped right into teacher mode. "We bow before we enter or leave the dojo."

"Got it." She nodded and pushed off the wall.

I took the lead, demonstrating the proper technique before stepping inside and onto the mats. Poppy followed, maintaining a three-foot distance between us as she took in the space.

"You'll be over there to bow in." I pointed to the back wall. "Just follow the instructions from Robert Sensei. After that, we'll do a workout. Do as much as you can but don't go overboard. Then you and I will work together the rest of the class. Sound okay?"

She nodded but didn't meet my eyes.

"Poppy." Her eyes rose to mine when I whispered her name. "It will be more fun if you just relax."

"I'm not really here for fun, I'm here . . . I'm just out of my comfort zone." As she spoke, she flailed her hands, her wrists spinning in circles.

Poppy Maysen talked with her hands.

And it was the most adorable thing I'd ever seen.

Unable to hide my grin, I stepped into her space, savoring the way her breath caught. She felt the electricity between us just as strongly as I did.

"If it gets to be too much, just give me a signal. Maybe that wrist spin thing you just did." Her eyes narrowed and I smiled wider. "Easy, killer. I'm just teasing you."

She cocked an eyebrow. "Do you tease all of your new students?"

"Maybe." I smiled. "So, what have you—"

"Line up!" Robert called.

Poppy spun around and dashed to the line with the other students, and I joined the instructors up front as class got underway. The entire time, my eyes stayed locked on Poppy. She was doing her best to hide it, but she kept glancing at me too.

That was, until her attention became solely focused on trying to keep up with the workout.

Robert had gone back into the office and picked a younger instructor, Danny, to lead the exercise. The punk had taken it as free rein to torture everyone. I wasn't having a hard time keeping up—hell, I'd barely broken a sweat—but Poppy and everyone else on that side of the room looked miserable.

There was no denying Poppy was fit. In those tight leggings and second-skin tank top, her body left little to the imagination, but a karate workout was a different animal. And Danny was pushing too hard, even for some of the senior students.

"That's enough," I told Danny when he called for another set of fifty push-ups. We'd already done a hundred.

"Having trouble keeping up, Cole Sensei?" The little shit puffed out his chest.

"That's good, everyone," I called, overruling Danny with a pointed stare. "Go ahead and get a drink."

Poppy pushed up from the floor to walk to the water fountain. Her face was flushed and her forehead sweaty, but damn if those pink cheeks didn't make her look even more beautiful. The image of her lying next to me in bed, her cheeks flushed from a different kind of workout, popped into my head.

Fuck.

The last thing I needed was to get a hard-on under my gi. Luckily, the top hung low enough to hide my quick adjustment while everyone was in line for water.

"Now that's an ass worth squeezing," Danny whispered, his eyes glued to Poppy's ass. I wasn't sure if he'd meant to say it out loud, but I saw red. He was right, her ass was spectacular, but he didn't get to say that out loud.

"Watch it, Danny." I clamped my hand on his shoulder and dragged him out of the line. "You went too far with that workout. We don't push that hard when we've got guest students

33

and you know it. I was willing to let that go, but you just crossed the line. You've got suicide drills and pull-ups for the rest of class. If I see you slacking, then we'll stay late and do another workout until you learn the limits. Understood?"

His face paled. "I'm sorry, Sensei."

"We treat women with respect, inside and outside of this dojo. Think it. Don't speak it." I pointed to the far side of the room and loomed to my full six-foot-two height. "Now get to work."

He nodded, his shoulders drooping as he walked away.

After everyone else had taken a drink, I slurped some water from the fountain and then motioned for Poppy to join me in the far corner of the room.

She wiped her brow with the back of her left hand, her wedding rings glinting in the overhead light.

"It's okay for tonight," I pointed to her ring finger, "but next time, you'll want to take those off. Better to leave them in the locker room than jam your finger and have them cut off at the hospital."

"Um . . ." She dropped her hand and inspected the emerald engagement ring and white-gold wedding band. "I haven't taken these off since Jamie . . . you know."

"Oh, uh, right." I guess I didn't need to ask if she'd gotten remarried—not if she was still wearing her late husband's rings. "Well, just think about it for next time. Are you doing okay after the workout?"

"I'm alive and I haven't fallen on my face." She smiled. "That's a win for me tonight."

I chuckled. "Then we'll make sure you get through the next thirty minutes on your feet and call it good."

"I'd like that."

I spent the next few minutes teaching her about her stances

and how to take the proper semicircular steps. When she had that down, I asked her to make a fist.

"Like this?"

"Not quite." I took her hands in mine to adjust her grip, but the moment we touched, I forgot all about karate.

My eyes locked with hers as both of us froze, and the other people in the dojo disappeared. Just like that handshake in the hallway, her touch blocked out the world and sent fire blazing through my veins.

And right to my cock.

I broke away fast, needing a moment to think asexual thoughts before I made things really awkward. "Um . . ." I motioned her forward. "Go ahead and practice a few more steps like I just showed you."

"Sure." Her musical voice didn't help my growing erection.

While she stepped toward the mirrors, I searched my brain for unsexy images and did my best to avoid staring at her slender legs. I stared at Robert's bald head. The sweat drops on the mats. Danny's hairy feet. I rotated through them all and by the time Poppy walked back to my side, the swelling in my boxers was at least manageable.

"Was that okay?"

"You did great. I'm going to go get us some pads." I gave her a wide berth as I walked to the stack of pads on the far wall, but her vanilla scent seemed to follow.

"Get it together," I muttered as I grabbed one large pad and one small.

"What was that, Sensei?" a green belt asked.

"Oh, uh, I said your kata is really coming together."

"Thanks!"

I did my best not to touch Poppy through the rest of class, but even with the pads as a barrier, we brushed every now and then. By the time our thirty minutes were up, I was desperate for a cold shower.

"How'd she do?" Robert asked, joining us before class ended.

"Good." I cleared the block in my throat. "She's a natural."

"Ha," Poppy scoffed. "More like a klutz. I kicked his fingers more than I kicked the pad." Her big blue eyes looked up to me for her hundredth apology. "Sorry."

"Like I said, I'm fine. It didn't hurt a bit."

She turned to Robert and smiled. "Thank you for having me tonight."

"Glad you joined us. Come back anytime."

"I appreciate the offer and letting me try this out, but I don't think karate is for me."

Robert nodded. "Fair enough. It's not for everyone. If you ever change your mind, you're always welcome." He shook hands with Poppy and then called for the entire class to bow out.

Without a word, Poppy scurried to the door, her hair swishing across her back as she disappeared into the locker room.

The sight of her retreating hit me in the gut. She wasn't coming back to the dojo and I didn't want to wait another five years to see her again. So instead of visiting with the other students, I hurried to the lobby and waited for Poppy to come out of the ladies' room.

It didn't take her more than a minute to emerge into the hall with keys in hand and sneakers on her feet. The moment she spotted me, her feet stopped short. "Oh, hi."

"I, um . . . I just wanted to say it was nice to see you."

"Thanks." She took a few steps toward the door.

"Wait," I blurted before she could leave. "Can I see you again? To catch up."

She stopped and turned, a war waging behind her eyes. She didn't want to say yes. She didn't want to say no. "I don't know."

It was honest.

Honest, I could work with.

"Will you at least think about it?"

"All right." She started for the door again, but just before she touched the handle, she paused, speaking over her shoulder. "Thank you for staying with me that night."

Then she was gone before I could even say *you're welcome.*

"Fuck," I grumbled and rubbed my face.

"What was that?" Robert had appeared by my side.

"Oh, nothing. Just a long day. I'd better get changed."

I hustled into the locker room, not wanting to stick around for the chatter tonight, and waved good-bye before heading home.

What I needed was a beer—or three—and some time alone to think.

Something about Poppy was different, and it wasn't just the extreme circumstances we'd met under. No woman had ever stirred my blood like she had tonight, not even Aly.

Aly, whose car was sitting in my driveway, blocking the garage, when I pulled up to my house.

"Damn it. Not tonight." I shook my head, parked my black truck on the street and stepped out just as she was coming through the front door with a box in her arms.

"Hey," Aly said, walking down the steps from the porch.

I crossed the short sidewalk and met her by her car. "Hey."

"Sorry. I was trying to be gone before you got home."

"It's okay. Here, let me help." I reached out and lifted the box from her arms.

"Thanks." She opened the back door of her car and I set the

box inside. When I stood, she was twisting my house key off her chain. "Here you go."

Our fingers brushed when I took it from her hand, but I didn't get even a minor jolt. Touching Aly, the woman I'd dated for two years and lived with for six months, wasn't anything compared to the touch I'd felt earlier with Poppy.

It cemented the decision I'd made last week. Breaking up with Aly hadn't been easy, but it had been right.

"Cole." She stepped closer, looking up at me with pleading eyes. The same eyes that she used whenever she wanted me to fuck her senseless.

"No, Aly." I stepped back. "We both know that would just make this harder."

Her shoulders tensed as she backed away. "Harder for me, you mean? Because you're just fine. One week after we're broken up and you're back to normal. Like the last two years together meant nothing. Meanwhile, I'm living in my sister's guest room, crying myself to sleep every night."

"I'm—"

"Sorry. I know." She slammed the car door closed and spun on her heel as she rounded the hood. She threw open the driver's door but paused, looking at me from over her car. Then she waited.

"Take care of yourself, Aly."

She huffed, then got in the car and backed out of the driveway, wiping tears off her cheeks.

I waited for her car to disappear down the street before going inside. Standing in my living room, I swept my eyes across the furniture. The toss pillows were gone. Aly had taken those, along with the throw blanket she had always used when we were watching TV.

I fucking hated that I'd hurt her. She was a good woman, just not the one for me. After two years, I'd never felt like she was the one. I'd never pictured asking her to marry me. Not once. We'd been on and off for our first year and a half together, but then she'd lost her roommate and moved in with me. Even after six months of Aly telling me she loved me, I'd never felt compelled to say it back.

I made my way to the kitchen for a beer, and as I opened the refrigerator door, my phone rang. I tugged it out of my pocket and pressed it between my cheek and shoulder. "Hi, Mom."

"Hi, sweetie. How are you?"

"I'm good." Or at least I was. The fridge was empty. Aly had taken all of my beer too. *Damn it.* Who took a man's beer? That was just mean. She didn't even drink beer—which I should have taken as a sign.

"I was calling to see if you and Aly could come over for dinner tomorrow. We haven't seen you both in weeks."

"I see Dad almost every day."

"That doesn't count. *I* haven't seen you both in weeks."

I took a deep breath and shut the door to the fridge. Mom was going to be pissed that I'd broken it off with Aly. She'd had her hopes up for a wedding and grandkids. "Mom, listen. Aly and I broke up."

"What?" she gasped. "When?"

"Last week," I muttered and braced.

"Last week!" she shrieked. "Why didn't you call to tell me? Is she okay? Where is she going to live?"

"With her sister until she can find a new place. She's hurt but it was for the best."

"And how are you?"

"Fine, but I feel like an asshole."

"Oh, Cole."

I sighed. "I tried, Mom. I really did. But I just don't . . ."

"You don't love her. I know. It wasn't hard to see."

I abandoned my fridge and pulled out a stool from underneath the island, slumping onto the seat. "I should have ended it earlier. I shouldn't have dragged it out this long and hurt her even more."

"Well," Mom said, "at least you didn't marry her."

"True."

My eyes landed on the laptop by my side and I slid it over. As Mom talked into my ear, my fingers pulled up Google. Then they typed in Poppy's name.

Her Facebook page popped up first. Instead of a profile picture, there was a logo for The Maysen Jar. What was The Maysen Jar? I clicked the picture to read the caption. *Grand opening tomorrow!*

Poppy had a restaurant and it was opening tomorrow?

"Cole!" Mom yelled into the phone.

"Huh? Oh, sorry. What was that?"

"I asked if *you* wanted to come over for dinner tomorrow."

I closed the profile picture and clicked on another Facebook photo. This one was of Poppy standing outside a restaurant. Her hair was swept up in a bun and her arm was looped with a brunette's. She was only five five or five six, but her legs went on for miles in her tight jeans and heels. The photo was stunning, but what really drew me in was her smile.

A smile I wanted to see for myself.

"Cole," Mom huffed.

"Sorry, Mom." I closed the laptop. "I can't make it for dinner tomorrow. I've got plans."

CHAPTER THREE

29TH BIRTHDAY: GO SKYDIVING

POPPY

"I love the name of your restaurant." My customer handed me her credit card.

I smiled and swiped. "Thank you."

"Except she spelled it wrong," Randall grumbled on the other side of the register.

He'd been camped out on "his stool" all afternoon and evening, offering commentary to people as they came to pay their tabs. He'd been talking and eating. Randall had walked in right before the lunch rush and had since eaten two quiches, a spinach salad, a chicken potpie, three apple pies and two peach cobblers.

"Mason," he muttered. "M-a-s-o-n. That's how you spell mason jar."

My customer looked at him, about to come to my rescue, but I just laughed. "Ignore him," I told her as I handed back her card. "He's just grouchy because I cut him off after *five* desserts."

Randall scowled. "Grown man can't even indulge in desserts these days without a lecture."

"You'll thank me later when you aren't in a sugar coma." I shot him my *so there* look and turned back to my customer with a smile. "Thanks for coming in! I hope you enjoyed everything."

"Oh, yes, it was wonderful. You've got a fantastic menu. And so creative." She glared at Randall. "Especially the name. I'll definitely be back."

"Thanks again!" I waved good-bye as she turned to leave.

When the door closed behind her, I surveyed the empty tables in the restaurant. For the first time since seven this morning, they were all vacant.

"Wow." Molly joined me at the register with a wet rag. "That was crazy. I figured we'd be busy, but never *that* busy. We're sold out of everything but one potpie and three salads."

"It's a good thing we're closing in," I glanced at my watch, "twenty-seven minutes."

Not that I'd be going home. I'd be in the kitchen all night making breakfast dishes for the morning and replenishing the dessert cooler.

The late-evening summer sun was starting to set, and the dinner rush had finally subsided. At nearly eight, closing time for my small café was just around the corner, and as much as I didn't want to turn customers away, I was hoping that my now-empty tables would remain that way. I didn't want to have to explain—again—why I had so few options to offer from the menu.

"I need to adjust inventory plans for this week. I felt like a chump telling people we had hardly anything left."

"Don't worry about it." Molly patted my hand. "People understood. You can make some adjustments and everything will be fine."

"Traffic will probably slow down once we're not the new thing anymore, but until then, we should plan for more."

She nodded. "I agree. I've already updated the budget and sales projections."

"You make sure to add a few extra pies to your tally for me." Randall pulled on his cap. "I don't want you running out if I'm here."

Molly rolled her eyes but I just smiled. "Okay, Randall. I'll make sure to save you some desserts."

He slid off his stool and grabbed his cane. "See you girls tomorrow." He gave me a pointed stare. "Don't stay too late."

I crossed my heart. "Promise."

Molly and I waited for him to leave before we both burst out laughing. Yesterday, I'd thought my chances of seeing Randall James again were slim to none. Now, I was thinking he'd be my most frequent customer.

"Today was a good day." Molly grabbed her rag and started wiping down the counter.

"A very good day." With the exception of running low on food, I couldn't imagine the opening having gone any better. Customers had been happy. Jars had been scraped clean. And I had found my rhythm quickly, balancing work in the kitchen and managing the counter with Molly.

And though he was a bit cantankerous, Randall had been a welcome and comforting presence today. Anytime I'd gotten flustered or started to stress, I'd found his eyes waiting for me with a small nod. His silent encouragement had saved me today.

Molly finished wiping the counter and started on the tables. "I'm glad we're bringing in a part-time helper soon. I don't think I can handle six in the morning until after eight at night on a regular basis. I'm dead on my feet."

"Me too." Except I'd been here since four and would probably stay until well after midnight.

As Molly cleaned, I took a tub of silverware and black paper napkins to a table and collapsed into the seat. Closing my eyes, I relaxed for a few seconds before getting back to work, rolling the silverware in the napkins and finishing them with a white paper ring.

Molly finished up with the tables and came to sit down, helping me with the silverware. "I'm going home, taking a long, hot bath and then going straight to bed. For once, I'm glad Finn has the kids at his place so I can crash."

Finn had come in earlier with Kali and Max so they could eat dinner. When Molly had joined them, I'd gotten a momentary swell of hope that the four of them might have a nice family meal, but then Finn had squashed it. He'd turned his chair sideways, away from Molly, with a two-foot gap between them so he wouldn't have to make eye contact. He'd literally given her the cold shoulder.

"Did you and Finn talk at all during dinner?" I asked.

Molly shook her head. "No. He won't talk to me. I've tried for months but . . . you know. He'll never forgive me."

I gave her a sad smile. She'd given up hope, but I hadn't. Not when there was still love there.

Because Finn and Molly did love one another. Anyone who spent thirty seconds with them could feel it. But their marriage hadn't been easy. A year ago, the two of them had been going through a rough patch. Finn had been working a ton and not spending much time at home. When he was there, he'd take his work stress out on Molly. They'd been fighting so much, Finn had actually moved out. They'd agreed on a separation and therapy, but Finn had never found the time to meet with their counselor.

Then Molly had made a mistake.

She'd been lonely and certain her marriage was over. She'd gone to a bachelorette party, gotten blitzed and had sex with some random guy from the bar. She'd messed up—big time—but to her credit, she'd owned her mistake. She'd told Finn the truth and begged for forgiveness. He'd told her to get a lawyer instead.

I'd had a hard time believing my friend could do that to my brother. I'd been angry and said some things I hadn't meant, but then I'd apologized and forgiven her. Things had been so hard for her when Finn had moved out. She'd been devastated.

So I'd assumed my role as Switzerland, supporting Molly as my best friend and Finn as my one and only sibling. Meanwhile, they were miserable. Finn was punishing Molly for one mistake. Molly was still punishing herself for losing the love of her life.

"I'm sorry, Molly."

She shrugged. "It's my fault. If I were in his place, if he had *cheated*, I'd be ruined."

Cheated. Why did she always say cheated? I hated that word. And the way she said it was worse than any four-letter curse. Molly wasn't a cheater. Molly was just human, dealing as best she could with a broken heart. "You weren't together."

"We were still married. I was—am—still in love with him. I understand why he's hurt and angry. Some mistakes you just can't forgive."

Or forget.

Molly would regret that mistake for the rest of her life.

"Enough about that." Molly forced a smile, steering the conversation away from her and Finn like usual. "How was your karate class last night?"

Unlike my brother, Molly was more accepting about my decision to work through Jamie's list.

"It was . . . interesting."

So interesting that I'd stayed up most of the night thinking about that class. My mind had run on a loop all night, but not about karate. About Cole Goodman. It had certainly been a shock to see him again, but more surprising was the rush of feelings he'd invoked.

Feelings—chemical, electric feelings—I hadn't had in a long time.

"So? What happened? Did you learn how to kick some ass?"

"Oh, yeah. I'm an expert ass kicker," I deadpanned, then laughed. "I'm just glad that I survived the workout. To me, that's a win."

"Did you mark it off the list?"

I nodded. "Last night when I got home."

"Are you okay?"

"I think so. I cried like usual, but when the tears stopped, I actually felt kind of good."

"I'm glad. That's what you were going for, right? Some closure?"

I nodded and rolled another bundle of silverware. "I've actually been thinking about trying to go through the list more quickly."

Finn's big objection was that going through Jamie's list would drag on for years, and I could see his point. Now that I was starting to cross off more items, I was feeling motivated to keep going.

"How quickly?" Molly asked.

"A year? Maybe less?"

She thought about it for a moment. "It's ambitious. Do you think it's even possible?"

The biggest item on Jamie's list had been the restaurant. It had also been the item requiring the most money. For the others, I mostly needed time. Luckily, some items I'd already set in motion.

"I think so. A year is going to be a push, but if I make the list a higher priority, I might be able to wrap up everything before Jamie's birthday." That would give me until New Year's Day.

"Well, you know I'll help with whatever I can."

"Thank you."

She moved her finished rolls of silverware into the tub. "You haven't eaten yet. Why don't you head back to the kitchen and I'll finish up out here?"

I glanced at my watch. 7:49. "We survived the first day. I think I'll head back and make a sandwich. I'm starv—"

The front door swooshed opened. *Damn. I spoke too soon.*

Turning to the door, I smiled, ready to greet my late-evening customer, but faltered as the door closed behind him.

Cole Goodman was walking my way.

My belly dipped as I took him in. His aviator sunglasses were perched on top of his chocolate-brown hair. A black polo stretched across his broad shoulders and pulled tight across his muscled arms. His pale-blue jeans molded to his Herculean thighs before draping down to his black, square-toed boots. The leather belt on Cole's trim waist held both a shining badge and a holstered gun.

Cole smiled and locked his light-green eyes on mine as he crossed the room.

His straight, white teeth made my breath hitch—something that had happened last night more times than I wanted to admit.

Molly, who had turned around from her seat to greet our customer, spun around so her back was to Cole. Her cheeks flushed as she whispered, "Wow."

Wow was right.

Cole Goodman was—simply put—gorgeous.

He could give a woman a speeding ticket and get a thank-you in return. He inspired women to attempt push-ups in a karate class just for the chance to watch him sweat through his gi. Cole made grown women blush like teenagers and giggle in corners, like those girls at the dojo last night.

Besides Jamie, I'd never seen a man so handsome. And if I were being honest with myself, Cole had even Jamie beat.

The blush in my cheeks paled as a knot of guilt settled in my stomach. I loved Jamie. Jamie had been a gorgeous man too. And as his wife, I shouldn't be attracted to another man.

My smile turned to a frown the moment Cole stepped up to our table.

"Hey, Poppy."

"Hi, Cole."

His smile fell. "You don't look happy to see me again."

"Again?" Molly asked.

Cole looked down to my friend and held out his hand. "Cole Goodman. I ran into Poppy at the karate school last night."

"Oh!" She stood and took his hand. "I'm Molly Alcott. Nice to meet you. Poppy was just telling me about your karate class." She turned to me. "But she didn't tell me she'd been bragging up the restaurant."

"I wasn't—"

"Actually, I heard about this place online," Cole said. "I saw Poppy's name and decided to check it out." He looked my way. "I hope you don't mind."

"No. Not at all." I stood, shaking off my strange feelings. I couldn't afford to turn away customers, even if they were handsome and made me feel uncomfortable things.

"I tried to get in earlier but I had something come up at work. I don't suppose you've got any dinner left?"

"Just barely. We had more of a rush than I expected and we're down to just a few things. Sorry."

"Don't be sorry. That's a good problem to have on opening day."

"You know," Molly said, standing too, "I was just telling Poppy she should eat. She's been running around like crazy all day. Why don't you eat together?"

My eyes snapped to my friend. "It's late and I'm sure Cole just wants to take something to—"

"I'd like that." He grinned at Molly.

She smiled back.

I looked from one to the other and back again. I held up a finger to Cole. "Would you excuse us for just a minute?"

He chuckled and pulled out a chair at our table, taking a seat. "Take all the time you need."

I grabbed Molly's elbow, then yanked her away from the table and back to the kitchen. When the door swung closed behind us, I let her go and planted my hands on my hips. "What do you think you're doing?"

"You like him."

"What?" I squeaked. My voice was so high it'd send dogs into barking hysterics.

"See?" She gave me her smug smile. "You like him."

I shook my head. "No, I don't. I don't like him."

"Liar."

I huffed. "It's complicated. I know him."

"Yeah. From karate."

"No." I shook my head and took a deep breath. "I knew him before karate. He was the cop that came to my house to tell me that Jamie . . ." I twirled my wrist instead of finishing my sentence.

"Oh, shit."

"Pretty much."

Molly paced back and forth by my prep table for a few moments, fidgeting with her hands. When she stopped walking, she planted both hands on the table. "Okay. I can see how that would be weird, but the fact still stands. You like him."

I shrugged. "He's cute. But I don't *like* him."

"Cute?"

"Smoking hot. Whatever. None of that matters. I am in no place to be liking a man."

She sighed and left the table, coming to stand right in front of me. Then she placed her hands on my shoulders. "Okay. I've been saving this speech for a day like today."

"I'm scared right now."

"Shush and listen up." She took a breath and started reciting something she'd clearly practiced a time or twelve. "You are my best friend and I love you. I want you to be happy and have love in your life. *Jamie* would have wanted you to be happy and have love in your life. And I think it's time for you to open your heart again to that possibility."

"It's too soon." I shook my head. Even thinking about being with another man made my heart hurt. I couldn't do that to Jamie. Not yet. Maybe not ever.

"Poppy," Molly whispered, "at some point, a man was going to come along and catch your eye. There's nothing wrong with that. There's nothing wrong with you exploring something with that guy. It's not a betrayal to Jamie."

The lump in the back of my throat started to choke. "It feels like it though. I can't do that to him."

"I understand. I really do. We all loved Jamie. We all miss Jamie. But it's been five years. You're going through his list to try and move on, right?"

I nodded.

"The list is a good thing, you know I support you in that. But just marking off all Jamie's check boxes isn't going to be enough. At some point, you have to live for you too. *That's* how you're going to move on."

"But I . . ." I wanted to move on, but I was scared to move on. As much as I wanted to be happy and let go of the past, I was terrified that I'd lose the piece of Jamie still in my heart.

"But what?"

I took a deep breath and confessed the worries that had kept me from sleeping last night. "What if I fall in love with another man and forget Jamie?"

She gave me a sad smile. "Do you really think that would ever happen?"

"No," I sighed. "Not really. I'm just scared."

"I get that. But I'm not saying jump into bed with Cole or have his babies. I'm just saying, you think he's *cute*. From the look in his eye, he thinks you're *cute* too. You two should spend some time being *cute* together."

"Okay. I officially hate the word cute."

"Me too." She laughed. "So what do you say? Have dinner with him. Do it for me. Pleeeeease?"

I groaned. "Stop that. Now you sound like Kali."

"Where do you think I learned it? She says 'please' so long and loud I always give in. Do you want me to do it again? I'll do it again. Pleeeee—"

"Okay! Since I'm already making myself a sandwich, I'll make him one too."

"Yes!" she cheered before pulling me into her arms. "Love you, Poppy-bear."

I smiled at the nickname she'd given me my freshman year in college. "Love you too, Molly-moo."

"How about I finish up out there and close up? Then you guys can eat back here."

I let her go. "All right. Will you give me a minute before you send him back?"

"I'll give you two."

As she disappeared from the kitchen, my hands came to my cheeks and I took a few long breaths.

Dinner. This was just dinner.

Dinner with an acquaintance at my new restaurant. Cole and I could chat and make small talk while we ate. Then he'd leave and I could get back to work. Dinner didn't mean anything. I was still Jamie's wife. I'd always be Jamie's wife, and there was nothing wrong with me cooking a meal for Cole.

This is just dinner.

My affirmations helped ease my anxiety but didn't erase it entirely. So I did the next best thing to settle my racing heart—I started cooking.

I dropped my hands and went to the large, stainless-steel refrigerator. Then I pulled out the ingredients for grilled cheese sandwiches, piling food on the prep table. I'd gathered all of my supplies when the door swung open and Cole stepped into the kitchen.

"I was told to get out of her dining room if I wanted food."

I giggled. "She has a way with customers, that one."

He smiled and stepped up to the prep table. "I can go if this is a pain in the ass. I really did just want to say hi and check out your place."

"You're hungry. I'm hungry. Making you dinner is not a pain in the ass. How about a grilled cheese? They aren't on the menu, but I've been told they don't suck."

"Considering I haven't eaten since ten this morning, I'd eat just about anything."

"Busy day?"

He sighed. "Busy year. Bozeman's growing so fast that we're a little understaffed with senior officers. I made detective last summer and it's been hectic ever since."

"Is that why you don't have to wear a uniform anymore?" I

waved at his casual clothes. When I'd seen him five years ago, he'd been in uniform.

"Yeah."

I nodded and started slicing a tomato.

"Can I help?"

"I've got this. You can just relax." I pointed to the stools next to the table.

Cole took his seat and rested his elbows on the table. As I cut slices off a block of cheese, his tan, sinewy forearms were right in my line of sight. On one wrist sat a watch with a huge silver face. I bet my fingers wouldn't touch if they took the place of his watch.

My eyes wandered up from his wrists and forearms to his biceps. Cole's arms were big but not bulky. The muscles were just perfectly defined, even underneath the cotton of his shirt. My hand would look tiny resting on his arm. My cheeks flushed when I realized I'd been staring for a moment too long.

I blinked and looked down at the table, then up at Cole's face.

Damn. He'd caught me staring. The smirk in his eyes was unmistakable, but I didn't look away. His eyes were too . . . fascinating.

I'd never seen green eyes like Cole's before. The color reminded me of dried sage, and his dark, thick lashes made them even more dramatic. His face drew you in with his chiseled jaw and straight nose, but those eyes were what made you stay.

My heart was pounding as I set down the knife, but I couldn't break away from Cole's eyes.

And he stared right back.

Molly came bursting through the kitchen door, making me jump. "All clean and locked up."

I scrambled to pick up my knife, then blinked a few times

before cutting a slice of bread. "Thank you. Would you like something to eat? I'm making your favorite sandwich."

Stay. Molly, stay. I willed her to come to my rescue, to take the stool next to Cole and be my buffer, but she kept on walking toward the office.

"Can't do it. My bathtub is calling my name. I'll see you in the morning. Cole, nice meeting you."

He waved. "Nice to meet you too."

She disappeared into the office, then came back with her purse slung over a shoulder. "Bye!"

"Night." The minute the back door slammed shut, a new rush of jitters hit. I was alone with a handsome man who was not my husband.

My kitchen, something I'd designed to be large and spacious, was suddenly too small. The air conditioning that I kept running on high must have just quit working because my entire body was on fire. And I had forgotten how to make a grilled cheese sandwich as the knife sat motionless in my hand.

"What did you think of karate last night?" Cole asked, breaking the silence.

Dinner. This is just dinner. Breathe.

I forced some air into my lungs, then pushed away from the table to turn on the flat-iron grill. "It was interesting but I'm already getting sore. Especially my arms. I imagine by tomorrow my entire body will be on strike."

He chuckled. "Yeah. It's a tough workout. Are you sure you won't try it again?"

"I'm sure." I went back to the table and brushed four slices of bread with some olive oil, then spread on a thin layer of homemade pesto before adding the cheese and tomato. "To be honest, I only came for a one-time deal. I hope that doesn't offend your instructor."

"Nah, he doesn't care. But why only the one time? Was it a dare or something?"

"It's, um . . . from this list."

"A list?"

Explaining Jamie's birthday list was so personal that only a few people knew about it. Even fewer knew I was going through it myself. Yet, for some reason, I wanted to tell Cole. "My husband, Jamie, he put together this birthday list. It was like his bucket list, except he separated out everything to do by year before certain birthdays. Taking a karate class was something he wanted to do before he turned twenty-six."

Cole nodded. "And you're going through his list."

"I am." I was ready to defend the list and why I was going through it, but his eyes weren't full of concern or judgment or questions. They just . . . understood.

He understood without a word.

"Interesting idea. What else is on this list, if you don't mind me asking?"

"Not at all." I resumed sandwich assembly. "Jamie put twenty-two things on the list. Most of them are silly, but totally him. He added some things he found on the internet he thought sounded cool. Others were goofy things he dreamed up or things he didn't get to do as a kid. Jump in green Jell-O. Have a paint fight. Things like that. Some were more serious, like buying me this restaurant."

Cole leaned over to pluck three oranges out of the fruit bowl on the table. "Have you done many of them yet?"

"No, not even close." I smiled as he started juggling the oranges. "I've only marked off three. The restaurant. The karate class. And skydiving."

Cole dropped an orange and it rolled across the table. "Skydiving?"

I laughed at the shock on his face. "You're not the only one surprised I did it. But yeah. I went last month."

While Cole picked up the fallen orange and resumed juggling, I took the sandwiches to the grill, setting them down on the hot metal. Then I rushed out of the kitchen and into the dining room, where all of the lights were off and the sign on the door had been flipped to *Closed*. With two sets of silverware and a couple of plates, I hustled back into the kitchen to set down the place settings and flip the sandwiches. Then I went to the fridge and got out a jar of salad.

"Here." I handed the jar to Cole. "Use those muscles and shake this up."

He grinned and put back his oranges before he started shaking. "Okay. Back to skydiving. You left me with a cliffhanger."

I smiled. "It was the one item on the list that scared me, so I decided to just get it over with before I chickened out."

He slid the salad jar across the table. The dressing that had been underneath a layer of vegetables and lettuce was now coating the glass. "And what did you think?"

"I actually loved it. The pilot said something before I jumped that really clicked. He said, 'If you want to go swimming, you get out of the boat. Same is true with flying. You have to get out of the plane.' So I did. I was strapped to this hippy with dreadlocks and bad breath, but he was so cool. The whole crew made it fun."

"Would you ever go again?"

"Nope." I popped the *p* to emphasize my point. "I had fun, but once was enough. Have you ever been?"

He shook his head. "No, but now I want to."

I smiled and went back to the sandwiches, taking them off the grill. Then I dumped half of the salad on Cole's plate and half on mine, sliding him his plate before taking the stool at his side. "Dig in."

"This looks great. Thank you for doing this."

"You're welcome."

We ate in silence, both of us concentrating on the food and listening to the hum of my kitchen appliances. But our meal didn't take long since both of us had been so hungry.

Cole swallowed the last bite of his sandwich. "So. Jars?"

"Jars."

"I like it. I'll have to come back and try your desserts."

I smiled. "I recommend the apple pie."

His eyes, locked on mine, darkened a shade. "I'll take whatever you'll give me."

CHAPTER FOUR

27TH BIRTHDAY: GO AN ENTIRE DAY
WITHOUT TECHNOLOGY

COLE

Two weeks had passed since the night I'd spent in Poppy's kitchen, and she'd been on my mind the entire time. One meal with her and I was completely under her spell.

After we'd finished our sandwiches, she'd set aside our dishes and filled the table with jars and baking ingredients. And I'd stayed in her kitchen, watching her cook until one in the morning.

When she had asked if I needed to get home, I'd said no. When she'd thanked me for coming in, I'd said you're welcome and kept my ass on that stool.

She'd never asked me to leave, and I'd never offered.

So while she'd made trays of pies, crumbles and quiches, I'd assumed dishwasher duty. I had done my best to focus on the sink rather than on the way her jeans stretched tight over her ass. I'd scrubbed pots to ignore the inch of her flat stomach she exposed whenever she reached for the top shelf of her storage rack. And when she'd licked apple-pie filling from a spoon, I'd scoured a pan until my knuckles were raw to resist the urge to kiss her pink mouth. When she'd declared she was done for the night, finally putting me out of my misery, I'd walked her outside and stood by the building while she'd gotten in her car and driven away.

Then I'd gone home to take a shower and relieve my aching dick. I'd come hard in my fist, thinking of the way Poppy's breath hitched whenever I'd gotten close.

My attraction to her was stronger than I'd ever felt toward a woman, which is why I'd backed off these last two weeks.

As much as I wanted to spend every night in her restaurant, it would only scare her away.

Poppy was attracted to me. She felt the chemistry between us.

And it terrified her.

If my intuitions were right—and they usually were—I was the first man she'd been attracted to since her husband, and if I wanted the chance to explore things with her, I couldn't spook her by moving too fast.

I didn't know where we'd end up. Maybe she'd be a clean freak and drive me crazy. Maybe she'd want to cuddle at night when I just wanted some space. Maybe she'd smack her gum too loud, something I couldn't fucking stand. I didn't know.

But I wanted the chance to find out.

"Hey, Cole."

I looked up from my desk—where I'd been daydreaming about Poppy and ignoring my paperwork—and nodded to Detective Matt Hernandez. "Hey, Matt. What's happening today?"

He dropped into the seat behind his desk adjacent to mine. "Not much." He slapped down a thick file on top of a stack five deep. "I've gotta get through all these today. You?"

"Same." I patted my own stack of files. "I've been procrastinating."

He chuckled. "Yeah, me too. I spent all morning running down some leads on a theft case assigned to Simmons."

I looked over my shoulder and frowned at Derek Simmons, who was sitting five desks down. When I turned back to Matt, he was frowning at Simmons too.

"That theft case might actually get solved if you're looking into it."

He huffed. "At least I'm trying."

I spun and glanced at Simmons again. He was shoving a donut—a fucking maple bar of all things—into his mouth. The arms of his desk chair were digging into his sides and his ass was ballooning through the small space between the seat and the backrest.

Simmons didn't have stacks of paperwork on his desk, just donut crumbles, because he was the only detective that put a priority on paperwork over fieldwork. It was no wonder his closed-case rate was the lowest in the department. He never left that desk to actually ask any fucking questions.

But he wasn't going anywhere, no matter how much the rest of us bitched. Simmons had been on the force for nearly thirty years. He'd die sitting in that chair while the rest of us busted our asses solving our own cases and picking up the slack on the ones assigned to him.

"Lazy," I muttered, turning back around.

"Uh-huh," Matt agreed, then jerked his chin at my files. "What do you have?"

"I've got one theft and six drug busts we caught last week on the task force."

"Nice. Sounds like you guys are off to a good start."

"Hell yeah, we are." I grinned. "I've got six busts, Higgins has four, Smith has five, and Colton two. I'm telling you, having an ex-dealer on our side has been gold. Now that we know what kinds of things to look out for, it's been a fuck of a lot easier to find out where deals are going down."

"That was a smart move on your part—getting that ex-dealer to come on board."

I nodded. "Without him, we'd be at square one."

I'd gotten lucky when we'd been planning the drug task force last year. Our focus was solely on the meth trade in Bozeman, and I'd known an ex-junkie/dealer who'd been needing some encouragement to get clean. I'd gone out on a limb and personally paid for his rehab. He'd cleaned up and come back a new man.

He'd also come back as my teacher.

I'd spent months with him, learning all about the meth trade and getting names of top producers and dealers. He'd taught me the clues. What to watch for on social media. Street lingo to listen for. Common places for quick exchanges.

Because of his help, my task force was finally starting to put a dent in the meth trade that had gone crazy in Bozeman over the last decade.

My dad had been begging the powers that be for years to get funding to start this task force. It hadn't been until a middle-school kid—a fucking eighth grader—had overdosed last year that the town had gone into hysterics and Dad had finally gotten some money to kick us off.

Our goal was to get the drugs out of the middle schools this year, then hit the high school hard next year.

"When you get an opening on your team, let me know," Matt said. "I'd be interested in joining too."

"You got it."

I made a mental note to ask for another team member at next month's task force committee overview meeting. With as much success as we'd had out of the gate, the council might actually consider adding to my crew, and Matt Hernandez would be at the top of the list.

"All right," he grumbled. "Time to get after it."

I smiled and swiveled my chair back to my own paperwork that I'd been working on all day—except for the time I'd spent thinking about Poppy.

An hour later, I'd only made it through one file because she'd been hounding my thoughts again. Was she at the restaurant today? Would she care if I came in for lunch? I was hungry and it was almost noon. Two weeks was enough time to give her some space, wasn't it?

"Hi, Detective Simmons."

Christ. Now I was even hearing her voice.

"Hello, Mrs. Maysen. How are you today?"

What the actual fuck? My head whipped up from my desk and over my shoulder toward Simmons.

And there she was.

My pretty Poppy, pulling up the gray chair across from Simmons's desk.

I was out of my seat so fast, my own chair went rolling backward and bumped into the wall. I weaved around the desks between us until I was standing behind Poppy's chair with my hands on my hips. "Poppy."

She spun around, her eyes wide as her breath hitched. *Damn, I liked that.*

Simmons stopped staring at her chest and looked up. "Hiyah, Cole. What can we do ya for?"

I ignored Simmons and focused on Poppy.

Her tawny-red hair was down today, something I'd never seen. It flowed down her back in loose waves, highlighted by a few strands of gold that framed her oval face.

"What are you doing here?" I asked. "Is everything okay?"

She nodded. "I'm just here checking in on Jamie's case."

My eyebrows came together. "Jamie's case?"

"His, um . . . murder." Her shoulders fell and she turned back to Simmons.

Simmons had Poppy's husband's murder case? I knew that they'd never found the person responsible for Jamie's death, but after all this time, they should have marked it cold and notified his family. Hadn't that been closed?

I didn't need to ask. Poppy's visit here answered my questions.

A rush of anger heated my chest. Had Simmons been leading Poppy on that he might actually find the killer?

I glared at my coworker as his eyes went back to Poppy's perfect breasts. She was wearing a simple black tank top with wide straps. It wasn't low-cut or indecent, but with the way Simmons was drooling, you'd think she was in a bikini.

And those breasts were not his to ogle.

"You and I are going to talk." I pointed at Simmons, then reached down and took Poppy by the elbow, pulling her from the chair.

"Cole!" she protested but stood.

"Come on."

"But I need to get an update on—"

"Do you have an update?" I barked at Simmons.

He shook his head and his splotchy skin reddened. "Uh, no."

"Okay. Update delivered. Let's go."

"Go where?" she asked as I dragged her over to my desk.

"To lunch."

I let her go and opened up my drawer to get out my keys and wallet.

"Taking off?" Matt asked.

"Yeah." I shoved the drawer closed and then did introductions. "Poppy, this is Detective Matt Hernandez. Matt, this is

Poppy Maysen. She owns that new restaurant on Seventh Street."

Matt stood and extended a hand. "Nice to meet you, Poppy."

She dropped the shocked look on her face and stepped past me to shake hands with Matt.

"My wife was telling me she wanted to head in for dinner there this week," Matt continued.

She smiled. "That would be great. Thank you. I'll look forward to seeing you."

"Be back after lunch." I grabbed my sunglasses off my desk and jammed them on my head. Then I slipped my hand around Poppy's elbow again, propelling her forward.

Her feet fell in step with mine. "Cole, what are you doing?"

"Taking you to lunch. I'm hungry." I led her out of the detective's office and toward the stairs that led outside. When we crossed into the marble-tiled foyer, I dropped her elbow.

She looked over her shoulder before we started down the steps. "But I needed to check in with Detective Simmons."

"Don't worry. He'll be right there at his desk when we get back."

The bastard was probably stuck in his chair. Usually he'd order in lunch and ask one of the receptionists in the lobby to bring it up. The man took the elevator up two flights of stairs and couldn't pass our physical to save his life.

Fucking tenure.

Five minutes ago, Simmons was an annoyance. Now, he was a major fucking problem. I wasn't sure why he was stringing Poppy along, but I was going to find out.

"Where do you feel like eating?" I asked as we turned the corner down one flight of steps. "Your restaurant?"

"No. I can't go in there today."

My feet slowed. "Say that again?"

"I can't go to the restaurant today." Her hands fluttered in the air. "Molly is an evil dictator and is making me take one day off a month. Since June is almost over, she declared this was my day."

I chuckled. Later, I'd have to thank Molly for keeping Poppy from burning herself out.

"Besides that," Poppy said as she skipped down the stairs, "if I went in there, I'd be tempted to check the sales and I am not allowed to use technology today."

My feet slowed again. "No technology? Molly won't let you watch TV or make phone calls on your day off either? She's gone mad with power."

Poppy laughed. "No, the technology isn't Molly. It's an item on Jamie's list. No technology for a day."

"Ah. That makes more sense."

We hit the landing on the first floor and I nodded toward a hallway that led to the back of the police station. "This way."

"But my car." She pointed toward the visitors' parking lot.

"I'll drive and bring you back."

Her hair swung across her back as she looked between me and the main exit.

"We're at a police station, Poppy. I'm sure your car will be fine."

I teased but I knew she wasn't worried about her car. She was debating whether or not she wanted to be in a confined space with me.

"That's not . . ." She threw up her hands and did her little wrist-circle thing. "Never mind. Let's go."

I grinned as she marched past me to the door.

Damn, she was something. For the life of me, I couldn't remember why I'd waited two weeks to see her again.

"How about Colombo's?" I opened the door for her.

"That sounds great. I haven't been there in ages." Her voice quieted. "Not since Jamie and I were in college."

"If it's a problem—"

"No, it's fine."

"You're sure?"

She nodded and smiled. "I love Colombo's."

"Okay." I slid my sunglasses off my head and onto my nose, then led her to the truck.

It couldn't be easy for her, living in Bozeman. I'd bet she was assaulted with memories of her husband everywhere she went. It was admirable that she hadn't let them chase her away.

Poppy was a fighter.

I beeped the locks on my truck and opened the passenger door. I took her elbow and helped her up. That familiar zing of electricity shot up my arm the moment my skin touched hers. Wanting to test her reaction, I leaned in, just a bit.

She didn't step away and her chin lifted an inch as her eyes landed on my mouth.

I wanted to kiss her. If we weren't in a parking lot, surrounded by patrol cars and the sounds of engines whizzing by, I might have given into the temptation. But now wasn't the time. Though there was lust in Poppy's cornflower blues, there was fear behind them too.

"Climb on in."

She dropped her eyes from my lips. "Thanks."

When she was in her seat, I shut her door, then rounded the hood to my side. Belted into the driver's seat, I backed out and pointed the truck down the road. "So, a day without technology. What exactly are you going without?"

She was smiling out the windshield. She'd thrown her hair over her shoulder and a couple of locks were trailing down her bare arm. Her delicate hands were folded in her lap.

That was Poppy's seat now. Any time I looked at the leather, I'd picture her riding shotgun.

"I'm basically cutting out screens," she said, reminding me that I'd asked her a question. "I've deemed modern-day appliances acceptable because I'm trying to get caught up on laundry. And kitchen appliances don't count, but other than that, nothing else. No TV. No phone. No radio."

"Oh, shit." I smacked the off button on the radio. "Sorry. Did I ruin your day? Do you have to start over?"

Her sweet laugh filled the cab. "I don't know what you're talking about. Wasn't that you singing? Has anyone ever told you that you sound a lot like George Strait?"

I grinned. "I think you might be the first."

She was witty too. This woman had it all. Beauty. Brains. And a sense of humor.

The drive to Colombo's was just a couple of blocks, but by the time I pulled into the parking lot, Poppy's vanilla perfume had infused the air. I hopped out and slammed the door in one motion, hoping to keep the scent from escaping.

"This place hasn't changed much, has it?" she asked as we walked to the door.

"Not a bit." My favorite thing about Colombo's was that it never changed. It was exactly the same as it had been when my parents had brought my sister and me here as kids.

Colombo's was a Bozeman institution. Located directly across the street from Montana State University, it was always packed with college students. I all but stopped coming during the school year, but in the summer, this was my go-to lunch stop.

Opening the door, I let her walk inside first. The minute I stepped in behind her, the smell of onions and garlic and tomato sauce filled my nose.

"Oh, god," she moaned. "I missed this place. It smells sooo good."

That moan and the smile on her face didn't help the problem in my jeans.

"You should know that I'm no good at sharing pizza," she declared. "You'll have to get your own."

I chuckled. "I can live with that. I'm more of a sucker for their pepperoni calzones."

We wasted no time ordering our meals from the walk-up counter and getting drinks from the fountain. Colombo's son was manning the open kitchen today and I waved to him before leading Poppy to a booth at the back of the narrow restaurant.

"How's everything going at the restaurant?" I asked as we sat.

"Good." She smiled. "Busy, but I'm getting the hang of how much food to make, and so far, I haven't had any complaints or bad reviews."

Not that she would. I doubted anyone would find fault with her food, and I'd only ever had a sandwich and salad.

"Are you getting any sleep or are you a slave to the kitchen?"

"That first week was rough, but we have a new part-time employee who started last week, so hopefully Molly and I can get into a better routine and not be there twenty-four seven."

"Good. I don't like the idea of you coming and going late at night by yourself. Make sure you're always parking in the space next to the door."

"I know," she muttered. "I'll park by the door. I won't take the trash out after dark. I won't forget to lock up the front the minute we close."

I took a drink of my water to hide my grin. She remembered my lecture from two weeks ago, and from the sounds of it, she'd been following my instructions. Setting down my glass, I leaned forward on the table. As much as I would have just loved to visit with Poppy, I needed some information before I went back to the station.

"So, before our lunch gets here, I have to know. What are you doing meeting with Simmons?"

She sighed and fidgeted with the discarded paper from her straw. "I've been coming in once a month ever since Jamie was killed to see if he's found out anything on the case. He never has information, but I just don't want him to forget that Jamie's killer is still out there."

Fuck.

She was hoping for something she'd probably never get. A five-year-old case without new evidence and Simmons as the lead? Her husband's killer was probably long gone.

Fucking Simmons.

"I'm actually surprised I haven't seen you before," she said before I could think of what to say.

I shrugged. "I don't love the office and avoid it when I can. Most of us usually only spend time there when we're doing paperwork." *Except for Simmons.* "We all started our careers in the field, doing patrols. Most of us like being out and about, asking questions."

Because fieldwork was how cases got solved—not by sitting in a chair, eating maple bars.

Poppy's eyes stayed locked on the rumpled paper in her fingers. "Do you think I should give up? Do you think there's a chance to find whoever killed Jamie?"

When she looked up, some of the light had dimmed in her eyes. For the first time in two weeks, she looked more like the woman I'd seen five years ago than the one who'd come to my dojo.

"I'll be honest," I said gently. "It's been a long time. Five years with no new evidence isn't a good thing. I haven't seen the case file, but my guess is that all of the leads are dead ends."

Her shoulders fell and she tucked her hands in her lap. She was shrinking right in front of me—curling in on herself. Is this what happened to her after every one of her visits with Simmons? Because I'd do just about anything to make it stop.

"I'll tell you what, when we get back to the station, I'll take a look at the file. I don't know what I'll find, but I'll check into the case. Okay?"

"You'd really do that?"

"In a heartbeat."

"Thank you," she sighed. "Don't get me wrong, Detective Simmons has been great. He meets with me every month and is always nice. But, I don't know. I guess I don't feel like this case is his priority."

She'd read that right. His priority these days seemed to be doing as little as possible. "Let me see what I can do," I promised just as our food was delivered.

"Thank you," she told me as I said the same to the waitress.

With my calzone and her pizza, we dug in and ate lunch mostly in silence—just like dinner in her kitchen.

Poppy didn't have to fill every moment with conversation. Aly had been a constant talker, always wanting to visit while we ate. It drove me nuts when I'd take a bite and she'd immediately ask a question. Sometimes, I just wanted to eat. Like my parents did for their meals. They talked, they knew about each other's days, but they were also content to just be with one another.

The quiet gave me time to enjoy my food and also a chance to think.

The first thing I was doing when I got back to the station was commandeering Jamie Maysen's case file from Simmons.

If all of the leads were dead, I'd do what needed to be done.

I'd sit Poppy down and tell her the truth. That her husband's killer was free and would remain so unless new evidence came to light.

But if the file had more, if Simmons hadn't dug into every lead and turned over every rock to find the murderer, I'd be pulling a favor from Dad. I'd do something I'd never, ever done: I'd use my position as the chief of police's son to handpick a case. I'd take the case away from Simmons and do my best to bring Jamie's killer to justice.

No matter how much stress it would add to my life, I'd do it because it was the right thing to do.

I'd do it for Poppy.

CHAPTER FIVE

36TH BIRTHDAY: LEARN TO PLAY THE UKULELE

POPPY

"Jimmy? I'm here!"

A week after my lunch with Cole at Colombo's, I was taking the afternoon off from the restaurant to visit Jamie's grandfather, Jimmy, at his retirement home, The Rainbow.

"Out in a sec." Jimmy's shout was muffled by the closed bedroom door.

I smiled and took a seat on the couch in the living room as I waited. The housekeepers must have swept through this morning because the normal stack of Mountain Dew cans and old newspapers on the end table was gone and the kitchenette was free of its usual Ritz cracker crumbs. They'd even hung up Jimmy's coats—the ones he normally just tossed on the couch.

"Gladys, you have *got* to see him," a woman whispered from the hallway.

"I heard all about it at breakfast," Gladys replied with a muffled giggle.

Were they talking about Jimmy? Because it sounded like Gladys and her gossiping friend were hovering right outside his open door. I hadn't bothered closing it when I'd come over. The door here was *never* closed. Why Jimmy liked his door open all the time I hadn't a clue. He treated this assisted living facility more like a college dorm than a place to settle down.

But at least the always-open door gave me a chance to see the women as they shuffled past.

"Hello!" I waved and smiled as two elderly women ignored me completely and craned their necks inside, searching the small living room for Jimmy. When they saw he wasn't in his recliner, they frowned and kept on walking.

I laughed when they were out of earshot. Every time I came here it seemed like a different resident was crushing on my grandfather-in-law.

"There's my Poppy." Jimmy's bedroom door opened and he emerged into the living room. "How are you today?"

"I'm goo—oh my god. What did you do?" I shot off the couch. My eyes were locked on his hair—hair that was normally snow-white, not hot pink.

Jimmy didn't answer. He just crossed the small distance from his bedroom and pulled me into his arms. When he let me go, his eyes gave me a thorough inspection from tip to toe before he sat in his navy plush recliner.

"Are you going to answer me?" I asked, still standing.

He frowned and motioned to his hair. "I lost a bet."

"A bet. You made a bet where the loser had to dye his hair pink?"

"Yeah," he grumbled. "I'll tell you, Poppy. You just can't trust some people. You know that new guy who moved in next door?"

I nodded even though I hadn't met Jimmy's new neighbor.

"He's a cheat. A lying cheat. I invited him to play in our

Tuesday afternoon poker club. Thought I'd be neighborly. He told me he didn't know how to play poker, but he'd like to learn." Jimmy's hands fisted on the chair's arms. "Didn't know how my ass. He's a damn card shark! Got us all laughing and joking around. Convinced us to make a bet. First one out of chips dyes his hair pink. That son of a bitch. Took me all in on the second pot and cleaned me out."

"So you got pink hair and lost a bunch of money. How much did you lose?"

He shrugged. "Eh, not much. We only play pennies. Maybe five bucks. But those ladies in the salon sure gouged me. Thirty bucks for pink hair. Can you believe it?"

"That's unbelievable." I pursed my lips to hide my smile as I sat back down. "I brought you your favorite peach cobbler if that will make you feel any better."

The scowl on Jimmy's face disappeared. "Just visiting with you will make me feel better, but I'll take that cobbler as a bonus. How are things going at the restaurant?"

I smiled. "Beyond my wildest expectations."

The Maysen Jar had been open for three weeks, and in that time, we'd sold twice as much as Molly and I had projected for its entire first quarter. I'd seen more repeat customers bring back jars for refills than I'd ever anticipated, and I'd closed down each night this week with a nearly full tip jar.

"I'm excited to come see it next week. Did Debbie and Kyle pick a night yet?"

"No," I sighed. "I texted Debbie but she hasn't gotten back to me yet. She doesn't text much these days."

Debbie, Jamie's mom, used to text me multiple times a day. Now I'd go weeks without hearing from her, and then it was only because I had reached out first. Kyle, Jamie's dad, I hadn't heard from in ages. Jamie's parents lived on their ranch about an hour outside of Bozeman, and when Jamie had been alive, they'd come to see us every couple of weeks. But since he'd been killed, their trips had all but stopped. Now, they rarely came to visit Jimmy—Kyle's dad and Jamie's namesake—and I only saw them for special occasions.

"They love you, Poppy. It's just hard for them."

"I know. I just miss them." I forced a smile as I looked at Jimmy—that pink hair making it wider.

I hadn't just lost Jamie when he'd died. I'd lost Kyle and Debbie too. They'd become surrogate parents for me in college. They'd had me to their house for holidays when I hadn't gone home to Alaska. They'd sat by my hospital bed during my junior year when I'd needed to have an emergency appendectomy, holding my hand until my own parents had arrived. They'd even co-signed on a car loan for me when mine had died one winter and I'd needed a replacement fast. After Jamie and I'd gotten married, our bond had grown even tighter.

Now it was nearly broken.

But at least I still had Jimmy. He was part of my family here in Montana, along with Finn, Molly and the kids, and I loved our weekly visits.

"It will be good for them to see your restaurant next week." Jimmy sat forward in his chair and patted my knee. "If they see that you're trying to move on, maybe they will too."

"Or else they'll get angry again."

"I'm sorry to say that's a real possibility too."

The last time Kyle and Debbie had come to see me, they'd arranged for dinner with me and Jimmy. I'd casually mentioned going through some of Jamie's things, asking if they wanted any of his old clothes or books I'd been keeping in the attic, and dinner had taken a nosedive. Debbie had burst into tears and Kyle had refused to look at me for the rest of the meal.

"Do you think they'll ever stop blaming me for Jamie's death?" I whispered.

After all, it had been my fault he'd even been at that liquor store.

Jamie had been standing at the register when a hooded man had come barreling into the store. The man had shot Jamie, then the cashier with no hesitation. Boom. Boom. Two shots, and my husband and a single mother to an eleven-year-old daughter had been murdered. The killer had loaded up cash from the register, then made his escape, disappearing without a trace.

No witnesses. No trail to follow.

No justice.

Jamie had been in the wrong place at the wrong time, all because I'd wanted to throw a party with something to drink other than tequila shots.

"They don't blame you," Jimmy said.

I gave him a sad smile. We both knew he was lying.

Kyle and Debbie had lost their oldest son. Since they couldn't blame the actual murderer, they blamed me instead. Kyle couldn't look me in the eye anymore, and whenever I tried to hug Debbie, she flinched.

But I understood. I blamed me too.

The guilt was part of the reason I'd been so diligent about visiting Detective Simmons. If I could actually find out who had killed Jamie, I might win his parents back. They could stop blaming me for his death.

Maybe I could stop blaming myself.

And now that Cole was looking into the case, I had a feeling we might actually make some progress. It was foolish to get my hopes up, but nevertheless, they were.

My faith in Cole's abilities unnerved me. It was the kind of faith I'd always reserved for friends and family, and at best, Cole was just a casual acquaintance. Yet somehow, after one karate class, one dinner and one lunch, he'd earned my complete trust and confidence. When he'd told me that he would look into Jamie's case, the deep-seated anxiety I'd felt for five years had eased—just a little.

Because if anyone could solve Jamie's case, it would be Cole.

Jimmy sat back in his chair. "What else is new?"

"Nothing much. I'm pretty much confined to the restaurant right now, though I am taking a ukulele lesson tonight." After leaving Jimmy's, I'd go to my lesson.

"Ukulele?" He got a faraway look in his eyes. "Jamie always wanted to learn the ukulele."

"Yeah, I know. I thought I'd give it a try for him."

All of Jamie's family knew about his birthday list—Jamie had practically shouted it from the rooftops when he'd came up with the idea. But while his family knew about the list, none of them knew I was working to finish it in Jamie's place.

I hadn't mentioned it to Kyle and Debbie because I knew they wouldn't react well. And I hadn't mentioned it to Jimmy because I didn't want to make him sad. In the last seven years, he'd lost his wife to cancer, then his grandson, and then both his sisters. He'd had enough sadness, so for now, the birthday list—and my real motivations for taking ukulele lessons—was something I was keeping to myself.

"Did Jamie ever tell you why he wanted to learn?"

I shook my head. "No. Do you know why?"

"It was for Debbie." Jimmy smiled. "She knew how to play and had always wanted to teach Jamie. Except in sixth grade, he decided on the drums instead so he could be in that awful garage band. Did he ever tell you his band's name?"

I laughed. "The Roach Eaters."

"Idiots," Jimmy mumbled with a grin. "I'm glad that was just a phase. Anyway, he played the drums but promised

Debbie he'd learn the ukulele someday, and you know how he was about his mama."

"She hung the moon," we said in unison.

Jamie had doted on Debbie, and except for me, his mother had been his favorite person in the world. A promise made to her was one only his death could break.

"Maybe next week you can bring your ukulele along and show me what you've learned."

"You bet." I nodded. "Now, before I have to head out, let's discuss this hair situation. How long, exactly, will you be pink?"

Jimmy grinned and stood, walking over to a grocery bag by the television. The plastic crinkled as he fished out a can of shaving cream and pack of disposable Bic razors. "However long it takes for you to shave my head."

"What?" My eyes got wide. "That's crazy! I'm not shaving your head. Just have it bleached back to white."

"And spend another thirty bucks? No way. This only cost me six." The gleam in his eye turned diabolical. "That cheating bastard thinks he's beaten me. Just wait until I show up in the dining hall tonight looking like Mr. Clean. That will show him. He's got a crush on Millie Turner, but I have it on good authority she's got a thing for bald guys. Let's see his face when I swoop in and take his girl."

"Jimmy, please don't get into a fight with this guy and get kicked out of The Rainbow. I'm begging you."

He grinned. "For Millie Turner, it might be worth it."

That grin was so familiar, I had to smile back. Jamie had inherited a lot from his grandfather. His grin. His romantic side. His wild and free spirit.

And a grin that was impossible for me to deny.

"Fine. Let's do this." I stood from the couch and followed Jimmy into the kitchenette. Then I spent the next twenty minutes helping a seventy-two-year-old shave his head and thinking the entire time that Jamie would have loved this.

And he would have loved learning the ukulele from his mom.

————

"IT'S OFFICIAL. I have no musical talent."

Two hours after I'd left Jimmy's apartment, any hope of becoming a ukulele virtuoso was lost.

"Oh, I disagree." Mia smiled. "You just need some practice. Let's give that last chord one more try."

"Okay." I picked up the ukulele off my lap and carefully placed my fingers.

She adjusted my index finger. "Move this one here."

I strummed the strings, and for the first time, the sound that came from my instrument was actually melodic. My eyes shot up to Mia's as a huge smile spread on my face. "I did it!"

"See? No musical talent," she scoffed. "Practice makes progress."

I liked that. *Progress.* Not perfect.

I strummed the strings again, then set down the instrument, wanting to end my lesson on a good note. "Thank you so much, Mia."

"You're welcome. Let me get you a few things. Sit tight." She set down her own ukulele and stood, disappearing into the back room.

My eyes wandered over the small, square space. Three guitars hung on the far wall, and the two perched in the corner were covered in bright patterned scarves. At my side was a black upright piano—the top covered with colorful frames and pictures of happy students. The floral couch I was sitting on took up the other free wall, leaving just enough space for the wooden chair Mia had positioned in the middle of the room so she could sit across from me during our lesson.

Mia's music studio was as eclectic as its owner.

I'd found Mia Crane through Google. She'd had so many five-star reviews for her guitar lessons I hadn't hesitated to ask if she'd be my ukulele instructor, and when I'd pulled up to her house an hour ago, I'd known I'd made the right choice.

Mia had been waiting for me to arrive, standing barefoot on her front porch. One look at her carefree smile and the nerves I'd had about these lessons had vanished. She'd wrapped me in a hug instead of a handshake, then led me to her music studio— this small, cute building she'd built next to her home.

"Okay, pretty Poppy." Her singsong voice preceded her as she came out from the back.

Pretty Poppy. My family had called me that as a child too.

The light scent of eucalyptus and cucumber lotion returned with Mia. Her long brown hair was braided loosely over one shoulder, and the number of bangles strung up one arm was nearly as impressive as her enormous hoop earrings.

"You can take that ukulele home." She set down a black case on the couch. "Here is a case and I included some notes on what to practice this week."

"Thank you." I stood and smoothed down my black shift dress. "I really appreciate you taking me as a student." She'd told me when I'd called that she was full but she'd find a way to squeeze me in.

"My pleasure. I love all my kids, but having adult students can be so much fun. Once we get you through the basics, we can jam."

I laughed. I'd never heard a ukulele "jam" before, but if anyone could make it cool, it was Mia Crane.

"Have you been teaching for long?" I asked as I packed up the instrument.

"For years. Ever since my kids started kindergarten. I was so bored and lonely while they were at school I decided to start teaching guitar during the day."

"Do your kids play?"

"My daughter." Her eyes softened. "Evie's a music teacher at the high school now. But I never have been able to convince my son. He was always too active in sports and wasn't really interested."

A car door slammed outside and Mia's smile got so big I couldn't help but smile back. "Speak of the devil. I guilted him into coming over for dinner tonight."

"Then I'll get out of your hair." I snapped the case closed and looped my purse over my forearm. "See you next week?"

"I'll be here. And if you ever need to adjust your schedule for the restaurant, just let me know. It's just me and my husband these days and he's always working." She grinned. "We can do a lesson later in the evening. I'll supply the wine."

I smiled. "I'd like that. And I'll bring the chocolate."

"I knew I liked you."

We both were laughing as we stepped through the door from her studio onto the pathway that led toward the front of her house.

"Mom?" a man's voice called from around the porch.

My feet stilled and my smile faltered. I knew that voice.

"Back here, Cole!" Mia yelled.

Cole was Mia's son?

Yep. He sure is.

He rounded the corner of the house and stopped. The shock on his face mirrored mine, but he recovered first.

"Hey." Surprise morphed into a slow grin as his eyes locked with mine and he started toward us again. He wasn't wearing his normal sunglasses today and his eyes were bright in the early-evening sun.

"Hi." *Damn that breath hitch!* I sounded like a lovestruck teenager.

My body's natural reaction to Cole was not in line with my mind. In the week since I'd seen him, I'd been trying to make sense of Cole Goodman. Of how he made me feel.

I'd been trying with no luck.

Cole brought up a lot of emotions that I wasn't quite ready to explore.

It bothered me that even after a week, I could close my eyes and still see his. That I could still smell his Irish Spring soap. Yet I couldn't remember what Jamie smelled like anymore.

So I'd resigned myself to keeping some space from Cole—to getting some distance until I had this attraction under control. I'd keep our relationship strictly professional as he looked into Jamie's murder case.

So much for my intentions.

I'd signed up for ukulele lessons from his mother.

"I see you know Poppy," Mia said as Cole reached her side.

He tore his eyes from mine to smile at his mom, then bent to kiss her cheek. "Sure do. Hi, Mom."

She patted his chest. "I'm surprised I even recognized you. How long has it been? A year? Two?"

He chuckled and pulled her into his arms. "So dramatic." His smile was wide as he looked over her head to the ukulele case in my hand. "You survived her torture chamber? I'm impressed."

"Cole!" Mia slugged him in the gut.

"Ouf. Jesus, Mom." He pretended to be hurt, letting her go and stepping back to rub his *extremely* flat stomach. "And you wonder why I don't visit more often."

She laughed and I looked to my feet, taking a few seconds to banish all thoughts of Cole's abs.

"So how do you two know each other?" Mia asked, looking between us.

"Uh . . ." How did I explain this? *Your son was there on the worst night of my life. Your son is looking into my husband's murder case. Your son makes me feel things I don't want to be feeling.*

Nope. Those wouldn't work.

Thankfully, I didn't have to explain because Cole came to my rescue. "Poppy came to the dojo the other night."

"Karate and ukulele?" Mia asked. "And a business owner. I'm impressed."

"Thank you." My eyes found Cole's, and I glanced back at Mia. "I'll see you next—"

"You'll stay for dinner," Mia interrupted.

"Oh, no. Thank you, but I don't want to intrude on a family dinner." The ukulele case swung wildly at my side as I waved my arms.

Cole stepped past his mom and right into my space, and —*damn it*—my breath hitched again. *Enough of that already.*

"Here." Cole reached down and took the case from my hand. The brush of his fingers sent a shudder through my shoulders. "You might as well give in now. She's more stubborn than me and Dad combined. You don't stand a chance."

"But—"

"Come on, kids." Mia marched toward the side door of her house. "Cole, you give Poppy the tour while I get started on dinner."

"Okay, Mom," he called and started to follow.

"I should really go."

He just kept walking. "You heard the woman in charge. In we go."

I stayed stuck on the pathway. I didn't want to be rude to

Mia but another personal dinner with Cole would only add more confusion to my already jumbled feelings.

"Poppy." When Cole hit the doorstep, he glanced over his shoulder. "Dinner. Come on."

"But—"

"If you don't come in here, she'll come after you, and trust me, you don't want that. It's just dinner."

It's just dinner.

I had told myself that weeks ago when Cole had eaten dinner with me at the restaurant. Except it wasn't just dinner. It was dinner with a man whose touch made me tingle. It was dinner with a man who seemed to bust right through my defenses. It was dinner with a man who stirred feelings I'd reserved for my husband alone.

"Hi, Son."

I broke my gaze away from Cole's back as another man rounded the side of the house. His necktie was loose and his suit jacket was draped over one arm. Without asking, I knew this must be Cole's dad. They looked nearly identical except for their age difference. Cole's dad had a liberal sprinkling of gray in his dark hair and he was a bit softer in the jaw than his son.

"Hey, Dad. Meet Poppy Maysen. She's staying for dinner." Cole nodded toward me, then stepped out of the way so his dad could go inside.

"Hi, Poppy. I'm Brad." He waved. "Come on in and make yourself at home."

"Actually, I should be . . ."

Brad disappeared into his house before I could finish my sentence.

"They'll be disappointed if you don't stay," Cole said.

Sheesh. "A guilt trip? Really?"

He grinned. "Whatever gets you inside."

TWO HOURS LATER, I stood on the front porch of Cole's childhood home with a huge smile.

Dinner had been . . . just dinner.

Cole must have sensed my internal turmoil because he'd focused mostly on his parents throughout the meal. He'd teased Mia about her two-decade obsession with *General Hospital*. He'd argued with his dad about the Montana State Bobcat football roster and their chances at making it to the playoffs in the fall. And he'd treated me like I'd been to dinner a hundred times before. Like I was a natural fourth at their dinner table who just needed the occasional explanation for an inside joke.

And his parents had provided the perfect buffer to the attraction between us.

"Thank you for joining us." Mia hugged me on the front porch.

"You're welcome. Thank you for the meal. I haven't had anything that delicious in a long time."

Cole laughed. "Now she's lying, Mom. You should eat at her restaurant."

"Oh, we plan to," Mia declared. "We're going tomorrow night. Got it, Chief? You be home by six."

"Yes, Ms. Crane," Brad agreed as Mia slid into his side.

I smiled at their endearments as I waved good-bye. At dinner, I'd learned that Brad and Mia had married young but she'd never taken his last name. She called him "Chief" because of his job and he called her "Ms. Crane."

"I'll walk you to your car," Cole said, carrying my ukulele case down the steps.

Brad and Mia disappeared back inside as Cole led me down the front walkway and toward my car a few houses down.

"Your mom is such a good cook."

Cole hummed. "You've got her beat."

"I don't know about that, but thank you."

I rolled my eyes at the sound of my breathy voice. Why couldn't I seem to fill my lungs when Cole and I were alone? He'd sat across from me at dinner and I hadn't had any problems breathing. But now? I felt like I'd just run five miles.

I took a few slow breaths, hoping that when I spoke again my voice would be back to normal. "Have you found out anything on the case?"

"Sorry." He shook his head. "Not quite yet."

His eyebrows were furrowed and a couple lines creased his forehead. There was something he wasn't telling me, but I didn't press. I was simply grateful he was assisting Detective Simmons.

"So the ukulele?" he asked, changing topics. "I'm guessing this is another thing on the list."

I smiled. "You'd be right. Though, I can't believe that of all the guitar instructors in Bozeman, I happened to pick your mother as my teacher." Or that I'd walked into his karate dojo.

"Coincidence." He chuckled. "It kind of seems like a recurring theme for us."

Was it ever. I was just grateful he hadn't mentioned all of these coincidences to his parents. Cole had stayed quiet all night about how we really knew one another, giving me a chance to enjoy the evening's conversation with people who hadn't known Jamie. It was nice to have a night when no one looked at me with pity or concern about my emotional state.

Tonight, I'd just been Poppy.

"My mother is kind of in love with you. Expect a dinner mandate after each of your lessons."

I was kind of in love with Mia too. "Then next week, I'll be sure to bring dessert."

"Dessert. That reminds me, I still haven't tried your famous apple pie."

"I'll be at the restaurant tomorrow if you want to swing by." The invitation popped out of my mouth before my head could intercede. And once it was out, there was no taking it back.

Cole smiled as we reached my car. "Then it's a date."

A date.

A date with Cole Goodman.

A rush of excitement and a chill of terror slid down my spine.

CHAPTER SIX

41ST BIRTHDAY: SAY YES TO EVERYTHING FOR AN ENTIRE DAY

COLE

"What the fuck?"

I hit the brakes hard, barely making the turn into the parking lot where a Bozeman PD cruiser was parked behind a seventies mint-green Oldsmobile. The patrolman had his ticket clipboard in one hand, while the other was making calming gestures to an irate woman with frizzy gray hair. Her teal muumuu was swinging around her ankles and fuzzy pink bedroom slippers as she poked one knotty finger into the patrolman's chest.

As I pulled in right behind the cruiser, I could hear her yelling and cussing over the sound of my diesel engine. Throwing the truck in park, I didn't bother shutting it off as I hustled out to the scene. Five long strides and I stood behind the patrolman—Officer Terrell Parnow. He was doing his best to hold his ground, but the woman wasn't small and her jabbing finger was going nonstop.

The woman glanced at me but kept on yelling. "I'm calling my damn lawyer and *you*, you son of a—"

"What seems to be the problem?" My voice held enough bark to shut the crazy lady up. Her eyes flew to mine as Terrell looked over his shoulder.

His frame deflated as his hand dropped to his side. "Detective Goodman. I was just writing a ticket because—"

"I'll tell you what the problem is here." The woman stepped right around Terrell and into my face. "This kid is trying to give me a speeding ticket when I wasn't speeding!"

"Ma'am, you were doing forty in a twenty-five." He looked to me with pleading brown eyes. "Honest, Detective. I've got her on radar."

She whirled around on Terrell—her muumuu whipping me in the shins—but before she could launch into another rant, I stepped between them. I stood my tallest, looking right down my nose into the woman's paling face. "Speeding and assault on a law enforcement officer. Not good."

She stuttered back a step, slapping a hand to her chest. "What?" she gasped. "Assault?"

"That's right."

"But—"

"Officer Parnow, mind if I borrow your cuffs? I left mine in the truck."

The woman gasped again.

"Detective, I don't, um . . ." He moved out from behind me to my side, speaking underneath his breath. "I don't think we need to charge her with assault."

"I'll take the speeding ticket." The woman flew to Terrell's side like he was her new best friend. "Please."

I held back a grin, fighting to keep the scowl on my face. "I don't know. It looked awful serious when I pulled up."

"I get carried away sometimes," she told me, then looked

over to Terrell, nodding fiercely. "I was going too fast. You were right."

Terrell looked to me and I shrugged. "It's your call, Officer."

He nodded, turning back to the woman who was now clinging to his arm. "Ma'am, if you'll get back in your car, I'll finish with the speeding ticket. Then you can be on your way."

"Oh, thank you." She squeezed his arm and then let him go, ducking eye contact with me as she scurried back into her Olds.

When her driver's door shut, I chuckled.

"Would you have charged her?" Terrell asked.

"Nah. I just wanted to shut her up."

Terrell grinned. "Smart."

I shrugged and jerked my chin to the Olds. "Give her the ticket and get her on her way."

"Yes, sir." He took his clipboard back to her window, returning her license and registration. Then he tore off a goldenrod speeding ticket and away she roared, pulling out of the parking lot with—careful—haste.

"Thanks." Terrell joined me by his cruiser and sighed. "That got out of hand. Seems to be happening to me a lot lately."

"Unfortunately, that's part of the job."

"Every time? I haven't had a stop in a month without getting a load of shit. Do you think I'm doing something wrong?"

"I doubt it." I clapped a hand on his shoulder. "Come on. I'll go out on patrol with you for a while."

His entire face lit up. "Really?"

"Really. Let me grab my keys." I walked back to my truck, leaning in to shut off the ignition and get my keys. Then I plucked my sunglasses out of the console and went to the cruiser.

Sliding into the passenger seat, I grinned at Terrell's excitement. His dark face was split with a wide, white smile, and his fingers drummed on the wheel.

"So you've been having some rough stops lately?" I asked as he pulled out of the parking lot.

"Yeah." His smile turned down. "No matter how polite I am, everyone fights the ticket. I asked a couple of the other guys on patrol, but none of them seem to be having the same problem."

I didn't want to be the one to break it to the kid, but his face was probably the reason he'd had such a hard time lately. Not because of the color of his skin, but because at twenty-something years old, Terrell Parnow had a baby face if I'd ever seen one.

Round, chubby cheeks. Soft brown eyes. There wasn't a thing hard or angular about him. Add to that his shorter stature and skinny frame, and the only intimidating thing about the kid was his gun.

But if someone didn't step in, his confidence would keep getting rattled and only make the situation worse. He'd either quit the force or someone would think they could push him too far.

"Look, Terrell. I'll be straight with you here." I slid off my sunglasses so he could see my eyes. "You're fighting an uphill battle. You're half the size of most guys on patrol, and people aren't going to take you seriously by default. You've got to figure out a way to be assertive but not come across as a dick. Find the balance between pushover and asshole. Understand?"

Terrell stayed quiet. The radio clicked on and off as dispatch made calls to other cars, but the kid didn't say a word.

Shit. Was that too blunt? Had I scared him? He had to know he looked like a teenager, right? I opened my mouth to tone it down a bit, but he spoke up first.

"What if I grew a beard?"

I grinned. "It's worth a shot."

"Thanks, Detective. I appreciate the honesty."

"No problem. And it's Cole."

He nodded. "Cole."

"One other thing," I said as we passed another patrol car heading in the opposite direction. "If the other guys on patrol say every stop is a good one, they're full of shit. With every four good stops, you'll have one bad. That's normal for everyone and we've all been there. Toughen up that skin and don't let the bad ones get to you."

"Okay." He nodded. We rode in silence for a few blocks until Terrell spoke again. "What should I have done differently with that woman?"

I rubbed my jaw, the stubble thicker than normal because I hadn't shaved this morning. "If I was in your spot today, I wouldn't have let her out of the car. I wouldn't have let her cuss at me, and I sure as fuck wouldn't have let her touch me. But when I was your age? When I was a rookie? I probably would have done the same thing as you. I would have stood there and taken her shit until she ran out of steam. Then I would have handed her the ticket and gotten back in my cruiser and had a beer when I got home."

"No shit?" His frame perked up.

"No shit."

For the next hour, we drove around Bozeman, staying fairly quiet. I'd been on my way to Poppy's restaurant for an early dinner break when I'd seen Terrell, but this hour or two was important for the young patrolman. So I rode along, marveling at how much my hometown had changed over the years.

Bozeman had once been a small college ski town, but the population had boomed these last ten years. Big-box stores and chain restaurants had flocked to this mountain valley.

Construction had reached an all-time high as builders replaced wheat fields with apartment complexes and townhomes. Open lots had been filled with tech centers and office buildings.

"Have you lived here long?" I asked Terrell.

"Just a couple of years. I moved from Arizona to Montana for the skiing, then decided to go to the academy."

"Bozeman is changing fast. None of this was here when I was in high school." I pointed to the new subdivisions on both sides of the street. We were at the far edge of town, miles from where I remembered the last stoplight being when I was a kid.

Terrell smiled. "I hear we might be getting a Best Buy."

I frowned. "Great." I could live without a Best Buy.

I missed the hometown feel that Bozeman once had. I ran into fewer and fewer familiar faces at the grocery store these days. I got stuck in traffic almost every morning. And walking down Main Street, something I remembered fondly as a kid, now just pissed me off. The local shops had lost some of their authenticity, becoming too fancy in an effort to mimic ski towns like Aspen or Breckenridge.

Out went the small-town charm and in came the higher crime rate.

Bozeman was getting to be as bad as a fucking big city. Drugs. Murder. We were even seeing a stronger gang influence.

"Whoa. What the hell?"

I was snapped out of my thoughts as Terrell's head whipped to the side. An orange Chevy Blazer streaked past us, speeding in the opposite direction.

In a split second, Terrell had the siren blaring and lights flashing and was flipping a tire-screeching U-turn. His foot dug into the gas pedal as the cruiser's engine revved. We caught the Blazer in no time, following it over to the shoulder.

"You take the lead," I told Terrell as I unbuckled.

He nodded and we both got out of the cruiser.

Approaching with caution, always at the ready like we'd both been taught, Terrell came up on the driver's side window while I took the opposite.

"Evening," Terrell greeted the driver. "License, registration and proof of insurance, please?"

I bent low to look through the open passenger window. The driver, a young college kid, was fumbling in his wallet. His shaking fingers had to try three times to get his license out of the plastic slot. "Here you go." His voice was as rattled as his fingers as he handed the card to Terrell.

"Do you know why I pulled you over," Terrell looked to the card, "Quincy?"

"I was, um, speeding?"

Terrell nodded. "The speed limit here is forty."

"Oh. Really?"

Come on, Quincy. Don't play dumb. Why did the young ones always try and play dumb?

Terrell frowned. "Go ahead and get me your registration and proof of insurance."

"Okay." Quincy reached across the dash, his gaze skidding away from mine. With a pop, he opened the glove box and set off a paper explosion. Receipts. Candy wrappers. University parking tickets. It all came spilling out—including an ID that landed right on the seat by my window, faceup.

My eyes narrowed at the Colorado ID. Quincy's picture was next to the name Jason Chen. I squinted and made out a birthdate. "Jason Chen" was twenty-seven.

Fuck that. If this kid was twenty-seven, then I was in my damn forties.

"Quincy, I think you'd better get out of the car," I said. "And bring that other ID with you."

Ten minutes later, Quincy was shaking my hand and promising never to buy a fake ID again.

"Thank you. Thank you so much, Officer."

I let his hand go. "Don't do it again."

"I won't." He shook his head. "I promise. I won't. It was stupid of me to get that fake ID in the first place."

"This is your once, Quincy." I held up one finger to his nose. "Your one free pass and your one chance to learn from your mistake. Don't take it for granted because you won't get a twice."

"Yes, sir. Thank you."

"Good." I jerked my head to the Blazer. "Now get out of here."

He nodded and rushed back to the SUV, waving to Terrell and me as he pulled back onto the road.

"Why'd you do it?" Terrell asked. "Why'd you let him off with a warning?"

I shrugged. "Way back when, I had someone give me a once and it changed my life. I pay it forward when I can. Besides, that kid was harmless. We took his fake ID. We could have written him up, but I think we made a more lasting impression this way, don't you?"

"I sure do. That kid was about to piss himself." Terrell nodded and started back to the cruiser. "A once. I like that."

I grinned, knowing Terrell would be stealing a term I'd stolen myself. "Just use them wisely."

———

FROZEN in the doorway of The Maysen Jar, I watched as Poppy smiled and laughed with an elderly man sitting by the register.

Damn, she was beautiful.

It was hours later than I'd planned to be at the restaurant. Terrell had dropped me off at my truck after the Quincy incident and I'd come straight here, so anxious to see Poppy that I'd had a hard time obeying the speed limit myself.

But I was here now and I couldn't get past the damn door. "Excuse me."

A lady stood behind me, wanting to get past. "Sorry." I unstuck my feet and stepped inside, holding the door open for her.

As the lady joined a friend at a table, I stayed at the back wall, watching Poppy work. Her hair was up, tied in a knot secured by two pencils. A black apron was tied around the waistband of her jeans. Her white V-neck tee with the restaurant's logo on the pocket draped perfectly down her breasts, hinting at just a bit of cleavage as it fell down her flat stomach.

Beautiful.

Her smile was so natural and charismatic. She mesmerized her customers, laughing and chatting as she worked. She mesmerized me.

So I stood at the back, doing my best to blend into the brick wall as I watched. I relished every second of her unguarded smile, because as soon as she spotted me, she'd be back on alert. She'd throw up her wall, just like she'd done last night when she'd spotted me outside of Mom's music studio.

I'd lectured Terrell earlier about finding a balance, but damn if I wasn't having a hell of a time finding one with Poppy. Was I pushing her too fast? Too hard? Not enough?

When I was around, she had a war raging inside her head. She'd look at me and I'd see that desire spark behind her eyes. But then she'd smother it, letting her face twist with guilt. I hated that look. I hated putting it on her face.

If I were a stronger man, I would have stayed away and given her time. But here I was, lurking at the back of her restaurant, so drawn to her that I'd barely blinked.

As if she knew I was thinking about her, Poppy's eyes

searched the restaurant. The second she spotted me, her body strung tight. She looked away, studying the counter for a moment as her shoulders rose and fell with a deep breath. But then she shocked me with a slow, gorgeous smile.

I was fucking doomed.

That smile—and the finger wave that went along with it—would have had me swaying on my feet if not for the brick wall at my back.

A customer snagged Poppy's attention and I took a moment to get my heart rate under control. Three deep breaths and I was steady, striding across the restaurant.

"Is this seat taken?" I asked the elderly man at the counter.

"No," he grunted.

"Thanks." I slid into the stool, catching Poppy's eye as she rang up her customer's order. "Hey."

"Hi. Give me one sec."

"Take your time." She went back to ringing up a customer's order and I turned to the old man. "Mind if I snag a menu?"

He grunted again as he lifted one off the stack by the register and pushed it down the counter.

I scanned the menu, debating my options. Maybe one day I wouldn't need a menu. Maybe I'd be around enough that I'd have all the choices memorized. And maybe one day I'd get a different greeting from Poppy. I'd be allowed behind the counter so I could tuck her into my side and kiss her hair as I said hello.

"Here's hoping," I mumbled.

"What was that?" the elderly man asked.

"Oh, uh, just hoping she's got more of that mac 'n' cheese." *Piss poor recovery, Cole. Piss poor.* "Have you eaten here much?"

"Every day." His chest puffed up as he made his declaration. "This is my seat."

"An expert. Nice. Any recommendations?"

"Meh. Her potpies are all right."

"All right?" Poppy stepped right in front of the old man and planted her hands on her hips. "Sheesh. Is that why you've had four of them today? Because they were just *all right*?"

The man glared up at Poppy as she scowled back. Was that what this guy did? He came into her restaurant and criticized her food all damn day? I opened my mouth to put this old geezer in his place—no one glared at Poppy—but the corner of her mouth twitched.

"Oh, stop." She waved off his glare and smiled. "Randall James. Meet Cole Goodman."

Randall turned to acknowledge me. He looked me up and down twice, each time his eyes lingering a bit on my gun.

I held out my hand first, and he shocked the shit out of me by actually taking it. "Nice to meet you, Randall."

"Same."

"Do you want some dinner?" Poppy asked me.

"Please. Surprise me, but don't forget my dessert this time."

"Last weekend I made up a new mixed berry pie in honor of the Fourth. I haven't added them to the menu yet but they're available. Do you want to try one of those or an apple pie?"

"What!" Randall nearly came off his stool before I could answer. "You said you ran out of those berry pie things earlier."

"No, I said *you* ran out." She pointed at his chest. "You know the rules. Five pies are all you get in a twenty-four-hour period."

"I don't know why I keep coming here and taking this crap." Randall spun around on his stool. "I'm leaving. Don't count on me coming back."

His threat didn't faze Poppy. "Don't forget your coffee." She turned and grabbed a to-go cup and filled it from the coffee pot on the back wall.

Randall grunted as he slipped on his cap and prepared his cane. Then he took the cup from Poppy's hand and started shuffling toward the door.

"See you tomorrow," Poppy called to his back.

Randall just shook his head and kept walking.

"Cheerful guy," I teased.

Poppy laughed. "And you caught him on a good day. Yesterday he threatened to leave me a bad Yelp review because I wouldn't make him six espressos. But he'll be back tomorrow to keep me and Molly company."

"Grouchy exterior, heart of gold?" I guessed.

"Exactly." She smiled. "Hang tight, I'll get your food. Do you want to sit up here or at a table?"

"Would you sit—"

"Poppy—" Molly came rushing out of the kitchen, interrupting my dinner invitation, but stopped when she spotted me. "Oh, hey, Cole. How are you?"

"Good." I returned her smile. "Just getting dinner."

"Perfect timing! Poppy was just going to take a dinner break too. You can keep each other company."

I guess I didn't need to ask Poppy to eat with me after all. *Thanks, Molly.*

"I never should have told you," Poppy muttered.

Told her what?

"Are you going to eat with Cole?" Molly's smile got wider as I looked between her and Poppy. "Yes or no, Poppy-bear?"

"Yes."

"And tomorrow, are you going to take the morning off? Yes or no?"

Poppy's teeth gritted. "Yes."

"And are you going to let me hire another part-time worker so you don't burn yourself out?"

"This is ridiculous."

"Answer the question," Molly pressed. "Yes or no? Are you going to let me hire another person?"

"Yes," Poppy hissed.

What the hell? I was definitely missing something here, but before I could ask, Poppy threw her hands in the air and stormed back into the kitchen as Molly burst into laughter.

When she'd caught her breath, Molly wiped tears from the corners of her eyes and leaned a hip against the counter. "She has to say yes to everything today, and I'm taking advantage because it's for her own good."

"Ah." I nodded. "Let me guess. Another birthday list item?"

Molly straightened. "She told you about the list?"

"Yeah. The last time I was here." *Shit.* "Should I have kept that a secret?"

"No, but it *is* interesting." Molly studied me for a long moment, then smiled. "I like you, Cole. Poppy does too, even if she won't admit it. Just go easy, my friend. Go easy."

"You don't beat around the bush, do you?"

She shrugged. "Takes too long."

"Agreed." I smiled, then slid off my stool and walked over to an empty table along the far wall.

The restaurant was busy tonight but not packed. Everyone seated had already gotten their meals so I sat and people-watched until Poppy came out of the kitchen with a tray of food and waters. She set down two steaming jelly jars filled with macaroni and cheese.

I inhaled the cheesy smell. "This smells great."

"Thanks." She handed me an unshaken jar of salad. "Shake that up and I'll be right back."

I did as I was told, shaking as she went behind the counter for plates and silverware. She came back and set the table, splitting the salad between us.

"I'll share the salad but you better not take any of my pie. I've been promised dessert and I refuse to share."

She giggled and did a mock salute. "Understood, Detective."

We ate quietly, each of us diving into our salad and pasta. The gentle hum of other conversations filled the room until Poppy broke the silence. "Can I ask you something?"

I nodded as I swallowed my bite of macaroni. "Shoot."

She waited a second before speaking softly. "Why did you stay that night? You sat with me for hours, even after my brother arrived."

I blinked, surprised by the serious question, then set down my fork and leaned in closer. "I stayed because I didn't want you to be alone. Your brother was on the phone and dealing with stuff. I just . . . I didn't want you to be by yourself on that couch."

She looked down at her plate, poking at her salad. "Thank you."

"You don't have to thank me. I was just doing my job."

It was more than that, but my real motives were damn hard to explain. Delivering the news of James Maysen's death had been fucking extreme, something I'd never done before. At the time, I'd chalked up my late-night vigil to the difficult situation. But now—now that I'd been around her again—I knew it wasn't just the circumstances that had made me stay.

It was Poppy.

I hadn't been able to leave her side until I'd known she was in good hands. So I'd sat by her side until she'd fallen asleep on the couch and her brother had taken my place.

"What made you ask?"

She shrugged and speared a bite of lettuce. "Just curious."

She may as well have said, "End of discussion." Not that I would have pressed anyway. I couldn't imagine how hard it would be for her to think about that night, let alone talk about it. And with a restaurant full of people, tonight wasn't the time for a recap.

If she ever wanted to talk about that night, I'd be all ears. If she never wanted to speak of it again, that was fine too.

"I hear you're saying yes to everything today?" I chased a bite of macaroni with some water.

She nodded, smiling again as she chewed.

"A guy could take advantage of that."

Her chewing stopped and her blue eyes snapped to mine.

"Me, for example. I could use this to get exactly what I want."

I didn't miss the way her eyes flared, and *damn*, it was sexy. If things were farther along—if this were a year from now and we were in a different place—I could have used this game to have her moaning *yes* all night long. But we weren't there, and I wasn't a complete asshole.

But I did love to tease.

"Poppy," I whispered, leaning closer.

Her breaths were shallow as she waited.

"Will you bring me both the mixed berry *and* the apple pie?"

She blinked twice, then a hand flew over her mouth—still full of salad—covering it as she laughed. "Yes."

I grinned, sitting back in my chair and digging into my food. "Maybe you can tell me more about this list too? It seems like every time I see you you're on to something new."

Her hand fell. "You really want to know?"

"I really want to know."

CHAPTER SEVEN

35TH BIRTHDAY: TAKE A PHOTO OF MYSELF EVERY DAY FOR A YEAR

POPPY

Cole's interest in Jamie's birthday list surprised me. No one but me had ever gotten excited about the list since Jamie had died, but Cole was genuinely curious. And eager, maybe? Whatever it was, I liked the sparkle it added to his eyes.

"Okay, um . . ." The best way for me to explain everything on the list was just to hand over the journal, except no one but me and Jamie had ever touched it before. Would it be strange to let Cole read it? Would that have bothered Jamie? I smiled to myself. *No.* Jamie had been so proud of his list, he'd have plastered it on a billboard.

"Be right back." I held up a finger to Cole, then got up from the table and walked to the register. Leaning over the counter, I dug through my purse, which I'd stashed underneath the register. When my fingers brushed leather, I pulled out Jamie's journal, stroking the cover once before standing back up.

The second I turned back to our table, I found Cole's gaze locked on the place where my ass had just been. His eyes were darker, the spark behind them now a blaze. He didn't even try to hide it as his gaze traced up my stomach and over my breasts. He lingered a bit on my chest, drawing out his inspection, until he finally continued to my face. When his stare found my lips, I fought the urge to lick them. When he found my eyes, I didn't want to blink.

Sexy. Cole was the epitome of sexy. The sexiest man I'd ever seen.

No, not Cole. Jamie. What was wrong with me? I blinked, forcing my eyes away from Cole's as I mentally chastised myself again. Jamie was the sexiest man I'd ever seen. *Jamie.* My husband.

Cole was just new. That's why I found him so attractive. I hadn't spent years with him, studying his face and finding flaws. I bet if I looked at him long enough, I'd realize that his ears were kind of pointed and his eyebrows were on the bushy side. And he had to have some imperfections underneath his jeans and black polo. No one was *that* cut—not in real life.

If I spent the time with Cole, like I had with Jamie, I'd realize he wasn't an Adonis. He was just a man. A man who wasn't Jamie.

A man who was now looking at me with furrowed eyebrows—which weren't bushy at all.

I unglued my sneakers from the floor and walked back to the table, holding out the journal for Cole. "Here. This was Jamie's birthday list."

He looked at it for a moment, not taking it from my outstretched hand. "Are you sure?"

I gave him a sad smile, glad that he understood how much trust I was giving him. "Go ahead."

Cole wiped his hands on a napkin before he took the book, then he carefully opened the cover. I sat back down, concentrating on my meal as he slowly flipped through the journal, and did my best not to stare with every swish of a turning page. Every once in a while, he'd let out a small chuckle. On other pages, I'd catch him frowning—I doubted he liked the fire alarm item.

When he reached the end, Cole surprised me by going back to the beginning, starting again.

"I'll get dessert."

Cole didn't glance up from the journal. "Thanks."

Clearing my plate and his, I went back to the kitchen and put the dishes in the sink. Then I went back out front to get Cole's desserts in the oven. Molly was busy clearing a couple of tables so I took a few moments to breathe and watch the timer on the oven tick down.

I'd figured out a way to partially bake my minipies when I was prepping them so that when a customer came in, they only had to wait five minutes instead of twenty. They weren't quite as good as they were completely fresh, but the only person who knew the difference seemed to be me.

So for the five minutes that Cole's pies were baking, I did my best to settle the anxiety that had grown ever since I'd handed him the journal.

My fingers tapped on the counter as I tried to make sense of my nerves. Was I nervous to hear what Cole had to say about Jamie's list? Or nervous that he'd think me doing the list was stupid? Or worse, was I nervous that Cole would think Jamie's ideas were stupid?

Given the short time we'd spent together, it surprised me how much Cole's opinion mattered. I knew he liked me, but I wanted him to like Jamie too.

And the birthday list *was* Jamie.

The timer dinged, ending my reprieve, and on autopilot, I took out the pies and wrapped them in napkins before adding a dollop of ice cream on both. Then I carried them on a tray back to the table, where Cole had closed the journal and was watching me with a seriousness that only made my anxiety spike.

"These are still hot." I set down his jars and took my seat. I slid my hands underneath my bouncing knees so I wouldn't flap them around as we talked.

Cole grabbed the apple pie first, taking a small bite with his spoon. "Wow. No wonder Randall wants ten of these a day." He took another bite, sucking in some air to cool down the crust. "This is amazing."

I smiled as pride swelled. I knew my desserts were good, but Cole's approval felt incredible. I hadn't been this excited about my silly little apple pies since the first night I'd made them for Jamie.

"That's quite a list." Cole nodded toward the journal in between bites.

"It is." My smile faltered at the way his jaw hardened.

"Are you planning on doing these all by yourself?"

"Um, yes." How else was I going to get through them all?

"That's going to take a while."

"I hope not," I sighed. "My goal is to get them done before New Year's."

"What?" His spoon dropped into the jar, clinking against the glass. "That's less than six months away."

"I know." Just thinking about all I still had to do made my shoulders fall. "I thought I could do it, but with the restaurant and some of the bigger things on the list, it will take longer. I was really hoping to have it done before Jamie's birthday."

That seemed impossible now. With the restaurant and all of the other things I was adding to my daily schedule, piling on more was going to wear me thin. If I didn't let up, my self-imposed deadline would stress me to the max.

Which meant it would take just that much longer to put

this list behind me. Could I do it if I added another year? Maybe two?

I didn't have to do this all so soon. But I wanted to. I wanted to do this for Jamie and let it go. Every day, I was getting stronger. I was getting back on my feet. I was starting to live again—for me.

And until the list was done, I'd still be living for Jamie.

"Look." Cole leaned his elbows on the table. "I don't want to step on your toes. This is an awesome list and he had some cool ideas. If you want to do them on your own, I understand. I get that this is incredibly personal. But if you'd like, I'd be glad to help you with some of these."

"What?" I didn't know what made me smile more. That he thought Jamie's list was cool or that he wanted to help. Regardless, I was beaming. "You'd really help?"

Cole's eyes were sparkling again. "In a heartbeat."

———

"WELL? WHAT DO YOU THINK?" I asked.

The restaurant was clean and closed, and while we'd been prepping in the kitchen for tomorrow, I'd been telling Molly everything about my dinner with Cole.

"I don't know." She grabbed another tomato to chop for the salad jars. "Do you want his help?"

"Yes," I admitted as I rolled out my piecrust.

Finn and Molly would help if I asked, but they each had so much on their plates already. And something about bringing Cole onboard felt . . . right. The instant he'd told me he'd help, a rush of confidence had spread through my veins. For the first time in weeks, I felt like this might actually happen. I might actually finish Jamie's list by the end of the year.

"I think it's a good thing." Molly grinned. "If he's willing, then take him up on his offer. And besides that, I think it'll be good for you to spend some time with someone else. A *man* someone else."

"That's not what this is about."

"I know. Your intentions are strictly platonic. But I also know that you've got the hots for the guy."

"I don't have—"

"And that scares you to death."

Denial would be pointless so I stopped rolling the dough to tell her the truth. "So much. And it makes me feel guilty. So guilty."

Molly set down her knife to look at me. "You have nothing to feel guilty about. Jamie would want you to be happy."

"But I don't want to forget him. Every day I feel like he's slipping further and further away from me." And every moment I spent with Cole, that slip happened faster and faster. Last night I'd broken down in tears because I couldn't get the picture of Cole's eyes out of my head. I'd ended up studying Jamie's picture for an hour, trying to re-memorize his eyes and block out Cole's.

But as much as I wanted to block him out, Cole Goodman was on my mind.

"Poppy, just because you find yourself attracted to another man doesn't mean you'll forget Jamie. It just means you're letting him go. Wasn't that what this whole list was about?"

I nodded. "Yeah. I just . . . it hurts."

My heart had been in pieces since the night Jamie had been killed. It had taken every day of the last five years for the pain in my chest to fade to a dull ache. Still, it was there. And after every one of my interactions with Cole, that ache flared. Because when I was with Cole, I wasn't remembering Jamie.

Cole made me forget the pain.

"I miss Jamie." My voice cracked as the burn of tears hit my eyes. "I miss him every day. At the same time, I want to move on with my life. I know Jamie would be pissed that I've spent the last five years crying for him. But if I move on, who will remember him? All he has is his family and me to keep him alive."

Molly rounded the table and pulled me into a hug. "Remember what you decided after Jamie died? How you'd get through?"

I nodded. "Minute by minute."

After Jamie's funeral, I'd spent months in bed. I'd sunk into a crippling depression, barely able to function on my own. Finally, Finn and Molly had gotten so worried that they'd flown my parents to town and staged an intervention. My parents had asked me to move home to Alaska, and I'd almost agreed, until Finn and Molly had announced they were pregnant with Kali. That was the first time I'd smiled after Jamie had died, and it had been my turning point. That day, I'd decided to stay so I could be here for Kali's birth, and I'd decided to take life minute by minute. Some minutes were better than others, but it was the only way I'd been able to live a life without my husband.

Minute by minute.

"My advice is to take things with Cole minute by minute. Can you try that? And remember, you have to say yes."

I smiled and hugged her tighter. "Yes. I'll try."

Molly's phone rang on the table, interrupting our hug. I sniffled as she let me go, and swallowed the burn in my throat, determined not to cry.

"Hey," Molly answered the call. "Okay, sure."

She lifted the phone from her ear and held it out as Finn's FaceTime request popped up on the screen.

"Hi, Mommy!" Kali's little voice filled the kitchen.

"Hi, sweetie!" Molly beamed at her daughter. "How are

you? You look so pretty and clean. Did you just have bath time?"

Kali nodded. "I'm in my bed too."

"I'm so glad you called. Did you have fun at Daddy's tonight?"

"Uh-huh." She smiled and snuggled closer into Finn's chest.

"Were they good?" Molly asked my brother.

"Yeah. Sorry, Max fell asleep early before we could call."

"That's okay."

"Mommy? Is tomorrow a Daddy night or a Mommy night?"

"It's a Mommy night."

I pulled my top lip between my teeth to keep from speaking up. *Mommy nights. Daddy nights.* I wanted to scream at Finn and pound on the table until Molly and my brother realized what they were missing. They were throwing love away. I'd give anything to have Jamie back, and here they were, wasting a happy life because they were too stubborn to look past some mistakes.

But as always, I kept my mouth shut and went back to my piecrust.

"Say good night, Kali," Finn ordered. "It's late."

Kali yawned. "Night night, Mommy."

Molly blew her a kiss. "Night night, Kali bug. I love you."

"Bye," Finn muttered and ended the call.

Molly tossed the phone on the counter and braced her hands on the metal, hanging her head between her shoulders.

Oh, Molly. Mine wasn't the only troubled heart in this kitchen.

When her shoulders started to shake, I abandoned my crust and went to her side, wrapping her in another hug. "I'm sorry."

She nodded and swiped away the tears. "It's my fault. I shouldn't cry."

"You can always cry, especially on me." I'd cried on her shoulder more times than I could count. "And it's not only your fault. You both made mistakes."

Molly shook her head. "No. This is on me."

"But—"

"I *cheated* on him, Poppy." I cringed as she stressed that ugly word again. "End of story. End of marriage."

End of discussion.

She stepped out of my embrace, drying her face as she went back to her chopping and I went back to the piecrust. We worked in silence for an hour, both deep in our own heads, until finally Molly spoke up.

"I don't know if I'll ever love anyone other than Finn. Maybe you'll never love anyone other than Jamie. But will you promise me something? I don't want us both to live our lives with broken hearts. If someone new comes along—if he already has—promise you won't let fear keep you from trying again."

I crossed my heart. "Yes, I promise."

———

A FEW DAYS after Cole had offered to help me with Jamie's birthday list, I was at Lindley Park with my phone angled up to my face as I attempted to take a selfie.

"What are you doing?" Cole asked.

I dropped my phone, surprised to see Cole standing a few feet away. *Damn it.* I'd hoped to have a few minutes alone to take my daily picture.

"Um, nothing. Just taking a selfie." *Or twelve.*

He grinned. "Pictures usually look better when you smile."

"I hate selfies." I grimaced. "My nose is too big for selfies."

"What? You do not have a big nose."

"I have nearly two hundred pictures proving you wrong."

I'd never thought my nose was big until I'd started this selfie ritual. Now I was finding props—a book, a coffee mug, my hand —to cover it for my daily picture.

"Give me that." Cole snatched the phone from my hand. "Now sit on that bench and smile."

I slumped on the metal seat, scrunching up my nose to give him an exaggerated toothy grin.

He dropped his arms and frowned. "I've seen mug shots better than that."

I laughed, and just as I did, he snapped a picture. "There. Was that so hard?"

I pushed off the bench and walked to his side, peering around his arms at the picture. "Not bad, Detective. Not bad at all."

"Picture a day for a year?" he guessed.

"Yep," I said, popping the *p*. "There were a couple of days where I almost forgot at the beginning but now it's habit."

My first picture had been on Jamie's birthday. I'd made his favorite chocolate cake and taken a picture with all his candles. Since then, I'd tried to take my selfies without tears and puffy eyes.

Today's picture would be my first nonselfie to add to the stack.

"Thanks for meeting me today." Since the restaurant closed after lunch on Sundays, I'd texted Cole and asked if he'd meet me at the park so we could make a plan to tackle some of the bigger items on the birthday list.

"Glad to. Do you want to hang out here or walk around?"

"A walk sounds good." I swung out my arm. "Lead the way."

Cole brushed past me and I caught a whiff of his natural scent mixed with traces of Irish Spring. My big nose acted on its own and followed that smell, sucking in so much air through my nostrils that they whizzed. To an onlooker, I probably looked ridiculous, following Cole's movements with my nose, but he smelled so good, so different, I needed just one more breath.

"Allergies?" Cole asked over his shoulder.

My hand flew to my face, rubbing my nose quickly as I lied. "No, uh, just an itch."

Smooth, Poppy. Real smooth.

I uncovered my nose and jogged to Cole's side, walking as close to the edge of the path as possible, hoping the distance would keep me from catching another intoxicating whiff.

"I can't remember the last time I walked through a park," Cole said as I fell in step with him. "College maybe."

"Did you go to MSU?"

He nodded. "Yeah. I got my bachelor's before going to the academy."

"We must have been there about the same time then. How old are you?"

"Thirty-one. You?"

"Twenty-nine. I wonder if we ever passed each other in a hallway."

He shook his head. "Doubtful."

"Were you not on campus much or something?"

"No." He looked over at me and smiled. "Doubtful because I would have remembered seeing you around."

Maybe it was the bright afternoon sunlight—or maybe it was because I was staring at his mouth—but for the first time, I noticed Cole had two small dimples when he smiled. And damn if they didn't make his smile just that much sexier.

Just when I thought I had the breath-hitching thing under control, he produced dimples.

"It sure is hot today." I fanned my face, hoping he'd think

my shortness of breath and flushed cheeks were from the weather.

Cole just chuckled. "Sure is."

We walked quietly for a few minutes, and with each step, I relaxed more and more in Cole's company. It was always like that. I'd need five to ten minutes just to calm my racing heart—to settle down and breathe easy again. Which is why I loved that Cole never rushed us into conversation. He set the perfect pace where I was concerned. Not too slow. Not too fast.

So we took our time, walking on the path through the park, enjoying the summer afternoon.

It really was hot today, the July sun shining high in the cloudless blue sky, and I was glad I'd changed into a pair of cut-off shorts and a green tank before I'd left the restaurant. My rubber flip-flops crunched along the gravel path that wound between the trees. Even Cole was in flip-flops; the tan canvas straps looked so small on his big feet.

Today was the first time I'd seen Cole out of his normal black Bozeman PD polo or T-shirt. He was still wearing faded blue jeans that hung perfectly from his narrow hips, but without the gun and badge attached to his belt, he looked different. Younger. Less serious. More handsome. Not many guys could pull off a coral T-shirt, but Cole did. The color brought out the dark green flecks in his eyes and highlighted the tan on his face and forearms.

I did my best not to stare but stole glances every few steps.

"The carnival is coming up in a couple weeks." Cole finally spoke up as we reached a part of the trail shaded by towering evergreens. "Want some company as you go on the rides?"

Jamie had always wanted to go on all the rides at the county fair. Every single one, including the kiddie rides. But while they'd been my husband's thing, carnival rides were definitely not for me.

"Would you mind? I get a little motion sick. I might need some encouragement to make it through them all."

Cole stopped walking. "Are you going to puke on me?"

"No." I laughed and kicked a pinecone. "Well, not intentionally."

He grinned. "I'll agree to go as long as you promise not to eat anything beforehand."

I crossed my heart. "Promise."

We both laughed as we fell back in step.

"I've been thinking a lot about Jamie's old truck. I called a couple of mechanics in town to see how much it would cost to get it restored, and it's a fortune. I don't suppose you know a decent mechanic who would cut me a deal?"

Jamie had bought an old truck in high school with the hope of restoring it. Since I knew nothing about fixing cars, I was going to have to hire out the restoration, but with everything I'd sunk into the restaurant, I couldn't afford to spend a huge amount. Definitely not as much as I'd been quoted over the past couple of weeks.

Cole rubbed his jaw. "I can probably handle the simple stuff. Replacing panels. Tuning up the engine. Things like that. My dad and I actually fixed up a couple of cars together when I was a kid, just as a hobby. I'll have to see the truck to know exactly what needs to be done, but if I did some of the work, you'd save some money."

"Cole, I can't ask you to do all of that. You're too busy as it is."

"I'll make time." He nudged my elbow with his. "Besides, I like fixing old classics. It will be fun for me too."

Having someone else restore that truck wasn't what Jamie would have done—he'd have done it himself—but I didn't have that luxury. It was either pay someone to do it for me or let Cole.

"I won't be able to help. I know absolutely nothing about cars."

"That's okay. I'll take care of it."

And just like that, Cole made one of the more daunting items on Jamie's list seen manageable. This was big, asking Cole to fix up Jamie's truck with little to no help from me. And after this, I wouldn't ask for more. I wouldn't take advantage of Cole's generosity. But I would let him take on the truck.

A surge of confidence hit me again. *I will finish Jamie's list.* I would do this for my husband.

"Thank you. For helping me. For looking into Jamie's case. I really appreciate it."

He stepped closer. "I'll do anything I can to help you."

His soft, intimate tone gave me heart flutters, but pain quickly chased them away.

My heart flutters were supposed to be for Jamie.

Guilt. Guilt was a heavy beast. It settled like a dead weight in my chest. I took a step away from Cole, retreating as far away from him as possible on the narrow path, in an attempt to lessen guilt's load.

Cole sensed it—the line I drew between us—and he stayed on his side of the trail.

We walked for a while, quiet again, watching as others enjoyed the summer day. Dogs were playing in the grass, chasing balls and each other. Kids were climbing all over the jungle gym as moms watched from nearby. A young couple cuddled on a large blanket, the woman reading as the man napped.

"Tell me about Jamie," Cole said, taking my attention from people watching.

"You want to know about Jamie?"

"Yeah. What was he like? He was a teacher, right?"

I nodded. "Seventh grade English and social studies. I

could never do that job, but he loved it. Kids that age were his favorite. Older than kindergarteners, not quite asshole teenagers."

Cole chuckled. "I do better with the asshole teenagers."

I smiled. "And I do better with the kindergarteners."

"What else?"

I thought about it for a minute, sorting through all of the wonderful things I could say about Jamie. "He was a joker. He loved making others laugh—probably why he was so good with preteens. He didn't care if he made a dork of himself. What you saw with Jamie was what you got."

Kind of like Cole. He didn't try to mask his feelings. He didn't pretend to be anything other than who he was.

"He loved teasing me." It was one of the ways Jamie showed people that he loved them. I missed the teasing.

Except for Cole, no one had really poked fun at me since Jamie had died. Everyone around me walked on eggshells. Molly would jest at times, but even then, she was always cautious. So was Finn.

But Cole, he just treated me like me. Not a broken Poppy. Or a sad Poppy. Just me.

And I could tease him right back.

"So, what's the future look like for you, Detective Goodman? Chief of police? Mayor? The White House?"

Cole chuckled. "No, I'm happy just being a cop. Though my dad has bigger plans."

"Oh? What does he want?"

"He wants me to follow in his footsteps, to be the next chief when he retires." He blew out a loud breath. "But I hate politics. I hate committees and all the meetings. I like being in the field and working cases."

"I can see that. I bet you'd suffocate if you were stuck inside all day, wearing a suit and tie."

He looked down at me and smiled, his dimples showing again. "Poppy Maysen, I think you've figured me out."

My heart thumped a bit harder. "Not quite."

"Give it time."

I'd try. Minute by minute.

CHAPTER EIGHT

38TH BIRTHDAY: GO ON EVERY RIDE AT THE FAIR

COLE

"Any questions?"

Matt closed the task force file I'd just laid on his desk. "No. This is all pretty straightforward. I'll get to work on this right now."

"Thanks. I really appreciate you digging right in."

He grinned. "Just glad to be a part of the task force."

I clapped him on the shoulder before going back to my desk. I'd recruited Matt to join my drug task force after I'd taken James Maysen's murder case away from Simmons.

Just as I'd suspected, the work Simmons had done to investigate the liquor store murder had been shit. Witness statements were thin, photographs of the crime scene were lacking detail, and the video footage from the area's security cameras had been reviewed by a rookie who was no longer on the force. Surprise, fucking surprise, they hadn't found a lead to track down Jamie's killer.

Five years later, there wasn't anything I could do about the witness statements and photographs, so my plan was to use the video footage in hopes I'd stumble on a lead. Maybe, if I was lucky, I'd find something Simmons had overlooked.

My desk phone rang, echoing in the quiet bull pen. I wasn't surprised when *Chief of Police* flashed on the caller ID—no one ever called me on my desk phone except Dad.

"Goodman," I answered, just in case it was Dad's assistant.

"Got a few minutes to talk?" Dad asked.

I checked my watch. "Yeah, but I've got to be out of here in fifteen."

I was leaving early today so I could meet Poppy at the restaurant at two, then head to the fair. That would give us a few hours to hit the rides before the Friday-night crowd got thick and the lines got long.

"Shouldn't be a problem. Come on up."

Hanging up the phone, I dug my truck keys and wallet out of my desk drawer.

"Summoned by the man upstairs?" Matt teased.

"Story of my life." I grinned. "See you Monday. Have a good weekend."

"You too."

I waved good-bye to Matt and a few other guys in the bull pen before taking the stairs two at a time to the fourth floor. When I got to the landing, I sidestepped a couple people passing by. Even on a Friday afternoon, Dad's office was busy. I had no idea how he got a damn thing done with people always rushing in and out of meetings.

Meetings. The idea of spending five days a week in back-to-back meetings made my skin crawl. I'd suffocate in a suit and tie, just like Poppy had guessed.

It had been almost two weeks since our walk in the park

and I'd been anxious for today ever since. We'd both been busy with work and I'd only seen her once these last couple weeks when I'd stopped by the restaurant for lunch with Matt and a few other guys on the force. I'd waved and introduced her to the guys, but she'd been busy so I hadn't stayed long.

But today it was just the two of us and there was no way I'd be late.

I checked my watch again as I walked down the hallway to the corner office. Dad always asked for just a few minutes but then I'd be up here for an hour. That was not happening on my day with Poppy. Dad had thirteen minutes and not a second more.

When I reached his corner, I nodded to his assistant but didn't stop to say hello—she was talking into her headset anyway. In all the years she'd worked for Dad, I'd probably only said twenty words to the woman, so I just walked through Dad's open door. "Hi."

He stood from the minifridge, holding up a bottle of water. "Hi. Want one?"

"Nah. I'm good. What's up?"

He sat in his desk chair. "Take a seat."

Shit. This was going to take longer than thirteen—now twelve—minutes.

"I can't stay long. Really, Dad. I have to leave at quarter 'til."

He nodded as he swallowed a drink of water. "This won't take long. I just want an update on the Maysen-Hastings murder."

I frowned. This was one of Dad's conditions for pulling strings with my boss and transferring the case from Simmons last month. Dad wanted to be "fully informed." I was learning that keeping him fully informed felt damn close to being micromanaged. But since I wasn't leaving this office until he had an update, I sat on the edge of his wooden guest chair and leaned my elbows on my knees.

"No changes to my theory since my last update. I still think the killer hid out in the shopping complex somewhere and then snuck out hours later."

The liquor store where Jamie Maysen and the cashier, Kennedy Hastings, had been killed was part of a grocery store complex. Either the killer had ducked into one of the smaller shops by the liquor store or he'd made it into the grocery store through a loading dock. Regardless, none of the witnesses or cameras had caught sight of him after the shots had been fired, which meant he'd probably been hiding in an employee area not monitored on video.

"This whole thing pisses me off," Dad said after another gulp of water. "We had responders on the scene within minutes after shots were fired. How'd we miss him?"

I shrugged. "Damn if I know, but somehow he got away. I'm guessing he hid out for a couple of hours and laid low. Then he waltzed out of the complex like just another customer. He probably strolled past the crime scene tape and right into a car."

Slippery bastard. The liquor store's camera had caught the suspect killing the cashier and Jamie, then nothing, according to Simmons's case file.

Having a rookie review the video feeds was probably Simmons's biggest mistake in the case. I was guessing the rookie only reviewed the timeframe directly after the murders, not hours later.

"So where are you on reviewing tapes?" Dad asked.

"I've watched everything we had in evidence, but it's not much. I'm still waiting to hear back from the grocery store and some of the other shops in the complex to see if they've got extended footage saved somewhere. Fingers crossed, we'll get something else. And I've requested all of the stoplight camera footage from that whole area too. It's getting pulled from the archives. They should have it early next week."

"I hope he pops up on a camera."

I nodded. "Me too, but if not, I'll go to Plan B."

Plan B was my Hail Mary.

The grocery store complex was next to one of the busiest streets in Bozeman. If we didn't catch the killer on camera leaving the complex, then Plan B was to catalog all of the cars that came through the area stoplights during a five-hour stretch after the murder. From there, I'd start matching cars to those seen on footage from the shops' various security cameras. I was hoping I'd be able to compile a short list of cars that had been in the complex and then run plates from the stoplight cameras. With plates, I could pull vehicle registrations and maybe find someone who matched the killer's description.

Plan B wasn't just a stretch, it was a really fucking big job that was going to take me a hell of a long time.

"Plan B is a big job, Cole." When I'd told him about it a week ago, he'd cringed at the number of hours I'd estimated Plan B would take.

"Let's hope it doesn't come to that, but if we don't see the guy on camera, it's the only angle I've got."

Dad sighed. "This is my fault. I should have done more to follow up on Simmons's investigation. I never should have let this go unsolved for so long."

"Well, it wasn't just you. We all got busy and this just got forgotten. By all of us." Everyone except for Poppy.

"When you asked me for this case a couple of weeks ago, I said you could have it but it was on your own time and you weren't getting any help."

Dad and my boss didn't want the momentum we had with

the drug task force to take a hit because I was wrapped up in this cold murder case that had a slim chance of ever being solved.

I respected where they were coming from, but that didn't make finding extra time any easier. I was already putting in long hours on the task force. Add to that time spent with Poppy to help her on this list, and I would be running on fumes for the foreseeable future.

"Yeah. I remember. But I'll find a way to fit it in."

"I'm changing my mind."

I blinked in surprise. "What do you mean?"

"You're still going to have to squeeze it in between task force work, but I'm calling in another favor to your boss and asking Matt Hernandez to pitch in too. Maybe between the two of you, the murder case can get more traction."

I sat back in my chair, stunned. "No shit?"

"No shit." He took another drink of his water.

"Why? What changed your mind?"

"I'm pissed this case wasn't handled correctly, and besides that, your mother is all kinds of infatuated with Poppy."

That makes two of us.

Dad loosened his tie. "She's all I've heard about since she came to dinner. Christ, we've eaten at her restaurant four times in the last ten days."

I grinned. "Sounds like Mom."

"And she's not the only one infatuated. Don't think I missed the way you looked at her over dinner either."

Damn. When I'd asked Dad to transfer the case, I hadn't exactly disclosed my feelings for Poppy. Hopefully, if I was honest with him now, I wouldn't get the case jerked away.

"I'm not going to lie and say this case isn't personal or say I don't have feelings for her."

"And I'm not going to lie and say my feelings for you aren't the reason you have this case in the first place. What I will say is that you need to be smart. I'm giving you Hernandez so he can take the lead."

Fuck no. This was my case. "Dad—"

"Think about it, Cole." He held up a hand to cut me off. "Do you want a relationship with this woman?"

I closed my mouth.

"Then this has to be done by the book. I'm not saying you'd fuck up the investigation, but put yourself in an attorney's shoes. Let's say you actually find the killer. How is it going to look to a defense attorney when the widow's boyfriend's name is all over the police report? Don't give the killer any more chances than he's already had."

I sighed and leaned back in the chair. Dad was right. If we actually found the killer, I wanted the fucker to hang, and in order for that to happen, the investigation itself couldn't be called into question.

"Okay. But can I still participate?"

"Participate," Dad nodded, "but stay behind the curtain. Do the grunt work. Spend your time staring at video footage, but let Matt run any and all questioning. Let him be the face of the investigation."

"Got it."

"And don't worry. Even if you're not the lead, this case could be big for your career."

"That's not why I'm doing this."

"I know." He held up his hands. "I'm just saying. It could be the case that guarantees you get my job when I retire."

I shook my head. "That's not—we don't have time to talk about that today."

"You're right. Let's talk about that later." His eyes glanced at the clock on the wall behind my back. "Quarter 'til. Out you go."

I pushed up from the chair. "Thanks, Dad."

"Say hello to Poppy for me."

"Will do." Dad had been a hell of a cop in his day—smart enough to know where I was running off to this afternoon without needing to be told.

But even good cops had blind spots, and my career was his. No matter how many times I told him, he just couldn't see why I'd never want his job.

Someday, I'd have to *make* him see. And hope like hell he wasn't disappointed in his son.

———

"HEY, Molly. Is Poppy in the back?"

"Yeah." Molly waved me closer to the register as she leaned across the counter. "Listen, she's had a rough morning. I know you guys were planning on the fair this afternoon, but she might not be up to it."

A rough morning? My heart rate jumped up a notch. "What happened?"

"I'll let her tell you." She nodded toward the kitchen door. "She's in the office, just head on back."

I didn't waste any time pushing through the swinging door and walking straight to the office, where I found Poppy with her head in her hands at the desk.

"Hey."

Her red and puffy eyes shot up to mine. "Hey."

Was her chin quivering? She was going to break my fucking heart. I'd never seen her cry, not even after her husband had been killed. Talk about a punch to the gut.

"What happened?" I walked to the desk, pushing aside a stack of papers so I could sit on the edge. I flattened my palms on my thighs, pressing them down, fighting the urge to pull Poppy into my arms.

Poppy wiped her eyes and sniffled. "I had lunch today with Jamie's parents and Jimmy, Jamie's granddad. We got in a big fight. I asked them if I could have Jamie's old truck, since technically it's mine, but they've had it at their ranch all these years. They asked why I wanted the truck, which led to me telling them I wanted to fix it up, which led to them asking why again and me finally admitting I was doing Jamie's birthday list."

"Didn't go over well, huh?"

She scoffed. "Not at all. Debbie, his mom, started crying. Kyle informed me that it wasn't my place to do *their* son's list and that I was crossing the line."

Assholes. I didn't personally know Jamie's parents, but treating Poppy like that spoke volumes. But calling them assholes probably wouldn't help. "Sorry."

"It's okay." She shrugged. "I'd expected them to be upset about it, but I guess I'd hoped deep down that they'd understand why I wanted to do his list. We all used to be so close once. Now . . . things are different. They blame me for Jamie's death."

"What the fuck?" Jamie's parents blamed Poppy for his death? That was bullshit. "You aren't responsible for his death." That responsibility belonged to the sick fuck I was becoming more and more dedicated to hunting down with every passing second.

Poppy looked to her lap. "No, they're right. I am partly to blame. I'm the one who asked Jamie to go to the liquor store in the first place. He didn't really want to go, but he did for me."

Did she seriously think this was her fault? "You are *not* to blame."

A couple of tears started to fall again, and she hurried to

wipe them dry. "I am. He'd be alive if I hadn't asked him to go to that store."

"No." I leaned in closer. "You are not to blame. The guy that pulled the trigger? He's got Jamie's death on his head. Not you."

She nodded but didn't look up.

"Poppy, look at me." I tipped up her chin with the side of my finger. "There are things in the world outside of our control. Other people's actions mostly. Nothing you did caused Jamie's death."

"I know," she whispered. "Logically, I know you're right. But I still *feel* like this is all my fault." Her shoulders began shaking as the hold on her tears broke, sending them streaming down her beautiful face.

Screw it. I grabbed her arms and pulled her out of the chair. Then I held her, whispering into her hair as she cried into my black shirt.

She didn't once try and push me away. Instead, she collapsed against my chest—her hands fisting the cotton at my sides as she let go. When she clung harder, I held on tighter. Every one of her tears sent a spear through my heart.

Had she been living with this guilt for five years? No wonder she'd been so diligent about visiting Simmons. She was looking for some answers—for a place to put the blame so she could take it off her own shoulders.

Poppy cried hard but it didn't last long. She pulled herself together, sniffling and taking a few deep breaths before she stood back.

"I'm sorry." She wiped at the wet spots on my shirt.

"Don't be sorry." I trapped her hand under mine until she looked me in the eyes. "No apologies for tears, okay?"

She nodded and I let her hand go so she could dry her face. Then she took another step back, standing tall. *Damn.* Even blotchy faced, she was beautiful. She let her grace—her incredible strength—shine through her sad smile.

My arms already felt empty with her standing three feet away. When her shoulders dropped, I had a brief flash of hope that she'd need me again, but she sat back into her desk chair instead.

"I'm okay." She nodded. "I'm okay."

She was. She would be okay. Somehow, I'd find a way to make it okay. I couldn't bring her husband back, but I could track down his killer. I could be the shoulder she cried on. And, maybe, I could be the man at her side as she started a new life.

"You know the worst part about lunch was Jimmy." She hung her head. "I should have told him sooner. I see him once a week and I never have told him I was doing Jamie's list. He looked so hurt at lunch. I should have told him."

"Give him some time and I'm sure he'll come around. They all will." I was talking out of my ass here—I'd never met these people—but I was grasping for anything to make her feel better.

"I'm going to pretend you know what you're talking about and just believe you."

I chuckled. "Good plan."

"Speaking of plans. We'd better get to the fair if we're going to get through all the rides today."

"We don't have to go. If you'd rather do it later, then we can wait."

She shook her head. "No, I want to go. It will be a fun distraction."

"All right." I held a hand out to help her stand. "Let's ride."

———

FOUR HOURS LATER, I was buckling my seat belt as a carnival worker locked us in a cage. A cage that had once been a clean white but was now spotted with rust.

"I fucking hate The Zipper," I muttered. "Are you sure about this?"

Poppy looked green. "I'm sure."

Liar. There wasn't an ounce of confidence in her voice. "Maybe we should take a break. Come back and do this in an hour or so." We'd saved The Zipper for last because it was the ride that had scared her the most.

"No." She clicked her own seat belt with shaking hands. "This is the last ride and then we're done. We just have to get through this, and we're done."

"Okay." I reached up and gripped the handle on the side of the car. My hand felt slimy because I was sweating my balls off. It was blistering outside, probably over ninety, and not a breeze to be found. Being trapped in this hot metal car wasn't helping.

I needed water. Better yet, a fucking beer. I hadn't gone on this many rides since I was a kid, and even then, Mom and Dad had limited my tickets. But there was no limit today. I'd spent almost two hundred dollars on tickets because I'd refused to let Poppy pay.

These fucking traveling carnivals were raking it in. *Bastards.* Even the kiddie rides had cost five bucks. You'd think they could afford some spray paint to spruce up these cages.

"Enjoy the ride." With our car locked, the worker smacked the side, then moved back to the control panel.

"Oh my god," Poppy groaned as the car rocked back, her face going from green to white, matching her knuckles on the bar across our knees.

"Tell me again why we're doing this?" I hoped a distraction would get her through the loading process. And then we'd just have to stick it out through the two-minute ride.

"Jamie never had a chance to do many fair rides. He was always showing livestock with 4-H, but he loved stuff like this. He even begged me to go to Disneyland for our honeymoon."

I swallowed hard, not wanting to picture Poppy on a honeymoon. A niggling prickle crept up my neck. I'd been pushing images of Poppy and her husband aside, compartmentalizing them in a box I had no plans to ever open, but the damn lid kept flopping open.

It didn't help when there were reminders everywhere, like her wedding rings always shining on her finger.

The worst part was, I'd asked her to tell me about him. And it wasn't that I didn't want to know. I did. I wanted to know everything about Poppy. I just didn't realize how hearing her talk about Jamie, seeing her face soften, would make me feel.

Jealous. Like an asshole, I was jealous.

The car rocked again and Poppy gasped, pulling my thoughts back into the cage. My free hand reached out and took one of hers off the bar.

She laced her fingers with mine and squeezed. "Keep distracting me."

I grinned, amazed again at how well this woman had me figured out. "Did you go on rides as a kid?"

"No. This was always more of Finn's thing."

I didn't remember much of Finn Alcott other than his hair, which was the same color as Poppy's, and how he'd stepped up for his sister five years ago. After she'd texted him, he'd come to her house and taken over, making the difficult phone calls so she wouldn't have to deliver the news of Jamie's murder.

"How's he doing?" I asked.

"He's okay." The car jerked and Poppy gripped my hand so hard my knuckles cracked. "Him and Molly are struggling to adjust to their divorce."

I tried to adjust my hand and restore some blood flow, but

she wasn't having it so I just let her squeeze. "I didn't realize they'd been married."

"Yeah. They got divorced not too long ago."

Below us, the carnival worker shouted something I couldn't make out and the car started to rock.

"Last ride. Last ride. Last ride," Poppy chanted.

"Just close your eyes. Two minutes, and this will all be over."

She nodded and squeezed her eyes shut.

Then we rode The Zipper.

While Poppy kept her eyes closed the entire time, I kept mine open and on our linked hands. By the time the ride was over and our car stopped shaking, I'd memorized the feel of her delicate fingers laced with mine.

"Poppy." Her eyes were still closed tight as our car stopped to unload first. "Poppy, I need my hand back so we can get out."

Her eyes popped open and her entire frame relaxed. "We did it," she breathed.

"You did it."

"No. We did it." Her eyes looked up to mine as she smiled. "I wouldn't have done this without you, Cole."

I leaned closer, not in a rush anymore to get out of this hot cage. Not with her eyes and hand holding mine. "I'm glad I—"

"Hey," the ride operator snapped. "You guys gonna get out?"

Damn.

"Sorry." Poppy wiggled her hand free and scrambled to unbuckle her seat belt.

I unbuckled too, stepping out onto the platform. My shirt was sticking to my back and I held on to the rail as I followed Poppy down the stairs to the dirt below.

"No matter what new rides they come up with, The Zipper always seems to ring my bell like no other."

She laughed and looked up at the ride. "Me and you are done, Zipper! You win."

When her smile came back to me, my heart jumped in a strange rhythm—almost like it skipped a beat. I'd never felt anything like it before.

"I could use a beer. What do you say, Detective? Can I buy you a cold one?"

My perfect woman. "Definitely."

CHAPTER NINE

43RD BIRTHDAY: GO TO A DRIVE-IN MOVIE

POPPY

Thirty minutes after we'd left The Zipper, I was on my second beer and feeling practically euphoric. The combination of alcohol and the fading adrenaline rush from the carnival rides had put a smile on my face that would stay all night. On top of that, Finn had just texted that he'd brought the kids to the fair, and I couldn't wait to see their happy faces.

"Hey, would you care if we met up with my brother and his kids?"

"Of course not." Cole grinned, then drained the last of his beer.

I smiled and did the same, tossing my plastic cup in the trash on our way out of the beer garden.

As we stepped through the gate, Cole's hand came to the small of my back. "Lead the way."

A tingle traveled from his fingertips to my neck at the unfamiliar gesture. Jamie had never done that for me—guided me as we walked. He'd been more of a grab-my-hand-and-drag-me-behind-him kind of guy.

But I liked this with Cole. I liked that it was different. I liked that it was subtle. I liked that in a sea of people, it tied us together. And when his hand fell away a few steps later, I missed the pressure of his fingers as we walked through the Friday-night crowd back toward the rides.

Unlike when we'd arrived at the fairgrounds, the sight of bright lights and spinning rides didn't make me nauseous. An enormous weight had been lifted now that we were done with this particular list item. From now on, I'd never feel compelled to do more than ride the Ferris wheel.

"Thanks again for coming with me tonight." If not for Cole's help, I doubt I would have made it through.

"Sure." He nudged me with his elbow. "Thanks for not puking on me."

I laughed just as I spotted Finn standing outside the gate to the small dinosaur-themed train. "There they are." I pointed and changed directions.

"Ugh," he groaned, glaring at the dinosaur cars.

He'd barely been able to fit on that ride. He'd had to sit in the caboose by himself because it was the only car big enough for his long legs. Even then, his knees had come up nearly to his chin. But he'd toughed it out through the four slow laps, and when we'd drawn a crowd of adults, staring at him with puzzled faces, Cole had just smiled and waved, pretending like it was no big deal that a grown man was on the kiddie train.

"You didn't like this one?" I teased. "I think this was my favorite ride of the day."

Cole scoffed. "My favorite part was when I got stuck trying to get out of the damn car."

I laughed. I'd had to help him off the ride by holding his arm so he could balance as he yanked his feet free. "I'm sorry. I shouldn't laugh." I tried to rein it in, but I couldn't stop picturing the faces of the parents who had been watching. They'd had vise grips on their children as they watched Cole curse at the triceratops. "Did you see that one mother? She looked like she was about to call the cops on you."

"Thank god she didn't." He shook his head. "I never would have lived that down at the station."

I smiled up at him, conveying silent thanks. It was hard to believe that I'd had such an awful lunch with Jamie's parents earlier. Cole had turned my whole day around by bringing me here.

Him, and doing this for Jamie.

Even though his parents were against it, today had reinforced my decision to finish the birthday list. No matter how much Debbie and Kyle objected, I was seeing this through. A year ago, nothing would have helped after such a bad encounter with Kyle and Debbie. I would have let it ruin my day, probably an entire week. But doing something fun, something for Jamie, had made it all go away.

"Aunt Poppy!" Kali screeched, waving wildly from her seat on the dinosaur train.

"Kali!" I waved back as I reached Finn's side. My brother gave me a quick hug before I bent down to Max in his stroller. "How's my Max?" I kissed his cheek.

"Pop, Pop." He pointed to Kali. "Wook."

"I see that. Isn't it cool?"

He stared at his sister with a dazed look, probably wondering what she was doing or wishing he were old enough to follow.

I smiled and kissed him again, then stood just as Cole and Finn were shaking hands.

"I know you," Finn said.

Cole nodded. "Cole Goodman."

"Right." Finn looked to me and then back to Cole, letting go of his hand. "Well, it's nice to see you again under better circumstances."

"Same to you. Is this your son?"

"This is Max." I patted the stroller, then pointed to the ride. "And that's Kali."

"The mini-Molly?" Cole asked.

I smiled. "That's the one."

"What are you two doing here?" From Finn's furrowed eyebrows, he wasn't quite sure what to make of me and Cole, but I'd explain later.

"Well, your sister spent the better part of the afternoon dragging me along on every ride at the fair. Every. Single. One." Cole circled his finger around, indicating each of the kiddie rides surrounding us.

"Yikes." Finn chuckled. "How'd you even fit?"

Cole and I looked at each other, then burst out laughing. "Finn," I held my side, "you should have seen him try and get into the little flying bumble bees. He had to beg the guy running the machine to even let him try. Then they had to balance the ride with me and a bunch of kids on the opposite arm. All of these people were standing around, glaring at Cole for being a pain. It was hilarious."

Cole shook his head at my teasing. "I knew I should have snapped a picture of your green face when we were on The Zipper."

"Sorry, Detective. You missed your chance, because that will never happen again."

"You got her on The Zipper?" Finn's eyes widened. "I'm impressed."

Cole shrugged. "I can't take much credit. She would have braved it with or without me."

He had no idea how much I'd relied on him today, but I wasn't going to debate that in front of my brother.

"So, you're a detective now?" Finn asked Cole.

"Yeah. I got promoted about a year ago. What about you? What do you do?"

"I own a landscaping company here in town. We mostly do new construction, some mowing here and there."

"Finn's being modest," I told Cole. "Alcott Landscaping is one of the biggest landscaping companies in the Gallatin Valley. And when he says new construction, he means that he designs the landscaping for some of the biggest homes in the area."

Finn just shrugged. "It pays the bills."

I was proud of Finn's success, but it had come at a price. In my opinion, his dedication to his company had driven the wedge between him and Molly in the first place. He'd taken his design assistants out to dinners instead of his wife. He'd made sure everyone else's lawn was mowed but forgotten to do his own, forcing Molly to do it herself. He'd spent late nights with his laptop instead of sleeping in bed next to her.

Alcott Landscaping had come above all others, except the kids. Finn might not have won awards as a husband, but he was a great dad. Even if their parents were divorced, Max and Kali had two parents who loved them unconditionally.

"Daddy! Aunt Poppy!" Kali screeched as the ride came to an end. She climbed out of her purple brontosaurus and came running down the platform and through the exit gate. "Did you see me? Did you see me?" She launched herself at Finn, giggling as he picked her up and threw her in the air.

"You did awesome! Was it fun?"

She nodded wildly. "Can I go again?"

"Sure. Did you want to do the dinosaur train again or try

something else?" Finn smirked at Cole. "Aunt Poppy's friend Cole said the bee ride was pretty fun."

Kali looked at Cole but dismissed him completely, much too concerned about her fair rides than another adult in our huddle. "Hmmm." She tapped her chin—something that was so stinking adorable I could hardly stand it. "Bees!"

"Bees!" Finn and I both cheered as Cole muttered, "Bees."

I laughed and took the handle to Max's stroller, leading the way to the other ride.

An hour later, Kali had been on every kiddie ride, I'd spent some quality time with my nephew, and Cole and Finn had made plans to meet up for a beer next week. My brother was man-crushing on Cole. Hard. And I couldn't wait to razz him about it later.

"Can I do that one, Daddy? Pleeeeease?" Kali pointed to the Tilt-A-Whirl.

Finn shook his head. "You have to be taller to ride that one, baby."

"But there's a kid." Kali's eyes zeroed in on a kid not much taller than her riding with his dad.

"Saw that, did you?" Finn muttered and knelt down to look at his daughter. "You can't go on that ride alone, and I didn't buy myself any tickets. I'm sorry."

"Finn, I've got a couple extra," Cole said. "You can have them or I can take her."

"Yay!" Kali squealed. "Can I go? Can I go, Daddy? Pleeeeease?"

Finn shook his head and clapped Cole on the shoulder. "She's all yours. Good luck."

Cole chuckled as Kali grabbed his hand and dragged him toward the ride. He smiled at me as my niece kept pulling. "At least I fit on this one."

"Have fun!" Finn and I called to their backs.

As Cole and Kali took their place in line for the ride, Finn stepped closer to my side. "I like him."

"No." I feigned shock. "Really? I couldn't tell by the way you were practically humping his leg."

"Tease all you want. You like him too."

Cole was still holding Kali's hand, smiling down at her as they waited in line. "Yeah. I like him too. He's a friend."

"A friend? Come on. What's going on with you two?"

I shrugged. "I ran into him at that karate class I went to last month. We've had a couple dinners together, and he's helping me with some of the stuff on Jamie's list."

"And."

"And he's also looking into the murder case."

"And."

"And . . . that's it. Nothing more. I just told you. He's a friend."

"Poppy," Finn chided.

I mocked his tone. "Finn."

"Be honest."

The downside of being extremely close to my brother was that I never could slip anything past him. "Honestly? I don't know."

"Fair enough." Finn waved to Kali as she smiled his way from the Tilt-A-Whirl car. She was sitting right next to Cole, her hands gripping the railing across their laps. And Cole was grinning at me.

The ride got started and I waved to them both as they started spinning.

"He likes you too. More than just a friend."

I sighed. "I know."

I didn't want to lead Cole on. I knew he had feelings for me, just like I had feelings for him. But since I wasn't sure how to deal with them, it was safer just to classify him as a friend.

Finn threw his arm around my shoulders and hugged me to his side. "It's okay to always love Jamie."

"I always will." Always.

"But maybe you can love someone else too."

Two years ago, I would have said absolutely not. I would have said that my love for Jamie was all-consuming and I'd never find room in my heart for anyone else. But now, I wasn't as sure. At some point, I wanted more in my life. A family. Children. Love.

So instead of saying absolutely not, I whispered, "Maybe."

Finn hugged me tighter. "Something to think about. Since Jamie was my best friend in the world, I feel like I'm qualified to say this. He would have liked Cole too."

Finn's right. You would have liked him, Jamie.

We stayed quiet as we watched Kali and Cole on the ride. By the time they came back, Kali had claimed Cole as her own, begging him to take her on one last ride. They did until all the ride tickets had disappeared and we were strolling through the midway, getting some drinks and buying the kids a late snack.

"We probably better get going," Finn said after the minidonuts and fresh-squeezed lemonades were gone.

Kali was still running around us in circles—literally racing around our legs—but Max was about thirty seconds from falling asleep in his stroller. And from the circles under his eyes, Finn's energy was fading fast too. He'd probably stayed up most of last night working.

"Do you want some help with bedtime tonight? I could come over and help with baths."

Finn's face lit up. "You wouldn't mind?"

"Not at all. You can spend some time getting caught up."

"I'll take you up on it. I'm behind on a bid."

That wasn't surprising. While Molly had more time on her hands since the divorce, Finn was struggling to keep up at work. I'd never say it out loud, but this had been a good wake-up call for him. He'd taken for granted how much Molly had done to manage the kids and run their household. Now he was having to do it all himself—be Mr. Mom three days a week and Finn Alcott, landscape designer and entrepreneur.

But he was still my brother and I wanted to help him before he got worn out.

"I'll walk you guys out." Cole placed his hand on my back as we all started for the gravel parking lot.

I got the same tingle that I had earlier when he'd touched me there, liking it more the second time than I had the first.

When we reached the parking lot, Finn jerked his chin to a long row of cars. "I'm this way."

"See you at the R Bar next week." Cole shook his hand.

"Looking forward to it." Finn smiled. "It was nice to see you again."

"You too." Cole looked to Kali and a sleeping Max. "Bye, kids."

Kali ran over and hugged his knees. "Bye, Cole!"

With one last wave good-bye, Cole and I turned and crunched along the gravel toward where we'd parked our vehicles.

"Thanks again for going with me. It was fun."

"You're welcome."

We reached my car and I stopped by the trunk. "So, what's next?"

"How about dinner?"

I hesitated. When we were spending time together for the list, I had an excuse to see Cole. But dinner? The way he'd asked seemed much more like a date. But before I could think of a dodge, Cole spoke up first.

"It's just dinner, Poppy."

Just dinner. He was right. I was making more of dinner

than it needed to be. "Sure. Any night next week you're free, just let me know. We can either eat at the restaurant or go somewhere else."

He grinned. "Not a lot of restaurants can compare to yours. In fact, I've pretty much lost my appetite for anything not served in a jar."

I smiled. "Then I'll see you next week."

"It's a date."

Just like the last time he'd said those three words, my heart jumped.

And maybe one day, the stitch of guilt that came with it would go away.

―――――

"HEY!" I greeted Cole as he came striding into the restaurant.

It had been three weeks since the carnival, and Cole had become my favorite dinner companion. If we weren't eating together at the restaurant, he'd meet me at Brad and Mia's after my ukulele lessons.

Three weeks, and there had been only a handful of times when we'd had dinner apart.

The way my breath hitched when he smiled didn't scare me anymore. I enjoyed the tingles he could conjure with the slightest touch. And I'd started to crave the way he sent my heart into overdrive with a heated stare from those green eyes.

It was a rush being around Cole. A rush I was learning to enjoy.

"You're here early." Not that I was unhappy to see his handsome face, but it was hours before our normal seven o'clock dinnertime.

"Change of plans."

My smile fell at the frown on his face. "Uh-oh. Is everything okay?" I tensed, hoping he wasn't here to deliver bad news about Jamie's case.

"Remember I told you last week that I found a drive-in movie theater?"

I breathed a sigh of relief that he was here about the list, something he'd become nearly as dedicated to finishing as I was. "Yeah. Can you not go next weekend? Do you want to reschedule?"

"Something like that. We're going now."

"Now? I can't go now." I was needed at the restaurant.

"It's now or never. I checked their schedule today, just to make sure we were on track for next weekend, and saw on their website that they're closing early for the summer. I guess there was some sort of emergency in their family and they aren't showing anything until next summer. Tonight's their last night."

"What? No!" The drive-in theater that he had found was the only one in the state, three hours from Bozeman in a small town called Lewistown. If we couldn't make it to a movie there, then finishing that item on Jamie's list was going to get a whole lot harder.

"We need to leave," he checked his watch, "in ten minutes."

"Shit." I threw my hands in the air. "I can't leave in ten minutes. Molly has the kids tonight and I'm the one closing."

"What about Helen?" Cole jerked his chin to the part-time college student Molly had hired a couple weeks ago. Helen was clearing a table and blushed when she spotted Cole looking her way.

"She's never closed by herself before."

"Do you think she can do it?"

I shrugged. "Yeah. I guess so." I'd trained her to close but most nights either Molly or I were here to help just in case.

"Then let her. What's the worst that could happen?"

"Uh, my restaurant could burn down."

He grinned. "That's a risk you're going to have to take if we're going to make the previews."

I sighed, weighing my options: trust my employee, or let Jamie down.

It wasn't much of a choice.

"Okay, we'll go. But I need a few minutes to walk her through it all."

Ten minutes later, Helen was thrilled to be running the show tonight and I'd called in the other part-time worker just in case. The two of them should be able to handle the Friday night dinner rush, and I just hoped that I'd made enough food to last until tomorrow morning.

Walking out of the kitchen, I slung my purse over my shoulder and joined Cole by the counter. He was talking to a man who must have come in while I was in the back.

Not wanting to interrupt, I just smiled, but the stranger pulled me into their conversation.

"Hi." He held out his hand but his eyes went to my chest. "How do you know Cole?"

Before I could answer, Cole stepped in. "This is Poppy Maysen, my girlfriend. She owns this place."

The smile on my face faltered as I shook the man's hand. He said something else to Cole, but I couldn't hear it. The only thing in my ears was the word *girlfriend* in Cole's deep voice.

"We'd better get going. See you around." Cole nodded to the man, then placed his hand on the small of my back, steering me toward the door. "Asshole," he muttered under his breath.

Too stunned to speak, I walked straight for the door, while that word just kept on ringing.

Girlfriend.

Was I his girlfriend? No, I couldn't be his girlfriend. It was too soon. I was married. I was a wife. Wives weren't girlfriends.

I couldn't do that to Jamie.

"Poppy," Cole opened the door to his truck for me when we got outside, "Helen has the restaurant covered tonight. You don't have anything to worry about."

I blinked at him but still didn't have anything to say, so I climbed in his truck.

He thought I was worried about the restaurant. He had no idea the bomb he'd just dropped on me. That with one word, he'd erased all of the comfort and ease we'd found with each other these last few weeks.

That he'd just brought back a surge of crippling guilt.

A guilt that consumed me as we drove three hours in complete silence.

By the time Cole pulled into the lot to the theater, I was about ready to break. My head was throbbing and my stomach knotted. I was on the verge of jumping out of his truck and walking back to Bozeman just to prove that I was loyal to my husband.

My head was in such a state of turmoil, I barely noticed as Cole paid for our tickets, parked in an empty spot and slung a radio box over his window. What I did notice was his hand coming across the cab and carefully prying my fingers off my jeans.

"Poppy, look at me."

I turned my neck and found his soft green eyes waiting. They were full of understanding. Of compassion. They made me want to cry just that much more.

"That guy in the restaurant is an asshole. I went to college with him, and the last thing I wanted was for him to hit on you or start coming to the restaurant on a regular basis because he thinks you're available."

"Okay." I relaxed a bit, glad that at some point in the last three hours, Cole had guessed why I'd shut down.

"Someday, I'd like to call you my girlfriend and have you not go comatose, but I know we're not there yet, so take a breath."

I obeyed, holding his eyes as I let go of some tension.

"I know this, me, scares the shit out of you. I know you've been sitting there for three hours worrying yourself sick. But, Poppy," he squeezed my hand, "this is just a movie."

I felt my throat start to burn and my nose sting. "It's not." My feelings for Cole made this so much more than just a movie.

"It is. Tonight, it's just a movie." He laced his fingers with mine and turned to the screen.

I stared at his profile as the radio box filled the cab with sound.

Just a movie. What happened after the movie? What happened when it wasn't just lunch or dinner or a movie? What happened when he wanted more?

Would I be ready?

I tore my eyes away from Cole's handsome face and turned to the screen, blocking out the unspoken questions.

Tonight, it's just a movie.

Except I never tried to take my hand away from Cole's.

And he never let me go.

CHAPTER TEN

37TH BIRTHDAY: RESTORE MY '79 FORD RANGER

POPPY

"Jimmy?" I tapped my knuckles on his doorframe.

"Hi." He waved me in but kept his eyes on the television. "Come on in. The show's on."

I sighed, walking into his apartment and taking a seat on the couch. It had been over a month since the awful lunch with Kyle and Debbie at the restaurant, and all of my weekly visits to The Rainbow had been like this: me sitting on the couch while Jimmy watched television.

I'd apologized over and over again for not sharing Jamie's birthday list with him, and Jimmy had promised it was fine. But the cold shoulder I'd been getting said otherwise.

Though his chilly attitude hadn't stopped my weekly visits. Jimmy was one of the most important people in my life, and I'd sit through season after season of HBO recordings while I waited for him to thaw out.

"How is your weekend going?" I asked. "Anything fun planned for your Sunday evening?"

Jimmy didn't look away from the screen. "So far so good. I think one of the neighbors is coming over later."

"That's nice." I waited, hoping he'd pause the show—or something—but he just kept on watching. His hair was growing back in thick, white spikes, and he looked more like the Jimmy I'd met years ago. Except for the smile that was missing from his face.

I sank deeper into the couch, turning to the TV, but since I didn't know anything about the show, it didn't catch my interest.

It was the week after my movie date with Cole, and I'd come to visit Jimmy before meeting Kyle and Debbie later this afternoon. I'd called them a few days ago and asked if I could come and collect Jamie's truck. Cole was taking me to get it from their ranch. He'd borrowed a trailer from a friend so we could haul the truck back to Bozeman and start fixing it up.

I hoped the month I'd waited since telling Kyle and Debbie that I wanted the truck had been enough time for them to adjust to the idea. Because a month was all the time I could wait. For Cole to even have a chance of getting the truck restored before the end of the year, I had to quit stalling.

"I'm heading out to the ranch later to pick up Jamie's truck."

That got Jimmy's attention. *Finally.*

He picked up the remote and paused his show. Then the Jimmy I loved and adored—the Jimmy I'd been missing all month—reached out and put his hand on my knee. "Do you need me to come along? I can cancel my plans."

I smiled and put my hand on his. "No, don't cancel. I'll be fine. But thanks for the offer." I took a deep breath. "I know I've said this before, but I really am sorry I didn't tell you about Jamie's birthday list. Please don't be mad at me."

"Oh, Poppy." He gave me a sad smile. "I'm not mad. It just surprised me is all."

"I'm sorry."

"Enough sorrys." He slipped his hand away and sat back. "We're just fine."

"Then why have you been giving me the silent treatment?"

He cocked his head. "Silent treatment?"

"Every time I've been here, you've had your eyes glued to the TV and ignored me."

"What? No, I haven't. I've been saving all the new episodes for your visits. Didn't you say this show was one of your favorites?"

"That wasn't me."

He studied my face. "Are you sure? I could have sworn it was you."

"Sorry. Not me. I'm not really into dragons and thrones and all that."

"Well, shit," he muttered. "I guess these last few visits have been kind of boring then. Sorry."

I smiled. "You don't have to apologize. *I'm* the one who needs to say sorry."

"Enough sor—"

"Please." I held out a hand. "Just let me say this one last time." He scowled but closed his mouth. "I hope you know that I didn't do it because I wanted to hide Jamie's list. I only kept it from you because I didn't want to make you sad."

Jimmy's scowl disappeared. "You don't ever need to keep things from me because you're worried I'll be sad. I'm sad every day. I've lost a lot of people in my life—it comes with age."

My heart broke just a little but before I could say anything, he kept going.

"But I'm happy every day too. I still have a lot of people in my life. Family. Friends. You. The trick is learning to let the happy outweigh the sad."

I sighed. "I'm still learning that trick."

"I know you are, and if going through Jamie's list will help, then I'm all for it. I just wish you had told me sooner. I'd have liked to help you with whatever he had on that list."

I should have known Jimmy would have wanted to help. Shame on me for not trusting he'd be supportive. "I'm not even close to being done if you want to help. There are a couple of them on there that I think are right up your alley. Want to see?"

He sat up in his chair, pushing down the footrest on his recliner and reaching for his reading glasses. "Hell yeah."

I dug through my purse, getting out Jamie's journal and handing it over. "I've checked the ones I've done already. All the others are still left."

He ran his finger down the leather spine, then opened the book. With every turned page, Jimmy's smile got bigger and bigger.

"Now that's a good one." He looked up over the rim of his glasses. "I'm helping with the paint fight."

I grinned. "I thought you'd like that one."

"Ha! Pull a fire alarm. I always wanted to do that too."

"Well, we can do it together. You can be my cellmate when they throw me in jail."

"*If* we get caught."

As his eyes brightened, page after page, I chastised myself again for not sharing earlier. The birthday list was helping me deal with Jamie's loss. Maybe it could help his family too.

"Do you think I should ask Kyle and Debbie if they'd like to see the list?"

Jimmy thought about it for a moment, then shook his head. "I had a long talk with Kyle after our lunch last month."

I tensed as he closed the journal and handed it back, then removed his glasses.

"I told him that you think they blame you for Jamie's death."

My frame deflated as I whispered, "I know they do."

"No, they don't." He leaned forward to speak softly. "But they do have a hard time being around you. When they see you, they expect to see Jamie right by your side. You two never went anywhere without the other. It's hard for them to see that missing piece."

I nodded but my heart was aching. I knew they had a hard time seeing me, but I wished that instead of finding pain in my face, they had found love. Maybe even some comfort.

"It's hard for me too. I feel that missing piece every day, but that hasn't stopped me from wanting to have them in my life."

"I'm not saying they're right. I'm just trying to explain. Kyle and Debbie might not ever be able to move on, but that doesn't mean you have to stay in the past. Deep down, they want you to be happy. To live a happy life. And for your own sanity, that might mean letting them go."

I sniffled, swallowing the lump in my throat before I could cry.

Jimmy got up from his chair and sat next to me on the couch, putting an arm around my shoulders. "They love you, Poppy."

Did they? If you loved someone, did you let a tragic experience drive you apart? Years ago, I'd believed that love prevailed above all. But now, I was learning that even love wasn't strong enough to mend some wounds.

I leaned my head on Jimmy's shoulder as I blinked away a tear. "It's not fair. I just miss them."

"I know. But you've still got me."

"Promise?"

He crossed his heart, just like I always did before making a promise. "Promise."

We sat together for a few moments, leaning on one another, until a grumble came from the hall.

"I see you're watching without me, asshole."

Jimmy scoffed. "Don't call me an asshole, asshole. I'm paying for the goddamn HBO, you leach. If you want to watch on your schedule, then you can shell out the cash."

I broke away from Jimmy and leaned forward, peering around him at his visitor. I gaped at the man walking into Jimmy's room. "Randall?"

"Huh," he muttered, then sat in Jimmy's recliner. "What are you doing here?"

"What am I doing here?" My hand waved back and forth between us. "What are you doing here?"

"I live here, stuck next door to this asshole." He jerked his thumb at Jimmy. "I don't care how far you watched, we're starting this episode over."

"Fine," Jimmy grumbled. "But you're not drinking all of my Mountain Dew like last week. You get one can. One."

I guess I wasn't the only Maysen limiting Randall's sugar intake.

Jimmy stood from the couch and glared at Randall. "And get the hell out of my chair, you poker cheat."

Poker cheat? "Was Randall the neighbor who beat you at poker and made you dye your hair pink?"

Randall snickered and Jimmy shot me his *shut up* look as they switched seats.

"Sorry to bring it up." Every ounce of willpower went to holding in my laughter.

"So Poppy is the granddaughter you're always talking about?" Randall asked as Jimmy fiddled with the remote.

My heart warmed whenever Jimmy told the residents at The Rainbow that I was his granddaughter.

"She is. How do you know each other?"

Randall shrugged. "I go to her restaurant every now and then."

"Every now and then?" I scoffed. "You come in every day."

"Interesting." Jimmy leaned forward and locked eyes with Randall. "I'll make a deal with you. If you want to keep watching my HBO, you'll bring me with you to the restaurant next time."

"Jimmy," I scolded. "I told you I'd come and get you whenever you wanted to come down."

He waved me off. "You're busy. He has nothing else to do, so he can drive me down there when he goes."

Jimmy didn't drive much anymore. His older sister had been killed in a car accident when she'd had a stroke behind the wheel and run into a tree. From then on, he'd only driven if there hadn't been another option. Which was why The Rainbow lifestyle suited him perfectly. They had meals, entertainment and a convenience store a few blocks away.

"I'll bring him," Randall told me, "but he's not taking my stool."

"I'll take whatever damn stool I want. She's *my* granddaughter."

I held out my hands, stopping their argument. "How about we decide who gets what stool tomorrow?"

"We'll be there for breakfast," Jimmy declared. "I haven't had breakfast there yet."

"Okay. I'll make you both something special." I stood from the couch and bent down and kissed Jimmy's cheek. "I'd better go."

Jimmy patted my arm. "Good luck tonight."

"Thanks."

I had a feeling I was going to need it.

———

"HOW'S THIS GOING TO GO?" Cole asked as he drove.

My foot bounced on the floor mat of his truck. "I have no idea."

After I'd left The Rainbow, I'd waited for Cole at the restaurant. He'd arrived with a long flatbed trailer hooked to the back of his truck. The closer we got to the ranch, the faster my foot bounced.

I wasn't just nervous about seeing Kyle and Debbie and taking Jamie's truck. I was also nervous about being there with Cole.

In the week since our drive-in movie, we'd resumed our normal dinner routine at the restaurant. I'd done my best to remember that he'd only called me his girlfriend to protect me from a potential creeper, but I still had fears.

Fears about where this thing between us was heading. Fears that we were getting closer and closer to that invisible line in the sand. The line that, when crossed, meant I'd no longer be Jamie Maysen's wife. I'd be some other man's girlfriend.

A part of me wanted to run away from that line. Another wanted to take a flying leap to the other side. As it was, I was just standing with my toes on its edge. Frozen.

Because I knew the man who'd pull me across was Cole. I wasn't waiting for some nameless, faceless man of the future. When I pictured kissing another man, it was Cole. When I imagined sleeping with another man, it was Cole.

He was the man of the future, patiently waiting on the other side of the line. I could imagine him standing there, holding out his hand.

I wanted to take Cole's hand. His fingers were so long, they threaded with mine and made my hands feel so small. His skin wasn't soft but it wasn't rough either. It was just a man's hand. Hard and warm. The perfect temperature to hold for hours and hours.

I wanted to take Cole's hand, but memories were holding me back.

Or a lack of memory.

I couldn't remember how my hand felt in Jamie's—I'd never really thought about it back then. I hated that I'd lost that part of him. That I hadn't taken the time to memorize the feel of his hand in mine.

Especially when I'd memorized everything about the feel of Cole's.

Every minute we spent together, Cole was taking more pieces of my heart.

Something that, if Kyle and Debbie picked up on it, would make this evening so much harder.

"You're going to take a left up here." I pointed out the turnoff to the ranch. "And then just straight down the gravel road until we get to their house."

Cole slowed and turned the wheel. "Is this where Jamie grew up?"

"Yeah. He didn't want to be a rancher, but his younger brother, Adam, still lives here with his girlfriend. Eventually, he'll take it all over from Kyle and Debbie, just like they took it over from Jimmy and Jamie's grandmother."

"Did you and Jimmy make amends?"

I smiled. "Yeah. And remember how I told you about the pink hair debacle? Guess who was the alleged poker cheat."

"Who?"

"Randall."

He chuckled. "No shit?"

"No shit." I laughed with him until the house came into sight after a bend in the road and anxiety shriveled my smile away.

"Nice place," Cole said as he pulled into the gravel area in front of the house.

Kyle and Debbie had built a new house about ten years ago and decked it out with all of the finest. Their old place, also nice, was now where Adam and his girlfriend lived. At least, I assumed that was where they both lived. Since Jamie's funeral, I'd only seen Adam once, and since Kyle and Debbie didn't talk to me much anymore, I wasn't up-to-date on the latest happenings at the ranch.

And probably wouldn't be in the future. If what Jimmy had told me today was correct, this might be my last trip to the Maysen ranch. To Jamie's home.

The nervous whirlpool that was my stomach spun faster. *Jamie, if you're listening, help this go okay. Don't let this be another good-bye.*

I pulled in a shaking breath as Cole's hand came to my shoulder. "We don't have to stay long. Use me as an excuse if you want to leave. Or if you want to stay for hours, that's fine too. Do whatever, but I'll follow your lead."

His beautiful green eyes were full of concern.

"Thank you. I'm sure this will be okay."

We both knew that was a lie, but he didn't call me on it. He just let go of my shoulder and shut off the truck before stepping out.

I took one more breath, then climbed out of the truck just as the front door to Kyle and Debbie's house swung open.

"Hi!" Debbie came down the steps of the wraparound porch and right into my space for a hug. "It's so nice to have you here."

I froze for a second, surprised at her warm welcome—one I

hadn't gotten since before Jamie had died—but the shock wore off fast and I returned her hug. "It's nice to be here."

"Hi, Poppy." I let go of Debbie as Adam walked out of the house.

I smiled to hide the wince at seeing his face. Adam looked more like Jamie than ever with his hair grown out long like his brother had worn it. "Hi, Adam. How are you?"

"Good. Damn busy, but good."

Behind him, Kyle came out of the house and waved. "Hi there."

"Hi." I stepped up for a hug. Kyle's was less enthusiastic than Debbie's but it was better than the handshake he'd been giving me lately.

"I see you brought reinforcements?" Kyle nodded to Cole.

"I did."

Cole stepped up to shake Kyle's hand. "Cole Goodman, nice to meet you."

Cole introduced himself to Kyle, then Debbie and Adam. My eyes darted back and forth between them, watching for an odd look or disapproving glance, but Jamie's family was pleasant and welcoming as they chatted with Cole.

Maybe this would go better than I'd expected. Maybe having Cole and Adam here would be a nice safeguard. Maybe we'd end up visiting for a while and get over the awkwardness from the past five years. Maybe they'd even invite us to stay for dinner.

"All right." Kyle nodded toward the large shop across the yard from the house. "Let's get this truck loaded up and then you guys can head back to town."

Scratch dinner.

"Lead the way." Cole nodded at Kyle, then placed his fingers on the small of my back.

I knew the second his fingers brushed my shirt that it was a mistake. Not that Cole had done it to cause problems—the gesture was innocent and habitual. But Debbie's entire body jerked as she gasped, while Kyle's face turned to stone. The only one who didn't look like I'd just slapped them across the face was Adam.

"Ready?" I took a huge step away from Cole and kept my focus on Adam as he spun on a boot heel and headed for the shop.

I could feel Cole's stare on my back as we walked, but I didn't turn. I just kept my eyes focused on the gravel and the shop, hoping that behind me Debbie wasn't crying and Kyle wasn't furious.

When we got to the shed, I took a spot by a row of toolboxes to stay out of the way as Kyle and Adam pulled a dusty tarp off of Jamie's yellow truck.

The side panels were spotted with rust. The front bumper needed to be reattached because it was hanging loose on one side. And the front windshield was cracked in so many places it looked like a spider's web.

But it was Jamie's. Something he'd bought as a teenager and driven until college when he'd bought a nicer car.

"I still can't believe Jamie didn't take this to college." Adam ran his hand along the yellow hood and smiled at me. "Remember how he said he'd never get a date to sit in here?"

I smiled back. "Well, considering the passenger seat is missing most of the cushion, I would have agreed."

"No way." Adam laughed. "You would have still dated him if he'd driven this old thing."

Jamie could have driven me around town on the handlebars of a bicycle for all I would have cared. "You're probably right."

"Should we see if it still runs?"

"Oh, it'll run." Kyle walked over to the driver's side of the truck. "I came out here a couple nights ago and made sure." He ran his hand along the open window, like he was saying good-bye.

At my side, Debbie sniffled. "It will be strange not to come out here and see Jamie's truck."

A wave of doubt hit me hard. *Maybe I shouldn't take the truck. Maybe I should say to hell with that one item on Jamie's list and let it go. Maybe Kyle and Debbie needed this truck in their shop more than I needed to check a box.*

I was just about to relent when Adam slapped his hand on the hood. "Thanks for getting this finished up, Poppy. Jamie always wanted to have it done."

He had. Jamie had talked about fixing it up all the time. We'd just never had the space and he'd never had the time. But now, I could see it through.

I had to see this through.

So I swallowed the lump in my throat and gave Adam a small smile. "Midnight blue. He always wanted it to be midnight blue."

"And cream interior," Kyle added as he opened the door.

I nodded. "And cream interior."

The sound of Jamie's truck filled the shop as Kyle started it up. As he drove it outside, we all followed behind as he steered it toward Cole's trailer.

"I guess I could have just come and gotten it myself," I told Cole as we walked. "Sorry."

"No, it's better this way. The last thing I want is for you to get stranded on the side of the road. The engine might run, but those tires won't last another fifty miles."

I didn't know if that was true, but it made me feel better.

Cole jogged ahead, pulling out the ramps on the trailer so Kyle could ease the truck onto the flatbed. Then together, Cole, Kyle and Adam all chained it down.

"Thanks, Debbie. It was nice to see you."

She nodded and forced a smile, then gave me a one-arm hug before turning and going back inside the house without a word.

I stared at the house, wishing there was something I could do to get an invitation inside. I stared at the house, knowing there wasn't. So I turned back to the guys, standing alone and waiting for them to finish.

"Thank you," I told Kyle as he and Adam came over.

Kyle nodded and looked back to the truck. "Take care of it."

"I will."

Then without a handshake, a hug, or even a good-bye, he went inside with Debbie. The click of the door's latch echoed for miles.

"Bye, Poppy." Adam waved at me, then Cole as he headed back to the shop. "Nice to meet you, Cole."

Cole nodded but Adam had already turned his back to us, done with that job and on to the next.

I glanced at my watch before they blurred with tears. Twenty-nine minutes. I'd been dismissed after only twenty-nine minutes.

Jamie's family didn't have to say it—I'd heard it loud and clear.

Good-bye.

Kyle and Debbie wouldn't be back to Bozeman to visit my restaurant. They wouldn't be inviting me back to this ranch to spend holidays like I'd done so many times before. They wouldn't be a part of my life.

Without a backward glance, I walked past Cole to his truck. "Let's go."

"You got it." He didn't hesitate to get us the hell off the ranch, driving in silence until we reached the highway. "Are you okay?"

"No."

I wanted Jamie to be alive so he could fix up his own truck. To do his own birthday list. I wanted him to be here so his parents weren't so heartbroken.

I wanted the ache in my chest to disappear. I wanted it to stop teasing me with reprieves, only to torture me with each return.

I want to be happy.

I couldn't remember how it felt to be truly happy.

"Give me your hand." Cole placed his hand, palm up, on the console between us.

I shook my head, knowing that if I touched him, I'd never keep the tears at bay.

"Poppy, give me your hand."

"I can't," I choked out.

"Poppy," he whispered. "Give me your hand."

I didn't have the strength to resist his gentle voice so I untucked my hand from between my knees and placed it on his. The second his long fingers closed over mine, the first tear fell. Then the second. Then the rest.

I cried for the loss of a family. For the loss of Jamie's parents as friends.

I cried because Cole's hand under mine made me feel better.

Better and worse, all at the same time.

CHAPTER ELEVEN

46TH BIRTHDAY: GET A TATTOO

COLE

"Nothing." I shut off the TV and tossed the remote on the table.

I had a bitch of a headache from staring at a small screen all afternoon, watching the surveillance tape of Jamie Maysen's murder for the tenth time today. Just like the nine times before, there was nothing to go on.

As I pinched the bridge of my nose, I closed my eyes, hoping the thumping in my skull would go away.

It had been two weeks since I'd taken Poppy to pick up that old Ford from her in-laws. Two weeks and I felt like all I'd done was sit in this goddamn conference room and watch security feeds. Every night, I went home feeling like my head was being split in two.

And tonight wouldn't be much different.

I pressed the heels of my hands into my temples and started rubbing just as the door opened.

Matt came in and took the chair at my side. "Anything?"

"No." I dropped my hands. "I've been studying the liquor store tape and running it against the parking lot footage we got from the grocery store. No one matching the killer's description comes in or out within five hours of the murder."

"Mind if I watch the liquor store footage again?"

"Go for it."

He swiped up the remote and rewound the video to the beginning, then pressed play. I was grateful there was no sound on the footage. Seeing what happened in that liquor store was gruesome enough without adding a soundtrack to the mix.

The TV screen filled with a grainy video taken from a camera that had been located in an upper corner of the store. The cashier, Kennedy Hastings, was smiling and chatting with Jamie Maysen as he carried over his haul—gin, vodka and margarita mix. He set them down on the counter, then took out a wallet from his back pocket, saying something to Kennedy that made her laugh.

She'd had a pretty smile. Kennedy's curly brown hair had been cut short but it suited her round, dark face and petite frame. And she was fumbling a little, probably nervous because Poppy's husband had been a good-looking guy.

Jamie had worn his blond hair a little long, but it went with his laid-back vibe. He was a big guy too, likely as tall as me and with just as much bulk. He was wearing flip-flops and cargo shorts with his Western pearl-snap shirt. And on his left hand, a silver wedding band reflected in the screen.

My insides twisted as the footage spun on. Tragic. That was the word I'd landed on to describe this video. Fucking tragic.

On screen, Jamie handed over some cash to Kennedy just as the killer came into the liquor store. The killer was barely inside the door before he started waving his gun in the air. Jamie said something, you could make out the word *don't*, and then took one step forward. The moment he moved, the killer gripped the gun with both hands and shot Jamie in the head. Kennedy's mouth was wide as she screamed before the killer turned the gun on her and shot her center mass.

Then, with no hesitation, as if he hadn't just taken two innocent lives, the killer reached across the counter and yanked out all of the cash from the open register drawer.

He'd kept his back to the camera as he backed out of the store. The angle of the camera had never caught his face—just hints of his profile. All we could see was the plain charcoal hoodie and jeans he'd been wearing. When he pulled the cash out from the register, we could make out a sliver of his light-skinned nose and a small tuft of brown hair at his ear. Black sunglasses covered his eyes and black gloves his hands.

With the register empty, he backed out of the store, leaving behind two dead bodies.

Leaving behind a young daughter without a mother and a wife who'd had to bury her husband in a closed-casket funeral.

Matt and I sat quietly, both staring at the screen as it played on. I'd seen a lot of fucked-up things as a cop, but this video was the worst. Maybe it was because I knew Poppy. Maybe it was because I knew what would happen hours later when I showed up on her porch. Maybe it was because the image of her heart breaking right before my eyes was one I'd never forget.

Besides delivering the news to Poppy that her husband had been killed, watching this video over and over was the hardest thing I'd ever done as a police officer.

Matt stopped the video and broke the silence in the room. "That is fucked up."

I nodded. "And for what? A couple hundred bucks from the register? Doesn't seem worth it, does it?"

Matt shook his head. "We've got to find this guy."

I dug my fingers back into my temples. "I've gone through

all the tapes from the complex, all the footage we got from the grocery store and all the other shops. I can't find a glimpse of this guy anywhere."

Matt sighed. "Which means we're on to Plan B. Stoplight cameras."

"Yep." I popped the *p* just like Poppy did. "Which means if you're looking for me anytime before eight or after five, I'll be in this room."

I had no fucking clue how long it would take me to start weeding through camera footage in my free time. A month? Maybe two?

But for Poppy, I'd do anything. I'd sit in this damn room and leave work every night with a headache just for the chance to give her some closure.

Because closure was the one thing she craved as much as love. She was desperate for someone to tell her it was okay to start living again. And since she sure as fuck wasn't going to get it from Jamie's parents, I'd do my best to give it to her myself.

These last two weeks, she'd built a brick wall between us. When I'd go to the restaurant for dinner, she'd be too busy in the kitchen to sit with me for more than ten minutes. When I'd text to check in, she'd respond with short answers.

ME: *How was your day?*
   Poppy: *Just fine.*

ME: *Do you care if I come by the restaurant for dinner?*
   Poppy: *Sure. That's fine.*

ME: *Are you doing okay?*

Poppy: I'm fine.

FINE. Things were not fucking *fine*. But if she thought she could shut me out, Poppy Maysen had something to learn.

I wasn't going anywhere.

I'd known going into this thing with her that the road would be rough. That she had more to overcome than I could possibly imagine. I had to give her time. So while waiting for her to realize that I was the new constant in her life, I'd been here, watching video footage.

And fixing up that old truck.

I'd forgotten how much I enjoyed tinkering on classic cars. How much fun I'd had as a kid working on old beaters with my dad. Besides my brief encounters with Poppy, that truck had given me something to look forward to at the end of each long day.

I'd ended up taking it to my parents' house because Dad had better tools and a bigger garage. He had been more than happy to part with the garage space, thrilled to jump into the project with me. Mom was happy because I'd been there almost every night for the past two weeks.

Every night except when Poppy had been there for her ukulele lessons.

Those nights, I'd given her some space.

"You should get out of here." Matt shut off the TV.

"I think I will." Leaving sounded like a damn good idea. I needed some time away from this room. Some time to think about the case. "See you Monday."

Matt nodded as we both stood and walked back to our desks in the bull pen. I didn't waste a second grabbing my keys, sunglasses and wallet from my desk and getting the hell out of the station.

The minute I pulled out of the parking lot, my headache started to ease. I debated going home, but when I passed a convenience store, I had a better idea. With a cold six-pack in the passenger seat, I drove to my parents' house to spend the evening working on Jamie Maysen's truck.

It was still early—only four in the afternoon—when I got to Mom and Dad's, which meant I had the garage to myself. Dad wasn't home yet and Mom was teaching in her studio. So I let myself in, stripped off my gun and badge, then traded my Bozeman PD polo for a plain white T-shirt I'd stashed in the back of my truck. I popped the top off a beer and got to work, letting the clank of tools on metal drown out the silent gunshots from the murder video I'd watched too many times.

Three hours later, I'd completely gutted the interior of the cab. The bench seat had been taken out, along with the floorboards. The steering wheel and door panels were gone. I'd even removed the radio, jockey box and driving gauges. The only thing staying was the black dashboard, which was in good shape but needed a thorough cleaning and conditioning.

With the inside basically a shell, I started on the smaller items, using a screwdriver to take out the driver's-side sun visor. I'd just loosened one screw when the visor fell open and a picture dropped to the floor.

I set aside the screwdriver and wiped my hands on my jeans before lifting up the photo.

It was a picture of Poppy and Jamie from college. Jamie had his arms around Poppy's chest, his chin resting on her shoulder. They were both smiling at the camera as they stood in a crowded row at the MSU football stadium.

Damn. She looked happy. So fucking happy.

My heart beat hard as I studied Poppy's face. She hadn't changed much since college. Some of the youth she had in the picture was gone—and pain had erased some of her innocence —but she was just as beautiful now as she had been back then.

Just as beautiful, but nowhere near as happy.

I wanted to see that kind of raw joy on her face again. I wanted to be the man that put it there.

Me. Not Jamie.

"Hey."

My eyes swung to the garage door. So lost in my inspection of her picture, I hadn't heard the woman herself walk inside. But there she was. My pretty Poppy. The sun limned her in an amber halo, and my heart did that weird double-beat thing before I found my voice. "Hi."

"Sorry if I startled you." She walked toward the far wall where all of Dad's tool benches were lined up.

"It's okay." I rounded the hood of the truck to join her, holding out the photo. "Here. I just found this."

She took the photo and smiled. "Look how young we were. This seems like a lifetime ago." With one finger, she touched Jamie's face, then set the picture aside on a workbench.

I waited, wondering when I'd run into the wall she'd constructed between us, but she surprised me by planting both palms on the top of the bench and hopping up to take a seat.

Did this mean she was done shutting me out? Done avoiding me? Because that would turn my long, shitty week all the way around.

"You know," she said, "I think that picture was the last time I went to a Bobcat football game. I kind of want to see the expanded stadium. Would you go to a game with me this fall?"

"In a heartbeat."

That got me the smile I hadn't seen for way too long.

Damn, I'd missed her these last two weeks. That smile. Her laugh. Her crazy hand gestures. The distance she'd put between us was killing me.

169

She pointed to the truck. "How's progress going?"

I turned and leaned against the bench, my hip next to her knee. "Good. I think I'll be able to do all of the interior myself. I was able to order a new seat and all of the parts. I've got a guy coming to replace the windshield next week, and I've asked a buddy of Dad's if he can help with the body stuff and paint."

"I'm sorry I can't help. But you're keeping track of how much I owe you, aren't you?"

"Sure."

Whatever the total ended up being, I was whacking it in half. There was no way she was going to pay for all of this truck, no matter what she said. Not when she was trying to run a new business, to support her employees and herself.

"I think I'd better have you save receipts."

I chuckled. It never ceased to surprise me how well she could read my thoughts. "So what's new? Everything going okay?"

"I'm good." She nodded. "I actually just finished a lesson with your mom and I saw your truck so I wanted to say hi."

My eyebrows came together. "I thought your lessons were on Tuesdays."

"They are, but I asked to switch this week. I took the whole afternoon off for an appointment." She reached to the collar of her shirt. She wasn't wearing her normal restaurant T-shirt today. Instead, she had on some sort of sports bra with a loose, short-sleeved sweatshirt on top. The collar had been cut so it draped across one of her shoulders, teasing me with a patch of flawless skin.

As she yanked the collar wide, I tucked a hand in my pocket so I wouldn't be tempted to see just how silky that skin was. My cock jerked against my zipper as she kept pulling that collar lower and lower, stretching it so her shoulder was completely bare.

"See?" She angled her back to me and I leaned closer.

"You got a tattoo today?"

She nodded and peered over her shoulder. "My first and only. That thing hurt like a mother."

I grinned. "I'll take your word for it."

"No tattoos?"

I shook my head. "Not yet. I just can't think of anything I'd want to get inked." I pointed to her shirt, wanting to hold it down so I could get a closer look. "May I?"

"Go ahead."

My fingers replaced hers at the collar and I gently tugged it lower. I was careful not to touch her skin, knowing it would be tender, but also so my dick wouldn't get any ideas about where this was going.

On her right shoulder, covered in plastic wrap, was a long string of delicate script—*the rest is still unwritten.*

"I like it." I had expected any tattoo she'd get to be something about Jamie, but this seemed more like something just for her. "What does it mean?"

"It's a song lyric. Something that has always stayed with me." She adjusted her shirt back over her shoulder as my fingers let it go. "The first few years after Jamie died were hard. I didn't see any of our old friends much. Mostly I just kept to myself. I worked as a receptionist for a dentist's office until I bought the restaurant, and if I wasn't at work, then I spent my time at home or with Finn and Molly."

I nodded and stayed quiet, not wanting her to stop.

"But after three years or so, I started to get out more. I started running into old friends. They'd always chat with me like old times, but as soon as I'd turn away, I'd hear them whisper *widow.* That was the first word they used to describe me behind my back. That poor widow, Poppy Maysen."

She stared, unblinking, at the truck as she spoke, while the anger flashed in her eyes.

"I hate that word. Widow." Her hands balled into fists on the workbench. "Every time I hear it I want to scream. People say widow like that's who I am now. Like it's expected that I stay in this permanent state of grief. Like it's unacceptable that I'd consider moving on with my life."

She didn't have to say their names, but I knew she was referring to Jamie's parents.

"Anyway." She relaxed her hands. "That's when I started to think about doing Jamie's birthday list. And that's what my tattoo means."

"That the rest of your life is still unwritten."

She nodded and locked her blue gaze with mine. "I've been thinking about you a lot these last couple of weeks."

"Yeah?" My chest tightened as I braced for her to throw up that wall. As I waited for her to tell me I wouldn't be part of her unwritten.

"Yeah." She looked to her lap. "You scare the hell out of me, Cole," she whispered.

"Is that why you've been avoiding me?"

"I'm sorry. I just needed some time to think."

I wanted to touch her, to tip her chin up so she'd look at me, but I kept my hands tight to my sides. "And what did you come up with?"

"I like you," she told her fingers. "I like you a lot."

The tension rushed out of my shoulders and I let out a breath. *She likes me.* This was good. No, this was fucking great. If she was actually willing to acknowledge her feelings for me, my uphill battle might start to level out. "I like you a lot too."

"But I—"

"Wait." My finger flew to her lips. "Let me say something before you take away the best feeling I've had in weeks."

She smiled against my skin.

"I'm not trying to take Jamie's place or erase his memory or make you forget that you loved him. I'm just trying to explore this thing between us." I stepped closer, resting my hip against her thigh.

Her breath hitched under my finger and I dropped it away, resting my hand on the other side of her lap, trapping her in my space.

"What I was going to say was," her eyes held mine as they smiled, "but I'd like to take things slow and just see what happens."

Slow. She wasn't going to back away or keep me at a distance. She just wanted to take this slow. And slow I could definitely handle.

"God, I want to kiss you." I wanted to strip her down and take her right here on this workbench, but since she wasn't ready for that, I'd settle for a kiss. "Does that scare you?"

She nodded.

"Do you want me to kiss you, Poppy?"

She didn't move. She just stared into my eyes as our breaths mixed. Then, she made my whole year by giving me the slightest nod.

I closed the inches between us until my nose brushed against hers. I stopped when she tensed, then waited, not moving a muscle. But just as I was about to step away and give her some space, she leaned into my lips with a hesitant brush.

"Cole! Do you want pizza?"

Poppy and I jerked apart, our heads turning toward Mom as she walked through the side door into the garage.

"Fuck," I muttered at the same time Poppy whimpered.

I stepped out of Poppy's space and frowned at Mom. She wouldn't have been able to see us from the side doorway, so I couldn't get too mad, but damn—kiss blocked by my mother. It felt like the time in high school when she'd caught me making out with my girlfriend in the driveway.

"Oh, Poppy!" Mom said, walking around the old truck. "I didn't realize you were still here. We're ordering pizza. Will you stay?"

She smiled. "Sure. Thanks, Mia."

"Cole and Brad both like meat lovers, but I get the veggie. Is that okay?"

"Sounds great."

"Okay! I'll call you when it gets here." Mom winked at me before she turned around and went back out the door.

I ran a hand through my hair and took a few seconds to get my dick under control. He'd gotten the idea that he'd be getting more than just my hand tonight and was jammed against my zipper, ready to come out and play.

Poppy's fingers were working themselves in tangled circles, her bottom lip between her teeth.

"Sorry." I held up my hands. "You said slow."

She shook her head. "It's okay. I'm just . . ."

"Hey." I stepped back toward the bench, trapping her hands between mine before they flailed. "We'll go slow until you're ready to pick up the pace. Just give me the signal when you're ready." I let her go and demonstrated my version of her wrist spin thing. "There. Give me that signal."

She laughed. "Okay."

I walked down the bench to the mini-fridge and took out another beer. "Want one?"

"Yes, please."

I opened the bottle and handed it over. Tipping the amber glass to her lips, she took a long swallow. The way her sexy throat moved as she drank wasn't doing anything to help the problem in my jeans.

She set down her beer and let her eyes wander over the tool

bench. They lingered on my gun and badge a few feet away. "Can I, um . . ." She pointed to my gun.

I set down my beer and picked up the Glock, sliding it out of the holster. "Sure. The safety is on and I unloaded it when I got here."

She held it carefully in her palm. "I don't know much about handguns. I've only ever used a rifle when I did hunter's safety as a kid. It's heavy." Slowly, she wrapped the grip with both hands. "Do you hold it like this?"

I shook my head and repositioned her hands so that one was around the grip and the other under the base to support its weight. "Like that. This gun would be way too big for you without a lot of practice. It's got a hell of a recoil and it's made for larger hands. Most of the female officers I know carry a smaller version of this."

This one would probably send her arms over her head and rock her back a foot or two.

Kind of like how the killer took the recoil in the liquor store shooting.

What the fuck? My mind started to race. How had I not thought of this? How had any of us not thought of this? What if Jamie's killer was a woman?

I ran a hand over my face as things dawned in a new light. Simmons hadn't royally fucked up this murder case. He'd just looked at it from the most obvious angle. He'd been searching for a man.

We'd *all* been searching for a man.

"Cole?"

I blinked and focused back on Poppy. "Sorry. I was just thinking of something." I took the gun from her hands and put it away.

"Is everything okay?" she asked, her eyebrows furrowed.

I smiled and lied. "Yeah. It's great. Do you want to hang out

175

with me while I work on the truck before dinner, or do you want to go inside and chat with Mom?"

"I'm good right here."

She was. She was perfect right here.

And she'd be even better if I could find Jamie's killer.

CHAPTER TWELVE

39TH BIRTHDAY: GET IN A TAXI AND YELL, "FOLLOW THAT CAR!"

POPPY

"I'm melting." Molly fanned her face.

"Me too. I just hope the cab has air conditioning."

It was three days after I'd gotten my tattoo and admitted my feelings to Cole, and Molly and I were standing outside the restaurant. Sweat beaded on my temples as we stared down the street, hoping to see a sedan with its taxi light on.

"Oooh!" Molly stood on her tiptoes and looked down the street. "Here it comes. Okay, I'm going."

With a huge smile, she jogged around her SUV, getting in and pulling onto the street the second the cab turned into the parking lot.

Okay, Jamie. Here goes.

I took a deep breath, then hustled into the backseat of the cab, throwing open the door and diving inside.

"Follow that car!" I shouted to the driver, pointing toward Molly's Explorer.

"What?" The cabbie looked over his shoulder.

"Follow that car!" I wagged my finger and gave him my *get going, buddy* eyes.

"Look, lady—"

"Just go! Please!"

He frowned but hit the gas, jerking the cab into traffic and zooming up on Molly.

"She could at least go a little faster," I muttered.

"What was that?" the driver asked into the rearview mirror.

"Nothing. Just please, follow that car."

And he did. He followed Molly around the block and right back to the parking lot of the restaurant.

"Thank you, sir."

"What? That's it?"

I nodded and reached into my pocket for a twenty. "That's it. Thank you."

Handing him the cash, I got out of the cab and walked back inside the restaurant, where Molly was waiting.

"So?" she asked. "How was it?"

"My one-minute cab ride? Expensive."

She laughed. "Well, at least that one was easy. Now you can cross it off the list."

Through the windows, I kept my eyes on the cab as he pulled back onto the street. "Jamie would have thought that was hysterical. He probably would have videoed the entire thing to post on Facebook."

"And he probably would have dressed up in a suit or something, pretending to be a secret agent."

I nodded. "Yep. He would have mapped out this entire route for me to drive so he could follow me all over town and end up at this sketchy place. He would have planned this epic chase."

"I think you're right."

Molly and I shared a sad smile. Our little adventure had

been tame compared to what my husband would have planned, but I was still glad that we'd done it together.

"Okay. Back to work." She turned and walked toward the counter.

"Yes, boss." I'd taken three steps away from the door when it opened behind us. I glanced over my shoulder and stopped when I saw Cole.

"Hi." My smile got bigger as my breath hitched.

It felt freeing to enjoy the hitch. To enjoy the acceleration of my heartbeat and the jitters I got when he was near. Because now that I'd laid it out there—now that I'd admitted to Cole my feelings—I'd given myself permission to enjoy it all.

What I'd told him was true. I'd thought a lot about him in the weeks after my trip to Kyle and Debbie's ranch. And though a part of me had thought life would be easier if I just cut him out, I couldn't do it.

During those two weeks, I'd found myself typing texts that I'd never sent. I'd made him special dinners that he'd never come to eat. And I'd realized life was too short to miss out on something . . . anything.

Because that was the point of Jamie's list. Not missing out.

So I wasn't going to miss this with Cole.

"Hi." He studied my face as he caught up to my side.

"What?" I stopped smiling so I could run my tongue over my teeth. I couldn't feel anything, but I kept my lips tight when I asked, "Do I have something stuck in my teeth?"

He smiled and shook his head. "No. It's just nice to see that smile. I haven't gotten to see it much lately."

My cheeks flushed as my smile came back. "That's sweet."

He nodded. "Sweet on you."

"Aww!" Molly swooned as she appeared at my side. "Say something else like that. I'm living vicariously through your romance."

"Ignore her," I told Cole, grabbing Molly's hand before she could start petting him. "Weren't you just saying we needed to get back to work?"

"Slave driver," she grumbled as I dragged her to the counter.

Behind us, Cole chuckled as he followed.

The restaurant was empty—hence our cab ride—but soon the takeout crowd would be coming in to pick up meals on their way home from work and the dinner rush would be in full swing. But for now, Molly, Helen and I were enjoying the lull and getting caught up on prep work.

"I'd better head to the office to pay some bills. Holler if you need help." Molly filled a glass from the large pitcher of lemon water, then smiled at Cole as she disappeared into the kitchen.

"Hi, Cole." Helen peeked out from under her eyelashes as she rolled silverware behind the counter.

"Hi, Helen." He smiled at her and the pink in her cheeks turned bright red.

"Can I get you something?" I asked Cole.

He sank into the stool across from me—the one next to Randall's, which Jimmy had claimed as his own—and sighed. "I've got a bitch of a headache. I thought some caffeine might help."

"Sorry." My hand reached for his temple but froze when I was inches away.

That's what I'd always done whenever Jamie had gotten a headache. I'd rubbed his temples and combed his hair with my fingers until the pain had eased away.

My eyes wandered from my hand to Cole's gaze. His eyes were waiting, quietly begging for my touch. With a racing heart, I placed my palm on the side of his face. My thumb was at his temple as my fingertips threaded into his hair and massaged his scalp.

Cole closed his eyes and relaxed his head into my hand. When he let out a sigh, the whole restaurant disappeared, leaving just me and Cole—my hand in his soft hair.

After a few minutes, he opened his eyes. "Thank you."

"Better?"

He nodded. "Much."

"Good." I reluctantly pulled my hand from his face. "What kind of coffee do you want?"

"Surprise me."

Smiling, I turned back to the espresso machine, getting to work on my personal headache killer—a triple-shot mocha with an extra pump of chocolate.

As I worked, a deep-seated contentment moved into my bones. Having Cole in the restaurant felt . . . right. In the two weeks that I'd tried to push him away, I hadn't felt like this except for the times when Cole had come in for dinner. Those nights I'd been too "busy" to sit with him.

Who knew what would happen between us. Maybe Cole and I would end up just being friends. Maybe he'd not want kids or turn out to be a slob or transform into a Fantasy Football fanatic during football season. No one knew what we'd become.

But I wanted to find out.

And I trusted that he'd take care with my damaged heart.

His coffee done, I set it down, then went to the fridge to get him one of the banana cream pies I'd made earlier. "Here. Caffeine and sugar. You'll be good as new before you leave."

He grinned and dug right into the pie. "Damn, woman, you can cook."

"I'm glad you came in. I need to ask you something."

He stopped chewing. "Uh-oh."

"It's not bad and you don't have to say yes. I can always ask Finn."

He shook his head and swallowed. "No, I'll do it."

"You don't know what it is."

Cole shrugged. "Doesn't matter."

"Sure it does."

He shrugged again. "Not really."

"What if I ask you to buy me tampons?" Jamie had always refused to go down the feminine products aisle at the grocery store. I was sure Cole would be the same.

"Text me what you need and I'll go to the store later."

As he took another bite of pie, I tapped my fingers on the counter. "What if I ask you to take me to a foreign film?" I was sure he'd pass on that one. I'd never met a man who liked foreign films, not that I was crazy about them either.

"They aren't my favorite, but as long as they have popcorn and Milk Duds, I'm in."

"Okay. I've got one." I gave him a smug grin. "What if I ask you to break the law?"

"Like pull a damn fire alarm?" He scoffed and pointed his spoon at my nose. "That's one you're not going to cross off the list, by the way. Not when you could end up with a huge fine or a year in jail."

I frowned. I had no idea how I was going to finish that item from Jamie's list, but clearly, I wouldn't be asking Cole for help. Maybe I'd see if Jimmy had any ideas.

Cole swallowed another bite of pie. "Are you going to ever ask me your question or just play hypotheticals all afternoon? Because at some point, I do need to get back to the station, and it would happen a lot faster if you just realized that outside of breaking the law, I'll say yes to anything you ask."

I smiled and leaned closer. Molly would definitely have swooned over that one. "I have to go to a wedding on Saturday. My freshman roommate is getting married and I'd like to go." I hadn't seen her in a few years but she was about the only friend from my past that didn't treat me differently because my husband had been murdered. "Would you go with me?"

Cole looked up from his pie. "Like a date?"

Date.

Maybe that word wasn't so scary, after all.

"Yes. Like a date."

———

"YOU LOOK," Cole swallowed, "stunning."

"Thanks." I smoothed down the skirt of my forest-green dress. It had a simple design but was fitted down the bodice to my hips and knees. I hadn't worn this dress in years, but it still fit perfectly and gave me the illusion of curves and cleavage.

I looked up from my patent nude heels, letting my eyes linger on Cole. "Not so bad yourself, Detective."

He was wearing a white button-down shirt tucked into some charcoal slacks. The leather belt cinched at his narrow waist accentuated his broad shoulders. And his legs looked long —really long—and his thighs thicker than they did in jeans.

I was shamelessly staring at his bulging quads when he cleared his throat. "Ready to go?"

I nodded, hoping that the heat in my cheeks wasn't too red, and stepped down off the porch. "This is kind of weird, having you here again." Tonight was the first time Cole had ever picked me up from home instead of the restaurant.

"Yeah." He held out his hand but didn't say anything else about that night.

When I slipped my hand in his, the nerves in my stomach settled the instant we touched.

An hour later, we were squished together in a wooden pew at the church. At the altar, my friend was saying her vows to a man who looked at her like she was the only person in the sanctuary.

I'd been fighting the burn and swelling in my throat since the moment she walked down the aisle. The moment she said *I do*, I lost the fight and tears flooded my eyes.

I'd never cried at a wedding before. Never. Not even my own.

Maybe it was because this was the first wedding I'd been to since Jamie had died. Maybe it was because the traditional vows that they'd exchanged were exactly the same ones I'd said to Jamie. Maybe I was just becoming more sentimental. Whatever the reason, I was about to lose it completely.

Breathe. Don't cry. Don't cry. But no matter how many times I told myself not to cry, I did it anyway. A steady stream of tears poured over my lower lids and I swiped furiously so they wouldn't smudge my makeup. I sniffled as I wiped my hands on my dress, drying them so I could go back to my face. Just as I lifted them up for the second time, Cole took one between his own.

I looked up through blurry eyes as he placed a handkerchief into my hand.

"Mom always cries at weddings," he whispered with a smile.

Cole didn't say *don't cry.* He didn't care if I lost it now and then. He just gave me some extra steel for my spine in the form of a plain white hankie.

I hiccupped a laugh, taking the cloth from his hands to blot my eyes dry. Then, leaning into Cole's side, I clutched the handkerchief and used it to keep my mascara from running as the ceremony concluded and the guests stood to clap for the newly married couple.

"She looks beautiful," I said as my friend and her husband walked by our row.

Cole's hand came to the small of my back as he inched closer. "So do you."

I was a wreck. I didn't need a mirror to know that my fair skin was splotchy from crying and my eyes were as red as my hair. But my heart still swelled with Cole's compliment and I smiled at him over my shoulder. "Thank you."

He lifted his hand, using his thumb to wipe a smudge on my cheek. "Want to hear a secret?"

I nodded.

He leaned down farther, pressing his warm chest against my back. His minty, cool breath feathered against my cheek as he whispered, "The guy in front of you has his fly undone."

I blurted a laugh, though it came out more like a snort, and I turned, trying to nonchalantly check out my neighbor's fly. Sure enough, it was undone. The blue tails of his tucked-in shirt were peeking out of his pants.

I looked back over my shoulder to a grinning Cole. With one silly joke, he'd made everything better. Jamie had always done that for me—given me brevity. Except where Jamie had always thought jokes were appropriate, Cole saved them for when the time was right.

As we slowly shuffled into the receiving line, the differences between Cole and Jamie filtered through my mind. I'd been dutifully trying not to compare the two, mostly because there wasn't any point—this wasn't a competition—but also because it sparked doubts about the relationship I'd had with Jamie.

He'd always been so relaxed, cavalier at times, which had driven me crazy. I'd been wondering lately how our relationship would have changed if we'd been given time. Would his constant jokes have gotten old? Would he have let go of some of his big-kid tendencies and matured? I'd always been the grown-up in our relationship. Would I have gotten sick of always having to be the adult?

No. We would have been fine. Thinking anything else just made me sad. And with laughing, happy people all around me, I didn't want to be sad. So I brushed off those thoughts and joined Cole as he visited with the other guests while we waited to congratulate the bride and groom.

Two hours later, we'd tossed the rice, we'd listened to toasts and we'd eaten our cake.

And now, it was time for dancing.

"What do you say, pretty Poppy?" Cole's hand skimmed my lower back as we stood by the bar. "Want to dance?"

"Sure." Then I let the soft pressure from his fingertips guide me to the dance floor.

Cole took me in his arms with one hand gripping my hip while the other held my hand between us. My free hand slid up his chest, resting on his sternum. Underneath the thin cotton of his shirt, his heartbeat seemed fast—harder than normal. I bet if I touched my own chest, my own would match.

"Having fun?" He swayed me with the music.

I nodded. "Thanks for coming with me. I haven't been to a wedding since . . . you know."

"Whatever you need, I'll be there in a heartbeat."

I relaxed into his arms, resting my head next to my hand. When his chin hit the top of my head, I let out a sigh.

This is nice. The fairy lights above us were twinkling. The singer's voice was soothing. And as cheesy as it sounded in my head, love was in the air. This dance with Cole was maybe the most romantic dance I'd had . . . ever.

I'd always had to beg Jamie to slow dance with me. His idea of dancing was a fast jitterbug or the bump and grind like we were at a club. The last time he'd held me close to dance had been at our wedding. Even then, he'd been so distracted—

waving to people as they'd watched us—our dance hadn't held much tenderness.

Nothing like this moment with Cole.

"What was your wedding like?"

"Hectic." I frowned. "Jamie had no interest in wedding planning so I did it all myself. I wanted a nice, small get-together in Alaska, but Jamie wanted a big party at the ranch. We actually got in a huge fight about it and ended up doing both. We got married in Alaska and then had a party at the ranch."

"Good compromise."

I scoffed. "Not really. It was twice as much work as it should have been. But Jamie wasn't known for his compromising skills. By the time it was over, we were at each other's throats."

As relaxed as Jamie had been, his competitive streak had been legendary. Sometimes, I think he liked to argue with me just to prove he could win. We'd get into innocent little debates that would turn into knockdown, drag-out fights because he'd never concede that I might have a point. After years together, I'd started to just let him win. I'd drop my stance and take his side to avoid the battle, even when deep down I didn't agree.

I leaned back to look at Cole. "Did you know I love playing board games?"

"No." He shook his head.

"Yeah, I do. But I haven't played since college. Jamie *had* to win. It took all the fun out of it. I hated—"

Stop. What was I doing? Bad-mouthing my husband when he wasn't here to defend himself? I was supposed to be honoring his memory, not questioning everything about him. About us.

"You hated what?" Cole asked.

"Nothing." I looked at the floor. "I shouldn't be talking

about Jamie like that. He was the best. He just liked to win and maybe I'm a sore loser."

Cole used his finger to tip up my chin. "No one is perfect. Just because he had some faults doesn't mean you loved him any less. We've all got our weaknesses. That's what makes us human."

"I shouldn't be complaining about him. It's not fair and I don't want you to think badly about him."

His finger left my chin as his hand framed my cheek. "I'll never think badly about him. I'll probably always be jealous. He had you first, and as much as I'm trying to be a grown-up about this, I've got a competitive streak myself. But I'll never think badly of him. He was special to you, which makes him special to me. Weaknesses and all."

I stared into his beautiful green eyes as the worries I'd had about Jamie all seeped away with Cole's words. "How do you always know what to say to make me feel better?"

"I'm *close* to perfect."

I smiled. "And very modest."

He shrugged. "Modesty is for suckers."

We both laughed and I leaned my head back against his chest to finish our dance. He'd been teasing, but from what I could tell, Cole Goodman *was* close to perfect. In our time together, I'd yet to discover a chink in his armor.

"What's one of your weaknesses?"

His hand at my hip moved up my spine so his fingers could play with my hair. "You."

I melted into him again, closing my eyes as we kept swaying. He was a weakness of mine too.

Soon, the music stopped and the couples around us came back into focus. When he offered me his arm, I looped mine with his as he escorted me back to our table.

"Do you want to stay?" he asked.

I looked around at the thinning crowd. It wasn't late, but my friend and her new husband were inching toward the exit, ready to make a quiet escape.

"Not really." I grabbed the clutch from my chair. "Let's sneak out."

Our escape was fast and the drive back to my house was quiet. I stared out my window as Cole drove, studying the stars shining brightly in the clear sky. My neighborhood didn't have streetlights, so when I climbed down from the truck, I took a moment to look up into the midnight sky. "I've never been able to find the North Star." No matter how many times someone told me the trick to finding it, I never could.

Cole joined me at my side and searched the stars. "It's right there."

I stepped closer, following his outstretched arm up to his pointing finger. "I still don't see it. People always say it's the brightest, but they all look the same to me."

Cole chuckled, dropping his arm around my shoulders.

Even in the dark, I could see the change in his eyes. The sparkle went away as the heat took its place. It was the same heat I'd seen in his parents' garage last week when he'd told me he wanted to kiss me.

His hand came up and, for the second time tonight, cupped my jaw. His thumb stroked across my cheek so gently that a shudder ran down my spine. And his mouth—those smooth, soft lips—began to drop.

Cole was going to kiss me. Did I want to kiss him? *Yes. No.* My breath started coming in pants as I flip-flopped back and forth. Cole wouldn't do anything until I gave him a signal. All I had to do was nod or reach up a bit and he'd take it as my yes.

Except my final answer was no. I couldn't kiss Cole. Not here. Not outside the house I shared with Jamie.

Cole sensed my decision—the one I'd made without a word

—because his lips changed course and landed softly on my fore-head. "Night, Poppy," he whispered.

I closed my eyes and leaned into him even further. "Good night, Cole."

He let me go, stepping backward twice before turning and getting into his truck.

I waved from my driveway until his taillights disappeared around the block. A slight breeze whooshed against my skin, bringing goose bumps and sending me inside. With the door locked behind me, I leaned against the wall in the entryway and slipped off my heels. Then I turned on the light and looked down the hallway that led to the living room and kitchen.

Pictures of Jamie and me lined the walls on both sides. There were pictures from college and our wedding. Pictures from our one and only year as a married couple. I glanced at the closet door on my left. I didn't need to open it to know there were a couple of his old coats I'd kept tucked at the back, along with his favorite hat. I could wander through every room in this house and find something of Jamie's.

This place was basically a shrine.

In the five years since I'd lost Jamie, I hadn't changed much. All I'd done was box up some of his old things for storage and sent some clothes to charity. If I truly wanted to move on, I couldn't do it here. Not in a place I'd spent hundreds of sleep-less nights, wishing for a life I'd never have back.

Which meant if I really wanted to let go—to explore this thing with Cole—it was time for me to move.

CHAPTER THIRTEEN

34TH BIRTHDAY: JUMP INTO A POOL FULL OF GREEN JELL-O

COLE

"Damn, I'm beat." Dad slung his bag over a shoulder. "You could have taken it easy on me tonight, you know."

"You held your own." I chuckled and followed him out of the locker room.

Dad had come to the dojo for sparring tonight, something he hadn't done in a while. And even though he'd been a little out of practice, he'd still managed to keep me on my toes. Probably because he wasn't the only one out of practice. With everything I had going on at work, fixing up that truck for Poppy and trying to squeeze in as much time as I could to see her, this was the first time I'd been to karate in almost a month.

"Do you guys want to go for a beer?" Robert Sensei asked when we met him in the waiting room. He was all smiles because Dad and I had both made it to karate tonight and given him the chance to kick our asses.

"I could drink a beer."

Dad nodded. "Me too. But one of you two is buying. It's the least you can do for kicking my ass tonight."

"Let me grab my stuff," Robert said, then disappeared into the locker room.

Dad and I walked out to the reception area and took a seat. "I'm glad I came tonight."

"Me too. That workout was long overdue."

Sparring had given me the chance to release some pent-up frustration. It wasn't how I'd preferred to burn my excess energy—having Poppy in my bed was my top choice—but since that wasn't going to happen anytime soon, karate would have to do.

That and my own goddamn fist.

It had been a week since I'd taken Poppy to her friend's wedding. A week since I'd nearly lost my patience and broken my promise to take it slow. A week since I'd been on the verge of kissing her senseless.

But I'd held off so she could dictate the pace.

Would she ever be as desperate for me as I was for her? Or had Jamie taken all of her passionate moments? Would she ever want me like she'd wanted him? This fucking jealousy was plaguing me. Every night, I'd go home to my empty house and remind myself over and over and over—*it's not a competition*. I just wanted Poppy to be happy. But no matter how many times I reminded myself of that goal, the jealousy wouldn't go away.

"I talked to the city manager today," Dad said. "Your name came up a couple of times as a potential replacement for when I retire."

I sighed. "Dad, no. I don't think that's the job for me."

"You say that now, but who knows what will happen. It's still years away, I just want you thinking about it. Just in case. Let's not close the door to that possibility until you're sure."

"I am sure."

He shrugged, still not hearing me. "There's no harm in keeping it as an option."

I clamped my mouth shut so I wouldn't say something I'd regret later. Dad was just looking out for me. He'd always been better at looking down the road than I was, and as much as I didn't want his job, I didn't want to disappoint him either. Luckily, he wasn't retiring anytime soon. We didn't need to wreck a perfectly good night because I'd told him how I really felt and let him down.

So we just visited about nothing as the rest of the students shuffled out of the dojo. With the last of them gone, Dad and I followed Robert outside.

"Where do you guys want to go?" I dumped my bag into the back of my truck just as I caught a flash of red out of the corner of my eye.

I know that red.

I did a double take just as Poppy disappeared into the apartment building across the street. "What the hell?"

What was she doing in a low-income apartment complex? I'd made two busts with the drug task force in that complex and it was on Bozeman PD's regular watch list. My Poppy had no business being in that building. It was unsafe and the last place I wanted her wandering around on a Monday night.

"Cole. Earth to Cole." Dad smacked my arm.

"Sorry. I'll, uh . . ." I waved him off and started jogging across the parking lot. "I'll catch up to you later!"

I heard them yell something back but I didn't turn. I just picked up the pace, hoping I'd catch Poppy before she vanished into an apartment.

I ran across the street and straight to the glass door she'd used, ripping it open, then listening for her voice.

"This is it." A man's voice came from the second floor.

"Like I told you on the phone. Six hundred a month plus utilities."

"Thanks," she said. "Can I look around?"

Was she looking to live here? *Oh, fuck no.* I took the stairs two at a time, hitting the second-floor landing just in time to see her walk through the doorway of an apartment.

"Poppy."

She spun around at my voice. "Cole? What are you doing here?"

I crossed the landing, taking her elbow and pulling her toward the stairs and away from the door. "Let's go."

"But—"

"Hey, don't you want to see the apartment?" the guy called from inside the unit.

"No," I answered for her, still pulling her to the stairs. When we reached the top step, I let go of her elbow and slid my hand down her arm to take her hand.

"Cole," she hissed, tugging her hand free. "What are you doing? I wanted to look at that place and tonight's the only night I have off this week."

I frowned and grabbed her hand again, this time with a firmer grip. "I'll save you the time. You're not looking at that apartment."

She grumbled something but followed me down the stairs, stomping a bit until we were outside. Then she yanked her hand free again and fisted it on a hip. "What was that about? And what are you doing here?"

I pointed to the karate school across the street, where my truck was alone in the parking lot. "I was just leaving the dojo and saw you come in here. Since this building is definitely not safe, I came over to check on you."

"Oh," she muttered. "Why is this building not safe?" She looked around the three-building complex. "It looks nice."

"Trust the cop on this one, okay? It might seem nice on the outside, but this is not a place you need to be hanging around."

She stared at me for a long moment, debating whether or not to keep arguing, until she tossed her hands in the air. "Fine."

"Why're you looking for apartments?" I fell in step at her side as she started toward her car, parked a few paces down the street.

"I decided it's time to move."

"Oh-kay," I drawled. I'd seen her twice for dinners this week and she hadn't said a word about moving. "Why?"

She shrugged. "I just think it's time."

There was more behind her motives but I wasn't going to push. Maybe it was too hard to live in that house, the one she'd shared with Jamie. Maybe all this work on his list really was helping her to let go. And if moving was what she needed to do, then I'd support her a hundred percent.

As long as it wasn't into a criminal cesspool.

Or a shit hole.

Or something full of college students.

In fact, there weren't many places I wanted her living. The only acceptable place that came to mind was my own house. There, she could use my kitchen to experiment with new recipes. She could stack her girly wheat beer next to my Bud Light in the fridge. She could share my bed.

But . . . slow. She needed slow.

So instead of moving her completely into my life like I wanted, I'd help her find a decent rental she could live in —for now.

"Is this the first place you've looked at?"

"You mean tried to look at?" She jabbed me in the ribs with her elbow.

I chuckled, fighting the urge to pull her in for a hug.

"No," she sighed. "I've looked at two other places this week. Do you have any idea how hard it is to find a decent rental in Bozeman? All of the good ones are already taken by college students and people moving to town. And since you just vetoed my best option, I'm back to square one."

"Sorry."

She smirked. "Liar."

"You're right. I'm not sorry. How about I make it up to you and help you scour the rental ads?"

"Riiight." She narrowed her eyes as we stopped by her car. "You just want to go through my list and filter it down to those you deem acceptable."

"Guilty," I grinned, "but my offer still stands. How about I come hang at the restaurant tomorrow for dinner and help you make a list?"

She gave me her brightest smile, making all the nights alone worth it. "It's a date."

———

"TRY THIS ONE NEXT." Poppy set a jar down in front of me. On the bottom was what looked like chili and, on the top, a layer of corn bread.

I picked up my spoon from the tiny jar of quinoa salad I'd just demolished and dove right in.

"Well?" she asked as I chewed. "Good enough for the fall menu?"

I swallowed my bite and nodded. "Good. Really good. Add it."

She smiled and took my jar away before I could take another bite.

"Hey! I was going to eat that."

"One sec." She held up a finger and disappeared back into the kitchen.

"Damn it, woman," I cursed as she giggled from behind the swinging door.

She'd been making me try new recipes since I'd gotten here thirty minutes ago. Now that it was September, she was on a mission to get her fall menu settled and I was her test subject. Except the only thing she'd actually let me eat was the fucking quinoa.

Not that it wasn't good. Just like everything she made, it was tasty. But I was a meat-and-potatoes kind of guy. I wanted the fucking chili and corn bread. Or the beef stew she'd brought out. Or the homemade chicken noodle soup. Not quinoa with red peppers and zucchini.

When she came back out a few moments later, she had three new jars.

"If you take these away from me," I gave her my best scowl, "I'm going to riot."

She laughed, setting down a jar of what looked like baked ziti. The next one had my favorite chicken potpie and the last was filled with cheesecake and some type of caramel sauce.

"I didn't want you to get too full during my tasting, but I'm all done. These you can just eat."

"Finally." I started with the cheesecake, polishing it off without delay before digging into the rest of my meal. When I was finished, she ran the dishes back to the kitchen and then came around to my side of the counter, bringing over a newspaper and her laptop.

"Okay." She handed me the newspaper first. "Green stars are the rentals I like. Red are the maybes."

It took me less than a minute to completely dismiss all of the red, since they were in mostly college-kid neighborhoods, and all but two of the green stars. "Don't use that property management company," I told her, pointing to one of the green stars that I'd crossed out. "I've heard they have a habit of keeping people's deposits and are assholes when it comes to maintenance."

She frowned. "Well, then we don't need to look online. There wasn't much else to see."

"How desperate are you to move?"

"Not desperate." Poppy studied my face, her eyes traveling from mine, down my nose and to my mouth. "Kind of desperate." She shook her head. "I don't know. I wish I had thought of it sooner before everything was taken by the college kids."

"Yeah. Your timing is off."

It was the beginning of September and college was back in swing. Coffee shops around town were packed full of studying students. Traffic was a nightmare if you got within a mile of the university. And available rental space was nonexistent.

"Sorry." I covered her hand resting on the counter.

She turned her palm up and threaded her fingers with mine. "It's okay."

"Cole?" a voice snapped behind us.

Oh, fuck. I knew that snap.

Aly.

Just as I'd expected, she was standing five feet away when Poppy and I turned. Her eyes were locked on our linked hands.

I smiled, hoping she'd be cool and not make this awkward. "Aly."

But no.

She screwed up her mouth and gave Poppy the death glare —the same glare I used to get whenever I left my towel on the bathroom floor.

Aly marched the remaining distance and stood right by my side. "Who's this?"

"Poppy, meet Aly. Aly, this is Poppy, and this is her restaurant."

Poppy untwisted her fingers from mine and stood, extending her hand to Aly. "Hi. Nice to meet you. Can I get you something to eat or drink?"

Aly glared at Poppy's hand, then crossed her arms over her chest as she turned that glare on me. "That didn't take you long, did it?"

"Aly, don't."

"No, you don't." She uncrossed her arms and jabbed a finger into my shoulder. "You could have at least waited a little while. We were together for two years, Cole. Two years. How could you have moved on already? Did our relationship mean nothing to you?"

I looked over at Poppy, hoping she could read the *I'm sorry* in my eyes. The last thing I wanted was to bring drama into her life, but knowing Aly, she wasn't going to make this easy on me.

"It's okay." Poppy's gaze softened "I'll let you guys talk." Then she backed away, disappearing into the kitchen and sending Helen out to watch the counter.

When she was gone, I stood, gesturing to the door. "Let's go talk outside." By some miracle, Aly followed me without a word, though she huffed behind me as we walked. By the time we reached the sidewalk outside, her anger had morphed to hurt.

"I'm sorry."

She nodded as the tears started to fall.

"Don't cry." My plea did nothing, but then again, Aly had always been a crier. Whenever Mom or my sister or Poppy cried, it damn near broke my heart. Aly's tears, on the other hand, had stopped bothering me a year ago—partly because she used them for manipulation, partly because she never tried to fight them back.

One of the reasons I admired the hell out of Poppy was because she worked so hard *not* to cry. And when she did? Shit was bad.

But still, I didn't want Aly to cry. I didn't want to cause her pain.

"I never meant to hurt you."

She nodded, reaching up to swipe a tear away. "Sure. Whatever you say."

"We just—we wouldn't have made it. I think deep down, you know that's true."

"Do I?" She looked into the restaurant and sniffled. "And what about her? Do you think you two will make it? Or are you going to do to her what you did to me? Make her fall in love with you and not even try to fall back."

"Aly," I whispered. "I did try." I'd tried for two damn years to say *I love you*, but it just hadn't been there.

Her chin quivered as she swiped at another tear. "Sorry. I just didn't expect to see you tonight. And with her. It was a shock."

"Don't worry about it."

She looked up to me with wet, pleading eyes as she leaned closer. "I really miss you." Her hand lifted between us, but before she could touch my chest, I took a step back.

"I can't touch you now?" Anger flashed in her teary eyes.

"No." The only woman whose hand belonged over my heart was inside.

With a murderous scowl, Aly spun on her heel and rushed to her car, then raced out of the parking lot.

"Fuck," I muttered, rubbing my jaw.

In time, I hoped Aly would find the guy for her. That she'd find the guy who'd give her his heart. It just wasn't me.

Through the restaurant's windows, I saw that Poppy had come back out to the counter. She was trying not to spy, but her eyes kept straying out front, searching for Aly. I hustled back inside and went right to the counter.

"Sorry."

"It's fine. Ex-girlfriend, I'm guessing?"

I nodded. "Yeah. Aly and I dated for a couple of years but broke up earlier this summer."

"Was it serious?"

"For her," I admitted. "We lived together for a while, but . . . it wasn't right. I finally ended it, but not before she got hurt." Not before she'd told me she'd loved me countless times and I hadn't said it back.

I tapped the newspaper we'd been looking at when Aly had come in. "Do you want to call either of these?"

"I'm not crazy about them. I think I'll just sit tight for a while."

"Okay. Let me know what I can do to help."

"Actually, there is something." She was unsuccessfully fighting a smile. "I went to three grocery stores earlier and bought each of them out of green Jell-O. Every single pan and pot and bowl I could find is currently in my walk-in filled with Jell-O."

I wasn't taking the bait. "Good for you."

Poppy had been trying to talk me into doing the Jell-O pool thing with her for the last couple of weeks, but I fucking hated Jell-O. The texture made me gag. The taste was awful. The idea of rolling around in a pool full of it? Not a chance in hell unless she was drowning in it and I had to drag her out.

I'd promised to help her with Jamie's list, but this was one of the two things where I'd drawn a line. I wasn't going to let her pull a damn fire alarm, and I wasn't getting in a pool of green Jell-O.

"Please?" Poppy gave me her best puppy-dog eyes.

Damn it. It was just Jell-O. I could probably make the sacrifice. If it made her happy, I could probably do it. If I kept my eyes closed and just got in real fast.

I was about to cave when she muttered, "Fine. I'll do it myself. Tonight, I guess. The Jell-O is made and I might as well get it over with."

"Did you get the pool?"

"No, not yet. I was going to duck out early and let Helen close so I could buy one."

"I'll get your pool." I stood up and pulled my keys from my jeans pocket. "You finish up here and I'll come back to collect you and your," I grimaced, "Jell-O. Would you care if we did this at my place? It's closer."

"That would be great. Thank you." Her face flooded with relief—a whole wave of it. Much more than saving ten minutes on a drive should warrant.

Was this why she wanted to move? Because she didn't want me in her house?

I kept the questions to myself as I waved good-bye, left the restaurant and went to a place I hated nearly as much as I hated Jell-O.

Walmart.

A couple hours later, I'd bought her a kiddie pool and taken two trips from the restaurant to haul over a shitload of green Jell-O. Then—gagging the entire time—I'd filled her pool with that damn neon gelatin and used a shovel to break it into small chunks.

By the time she'd finished up at the restaurant and come over, the sun was starting to set. We skipped the house tour and I shuffled her straight to the backyard.

She'd changed at the restaurant. I was sure she was going for practical with her tight running shorts and plain white tank top over a strappy sports bra. But she'd sailed way past practical and landed on sexy as fuck.

"You set it all up, even though you hate Jell-O?" She smiled up at me and I fought with every cell in my body not to kiss her. "Thank you."

I cleared the rasp from my throat and pointed to the pool. "You'd better get in there before it gets too dark."

She took a deep breath, then put a foot in the Jell-O. "Oh my god, this is cold."

"No turning back now." I had my phone ready. "Smile for your picture."

She scowled over her shoulder—a look I caught perfectly with the camera—then put her other foot in the pool. She hissed as she dropped to her knees, and then in one graceful twist, she sat down.

Her legs flattened just enough so the green could coat her thighs. "This feels weird." She picked at the Jell-O with her fingers before planting her palms on the base of the pool and pushing herself up. Then she swiped the green bits off her legs.

"That's it?"

She shrugged. "It's freezing. I'm calling this one done, unless you're going to get in here with me."

I shook my head and took a step back. "Not a snowball's chance in hell."

"Are you sure?" A slow grin spread over Poppy's face. She took one step, then another, moving to the edge of the pool closest to me.

"Poppy," I warned.

She shot out a hand and made a grab for my wrist.

I jumped backward, barely dodging the green bits that flew off her hands. She'd used too much momentum trying to grab me though, because as her hand kept traveling, her feet began to slide. Like a drunken man on ice, her torso twisted, her arms pinwheeled, and her legs wobbled as she tried to keep her balance.

I was sure she was going down, but then somehow, she managed to find a grip.

"Oh my god," she panted, looking up to me as she steadied her legs. "That was close. I almost came out of here looking like Kermit the Frog."

I laughed. "Or the Hulk. Can you imagine going into the restaurant tomorrow looking like a pissed-off Bruce Banner?" Randall would have a field day if Poppy came in with a green face.

I was still laughing as Poppy planted her hands on her hips. "The Hulk? I remind you of The Hulk?"

My laughter died. "What? No! Of course not." *Oh, shit.* "You'd be like a small green person. Like, uh . . ." *Think, Cole.* What the fuck else is green? The Jolly Green Giant. Godzilla. The Grinch. "Yoda." I snapped my fingers. "You'd be like Yoda. Except not old. Or bald. Or wrink—"

"Cole." I stopped talking as Poppy grinned. "Mouth shut, you should keep."

I nodded. "Good idea."

"Okay. I'm getting out of here."

I stepped forward and held out my free hand to help her out, but before she could get a grip on my palm, she shifted her weight. One second she was standing, the next she was flying through the air.

Splat.

Green Jell-O flew everywhere as Poppy screamed. She gargled as a chunk landed in her mouth—I gagged—then spit it out, struggling to sit up. Goo dripped from her fingertips and the knot of her hair. Her tank top would never be white again.

And I couldn't resist. My phone was still in my hand and I lifted it up for a photo burst.

"Are you kidding me right now?"

I grinned. "Just in case you want proof." I tossed my phone aside and bent down, helping her back up on her feet. "Here."

This time when she stood, Jell-O covered her from head to toe.

Don't laugh. Don't be an asshole. It was no use. A snort escaped, followed by a fit of laughter as Poppy glared and gripped my hand with all her might.

"Sorry." I stopped howling—though my chest was still heaving—as I helped her from the pool.

With a green finger shoved in my face, Poppy spoke through her clamped teeth. "Mention one thing about Yoda or Muppets or leprechauns and you're dead."

"Yes, ma'am. Not a word."

She dropped her glare and my hand so she could rub the spot on her ass where she'd taken maximum impact. "That hurt. Jell-O is not a good cushion."

"Sorry." I swiped the towel I'd brought down off a deck chair. "Want to take a shower?"

She nodded as she wiped her face, then darted past me toward the door.

"The shower is upstairs. Last room on the right!" I called to her back.

She waved and kept on running inside.

I smiled, shaking my head as I examined my yard.

It was a mess. That pool was going to be a bitch to clean up, and I hoped the Jell-O chunks would dissolve into the grass, but still, I was glad Poppy had come here to do this.

Deciding I'd clean up the pool tomorrow, I grabbed my phone and went inside, plopping down on the couch to look through the pictures I'd taken.

Before the water turned on upstairs, I found my favorite photo.

My beautiful, green leprechaun, Poppy.

I loved her. Staring at her picture on my phone, it hit me square in the chest.

I was in love with Poppy Maysen.

The irony hit me next.

Aly had told me she loved me countless times and I'd never said it back. Not once. And now, I was finally ready to say those three words to a woman who couldn't say them back.

CHAPTER FOURTEEN

32ND BIRTHDAY: HAVE A PAINT FIGHT

POPPY

Cole's shower was fancy. And huge.

Floor-to-ceiling tiles extended from a bench seat at one end to the doorway at the opposite side. There wasn't an actual door because the space was so big—the water coming from the three bronze showerheads didn't come close to escaping. But as gorgeous as the ivory marble tile was, the best part of Cole's shower was the smell.

Just as I'd suspected, on a cutout shelf was a bottle of Irish Spring body wash. The smell had seeped into the tile, so as the shower filled with steam, I was engulfed in Cole's clean, manly scent.

I laughed as I stared at the bottle. Its dark green coordinated perfectly with my light-green skin.

I'd done my best—scrubbing with fury—to get the color off my arms and hands, but I would need a thorough exfoliation with some sugar scrub and my loofah to get back to my normal shade.

Doing the Jell-O pool at Cole's had its drawbacks. I didn't have any of my normal beauty products or a hair dryer. I'd be putting back on the clothes I'd worn earlier at the restaurant even though I longed for something fresh and clean. But still, I was glad we'd done it here. Not only was I avoiding bringing him to my house, it was nice to have company instead of doing it alone.

I'd always known the Jell-O item was going to be hard—since Jamie had added it on the day he'd died. But with Cole teasing me about being green, plus his weird aversion to Jell-O, it had been bearable.

His steady hand helping me out of the pool had eased some of the sting away.

I was really coming to rely on his hands. Probably too much.

But without them, I don't know how I would have ever come this far. I'd promised myself I wouldn't keep asking for Cole's help, but just tonight, I'd let him do all that work to set up my Jell-O pool. Every time he offered his assistance, I agreed. I had to stop taking advantage before he came to resent me—I just didn't know how.

Because of Cole, I was getting closer to the end of Jamie's birthday list without being in a constant state of tears. Instead, he was helping me find the joy in each item. The fun that Jamie had been after in the first place.

I smiled down at my green cuticles as the water ran over my body to my green-tinged toes. *You would have loved this, Jamie.* Where I wanted to scrub away the green, Jamie would have let it stay. He'd have worn this Jell-O color like a badge of honor until it faded.

The water started to turn cold so I did one last scrub, then shut it off, stealing a fresh towel from Cole before pulling back on my flour-dusted jeans and The Maysen Jar T-shirt. I tied up my damp hair in a knot, then came out of the bathroom into Cole's bedroom.

I'd been in such a rush to get out of my Jell-O clothes, I hadn't really studied his bedroom earlier when I'd sprinted for the shower. But now, I couldn't help but let my eyes linger on his sleigh bed right in the middle of the room.

Just like his shower, it was huge. The espresso wood of the footboard and headboard gleamed under the recessed ceiling lights. The simple khaki bedding went well with the white walls and chocolate-brown wood floors.

Had Cole decorated in here? Or had his ex? My lips thinned as I thought about the encounter with Aly earlier.

She was beautiful. Of course she was beautiful. Cole was hotter than the vast majority of male specimens on the planet. Of course his ex-girlfriend was gorgeous.

And clearly still in love with him.

Had he loved her too? Had he whispered those three words into her hair as he'd held her in his strong arms in this massive bed?

Before my head could wander too far down a green-eyed—er, toed—path, Cole knocked on the door. "Poppy?"

I jerked out of my daze, whipping my eyes away from his bed. "Come on in."

His feet were bare as he came into the room. "I just wanted to see if you needed anything."

"No." I smiled. "Thank you for your help. I left your towels in the bathroom, but I'm not sure that green is going to come out."

"I don't care about the towels." He stepped past me and sat against the footboard. His hands were braced on the wood at his sides, making the muscles of his arms pop. When he crossed one ankle over the other, I spun around so he wouldn't see my heated cheeks.

Damn, he was sexy. The image of Cole in that seemingly casual stance would forever be stamped on my brain.

I took a few long seconds to collect myself as I pretended to study his decor. "I like your house."

"Thanks. I got lucky and bought it for a steal because it was the last house on the block that hadn't been restored yet. It's taken me a while, but I'm finally getting it fixed up to this century."

I nodded and smiled, peeking over my shoulder to see he hadn't moved. Back came the heat to my face, but this time it didn't stop at my cheeks—it went all the way down to my core, stirring a desire that had been dormant for a long, long time.

He pushed off the bed. "Want the full tour?"

"Yes, please." *Sheesh.* I'd hid my flaming cheeks, but there was no mistaking my breathy voice.

But Cole—in true Cole fashion—just grinned his knowing grin and crossed the room without a word.

I took one last look at his bed. The image of me sleeping naked under his sheets popped into my head, but I shook it away. Why was I thinking about sex with Cole? We hadn't really even kissed yet—unless you counted the brush of our lips in Brad and Mia's garage. And even then, that hadn't been the type of kiss that led to a long, sweaty night together and me waking up in his arms.

My body was getting in front of my head and it needed to slow down. Way down. Which meant I needed to get the hell out of Cole's bedroom.

Slamming the door on all things sex and kissing and the way Cole's ass looked in his jeans tonight, I followed him into the hall as he started his tour.

"The master used to be two rooms." He knocked on the wall as he led me down the hall. "I had one converted into the bathroom and closet."

I ran my hand along the door as I peeked into the guest bedroom. "I love that you kept all of the original doors and trim."

"Me too. It was a bitch for the construction crew to get cleaned up but worth the added time."

Cole lived in an older downtown neighborhood in Bozeman. Unlike my house, located in one of the newer, cookie-cutter subdivisions, homes in this area were filled with character and surrounded by hundred-year-old trees.

The trim and doors were a rich brown, similar to the color of the restored hardwood floors. The crown molding, painted white to match the walls and ceilings, was thick and carved with an intricate pattern absent in new homes. And the old brass-and-glass doorknobs were something people would spend a fortune on now.

After showing me another spare bedroom and bathroom, Cole led me down the staircase situated in the center of the house. Just like upstairs, the old-style charm had been restored and mixed with the luxuries of modern-day life.

The fireplace in the living room had all of the original brick but the mantel had been changed to fit a wide TV. He'd kept the antique chandelier in the entryway but added recessed lighting to brighten the space. And he'd had a couple of walls knocked out, opening up the floor plan to fit larger, more comfortable furniture.

Everything in Cole's house flowed seamlessly, from the living room to the dining room, then to the kitchen of my dreams.

"This is beautiful." I ran my hand along the gray-and-white marble counter. He had it all. Shining stainless-steel appliances. A top-of-the-line gas range. Pristine white cabinets. The moment I set foot on the black-and-white checked floor tile, I'd gotten the urge to start cooking.

"I'm afraid to tell you that I've hardly used this kitchen since I had it updated."

I gasped. "Shame on you, Cole Goodman."

"Maybe you can help me break it in."

Break it in.

He was referring to my cooking skills, but the visual that flew into my head had nothing to do with food. I saw myself sitting on the counter, naked, with Cole between my legs, his cock buried deep inside of me as I moaned to the ceiling.

A hot wave spread over my shoulders and down my back as I throbbed between my legs. My nipples hardened against my bra, straining against the thin padding, as my eyes wandered to Cole.

He was watching me, his eyes darkening as if he'd seen the same naughty image in his mind. His chest was rising and falling with short breaths and his hands were fisted at his sides —like he was holding himself on his side of the kitchen.

My gaze dropped to his mouth, unable to look away from his soft, pink lips.

I wanted to kiss him. I wanted to kiss him so badly, all of the worry, the indecision I'd held on to these last couple of months just . . . disappeared. There was no room in my head for anything other than getting Cole to kiss me.

Slowly, my hands came off my sides, and with my eyes locked on his face, I twisted my wrists in a slight circle.

My signal.

Cole watched my hands as I twirled once, then twice, before he swallowed hard. "Poppy." His voice was rough and deep. "Are you sure?"

I nodded. "Kiss me, Cole."

In two huge strides, he erased the distance between us. His hands dove into my damp hair as his palms pressed against my jaw. Then his lips molded to mine.

A zing shot through my body as his tongue stroked across my lower lip, coaxing my mouth open. When my lips parted, his tongue swept inside. And he tasted so good—better than anything I could ever make in this kitchen.

I moaned into his mouth as his tongue started exploring. My hands gripped tight to his shirt, holding on as his hands left my face and banded around my back.

Cole pulled me so close that every inch of him was pressed up against me. His solid chest. His muscled thighs. His cock straining beneath his jeans.

With his mouth devouring mine, Cole sparked a fire inside of me that had been only embers for years. The burn was so hot, I could barely stand it. So with desire in charge, I kissed Cole with everything I had. I held him closer, pulling and sucking him in, but it wasn't enough. I thrust my hips forward, grinding against his, hoping for relief, but the friction only fanned the flames.

I released Cole's shirt and ran my hands down his backside, squeezing hard when I reached his perfect ass. When Cole groaned, the rumble vibrated down my throat, making me squeeze again, this time even harder.

One second his tongue was working magically against mine, and then it was gone. He broke away from me, panting for breath as I did the same.

"Fucking hell, woman." He dropped his forehead to mine. "God, I could kiss you forever."

My lungs heaved as I tried to fill them with air.

Cole's hands smoothed away the hair that had fallen onto my cheeks, pushing it back behind my ears. "But we'd better slow down."

He was right—we should slow down—but I missed his lips. I wanted them back so badly I nearly cried.

Because that was the best kiss I'd ever had in my life.

My *entire* life.

No man, not even Jamie, had ever kissed me with that much passion.

A surge of emotion exploded in my chest and came out of my mouth as a sob. Between the intensity of the kiss and the realization that I'd just broken free from my husband, I couldn't contain the cry that followed. Or the one after that. Or the tears welling in my eyes.

I slapped a hand over my mouth as the first tear fell. And when the second dripped down my cheek, Cole pulled me into his arms.

"I'm sorry," I cried, burrowing my face into his shirt.

I was sorry for crying after our incredible kiss. I was sorry for ruining our intimate moment. But mostly, I was sorry that I *wasn't* sorry for kissing Cole.

I was letting Jamie go.

And it broke my heart all over again.

"It's okay," Cole whispered into my hair. "It's okay. I've got you. Let it out."

With his permission, I didn't try to fight the pain. I cried into his shirt, wetting his shoulder with my eyes and damp hair. I soaked up the comfort of his arms until I was strong enough to stop.

"I'm sorry," I whispered into his shirt before leaning back and wiping my eyes.

He placed his palm on my cheek. "Never be sorry."

"I don't regret that kiss. Please know that. It's just . . . hard."

"I know."

I looked up into his eyes, so kind and compassionate, and nearly cried again. He was a dream. How had I found a man who was so understanding and patient, who saw me so clearly? It was nothing short of a miracle.

I inhaled a shaky breath, holding it for a long moment as I

reined in my emotions. When I blew out the breath, I let my shoulders collapse, then stood tall.

I hated crying in front of others. I hated feeling weak and pathetic. I hated that I felt so out of control of my emotions. For five years, I'd felt out of control, and every time I started to take back that control, it so often ended with me in tears.

I was exhausted. The tears were exhausting.

I didn't want to cry anymore. I didn't want to be sad anymore. I didn't want to hurt.

When would it go away? When would I find the strength to put the pain in the past and stop letting it tarnish the present?

Disgusted with myself for ruining what had been a magical moment with Cole, I shook my head. "I'm so, *so* sorry."

"Look at me," he ordered and my eyes went to his. "No apologies. You're the strongest person I've ever met. A couple of tears are no big deal."

I scoffed, waving my hand at his shirt. "I was bawling, Cole. That wasn't just a couple of tears. You're practically soaked. I don't think that constitutes being strong."

He stepped closer, his palm again finding my cheek. "Crying doesn't make you weak, Poppy. Sometimes, it takes more strength to let go than it does to keep it all inside."

I didn't know if that was true, but the words felt wonderful as they settled in my heart. "Thank you."

"You're welcome."

His hand fell away from my face and I motioned toward the hallway. "I'd better go."

"Okay." He followed me into the living room where I grabbed my purse and backpack from his camel leather couch. "Are we still on for the paint fight on Sunday?"

"Yeah. I've got everything ready to go. Molly, Finn and the

kids are going to be there. And you'll finally get to meet Jimmy."

"I can't wait." He escorted me to the door, opening it up so I could step out onto his porch.

The red brick exterior of his house was trimmed with white. The square pillars around the porch were thick and adorned with gables. A weaving vine snaked up the far corner to the second floor. All that was missing were two white rocking chairs and this porch would be the perfect place to watch children play in the front yard.

"See you Sunday." Cole bent down and kissed my cheek.

"Bye." I stepped outside but paused, looking over my shoulder. "Thank you." I swallowed hard. "Thank you for kissing me. For being the one."

His eyes softened. "It will always be me."

I hope so. I gave him a tiny smile before turning and walking to my car. With a quick wave, I pulled away from the curb and drove straight home. But instead of taking the shower that I'd planned, I went inside and flopped on my bed. Then I grabbed Jamie's picture off my nightstand.

I stroked his face in the frame.

His smiling face, frozen under the glass, soothed the ache in my chest. Jamie would never want me to be sad. He wouldn't want me to be alone. If he couldn't be here with me, then he'd want me to find happiness.

I knew it down to my bones.

I set down the frame and dug into my purse next to me on the bed. With Jamie's journal and a pen in hand, I flipped to his Jell-O page and checked the box.

We're almost done, Jamie. Just a few things left to do.

I closed the journal and hugged it to my chest. I'd cried myself out at Cole's, so I just smiled.

Was Jamie somewhere, looking down and smiling too? Was

he glad that I was doing the things he'd wanted to most? I hoped that this list was his way of guiding me through the grief. I hoped that this was his way of helping me say good-bye.

I hoped that this was his way of leading me to a new life.

One filled with smiles. With laughter.

One filled with love.

———

TWO DAYS LATER, the green had vanished from my skin and I was at Jimmy's apartment, filling up biodegradable water balloons with paint. I'd spent the last thirty minutes working up the courage to tell him about me and Cole so he wouldn't be surprised when we arrived at the park later this afternoon.

"So, um . . . I invited Cole to do this paint fight with us."

"Yeah, I know." His fingers were covered in blue paint as he tied a balloon closed. "I remember when you told me the same a week ago. Are you worried I'm getting senile or something? Because I'm not. No matter what that asshole Randall says, my head's as clear as it was when I was your age, got it?"

"Got it." I giggled, tying off my red balloon and dropping it in the tub with the others. "But I wanted to tell you something else. Cole's not just a friend helping on Jamie's truck. We're kind of dating."

"You really do think I'm senile." He chuckled. "Relax, Poppy. I figured as much."

"You did?" I gaped at him as he filled another balloon.

He nodded. "You talk about him a lot. Seems like you spend a lot of time together. Molly told me he comes into the restaurant most nights. I'm old, not blind. I assumed there was something more going on with you two."

"And that doesn't bother you?"

He shook his head, dropping the paint bottle in his hands to give me his full attention. "I just want you to be happy. And if you like this guy, I'm all for it."

"You think it's okay to start dating again?"

Maybe it was because Jimmy and Jamie had been so close, but I needed Jimmy's blessing. It was the closest thing I had to Jamie's blessing. I needed him to tell me that it was okay to date Cole.

He nodded. "I don't just think it's okay. I think it's time. Five years, Poppy. It's time to move on. And you know just as well as I do that Jamie would want that for you too."

I looked down at my paint-covered fingers. "Thank you," I whispered. He couldn't know how many fears and anxieties he'd just eased.

His blue hand closed over mine. "It's the truth."

I looked up at him and smiled.

"Are you two ready to go or what?" Randall grumbled from the hallway as he walked into Jimmy's room. "I want to get this over with so I can be back in time for dinner."

I started filling another balloon. "Just a few more of these and then we can go."

"Fine," Randall muttered as he came into the kitchenette. He was wearing head-to-toe coveralls, and in one gloved hand was a shower cap.

"Look at this guy." Jimmy rolled his eyes. "A jumpsuit? Really? You pansy. It's just a little paint."

"I'm not wrecking my clothes. Some of us take pride in our appearance." Randall's eyes narrowed as he and Jimmy went into one of their usual stare-downs.

Jimmy came to The Maysen Jar with Randall nearly every day now, and one thing I'd learned was that they lived to bicker. Those two would come to the restaurant midmorning and argue about anything until well past lunch.

At first, I'd tried to intervene—to play peacemaker—but after my fiftieth failed attempt, I'd given up.

So I just shook my head and kept filling my balloon. "Can you at least save the fight for the park, gentlemen?"

"Always taking his side," Randall muttered and turned around to the living room.

"She's my granddaughter!" Jimmy called to his back. "Of course, she takes my side." He looked to me. "What a dumbass."

"You two are worse than little kids."

Jimmy chuckled and waved me closer to whisper, "Look."

He double-checked that Randall was out of sight, then reached into a cabinet. Out came a full-sized balloon, ten times the size of the miniballoons like we'd been filling.

"Jimmy," I hissed.

He snickered. "No way that jumpsuit and shower cap will save him from this big ol' bastard."

I snorted, trying to swallow my laugh. Then I bent down to the tub and started making room for his monster balloon. "Get it down between the little ones so he won't see it."

Jimmy smiled. "That's my girl."

An hour later, I was standing in a huddle, having just gone over the rules for our paint fight. No direct shots in the face. Take it easy on Max and Kali. Go until all the balloons were gone.

On my left stood Jimmy and Randall, Cole on my right. And across from me were Finn, Molly and the kids.

"Everybody ready?"

I got cheers all around as we broke apart to load up on balloons.

"Okay. On the count of three. One. Two. Three!"

Pandemonium ensued. Balloons started flying, people started running, and paint splattered everywhere.

"Get Aunt Poppy!" Finn yelled to Kali, who immediately started chasing me.

"No, Kali! No!" I pretended to run fast but let her catch up and lob a yellow balloon at my back. The sticky paint instantly soaked through my thin white tank and coated the backside of my arms. "You got me!"

She giggled, then raced back to the bucket to reload. "Get Daddy!" she squealed, aiming a green balloon at Finn. She took off, joining Molly and Max as they chased Finn and pelted him with balloons.

For the first time in months, Finn and Molly were actually smiling at one another. Genuine smiles. I wasn't sure if they were getting along because this paint fight was for Jamie, or maybe they were putting on happy faces for me. Regardless, it made this whole idea just that much more fun.

I was so lost in watching the smiles on their faces that I didn't notice Cole sneaking up behind me. One second, I was watching Kali toss the green balloon at Finn's white T-shirt. The next, blue paint was streaming down my hair.

"Gah!" I spun around just in time for Cole to break another on my head, this one orange. "You!" I pointed a finger at his smile, then raced back to the tub for a handful of balloons.

I tried to hit him, but he was too nimble. He dodged each of my shots until the grass around him looked like a rainbow unicorn had puked at his feet.

"I give up," I pouted at Cole, then went back to reload. When I came back to the fight, I chose a different target. "Gotcha!" I cheered as the red balloon I'd thrown burst against Randall's chest.

He looked to his jumpsuit and sneered. "You'll pay for that."

I stuck out my tongue, daring him to come after me, just as

Jimmy snuck out from behind a tree carrying the huge balloon he'd hidden when we'd arrived.

I braced, waiting for the inevitable, but just as Jimmy was lifting up the balloon high, Randall turned. With agility I never would have expected from the old man who walked with a cane, he skittered backward, throwing the balloon he'd been carrying at Jimmy's monster.

Hot pink paint flew everywhere.

Jimmy's short white hair was covered. His face. His shoulders. Everything was dripping pink.

"You *son of a bitch*," he spat, sending pink splatters to the ground.

"Ha!" Randall laughed. "That backfired on you, didn't it?"

At my side, Cole started to laugh. Then Finn and Molly joined in. I tried to keep a straight face, but as the pink paint kept dripping off Jimmy's nose, I lost the battle. I laughed so hard and so long my sides ached.

I bent over in half, fighting to get my breath back as happy tears mixed with the paint smears on my face. "Oh my god. That was hilarious."

When I stood, Cole handed me one of the towels I'd brought. "Here."

"Thanks." I used it to dry my face and then handed it to Cole so he could wipe his hands. He'd gotten hit with a green balloon right in the middle of his chest. The color and the bright afternoon sunlight made his eyes fiercely bright as he grinned.

Those beautiful eyes held mine as he stepped in closer, taking the towel and dabbing the side of my face. "You missed a spot."

Without thinking—or caring—about our audience, I stood on my tiptoes and touched his mouth with my own. "Thanks for coming today."

"Sure."

I'd shocked him a bit with that kiss, but I was glad I'd done it. Especially here. In front of family and friends, I wanted them to know that he was someone special.

After all, that was what today was all about. Today was to have fun with the special people in my life and honor someone who'd been special but was no longer with us.

"That was fun." Jimmy came over and I handed him a towel. "I think we did my boy proud."

"Me too," Finn said as he cleaned off Max's face.

"Agreed." Molly nodded. "Jamie would have loved this."

I smiled up at Cole, then looked into the blue, cloudless sky.

"Yeah. He would have."

CHAPTER FIFTEEN

31ST BIRTHDAY: HIKE GLACIER

POPPY

"I'm forgetting something."

I was staring at my stuff in the backseat of Cole's truck, sure that I'd forgotten to pack something important. It was the weekend after the paint fight and Cole and I were driving up to hike in Glacier National Park.

What am I forgetting? I had my bag of clothes and toiletries with extra panties, pajamas, socks and a T-shirt, just in case. I had my hiking boots, hiking socks and canteen that I'd dragged out of storage. I had my purse with wallet, phone, phone charger and the lip balm and hand cream I used before bed each night.

Still, I couldn't shake the niggling feeling that something was missing.

"Poppy!" My eyes snapped up to Cole in the driver's seat, his fingers tapping the steering wheel.

I waved him off. "I'm forgetting something!"

"Poppy, you've been staring at that pile for five minutes.

You're not forgetting anything. We're only going for one night. We'll be back tomorrow."

"Fine." I huffed and slammed the back door. Then I jumped into the passenger seat and slammed that door too. Nothing bothered me more than being unprepared for a trip, but since I couldn't remember what I was missing, I had no choice but to go without.

With me finally ready to go, Cole wasted no time backing out of the driveway and pointing us down the road.

It was still early, only six in the morning, but the mid-September morning light was beginning to shine.

"Wait!" I threw my hands out as Cole slammed on the brakes. "My sunglasses. I forgot my sunglasses."

He grumbled and shoved the truck in reverse, speeding backward to my house.

I dug the keys from my purse and jumped out, rushing inside to grab my sunglasses from the kitchen counter—right where I'd left them so I wouldn't forget. I smiled as I walked back to the truck, feeling much better about starting the weekend off right.

Thanks to a last-minute cancelation, Cole and I had scored a room at one of the nicer lodges in the park. We'd be able to make this trip—without sleeping in a tent—and cross this item off Jamie's list.

"Okay. I'm ready now."

Cole was shaking his head as I got back into the truck. "Are you like this for every trip?"

I shrugged and buckled my seat belt. "I don't believe in packing light."

"Noted." He smirked. "Are you sure you're ready to go? We could take another lap through your house. Maybe box up some more clothes. Pack up a cooler in case we get stranded on the side of the road. We should probably take some extra gas too. Maybe another spare tire."

I fought a smile and slid my sunglasses onto my nose. "Are you done teasing me so we can get on the road?"

He chuckled. "For now."

"Good. Then let's do this." I smiled, practically bouncing in my seat. I couldn't wait to do this hike.

―――――

MY EXCITEMENT WAS GONE eight hours later.

Every step was excruciating. Pain shot through both of my feet as I followed Cole up the trail toward the peak.

Damn it. Damn it! This was not how I'd envisioned the day going.

We'd made it to the lodge just after lunch and immediately gotten ready to hike this trail. The sun was shining. The air was pure. I'd never expected to be in this much pain hours later.

I'd chosen this trail because it was rated as one of the most beautiful. The relatively short hike—only about eight miles round trip—would lead us to a small lake surrounded by high peaks and a couple of glaciers.

But now, I had no idea if I'd actually make it to the end or be able to cross this item off Jamie's list.

I could see the crest in the distance, and according to my pedometer, this was the last stretch before we reached the lake. I only had to make it another hundred yards, but it might as well have been ten miles.

I was ready to collapse.

My lungs were burning and my legs were turning to mush. I could have pushed through that kind of pain, but my feet? The agony with every step was going to bring me to my knees.

Fuck. Fuck! I cursed and winced with every step. All because of these *fucking* boots.

My feet had grown since I'd last worn these boots in college. Not by a lot—I hadn't gone up a size in my regular shoes—but enough that these boots no longer fit.

My heels were rubbed raw. Blisters were growing on blisters. It had gotten so bad on my right foot that with every step, blood squished between my toes.

How could I have been so stupid? Why hadn't I tried these on before we'd left Bozeman? I grew up in Alaska—*hiking* in Alaska. I'd learned young how important it was to have good hiking boots.

I wanted to scream. I wanted to cry. I wanted to throw something. I was close to the end. So *fucking* close, but all I wanted to do was turn around.

I took another step and a fresh stab of pain shot through my foot, causing me to falter and my ankle to twist. "Ahh!" I let out a strangled cry as I dropped to my hands and knees. Bits of gravel dug into my palms as I closed my eyes and took a breath.

I had to keep going. I had to finish this hike.

I whimpered as I tried to stand, struggling to find my balance on two aching feet. I would have dropped again if not for the two large hands that came under my arms and helped me up.

"What's wrong?" Cole's face searched mine. "Are you hurt? Did you twist your ankle?"

I looked to my traitorous feet. "No, I'm okay."

"Bullshit," he clipped. "What's wrong?"

He was wearing a hat today, an old Montana State baseball cap, but it didn't hide the worry pinching his green eyes.

It was his concern for me that broke the thin hold I'd kept on my emotions. Frustrated tears welled and my chin quivered as I looked back at my boots. "My boots are too tight. My feet must have grown. These were my hiking boots from high school and college, and I . . . I didn't know."

"Hey." Cole tipped up my chin. "It's okay. We'll just go back down."

"No!" I shook my head frantically. "We're so close. I need to do this. I can do this." I tried to take a step past him but his hands clamped on my biceps and didn't let me pass.

"Stop," Cole whispered. "You've hiked Glacier. Maybe not to the lake, but you did it. You can mark this off the list, even if we turn back now."

"No, I need to do this." My voice cracked in despair. "Not just for Jamie's list, but for me. I need to finish this hike."

Every agonizing step up this mountain had become so much more than just marking a box on Jamie's list. This was a chance to prove to myself that I had the strength Cole saw in me. To prove I could overcome any pain.

That no matter what life threw at me, this was my chance to prove I could handle it all. Blistered feet, shattered heart—I could survive it all and keep marching on.

"I can do this." I held my breath, ready for the inevitable pain as I stepped past Cole. He let me go this time but I felt his eyes on my back as I took one step, then another. My hopes soared when the pain didn't bring me down.

I'd almost convinced myself I could make it this last stretch when I took another step and my foot slipped again, forcing me back to my hands and knees. "Damn it!" I cried. "I'm so close."

Cole's hand came to my back as he knelt by my side. "Let me help." Gently, he positioned me so I was sitting on the narrow trail for an overdue break.

"I just need a minute, then I'll be okay." I sniffled and wiped away a fresh batch of tears.

He sighed, but instead of taking a seat next to me, he knelt by my outstretched feet as he started untying the laces on my boots.

"What are you doing?"

"Assessing the damage." With a tender touch, he tugged off my boots.

Even though he'd taken care, I winced as they pulled free. Just as I'd suspected, my socks were spotted with blood. My heels were the worst, nearly the entire area covered in red, with my toes a close runner-up.

"Fuck, Poppy." Cole shook his head. "Those boots are not going back on."

"But—"

He held up a finger, cutting me off. "I want to take these socks off too, but it's going to hurt."

"Okay." I sucked in a huge breath and held it as Cole's fingers stretched my socks wide, peeling them away from my raw skin. The cotton stuck in a few places, and as it pulled free, a pained cry escaped my lips. Blood rushed to both feet, causing them to swell immediately.

My feet were wrecked. There was no way I'd be able hike up any farther and I had no idea how we'd get back down. The soles of my feet were surprisingly unscathed. Maybe I could pull back on my socks and just go down in them. Because at this point, anything was better than the boots.

I opened my mouth to tell Cole my plan, but he talked first. "Can I see your backpack?"

"Sure." I stripped it off my shoulders and handed it over. There wasn't much in it, just my canteen and a couple of granola bars.

Cole shoved my boots and my socks into the backpack and then loosened the straps before putting it over his own shoulders.

"I'm going—"

—to need those socks. But before I could get the words out, he scooped me off the ground, bouncing me a bit as he situated me in his arms.

"Cole! What are you doing?"

"Carrying you."

"You can't carry me."

He looked down at me and smiled. "Sure, I can."

"I'm too heavy."

"You're light as a feather, besides, it's not much farther."

Not much farther? "It's miles." Four point two miles, to be exact.

"It's just up this incline." He took a step in the wrong direction. Instead of turning and taking me back down the trail, he started marching forward, carefully navigating the rocky trail as he carried me toward the peak.

"Where are you going?" I squirmed, trying to get down but he just gripped me tighter. "Cole, no! You'll hurt yourself. It's too steep."

He paused and considered my words. "You're right." He set me down on my bare feet and unslung the backpack. "Put this on for me, would you?"

"But—"

"Now, Poppy. I want to get back before dark."

I didn't argue—I just strapped on the pack. With him carrying me, our descent would be much slower and I didn't want to delay us getting back on the trail. The last thing I wanted was to be out here at night with the bears.

He tapped his back and crouched. "Climb on."

"Okay." With a tiny jump, I wrapped my arms around his shoulders and my legs around his waist. He boosted me higher so his arms were cupped underneath my knees.

"Are you good?" When I hummed an *uh-huh,* he took a step, again in the wrong direction.

"Cole, what are you doing? We need to turn back." I swung an arm behind us, in the direction we were supposed to be going.

"Hold still, Poppy." He took another step. "And clamp tight with your legs."

"Cole," I pleaded. "It's too much. Turn around."

He ignored me, moving forward on the trail without so much as a backward glance or a labored breath.

"Please?" I whispered into his hair.

"Not a chance. Just hold tight."

No amount of pleading or begging would change his mind so I stayed quiet, doing what he'd asked. I clamped my legs tight and did my best to hold still, making it as easy as possible for him to get up the trail.

Which he did. He carried me up the trail and right to the shore of the icy mountain lake.

Cole set me down on my bare feet and stepped behind me to open the backpack and dig out my canteen. As the cold from the ground seeped into my aching feet, dulling some of the pain, he took a long drink of water. Then he put the canteen back and stood at my side, staring out to the lake.

"Look at that." He pointed to the glaciers cutting their way through the valleys of the high peaks. "Incredible."

I was too fixed on his profile to take in the scenery. "You carried me."

Cole's eyes broke away from the view. "I'll carry you back down too."

"But why? Why didn't you just turn back?"

He shrugged. "You said you needed to do this. Now you have."

This man took my breath away.

"Cole, I . . ." As much as I wanted to thank him, to say

anything, none of the words in my head were enough to convey how much this meant.

When I hadn't been strong enough to do something myself —when the pain had been too much—he'd done it for me.

"It's okay, Poppy." He turned back to the view. "Just enjoy it."

"All right." I turned and let my eyes take in everything before us. And as I studied the lake and the glaciers and the mountain, I realized something.

Maybe I didn't have to be strong enough to banish the pain away all by myself.

Maybe being strong meant learning to lean on those who would take some of the pain away.

Like the man at my side.

———

BY THE TIME we made it back to the lodge, the sun had begun to set. Cole had carried me all the way down the mountain—he'd endured over four miles with me on his back. When we'd gotten to the easier part of the trail, I'd offered to walk in my socks but he'd refused to set me down no matter how much I had pleaded.

Finally, my feet hit the ground when we reached a bench outside the lodge.

"Do you want to go up to the room or would you like to grab dinner first?"

He ran a hand over his face. "I need a shower, but I'd really like to eat first so I can crash after I get cleaned up. I'm wiped."

"Dinner it is. Just let me go grab the flip-flops I left in the truck."

"I'll go get them."

"Cole, sit and take a break." I pointed to the bench. "I can walk across a paved parking lot in my bare feet."

He relented, digging his truck keys out of his pocket.

I took them and hustled toward the parking lot, looking over my shoulder to see him slouched on the bench. He looked more exhausted than I'd ever seen before.

All because of me.

I walked faster, my pace matching the speed of my racing thoughts.

Was I taking too much from Cole? He'd offered his help freely, but was I taking advantage? First, he'd taken on Jamie's murder case at work. Then the birthday list and everything that came along with it. The truck. The weekend activities. The hike.

I didn't want him to resent me by the time we'd finished the list. I didn't want him to think that all I wanted from him was his help.

My worries were put on hold as I reached his truck. I slipped on the flip-flops I'd tossed in the backseat just in case, then hurried back so we could get Cole some much-needed calories and a well-deserved beer.

An hour later, Cole patted his stomach, having just polished off a plate of home fries and an enormous rib eye. "That was good. Not as good as your food, but still. It hit the spot."

"Thank you." I smiled. "Too bad there isn't a way to serve steak in a jar."

He chuckled. "If anyone could figure it out though, my money is on you."

"I think I'll just save the steak recipes for home. I'll dig them out when I come over to break in your kitchen."

His hand covered mine on the bar between us. "I'd like that."

"Me too." I turned over my hand to thread my fingers in his.

We hadn't discussed the kiss we'd shared in his kitchen and we hadn't had another since. I just hoped he knew that the tears that had followed were not because I'd regretted that moment.

I could never regret that kiss.

"I hope you—"

"Do you want another beer?" The bartender, a young woman with spiked black hair, interrupted.

Cole let go of my hand and reached into his pocket for his wallet. "No. Just the check. Thanks."

"You got it." She tapped a cardboard coaster on the bar and walked to the register.

"Here." He handed me a stack of twenties. "I'll be right back."

He stood from his stool, leaning down to kiss my forehead, then walked toward the restrooms. His footsteps were slow and heavy. His broad shoulders stretched the white cotton of his T-shirt as he hunched forward. And the way he was rolling his neck, he must be getting one of his headaches.

"Here you go." The bartender leaned her arms on the bar after setting down our ticket. "Your husband looks like he had a rough day."

"Oh, um," I fumbled the cash as I handed it over, "he's not my husband."

Her eyes darted to my left hand, zeroing in on my wedding rings. "Oh-kay." She pushed off the bar and held up her hands. "No judgment here. Just assumed."

"No!" My hands flailed as I did my best to explain I wasn't having an affair. "It's not like that. I'm . . . I'm not married. My husband passed away and I just haven't taken off my rings."

"Sorry." Her face softened before she spun around and went to the register to make change.

Okay, that was awkward. I twirled the rings on my finger. Was it time to take them off? If I really wanted to move on, I couldn't keep wearing them.

Before I could work up the courage to pull them off, Cole's hand landed on my shoulder. "All set?"

I nodded. "She's just bringing back the change."

The bartender appeared with cash in hand, but Cole just waved her off. "Keep it. Thanks."

I hopped off my stool, then followed Cole as we made our way to the front desk to collect the bags we'd dropped off earlier. We took them from the desk clerk, then made our way to the second floor and down a long hallway to our room.

I tossed my bags on one bed as Cole did the same on the other before sinking into the chair by the balcony door. "Go ahead. You can take the first shower."

"Are you sure?"

He nodded and rested his head against the back of the chair.

"Okay. I'll be fast." I swiped my bag off the bed and hurried to the bathroom, knowing that the faster I showered, the sooner Cole could get in here and get some sleep.

I turned on the water and stripped off my clothes. The blisters on my feet had started to dry thanks to hours of being exposed to the air, but still, when I stepped under the water, I hissed at the sharp sting. Luckily, it faded fast as I took the fastest shower of my life.

With my hair wrapped in a towel, I emerged from the bathroom, dressed in maroon sleep shorts and a matching camisole. "All done."

My feet stopped as my eyes landed on Cole.

He'd fallen asleep in the chair.

His hat was resting on one knee and his hair was matted

down. His neck and jaw were covered in stubble, and his clothes were dirty and wrinkled. He was a mess.

He was a mess and the most handsome man I'd ever seen.

Cole was simply breathtaking.

Quietly, I set down my backpack on the floor and crossed the room. "Cole." I touched a hand to his shoulder.

He jerked awake, blinking a couple of times to clear the sleep away. "Sorry."

"It's okay. Go take a shower and then get into bed."

He nodded, easing up from the chair, then striding to the bathroom.

I took the towel off my hair, quickly combing it out and leaving it to air-dry. When the shower turned on, I opened the balcony door and stepped outside. The night air was cold and gave me goose bumps, but I ignored the chill and focused on my left hand.

Carefully, I slid the ring that Jamie had given me the day we'd gotten engaged off my finger. Then I slid off the simple band he'd given me on our wedding day.

I'll always love you, Jamie, but it's time to let these go.

I couldn't wear his rings anymore.

Not when I was falling in love with Cole.

CHAPTER SIXTEEN

44TH BIRTHDAY: GET A DOG TO KEEP FOR ITS ENTIRE LIFE

POPPY

I was just sliding the balcony door closed when the bathroom door opened.

"I feel like a new man."

"Good." I had a smile on my face when I turned around, but it faltered as Cole crossed the room.

He was towel drying his hair, wearing nothing but a pair of black pajama pants that hung low—unbelievably low—on his hips.

My breath didn't just hitch, it vanished. Every molecule of oxygen evaporated with a single glance.

Because Cole was cut—really cut. His arms were so chiseled, the dips between his muscles resembled the mountain valleys we'd seen earlier on our hike. Hours wouldn't be long enough to trace all of those dips. His chest was dusted with just a bit of hair, but plenty to entertain my fingers for days. And his abs belonged on the cover of a romance novel. I'd expected his stomach to be flat. His T-shirts and polos were never puffed out around the middle, not even after a large meal. But Cole's abs weren't flat—they were ripped. The skin covering the muscle was so lean his stomach was the definition of a washboard.

If I knew who'd invented karate, I'd send them a thank-you note.

Cole dropped the towel and I snapped my eyes to the floor, trying to hide the fact that I'd just been drooling over his upper body.

"I don't suppose you have any painkillers in that massive purse of yours."

"Sure," I panted, remembering to breathe again. My arms led the way to my purse on the bed, digging frantically for the pill bottle at the bottom. "Here you go."

"Thanks." He popped the cap, shook out some pills and grabbed one of the water bottles I'd brought along.

The cords of his throat mesmerized me as he tipped the bottle back to his lips and started gulping. As if I were watching the water on its path, my eyes traveled down his throat, skimming over his collarbone and down the center line that cut between his pecs and stomach. I watched it flow all the way down to the V that disappeared between the waistband of his pajamas, then down a little farther, to the bulge no cotton could conceal.

Cole dropped the water bottle from his lips. I turned back to my handbag, pretending to organize it while my cheeks cooled. "Headache?" I asked, pushing things around on the bottom of my purse.

"I'll be fine." He set the pill bottle by the TV and rolled his neck.

He was trying to play it off, but I knew he was in pain. Setting my purse aside, I pointed to the end of my bed. "Come sit down."

Without question, he sank into the mattress. His shoulders rolled forward as he hung his head.

I climbed on the bed behind him, staying on my knees as I scooted my way to his back. With the slightest touch, I placed my hands on his bare shoulders. A zap of electricity shot up to my elbows and the heat from his skin infused my cool fingers.

Cole tensed and the muscles in his back became even more pronounced—he'd felt that zap too.

My heart was racing but I ignored its drumming beat and began kneading my thumbs into the base of his neck.

"You don't have to do this."

I added more pressure. "Just close your eyes and relax."

Cole gave me a faint nod and then hung his head again, relaxing with every passing second as I worked up and down his neck, then back and forth across his shoulders.

"Is it helping?"

He nodded. "You have magic hands."

"If the restaurant doesn't work out, maybe I'll become a massage therapist."

A quiet laugh came from deep in his chest, the rumble sending tingles skittering over my forearms. "Talk to me about something. Your voice is soothing."

My hands paused. No one had ever complimented my voice before. It was funny how a little bit of his praise made me like something about myself I hadn't really considered special before. So if my voice would help soothe Cole's headache after a long day of literally hauling me around, I'd read him my grocery list. "What do you want me to talk about?"

"Anything. How about your family? Are you close with your parents?"

The thought of them warmed my heart. "I am. We don't get to see each other much but I talk to them both a couple times a week. And they always come down for Kali's and Max's birthdays and for Christmas too."

"When was the last time you were in Alaska?"

"Two years ago. I went up not long before I bought the garage and started renovating it for the restaurant. I spent a couple of weeks up there getting my dad's advice on my business plan and having my mom help me brainstorm a full menu."

My hands dug harder into Cole's neck, working away one of the knots.

"What do your parents do?"

"Dad is a pilot. He has his own business flying supplies into northern Alaska. He's built it up over the years and has a bunch of pilots working for him now. He could retire anytime, but he loves flying. And Mom is a private chef in Anchorage."

"Is that where you got your love of cooking?"

I smiled. "Yes. Mom taught me how to cook." She had passed down her passion for food, while Dad had paid for my business degree from Montana State. They'd both given me the tools to make food my career.

"What about your grandparents?"

My hands moved down Cole's neck to his shoulders again. With every circle of my thumbs, the tension eased away. "They're all still in Alaska. Dad's parents live in the same place they have for fifty years, three blocks away from my parents' house. And Mom's parents are in a nursing home. They're in their nineties now but otherwise in good health. Though neither of them can hear very well anymore."

He sighed. "It's nice that you still have all of them. My grandparents all passed when I was younger."

"I'm sorry."

Before Jamie, I'd never lost anyone. Maybe that was a tiny part of why his death had been so devastating. So shocking. It had been a wake-up call that the time we had with our loved ones was fleeting.

As if he could feel my moment of sadness, Cole reached up and put his hand over mine, squeezing once before dropping it back to his lap.

I rubbed his shoulders and neck for a while longer until my fingers finally wore out. But I didn't want to stop touching Cole, so I inched my knees closer. My hands slid up his neck, past his ears and into his hair. "Lean back."

Cole looked up at me through dark lashes, watching as my fingers massaged his scalp. "Magic fingers," he whispered, "and beautiful eyes."

My hands kept working at Cole's hair as I held his gaze. The intensity between us grew with every passing second that we refused to break apart—refused to even blink.

And in that moment, I opened myself up completely to Cole. Without words, I told him how much he meant to me. How he'd stitched my broken pieces back together. And in his tender gaze—deep in his pale-green irises—he showed me a vulnerability I'd never seen. His eyes pleaded for me to take care of his heart.

I'd protect it always.

The heat between us grew as the seconds passed, but still, we didn't break our stare. My hands stopped moving as my chest heaved with choppy breaths. Cole sat frozen against me —waiting.

Waiting for my signal.

I blinked before filling my lungs with a jagged breath. "Will you do something for me?"

"In a heartbeat."

"Kiss me."

His head came off my shoulder as he twisted. With his arms bracketing my knees, Cole leaned forward, fitting his naked chest against my front. His hands left the bed, traveling up my sides with the lightest touch. Those long fingers grazed the sides of my breasts before running over my bare arms and up, into my damp hair.

The entire time, Cole's eyes stayed glued to mine.

When his face came closer, I dropped my gaze to his lips. I only had a second to study them before he kissed me. The moment we touched, my eyes drifted shut and my lips parted for his tongue. It touched the tip of mine before darting back out to trace my lower lip.

A greedy moan came from the back of my throat as Cole teased. He nipped and sucked on my lips but he was holding back. My hands, dangling limp at my sides, reached for his waist, but he jerked his hips back, not letting me get a grip.

"Cole," I pleaded when he broke away.

He was panting as he searched my eyes. "How far do you want to take this?"

The answer came without hesitation. "All the way."

He leaned back, like he didn't trust himself to be too close. "Are you sure? Because once we do this, once we cross that line, we aren't going back."

I cupped his jaw. "I'm as sure as I've ever been. This. Us. I want this. I want *you*."

I'd barely gotten the last word out before Cole's mouth slammed down on mine. This time, there was no teasing. No playing. No holding back. Cole kissed me so deeply that I was lost to anything other than his mouth.

My hands clung to his back as I pulled him closer, needing more. I was dizzy from the throbbing between my thighs and the lack of oxygen, but I just held tight, desperate to consume him completely.

On a groan, his hands left my hair and moved down to my ass, squeezing tight as he picked me up off the bed and laid me on my back, and not once did he break the latch he had on my mouth. As my hips cradled his, his hard length rubbed against my aching clit. I arched up, rubbing myself against the thin cotton that separated us.

Cole's tongue dove back into my mouth, plundering relentlessly as his hands roamed to my breasts. He squeezed them over my camisole before yanking it down, freeing them so he could fill his large hands.

I arched my chest into his hands, craving a harder touch on my pebbled nipples. And Cole didn't disappoint. With his palms still cupping my breasts, he used his thumbs to flick and tease my hard buds. Every tug and roll sent my pulse shooting directly to my center. Surely my wetness had seeped through my panties and sleep shorts. Surely Cole could feel just how much I needed him inside.

My hands slid between us, working their way toward the waistband of Cole's pants, but before they could slip inside, he broke away, cursing.

"Fuck. Fuck. *Fuck.*"

"What?" I breathed.

He collapsed onto my chest, panting and still cursing into a pillow. When he lifted his head, his jaw was clenched tight. "I don't have any condoms."

Fuck.

Before I could say anything, Cole rolled over me, reaching for the phone on the nightstand. "I'm going to call the front desk."

"Wait!" I smacked his hand away from the receiver. The last thing I wanted was for a bellhop to bring up a condom that had been sitting around an old mountain lodge for who knew how long. "I'm on birth control, and I haven't been with anyone since . . ."

His hand came back to the bed. "I just had my annual physical and I get tested every year. I'm clean."

I lifted my head from the pillow, pressing my lips to his. "Then what are you waiting for?"

He grinned, the light in his eyes sparkling brighter than I'd ever seen. "My perfect woman."

My heart flutter was so strong, it was nearly all I could feel. And with that feeling came something else, a realization. I shouldn't feel guilty for having heart flutters with someone other than Jamie. I should feel lucky—incredibly, unbelievably, magically lucky. I'd found someone else who made me feel cherished and loved and protected.

Cole had earned these heart flutters.

And he should have them.

As he fit his lips back to my smiling mouth, I closed my eyes, savoring the realization. Savoring his kiss and the heat between us that scorched my skin. I craved more of the burn, more of his skin and his body, so I slid my hands into the waistband of his pants. With a relentless grip, I filled my hands with Cole's ass.

"Poppy," he groaned as I squeezed. Even with my fingers digging in hard, they barely made a dent in the muscle. Cole's body was too solid. Too hard. Every inch.

And I was done with these clothes keeping it away.

My hands traded his waistband for my own. I hooked my thumbs into my shorts and did my best to wiggle them free, but with his weight on top of me, they barely slid down an inch.

I tore my lips away from Cole's and huffed.

He chuckled against my cheek. "That's my job." Starting at my jaw, he began peppering kisses down my neck.

I abandoned my undressing efforts and let my hands fall to my sides, enjoying the way Cole's tongue licked and his mouth sucked on my skin.

Down he moved, to the dip between my collarbone, then to the swell of one breast. His hot mouth found my hard nipple and he sucked it inside, rolling it once with his tongue before letting it go with a pop.

He did the same to the other nipple as his hands came to the hem of my camisole. By the time he'd dragged it up my torso, I was writhing beneath him. The torture was agonizing. Beautiful. It was driving me crazy but I didn't want him to stop.

"Cole," I pleaded. "More."

He hummed and broke away from my breast, finally whipping my camisole over my head and tossing it to the floor. He leaned back on his knees, his eyes darkening as they feasted on my naked skin. "You are so beautiful."

My heart swelled as I pulled in a shaking breath. There was so much I wanted to say, to tell him how special he made me feel, but I was lost for words. All I could do was hold his eyes as he slowly stripped off my shorts and pink lace panties.

His mouth came back to my skin and began exploring. His tongue licked the swells under each of my breasts before his lips tickled down my ribs on one side. Cole sucked and nipped at the soft curve of my hip. He kissed the inside of my thigh, down to the bend in my knee. Then he moved back up my body to do the whole thing again, this time on the side he'd neglected.

He was on a quest to devour every inch of my skin just to see if one part tasted differently than the rest. By the time he reached my center, dragging his tongue through my slit in one long, euphoric lick, every nerve in my body was pulsing, desperate for release.

Cole stepped off the foot of the bed and shoved down his pants. When he stood, my eyes dropped straight to his thick, hard cock. My heartbeat kicked up another notch as I took in his size. It had been so long since I'd had sex and Cole was big.

Crawling back into bed, Cole covered me with his body, wrapping one arm around my back while the other threaded in my hair. He pressed a soft kiss to my lips, erasing my worries with that one sweet caress.

As his tongue stroked my bottom lip, his hand abandoned my hair and came between us to fist his cock. He pulled it through my slit, spreading my wetness up to my clit. My hips arched when he did it again and again—my body begging for more.

Finally, he positioned the tip at my entrance and brought his hand back to my face. Then with one smooth glide, Cole filled me completely. He stayed still for a moment, giving me a chance to stretch around him, but then he began stroking. His deep, deliberate rhythm brought me higher and higher until my legs were trembling and my skin was on fire.

I couldn't last. As much as I wanted to drag out this incredible feeling, my body was leading the way. So I closed my eyes, blocking out everything but the feel of Cole inside me. And I let go. I moaned as my orgasm ripped through me in waves, my inner walls clenching hard around Cole until I was boneless beneath him.

"God, you are perfect." Cole kissed me again, then started stroking faster.

I'd expected him to find his own release soon, but he just kept going. Over and over he moved, building me back up. Showing me that, even exhausted, he had the stamina to go for hours. He kept thrusting, his hips setting an erratic rhythm I couldn't predict, until I was shaking underneath him, ready to come all over again.

"Come, beautiful," he panted. "I'm there."

With his gravelly voice in my ear and his hot mouth on my neck, I gasped his name just before my second orgasm broke hard.

I pulsed around him, my hips bucking against his. He tipped his head back and let out a loud groan as he came, hot and wet inside me. I was still coming down but forced my eyes open, wanting to see his face—his breathtaking face.

His dark lashes squeezed together. The cords of his neck flexed tight. His stubbled jaw clamped shut.

Breathtaking.

So much had happened since the day Cole had come back into my life. The highs and lows of my emotional roller coaster had been almost too much to handle. But I couldn't regret a second of that ride—not if this is where I got to step off. Here, in the arms of this incredible man.

Cole collapsed on top of me, holding me close, as we panted for air. I pressed my hands flat onto his back, not wanting to let him go quite yet, until, finally, we'd regained our breaths and the room had stopped spinning. He slid out and fell onto the bed at my side. Then with a fast tug, he pulled me onto his chest.

"*Now*, I'm wiped."

I giggled into his neck. Between the hike and the sex, I bet he'd be dead to the world in less than five minutes. "I'm going to clean up. Be right back." With a peck on his cheek, I rolled out of bed and went to the bathroom. I hurried to clean up, wanting to make it back into his arms before he fell asleep.

Cole was waiting when I slipped under the blankets he'd turned down. He pulled me into his side and nuzzled his nose into my hair. Then he took my hand and laced our fingers together. "Are you okay? Being with me?"

Since I'd completely broken down after our first kiss, his question didn't surprise me. He was probably waiting for me to have another crying jag. But there was nothing about sex with Cole to cause anything other than tears of joy.

"I'm better than okay." I kissed his chest. "I'm wonderful. And you're the only one I want to be with."

"Good." He blew out a relieved breath. "Do you want to talk about why your rings are gone?"

I should have known he wouldn't miss that. "It was time."

"You can always talk to me about him. About how you're feeling. Promise you'll tell me if it ever gets to be too much."

"I promise, just not here. This bed, it's a place that's just for us, okay? This is only ours."

He kissed my hair. "Okay."

I closed my eyes and snuggled closer, glad that he liked to cuddle. "Good night."

He yawned. "Night, my pretty Poppy."

Then I fell asleep next to the second man I'd ever had sex with. The man who had set out to win my damaged heart. The man who had been healing it ever since.

The man I saw when I dreamed of the future.

———

THE NEXT MORNING, Cole and I were slow to start the day.

Since I didn't have boots, we couldn't take the morning hike I'd originally planned, so instead, we lazed in bed. After he'd made me come—twice—and shared my shower, we forced ourselves apart and left the lodge, making a stop at Lake McDonald.

"I've seen so many pictures of this lake, but none of them do it justice." Leaning into Cole's side, I couldn't believe this place was real.

The glassy water reflected the blue mountains in the distance. Some of the trees had started to turn, their yellow and amber leaves contrasting with the surrounding evergreens. But my favorite part was the lake rocks. Round, smooth stones of every color—red, green, blue and yellow—rested under the water's surface.

"I want to come back here some day and take a canoe out on the lake."

Cole's arm around my shoulders pulled tighter. "Maybe we should come back every year. This could be our annual vacation."

I smiled. "I like that."

This park would always be special to me, mostly because this was the place where Cole and I had really started. I'd happily come back every year to spend a weekend together. And I loved that Cole assumed—just like I did—that we would be together. That I'd be the one he'd spend his annual vacations with.

"Give me your phone. I'll take your picture." He let me go and held out his hand.

"Okay." I dug it out of my back pocket and handed it over.

Cole backed up, but I didn't turn right away. I kept my eyes on the lake and threw my arms out to my sides, tipping back my chin to let the sun warm my face.

"All right." He chuckled. "Turn around and smile."

I dropped my arms and turned, but instead of smiling, I blew Cole a kiss.

He clicked a few pictures, then gave me back my phone. "Do you want to stay or should we head back?"

I looked over my shoulder at the lake one last time. "We'd better go. It's a long drive."

"Okay." Cole fell in step behind me as we walked up the dirt path to the truck. He opened my door, then went around to his own. His movements were stiff today, the aches from our hike yesterday likely setting in, but he hadn't complained.

As we pulled onto the highway, he took my hand. "When

we get back, how long do you think it will take you to pack up stuff for a few days?"

"Pack? Where exactly am I going?"

"To my house." He grinned. "You're stuck with me now."

I smiled at Cole's profile. He hadn't shaved today and his jaw looked sexier, more rugged with his thick stubble. When we got to his house, my tongue was going to get up close and personal with that jaw. Packing light—or fast—had never been a strong suit, but tonight, I'd be setting a personal best. "Ten minutes. Fifteen, tops."

And if I forgot something, I'd just swing by my place tomorrow before work. I was more than willing to get up thirty minutes earlier if that meant I got to sleep in Cole's sleigh bed.

The only down side was that I'd have to block out the image of another woman having slept there first. "How attached are you to your bed?"

"My bed? Well, considering I just bought it a few months ago, pretty attached."

That wasn't what I'd expected. "You just bought it?"

"It was time for an upgrade. That one is brand new. Why?"

"Oh, just curious." I covered my mouth, pretending to yawn, when really, I was hiding a huge smile. *Cole's house, here I come.* He didn't know it yet, but I'd just claimed that bed as mine.

His kitchen too.

We drove awhile in silence, taking in the scenery as we navigated the windy roads out of the park until we hit the main highway that would lead us back to Bozeman. Cole pulled into a gas station to fuel up and I hopped out, wanting a drink for the ride home. "I'm going to get a water. Want one?"

He nodded, digging his wallet out of his back pocket and tossing it over. "Thanks, beautiful."

Beautiful.

I smiled at his new endearment. Pretty Poppy was still my favorite, but beautiful was a close runner-up.

Hurrying inside, I used the restroom and then got Cole and I both waters and some licorice for the rest of the trip. Just as I was coming outside, I heard a yelp from the parking lot of the farm and ranch supply store next to the gas station.

I searched for the sound just as I heard it again. The yelp was coming from an old red truck where a woman was setting out a sign next to a tire.

Puppies for Sale. $1500. Purebred German Shepherd.

My feet immediately changed direction. Fifteen hundred dollars was *way* too much to spend on a dog, but since looking was free and I loved puppies, one glance wouldn't hurt.

"Hi!" I waved to the woman as I approached her truck. "Would you mind if I looked at your puppies?"

She smiled. "By all means. Please."

I leaned over the tailgate and five pairs of brown eyes all came to me, tails wagging frantically as they licked their metal crate. "Oh my god." Now I knew why people spent fifteen hundred dollars on a dog. One look, and I was in love. This woman could have my car if that meant one of these fur babies could come live with me.

"Pop—oh, shit," Cole muttered, walking up. The minute he spotted the puppies and the look on my face, he knew exactly what I was planning. "So much for going to the pound and getting a rescue pup."

I'd told Cole that I was planning on getting a puppy from the pound to satisfy Jamie's list, but that plan was history. My next dog would have to come from the pound, because I was buying one of these puppies today. Besides . . . "These dogs need good homes too, don't they?" I asked the woman, hoping for some support.

She just backed away, not making eye contact with a scowling Cole.

Chicken.

I'd expected her to jump right in and help me make my case to Cole as to why I was going to spend a ridiculous amount of money on a puppy.

"Cole, look how cute they are." I turned back to the puppies. One of them—the cutest one—had retreated to the back of the cage, lounging while its siblings were still licking the crate. "Besides, it doesn't matter where the puppy comes from. The list just said to get a dog to keep for its entire life."

Jamie's family had always had ranch dogs, but he'd always wanted a pet. A dog that could come inside or that he could take on jogs around the neighborhood. He'd wanted a dog to become man's best friend, not be another employee of the Maysen ranch. This puppy was just the kind he would have gone for—probably because this was exactly the type of puppy *I* would have gone for.

I had no idea how I'd fit a puppy into my life, but the little one in the back, the one more interested in watching the activities than being front and center, was my new dog.

"Do you take credit cards?" Cole asked the woman.

My head whipped away from the dogs as Cole stole his wallet from my hand.

The woman grinned. "I sure do."

And just like that, I had a puppy.

An hour later, my new dog was on my lap and the back of Cole's truck was filled with pet supplies we'd bought at the farm and ranch supply store.

"What should we name you?" I cooed as the puppy perched her paws on the door to look out the window. "I'm thinking . . . Nazboo."

"What the fuck?" Cole muttered. "No, Poppy."

"What's wrong with Nazboo?"

He frowned. "I don't want to be outside yelling 'Come here, Nazboo.' 'Sit, Nazboo.' 'Don't fucking eat that, Nazboo.' Pick a normal name."

I laughed but shook my head. "No. Nazboo is cute. It's from one of Kali and Max's cartoons and it's unique."

"Veto."

"Fine. If you're so particular about the names, let's hear your pick."

"Hmm." Cole rubbed his jaw with one hand, brainstorming quietly as he drove with the other.

While he attempted to come up with a better name, I stroked Nazboo's back. She was, by far, the most precious dog I had ever seen. Her coat was mostly black, but she had the typical German shepherd tan spotted on her legs, her belly and the sides of her face.

And now she was mine to love and cherish until the end of her days.

"Well?" I asked. "What do you think we should name her?"

Cole looked over at me and my girl, then shook his head before admitting defeat. "Nazboo."

CHAPTER SEVENTEEN

45TH BIRTHDAY: PULL A FIRE ALARM

COLE

"Thanks for coming up." Dad leaned his forearms on his desk. "Ready when you are."

Matt, in the chair at my side, dove into his update for Dad on the liquor store murder case.

"We've gone through the video footage and narrowed our search down to six vehicles in the shopping complex at the time of the murder. All were driven out of the complex by women fitting our rough description. We weren't able to get all of the plates from the security camera footage, so we crosschecked the ones missing plate numbers with stoplight cameras. Before we came up here, I sent a request to the DMV to get registrations. Hopefully by Monday we'll have names and I'll start bringing people in for questioning."

Dad nodded. "Good. I hope you two are onto something."

"Me too," Matt and I both said in unison.

It had taken nearly two months—two long months—of digging through the camera footage to get this far. Ever since the night in the garage when I'd shown Poppy my gun, Matt and I had looked at the case from a new angle. This time around, we'd searched the footage for a woman.

It hadn't been easy. Between balancing my work on the drug task force, my normal caseload and everything else that was happening in my personal life, the last thing I wanted to do most mornings was lock myself in the conference room and scour camera footage for a couple hours before a full day's work.

But if this paid off—if we actually found Jamie Maysen's murderer—it would all be worth it. It would be worth every minute if we could give Poppy some peace.

It had been a month since we'd officially gotten together up at Glacier. A month and we hadn't spent a night apart. She'd get up early and go to the restaurant. I'd get up early and come to the station. We'd text throughout the day, and if I had free time, I'd stop by for lunch. And in the evenings, I'd spend a couple of hours working on that old truck while I waited for her to finish up at the restaurant.

Basically, we'd both work our asses off until we could quit for the day and meet up at my house. Then we'd spend the rest of the night unwinding in my bed.

Our bed.

One thing I'd learned this past month was that Poppy belonged in my house. With her there, it felt like home.

"Where's Nazboo?" Dad asked.

"I dropped her off with Mom after lunch."

Dad grinned. "She loves that puppy."

"Yeah." I grinned back. Nazboo was a keeper, even if she did have a dumbass name.

A dog like her should have a name like Sadie or Bailey. Instead, she was named after some weird pet dragon from one of Kali's cartoons. But I seemed to be the only one who thought

Nazboo was a ridiculous fucking name. Everyone else loved it, especially Poppy. So I hadn't put up much of a fight and started calling her Naz, which was easier to swallow.

"I think she might be the best puppy I've ever seen," Matt said. "I told my wife I'd consider getting one too if I could guarantee she acted like Naz."

"We lucked out, that's for sure." Naz rarely had an accident, she didn't nip at fingers, and she'd only chewed one of Poppy's shoes. After that, we'd made sure to always have a rawhide nearby, and from then on out, Naz had never chewed on anything else. But it was her personality we all loved the most. She was mellow—for a puppy—and as sweet as sugar cane.

Naz had become my sidekick during the day, hanging out with me at the station or riding around in my truck if we were doing fieldwork. Bozeman was a dog-friendly town, and a couple of years ago, the station had started allowing senior officers to bring their dogs to work. Naz was now one of three dogs in the bull pen on a regular basis, and the times that I couldn't bring her with me, she stayed with Mom.

"All right." Dad checked his watch. "I've got another meeting in five. Keep me posted on how your interviews go."

Matt nodded. "Will do."

We all stood and Dad shook Matt's hand. "Nice work, Matt."

"Thanks, but I can't take all the credit." He clapped me on the shoulder. "This guy has been doing most of the work."

I scoffed. "I don't know about that."

I'd been the one to watch the majority of the camera footage, but Matt hadn't been sitting idle. He took his role as lead seriously and he'd done a lot of fieldwork while I sat behind the scenes. He'd interviewed all of the original witnesses again. He'd spent hours at the shopping complex, learning all of the ins and outs of the area so we could zero in on potential blind spots the suspect could have hidden in. Matt had even spent hours going over the case with Simmons.

Surprisingly, Simmons had memorized a lot from the case. He might have delegated things too far down the chain and his documentation skills were shit, but what he hadn't written down, he'd kept in his head. I was still pissed at Simmons for being lazy these last few years, but he wasn't the one to blame for letting Jamie Maysen's killer walk free. He'd just looked at the investigation like the rest of us had.

For a man.

Female killers were rare, and even though we'd been trained to keep our eyes open to any possibility, I couldn't blame Simmons for spending his time focusing on a male suspect. The camera footage from the liquor store was deceiving. The killer looked like a man.

But maybe we were finally getting somewhere.

"It's been a team effort," Matt said. "I'd better get back to it. Bye, Chief."

"Bye, Dad." I turned to follow Matt out the door but Dad stopped me.

"Cole, stick around for a sec."

I sighed, jealous that Matt had made his escape. *Lucky bastard.* "What's up?"

Dad pointed to the chair, so I resumed my seat. "I've decided on something and wanted to tell you before the announcement is made next week."

The muscles in my shoulders tensed at his tone. "Okay."

"I've set my retirement date. Two more years, and I'm done."

"Wow." I'd expected Dad to work for at least another five. Maybe ten. He loved his job. "That's . . . soon."

"It is, but your mom and I have been talking a lot about how we want to spend the remainder of our years. Both of us are in good health. We've been careful with our money. So rather than waste these next ten years in the office, we want to have some time together. Maybe travel. And we want to be close with our grandkids."

Grandkids. That was the reason behind the sudden short timeline. My sister had stopped by the station two weeks ago and told me she was pregnant. I was fucking ecstatic for Evie and her husband, Zack. They'd been trying to get pregnant for years until they'd finally resorted to IVF. Now my sister was as happy as I'd ever seen her and the early ultrasounds showed they were expecting triplets. It made sense that Mom and Dad would want to be around to help with three grandbabies on the way.

"Congratulations."

"Thanks." He nodded. "But that means we need to get serious about making transition plans. Two years is going to fly by and we've got to start prepping you to take over as chief. We should get you involved in more committees. I'd like you to get more play in the politics and—"

"Hold up." I raised my hands. "Dad, we talked about this. I don't want to be the next chief of police."

"Right. I know you're still considering things." He nodded but he wasn't hearing me. "We've got time, but what's the harm in learning more about what I do? Just in case."

Just in case.

Three words I was really fucking sick of hearing.

"Look, Dad—" My phone rang in my pocket before I could put my foot down. "Sorry," I muttered, digging it out.

"You go ahead. I've got another meeting coming in."

"Okay. We'll talk later?"

"You got it."

I waved good-bye as I pressed the phone to my ear, walking down the hallway toward the staircase. "Hello."

"Hey, Cole, it's Finn."

"Hey. What's going on? Up for a beer tonight?"

I'd met Poppy's brother for beers twice since the fair. He was a stand-up guy and easy to hang out with, but what I liked best about Finn was how he adored his little sister. The first time we'd met up, he'd told me point-blank that if I ever hurt her, he'd gladly serve life in prison for my murder.

"That's not exactly the reason for my call."

My feet froze as my heart rate spiked. "Is it Poppy?"

"Yeah. She's fine, but she's in some trouble."

"What kind of trouble?" What the fuck was going on that she couldn't call me herself?

"She just called me to bail her and Jimmy out of jail."

"Motherfucker." The word came out of my clenched teeth. "It was that fucking fire alarm, wasn't it?"

"Yep." He popped the *p* just like Poppy did. "I guess she decided not to listen to either of us on that one."

"Goddamn it." I jogged toward the stairs. "I'll take care of it."

Finn chuckled. "I figured you would. She's going to be pissed at me when she finds out I called you on the sly instead of coming down to bail her out."

I huffed. "She's got bigger problems to worry about right now."

"Good luck."

"Thanks for calling." I shoved my phone back in my pocket and hustled downstairs to the bull pen. "I need to head out," I told Matt. He was standing by his desk, talking to a couple of the other guys. "Something personal came up."

"Personal, as in your girlfriend and some old guy getting hauled in for pulling a fire alarm at an old warehouse?"

"Fuck." I swiped my keys off my desk. "Does everybody know?"

The huddle immediately started laughing.

"I'll take that as a yes." *Fucking gossips.* This place was worse than a high school locker room. I ignored my coworkers and turned to leave, but one of the guys stopped me.

"Hey, Cole."

"Yeah?" I looked over my shoulder just in time to catch the handcuffs he threw my way.

"You might need these." He snickered along with the other assholes laughing at me.

I glared at him, about to toss them back, but stopped myself. Maybe a night spent naked in handcuffs would teach Poppy to listen. So without a word, I shoved them into my back pocket and stormed out of the bull pen.

Short-term lockup was on the other side of the law enforcement complex, so when I exploded through the door, I turned in the opposite direction of the parking lot. The short walk down the long sidewalk did nothing to cool my temper, and by the time I reached lockup, I was fuming.

How could she be this stupid? Didn't she know that this was a serious crime? It was a misdemeanor at least, but if she'd caused any property damage or an injury, she could be facing a felony. Something I'd told her more than once.

For the first time, I wanted to take a match to that goddamn birthday list.

"Hi, Detective Goodman." The officer sitting behind the plexiglass window smiled but it fell as he read my angry face.

"I'm here to cover the bail for Poppy Maysen and Jimmy Maysen."

His eyes widened. "Oh, um . . . okay." He shuffled some papers on his desk. "It's set at five hundred each."

My nostrils flared. *A thousand dollars.* I grabbed my wallet out of my back pocket and dug out a credit card.

"There's an extra fee for cred—"

I held up a hand to shut him up. "I know. Just put it all on there."

"Yes, sir."

I pointed to the door in the corner. "Can I go back?"

"You'll just need to sign some paperwork before they can be released."

No shit.

He cowered under my glare and reached for the buzzer to let me through to the cellblock.

The first cell I passed was occupied by a drunk who had puked all over himself and the floor. The next had a guy covered in tattoos, most of which were gang symbols.

I didn't want Poppy in this place. She didn't belong in this hellhole. And she wouldn't be here if she had just *fucking listened.*

My hands were fisted as I walked down the hall to her cell, where she was talking to Jimmy.

"I don't like this idea."

"Too bad," he hissed. "I'm taking the blame. Like I told the cop, you were just trying to stop me."

"But—"

"No buts. This is how it's going to be. Let me do this."

I cleared my throat as I came up to the bars.

Poppy's wide eyes were waiting.

Jimmy's darted to the floor.

I stepped up to the door, planting my hands on my hips, and glared down at them both sitting on the metal cot. "How about you both stop talking where anyone can overhear your conversation?"

"That's what I tried to tell her." Jimmy stood from the cot. "But she's a bit on edge."

"On edge!" Poppy shot up. "We're in jail, Jimmy." Her eyes came to me. "Cole, I can explain."

"Not now." I looked down the hallway to see the cop from the front desk coming down with a fistful of keys. "Both of you stay quiet until we get out of here. Then you'll have your chance to explain."

Poppy and Jimmy stayed quiet as the officer and I escorted them out of the cellblock. They didn't mutter a word as I signed their bail papers and the credit card receipt. And they nodded in silence as the officer told them that they had to appear at the arraignment or I'd lose my bail money and they'd have warrants issued for their arrest.

"Where's your car?" I asked Poppy as we stepped outside.

"At the warehouse."

"Let's go."

I marched back across the complex with Jimmy and Poppy following behind me like children after being scolded by an angry parent.

We went straight to my truck and got inside, with Jimmy riding shotgun and Poppy in the back. When the doors were closed, I took a deep breath, trying to calm down. But not even the white-knuckle grip I had on the steering wheel eased the anger flowing through my veins, and the hold I'd kept on my temper fell to pieces.

"What the fuck were you thinking?" I roared, twisting toward Poppy in the back. "Is checking some goddamn check box really worth a criminal record? Jesus Christ, Poppy. We've talked about this. You could get charged with a felony. A *felony*! That stays with you forever."

"I know." As Poppy's frame crumpled, my anger fizzled.

"This is my fault." Jimmy came to her rescue. "But we've got a plan."

"A plan?"

Did Jimmy actually think he could beat the system? If we were lucky, these two would only end up with misdemeanors.

"I'm taking the blame for this whole thing," Jimmy declared.

"Jimmy, no!" Poppy protested. "I pulled the alarm. It's my responsibility. I won't let—"

I held up a finger, silencing her rant, and kept my eyes on Jimmy. "Keep going."

"I pulled the alarm. Poppy and I were at the warehouse. We went to coffee at the place next door, I've got the receipt to prove it, and then I told her I wanted to check out the warehouse. I wanted to see how it had changed over the years since I knew who used to own it. We snuck inside and I pulled the alarm. On accident."

"An accident." I deadpanned. "That's your plan?"

He nodded. "Yep. I tripped, grabbed the wall and yanked the alarm."

I sighed and looked back at Poppy. It killed me to see her beautiful cornflower blues filled with worry. "How about the truth this time?"

She nodded. "Jimmy found out that the sprinkler system had been turned off in the warehouse because they're getting ready to do a renovation. We went for coffee—that part is true—and then walked across the street to the warehouse. We snuck in and I pulled the alarm."

"The sprinklers were all shut off, but the alarms were still active." Jimmy shook his head. "Bad intel on my part."

Intel. Jimmy was acting like this was some fucking covert operation and he was a secret spy, not something that could ruin my girlfriend's reputation as an upstanding citizen.

Poppy touched my arm. "We thought doing it this way would be no big deal. That I'd be able to pull a pointless alarm and finish the item for the list without actually committing a crime. Neither of us had any idea the alarm was still active. I swear, this was all an innocent mistake. We didn't even run after the alarm went off. We just waited until the fire department arrived so we could tell them we'd pulled the alarm. They called the cops and . . . you know the rest."

"Okay." I closed my eyes and took a breath, then turned the truck key and backed us out of the parking lot. I used the drive to The Rainbow to think of how we were going to deal with this before the arraignment next week.

Parked in front of the retirement home, I looked at both Jimmy and Poppy, telling them with my scowl that I was in charge. "Here's what we're going to do. First, you're going to tell the judge the truth. All of it. Starting with the list and why you pulled the alarm in the first place. Then you're going to promise to never, ever break the law again and hope that the judge is a bit sentimental and gives you a fine instead of jail time." My eyes snapped to Jimmy. "But we're sticking with the truth here. Not some crazy story."

Jimmy surprised me when he didn't argue. He nodded at me and reached back to pat Poppy's knee. "I'm sorry. I'll see you soon."

As he disappeared inside, Poppy climbed over the console and took his place in the passenger seat. "I'm sorry, Cole. I know you're mad. I know you told me not to do it, but we honestly thought it would just be pulling a switch that didn't work anymore."

I took her hand. "I didn't realize pulling a disabled alarm was an option. I thought you'd want it to be real. If you had just asked me, I could have talked to the fire department and gotten you a whole list of buildings where the alarms didn't work."

She hung her head. "I just . . . you've been doing so much for me. I can't keep taking from you."

Huh? "What are you talking about? And where is this coming from?"

She shrugged. "You've been so busy lately and it's my fault. I can't keep piling it on. With the truck and the hike and now you've got Nazboo all the time. I don't want you to resent me by the time we get this all done. I'd rather have *you* than your help on this list."

"Poppy, look at me." When she did, I let her hand go to run my thumb up her cheek. "You have both. Me and my help. I want to fix up that truck. I want to be with Nazboo. I want to do whatever *you* need me to do. Okay?"

"I don't want the list to come between us," she whispered.

God, I love this woman. I loved her heart. Her dedication to see things through. I loved that she was trying to put me first. And even though it had backfired, I loved that she'd done this today because she was trying to lighten my load.

Those three little words almost slipped out of my mouth, but I swallowed them back. Maybe I'd muster the courage to say them when the list was over—when all of this was behind us. She wasn't ready for them yet.

And I needed to know that when I said *I love you,* I'd hear it back.

Today wasn't that day. We needed more time.

"I love that you're dedicated to the list and I'm so damn proud that you'd do that for Jamie. But that list will never come between us."

She relaxed, leaning further into my hand. She'd needed to hear those words just as much as I'd needed to say them.

Jamie's list wasn't going to come between us. I just had to make sure his memory—and my own insecurities—didn't either.

CHAPTER EIGHTEEN

33RD BIRTHDAY: THROW A DRINK IN SOMEONE'S FACE

POPPY

"Are you ready?" I asked Finn.

He rolled his eyes. "Is anyone ever *ready* to have water thrown in their face?"

"Okay. Here goes."

With a flick of my wrist, I threw the water in my glass into my brother's face. He frowned, blinking it out of his eyes before grabbing the towel off the kitchen table.

Behind me, Molly silently slid me another glass of water. The moment the towel dropped from Finn's face, I threw the second glass.

"Hey!" he shouted, sputtering the water out of his mouth. "What was that for?"

I grinned, glad my secret attack had worked. "That was for calling Cole to come bail me out of jail."

Finn shook his head and went back to the towel.

It had been a week since my time behind bars—something I didn't care to ever repeat. I'd been a nervous wreck the entire time, wondering what the judge would do to punish Jimmy and me, and by the time I'd arrived at the courthouse this morning, not even Cole's touch could settle my anxiety.

"You should be glad I called Cole." Finn tossed down the towel. "If he hadn't convinced you and Jimmy not to commit perjury, things would have turned out a lot worse."

I scoffed. "I never would have let Jimmy take the blame."

No matter what Jimmy had wanted, I'd always planned to tell the truth and plead guilty—something else I didn't care to ever repeat.

Never in my life had I been more humiliated than this morning as I'd stood in front of a judge and admitted to pulling a fire alarm, all because I was trying to honor my late husband's birthday list.

"It's over now." Molly patted my shoulder. "You've paid the fine and marked the item off the list. Fire alarm," she made a checkmark in the air, "check."

After the hearing, Cole had gone back to the station while Jimmy and I had waited to pay our fines. I'd handed over a two-thousand-dollar check to the courthouse clerk, then taken Jimmy back to The Rainbow. The minute I'd gotten back to the restaurant, I'd pulled out the journal and crossed that item off the list. No tears. No twinge of sadness or longing. Just a grimace followed by pure joy that I'd never plot a crime again.

"No more misdemeanors, okay?" Finn asked.

"Promise." I crossed my heart. "Thanks for letting me throw water in your face. I'm glad to know my brother is here to support me when my *friends* let me down."

I shot an exaggerated glare at Molly but she laughed it off. "Some of us require makeup to get through the day."

I'd begged Molly to let me do it, but she'd refused, claiming her mascara and foundation would not be victims of Jamie's birthday list. So when Finn had come in with a clean face and a hungry belly, I'd given him a free lunch in exchange for his assistance.

"Okay. I'd better get back to work." Finn came around the table and gave me a hug. Then he smiled at Molly. "See you tonight?"

Tonight? What was happening tonight?

She nodded. "Come over whenever. The kids are really excited."

"I'm excited too." He waved to us both before leaving the kitchen.

The second the door swung closed behind him, I spun on Molly. "Tonight?"

"He's coming over for dinner."

"What? That's great!" My arms shot in the air. "Why didn't you tell me earlier?"

She shrugged. "It's no big deal."

"Yes, it is. You two seem to be getting along great lately and now dinner. What if he wants to get back together?" My spirits nearly shot through the roof at the possibility of a Finn-and-Molly reconciliation.

"Poppy," she sighed, "this is just a dinner for the kids. We're not getting back together."

"But you might."

She shook her head. "No. We won't. Finn is coming over for dinner tonight so we can show the kids that we can all get along, even if we don't all live in the same house anymore."

"Oh." My spirits came crashing down. "Sorry."

"It's okay. We had a long talk a while ago and decided that we need to do a better job of putting the past behind us. We're divorced but that doesn't mean we can't be friends."

"Friends?"

"Friends," she declared with a nod.

I didn't buy Molly's confidence. This friendship idea was

Finn's—I'd bet the restaurant on it. "Is that really what you want?"

"I'll take anything he'll give me just to get us past these awful last few months. He's looking at me again. He's starting to talk to me. And at the end of the day, if it makes it easier on the kids, then I'll do whatever I have to do."

Molly would put her heart through a meat grinder if that meant making Kali and Max smile. "Those kids are lucky to have such a wonderful mom."

She smiled. "Finn and I love them so much, and they deserve better than we've given them lately."

"Don't be so hard on yourself. You're doing your best."

"We can do better." She stepped away from my side to take a seat on one of the stools. "I actually have you to thank for Finn's change lately."

"Me? What did I do?"

"A lot, really. The night of the paint fight last month was the night he came over to talk about us being friends again. The kids had so much fun that day, laughing and playing. Maybe it was because we were there for you or for Jamie—I don't know— but that was the first day in a long time that he acted like himself. No anger or resentment. Just the Finn I remembered."

It had been like old times with them that day. We'd all had fun, and I was thrilled that Jamie's list had given their family one day of joy. I just wished they could get over the past and find that joy every day. Did they even know how much they were missing?

Molly started fiddling with the towel Finn had used to dry his face. "I think he finally clued into how much the tension between us was impacting the kids."

"He's only got himself to blame for that. You're always nice when he's around, even when he's acting like a jerk."

"Don't blame him. He's just hurt." Molly always defended

Finn's bad behavior, but I wasn't quite as generous with my loveable, yet infuriating older brother.

"So you guys are going to start doing family dinners?"

"That's the plan. Dinner a couple times a month. Trips to the museum. Things where the kids are the focal point and they can see us getting along."

"Well . . . I guess the paint fight was more of a success than I'd thought. Maybe Jamie was watching down on us and was getting sick of Finn's attitude too."

Molly gave me a sad smile. "It definitely helped him open his eyes. But like I said, you're the one I have to thank."

"Because I filled the water balloons with paint?"

She shook her head. "Because you invited Cole."

"I know Finn has a man-crush on Cole, but what does that have to do with his attitude adjustment?"

Molly set the towel aside to look me in the eyes. "Finn's proud of you. We both are. You've overcome more than either of us can fathom. Losing Jamie, you could have lost yourself too. But you didn't. You could have shut down and pushed everyone away—no one would have blamed you for it—but you didn't. You put the pieces of your heart back together and are strong enough to trust Cole not to break it again. When Finn came over the night of the paint fight, he told me he wants that too. He wants to put the past behind us."

Up went my spirits again. *I knew it!* Finn did want to work things out with Molly. He wanted to put their family back together. He was finally seeing how much he was missing. Molly was downplaying dinner, maybe she didn't want to have false hope, but I think it was Finn's way of slowly making amends.

I just wished he'd told me about it. I would have skipped that second glass of water to his face.

Molly read the hope on my face but shook her head. "Finn

wants to move forward, but not with me. He told me that he's ready to start dating again."

And just like that, the hope I'd been clinging to for months and months was gone, leaving an empty hole inside my chest.

"No." My voice cracked. Finn and Molly loved each other. They belonged together. "But . . . you're Finn and Molly."

Molly's eyes flooded. "Not anymore. Now he's single. And I'm a *cheater*."

That word. Damn that word! Months and months of restraint—of being neutral and supportive—fizzled with a word I hated just as much as *widow*. "I hate that word! Why do you always say it? God, you toss it out all the time and it's driving me crazy!"

"Me?" She jerked back, and the sadness on her face twisted into anger. "That's your word."

"My word?" My mouth fell open. "You think *I'm* a cheater?"

"What? No—"

"So all this time—all this time you've been telling me to go for it with Cole, but deep down you really think I'm *cheating* on Jamie. Nice."

She'd pretended to be so supportive, but now I knew how she really felt.

I pushed away from the table, tears flooding my eyes, but before I could run for the office, Molly shot her hand across the table. "Poppy, wait! That's not what I meant."

My feet stopped as I met her gaze.

"You don't remember, do you?" she whispered.

What was she talking about? "Remember what?"

"The day I told you that I'd had a one-night stand, you called me a cheater. You said, 'How could you? I never thought my best friend would be a *cheater*.' "

I gasped and slapped my free hand over my mouth. I'd been

so upset, so angry at Finn and Molly both, that I'd said a lot that day I hadn't meant. And Molly had been holding on to that awful word all this time.

"Oh, Molly. Oh my god. I'm so sorry. I didn't mean it like that. You're not a cheater."

She shrugged. "Sure I am."

"No, you're not. Not even close. You and Finn were all but divorced at that point. And you were so hurt. It was a mistake, not cheating."

Molly studied my face, taken back by my declaration.

Had she spent all these months wrapping herself in my haphazard label, convincing herself she was a cheater? Had she been thinking less of herself all this time?

I wanted to go back in time and slap myself for being so careless with my words. For so deeply hurting my best friend and sister. But since that wasn't possible, I wasn't letting her leave this kitchen until she realized the truth.

Moving to her side, I lifted her hand off the table and pressed it between mine. "You are *not* a cheater."

"I am." Her chin started to quiver as she picked at a spot on the table with her free hand. "You said so yourself. Finn thinks it, even if he's never said it. I am a cheater. That's who I've become."

"Molly, please look at me."

Her eyes, swimming in tears, tipped up.

"You're not a cheater. I don't think that. No one does. Not even Finn."

"He does."

I shook my head. "He doesn't. Never, not once, has he used that word around me. Has he ever said it to you?"

"No," she whispered.

"Because you're not. He might be hurt and still trying to figure things out, but Finn would never accuse you of cheating.

He knows that you both made your mistakes. And I was wrong to call you a cheater. So, *so* wrong. And I'm so, *so* sorry."

Her focus turned back to the table as she considered my apology. "Maybe you're right. Maybe I just latched on to that word as a way to keep punishing myself. I don't know. Regardless of what I call it, mistake or cheating, I'll always be sorry."

I let go of her hand to tuck her into my side and rest my cheek to her hair. "I'm sorry. For everything."

She leaned further into my side. "I appreciate that. It's time to let it go and move on. That's what Finn wants. I should try and do the same."

We stayed still, listening to the hum of the appliances and the noise filtering through the door from the dining room. And, though her heart was still hurting, I knew that after today, I wouldn't be hearing the word cheater again.

I unwound my arm and leaned back against the table. "Why didn't you tell me about your conversation with Finn sooner? The paint fight was last month."

She caught a tear before it could smudge her mascara. "I just needed some time to process it all. Saying it out loud makes it real."

"I'm sorry, Molly-moo," I whispered.

"Me too." She sniffled, fighting hard not to cry.

And if I cried, she'd cry too. *Breathe.* I needed to be strong for Molly. I gripped the table behind me, sucking in some air as I reined in my emotions. But on my exhale, my heart sank. I was just so . . . disappointed. In my brother. In my friend. In this whole situation.

These two were wasting love. They were throwing it all away because of some mistakes. Finn hadn't learned anything from me. He hadn't been paying attention at all these last five years. Because if he'd really been paying attention, he'd realize just how lucky he was.

He had someone he loved right *here*. Right here, waiting to love him back. He could hug her. He could kiss her. He could tell her things—things I'd never get to say to Jamie again.

Instead, he wanted to date.

Disappointment shifted into anger as I pictured Finn out with another woman. Dating.

Fuck dating. Fuck this whole thing. I loved my brother fiercely but he was making a huge mistake. And Molly didn't need him if he didn't see her for the flawed, beautiful, wonderful woman she was.

"You'll be okay," I declared.

Her shoulders pulled back. "Yes, I will. I have two beautiful children. I love my job. I get to work with my best friend every day. I'll be more than okay. I just need to get through this."

I reached out and took her hand. "Minute by minute."

"Minute by minute."

"Does this mean you're going to start dating too?" Just the words made my stomach tense. In my eyes, Molly would always be Finn's.

She shook her head. "If Finn wants to move on, I won't hold him back, but I don't have any interest in other men. Contrary to my mistake, he's the only man in my heart."

"I'm sorry."

She gave me a sad smile and did what Molly did best— steered the conversation away from Finn. "Why would you ever think I'd accuse you of cheating on Jamie with Cole? You realize how ridiculous that sounds, don't you?"

I ran both hands over my ponytail as I sighed. "Yes. Sorry. It just came out." Apparently, I had a really bad habit of spewing nonsense when I was angry.

"Is there something going on we should talk about?"

"No." I shook my head. "I just . . . things have changed so

much with Cole. Between the kissing and sex. It's just an adjustment." One I didn't regret, but still, an adjustment.

"It's a big change."

"A good one, though." I reached across the table for her hand. "I'm sorry for getting angry."

She nodded. "Me too."

The kitchen door swung open, interrupting our conversation as Helen carried in a tub of dirty dishes.

"I'll do those for you, Helen." Molly sprang off her stool, forcing a smile as she took the tub from Helen. Without another word, she went to the sink and started washing.

Our conversation was over.

Finn and Molly Alcott were over.

I left Molly to her chore, returning with Helen to the front. I took up one of the back-corner tables and rolled silverware, attempting to process my swirling emotions.

Disappointment filled the empty hole where I'd once had hope. It settled heavily along with anger and sadness.

And loss.

Finn and Molly had started dating at the same time Jamie and I had gotten together. I couldn't think of a party in college where the three of them hadn't been by my side. Our foursome had done everything together. Made countless memories together.

But everything from back then was gone now. Jamie. His parents. Now Finn and Molly. *Gone.*

My mood was nearly black by the time I rolled the last bundle of silverware. I did my best to hide my feelings from Molly, but when she finally left to pick up the kids, I was relieved to see her go.

I plastered on a smile for the dinner crowd, but as customers began to dwindle, I took Helen up on her offer to close. I fled from the restaurant, wanting nothing more than a beer, some time cuddling with my puppy and Cole.

Driving straight to his house, I hoped he'd hold me for a while, but for the second time today, my hopes were dashed. When I used the remote he'd given me last month for the garage, I was greeted with an empty space where his truck should have been.

No Cole. No Nazboo.

But at least there was beer.

I went inside and grabbed one of my wheat beers from the fridge. I drank half the bottle just standing in the kitchen before going upstairs to take a long hot shower, hoping it would wash away my bad mood before Cole got home.

With the bottle tipped to my lips, I wasn't paying attention as I walked into Cole's bathroom. So when my feet got tangled in something on the floor, I let out a gurgled cry as I choked and tripped. I managed to keep my feet, stumbling but staying upright. However, the same could not be said for my beer. The bottle dropped from my hands and shattered on the marble tile, sending fizz everywhere.

"Grrr!" My yell echoed in the bathroom as I balled my hands into fists. "Hang up your damn towels!"

I spun around and marched downstairs to get a broom and dustpan. With fast, angry strokes, I swept up the broken glass and then used Cole's towel to mop up the beer. I was just dumping the glass shards into the kitchen trash can when the door leading to the garage opened and Cole stepped inside, carrying Nazboo.

"Hey." He smiled. "You're here early. Slow night?"

I tossed the dustpan on the counter. "Would it kill you to hang up your towel in the morning instead of tossing it on the floor for me to trip over?"

The smile on his face disappeared as he blinked at me

twice. Nazboo wiggled wildly in his arms, so he set her down. She romped over and licked my bare feet.

But not even my cute puppy snapped me out of my anger. I let her lick while I planted my hands on my hips and glared at Cole.

He ignored my scowl and took a step toward me. "What happened?"

I threw out an arm. "I went upstairs to take a shower but I tripped on one of your towels and broke the beer bottle I was carrying."

"Did you get hurt?"

"No, I didn't get hurt. This time. But what about tomorrow? Or the next day?" With flailing arms, I let go of a rant that had more to do with my emotional state than Cole's towel. "You're a slob. You leave shit all over the house and I'm sick to death of cleaning it up."

"Slow down." His jaw clenched as the gentle vanished from his voice. "I don't expect you to pick up after me. But I'm not a slob. I'm just not a clean freak."

"You think I'm a clean freak?" I didn't give him a chance to respond. I bent down and scooped up Nazboo, then marched toward the door. "Fine. I'll be a clean freak in my own house."

I didn't make it two steps before two strong arms banded around my shoulders, pulling me back.

One second Nazboo was in my arms and then she was back on the floor. The next second, Cole spun me around and slammed his mouth on mine.

I fought his kiss, keeping my lips pursed as he ran his tongue along the seam. But with every touch, the fire he stoked melted my resolve.

He growled against my lips—the vibration sending a shudder down my back—then his arms banded around me so he could hoist me up and haul me to the counter.

The cold from the marble seeped through my jeans, but it did nothing to temper the hot throb at my core. My fingers plunged into Cole's hair, tugging and pulling his thick, dark strands. As I slanted my face, he took control of my mouth.

I moaned as his hands ran down my sides, pawing my breasts through my T-shirt and bra, then trailing down to the button on my jeans. There was no fumbling when it came to Cole's hands. He flicked the button with one twist while sliding my zipper down with the other.

Five seconds was all it took him to unfasten my jeans, fist the waistband and yank them down over my ass and thighs. He did it all without breaking his mouth from mine. As his hands came to the hem of my shirt to whip it off, I kicked my jeans off my calves and onto the floor.

Naked except for my bra, Cole shoved my knees apart. His rough grip on my thighs pooled the desire between my legs. He released his hard clasp on my thighs, and with the lightest touch, he traced his fingers from my knees to my hips. I loved when he did this—when he'd alternate between reckless abandon and measured deliberation. The combination left me limp and pliable under those large hands. Completely at his mercy.

His fingertips changed directions, feathering down to my slit, as his tongue plundered my mouth. When he dipped his middle finger into my wetness, I moaned into his mouth. When he added his index finger, stroking me on the inside at the same time his thumb found my clit, I broke away from his lips, barely able to breathe.

"Cole. I need you."

His answer was to plant his lips on the side of my neck and suck. Hard.

As his fingers worked in and out, my head lulled to the side. My legs trembled as they dangled off the counter, and with every stroke of his long fingers, he pushed me farther and farther to the edge. I was just about to come when Cole's mouth left my skin and his fingers slid out.

My whimper just made him smile. He took a step back as I reached for him, smirking as he brought his hand to his mouth. Then, with his green eyes locked on mine, he sucked me off his fingers.

"Oh my god." My pussy clenched.

Cole's smirk grew as his fingers popped free from his mouth. Off came his shirt, the shallows between his peaked abs more pronounced than normal. He'd probably been at karate when I'd gotten here, working those muscles hard. But I didn't let his abs distract me for long. Instead I followed the lines down and waited as Cole jerked off his jeans and black briefs.

When his hard cock sprang free, my pussy clenched again. I was so on edge—literally almost falling off the counter—I'd be coming around him by his third stroke.

It only took him two.

With one big stride forward, Cole grabbed my hips, bringing me onto his cock as he thrust inside, stretching me with a luscious burn.

When he pulled out and slammed back in, I cried out, the kitchen filling with sound as my orgasm washed over me in pulsing waves. My heels pressed into the cabinets underneath me as my toes curled in ecstasy.

"My pretty Poppy." Cole ran his tongue along the shell of my ear, sending tingles down my neck.

I moaned again, clenching around Cole as his strokes picked up speed. My arms held on to his shoulders as he pounded hard, erasing all of the bad from my day. Because right here in this kitchen, all I cared about was us. Cole's body inside mine. Him inside my heart.

He didn't hold back as he kept thrusting. He didn't take his time to build me up again—he was probably saving energy for a second round later. Cole squeezed his eyes shut and found his own release, spilling his hot come inside me as he tipped his head back and roared my name.

My arms wrapped around his neck as he fell into my chest. "We finally broke in the kitchen."

He chuckled and held me tighter. "You're not a clean freak."

I kissed the top of his shoulder. "You're not a slob."

We stayed like that for a few moments, holding one another while Nazboo was off somewhere exploring the house. When she came back into the kitchen, Cole leaned back to meet my eyes.

"I'm sorry you tripped. I'll work on the towel thing if you promise to work on the gum thing."

"Gum thing?"

"You smack your gum. It drives me crazy."

"What?" My eyes got wider. "I do not smack my gum." *Do I?*

He grinned and kissed my forehead. "Do you still want to take a shower?"

"No." I slumped against his chest. "I just want to go to bed."

"All right." He slid out and went to the towel drawer for a fresh washcloth. After he'd dampened it with warm water, he came back and cleaned me up. Then he scooped me up in his arms and carried me through the living room toward the stairs. Nazboo followed behind.

"We need to let her out."

"I'll do it."

"Thanks." I rested my head against his shoulder as he took me upstairs. Carefully setting me in bed, he went to the closet, coming back wearing a new pair of briefs and tossing me one of his T-shirts. I pulled it on and snuggled into bed while he went downstairs to take care of Nazboo and kennel her for the night.

When Cole returned, he brought all of our clothes with him, and I smiled as he dumped them into the hamper instead of on the floor of the walk-in closet. I kept my smile as he climbed into bed and tucked me against his naked chest.

"Do you want to tell me why you picked a fight with me tonight?"

I snuggled deeper. "My day went downhill after I left you at the courthouse."

"I gathered that. What happened?"

As much as I hated to talk about other people while we were in bed, I also didn't want to shut Cole out. I didn't want him to think that he was the cause of my frustration, so I sighed and admitted why I'd been so upset. "Me and Molly kind of got into a fight."

"Why?"

"Because I said something stupid. And because she and Finn aren't getting back together."

"Did you think they were?"

I nodded. "I had hope. Now it's gone."

"Sorry, beautiful." He kissed my hair. "But don't give up hope. They were right for one another at the time. They've got two awesome kids to prove it. It's just, maybe the person they'll be right for in the future is still to come."

I closed my eyes and let out a breath as I contemplated his words.

Cole might be the most insightful person I'd ever met. It made him a great cop. A good man. The perfect one for me. And he was right. Just because Finn and Molly weren't together, didn't mean they wouldn't find happiness with someone new. A happiness that would be the lasting kind, this time around.

Just like the kind of happiness I'd found with Cole.

I hadn't understood it earlier at the restaurant—I'd been too upset to see things from Finn's perspective—but now I understood why my brother wanted to date again. He knew he'd never get over Molly's affair, and he didn't want to spend his life alone.

He wanted to find love again too.

I snaked my arm across Cole's waist and hugged him tight, breathing in the smell of his skin. "I'm glad you like to cuddle."

"I don't."

I shot off his chest as my chin fell open. "What?"

"I don't like to cuddle. Never have, not even with my mom when I was a kid." He smiled at my wide eyes, then tugged me back down. "But I do like to cuddle with you."

I collapsed back onto his chest. "Tonight has been . . . informative. Is there anything else I should know besides the gum smacking and cuddling?"

"I'll keep you posted."

"Thanks, Detective." I patted his stomach, then began playing with the hairs on his chest. "How was your day?"

"Long," he sighed, drawing circles on my hip. "But good."

Cole had been working so hard lately. He'd get up just as early as I would and head into work while I went to the restaurant to bake before six. He was swamped with the drug task force and the other cases he had on his plate. But in these recent months, I'd avoided asking him about Jamie's murder case.

I didn't want him to think I didn't have faith in his investigative skills. I didn't want him to think I had false hope. But I was curious. I'd spent years getting updates from Detective Simmons—albeit the same update—every month. And though I trusted Cole to tell me if he'd learned anything, tonight, curiosity beat out patience.

"Have you, um, made any progress on the murder case?" I tensed as I waited for his response.

Cole's hand on my hip froze. "There isn't much I can share, but we're doing our best. And we are working on it."

"Okay." His limited update was enough. "I've been thinking about something for a couple of weeks. I was wondering if you could do me a favor. A police kind of favor."

"Okay," he drawled.

"I want you to find the daughter of the woman that was killed with Jamie. The cashier."

"Poppy—"

I lifted my head and cut him off. "I just want to know if she's okay. I don't need details or anything like that. Just a yes or no that she's okay."

His hand came to my face. "Why?"

I shrugged. "I've thought about her from time to time over the years. I've wondered where she was and how she dealt with the loss of her mother. I guess finishing Jamie's list, letting go and getting on with my life has made me wonder if she's found some closure too. I don't have any power to find the man who killed them and make him pay, but I can at least make sure that her life hasn't been ruined. Would you help me check on her?"

His thumb stroked my cheek. "In a heartbeat."

CHAPTER NINETEEN

48TH BIRTHDAY: BUY A STRANGER A CAR

POPPY

"You two kiss like teenagers."

I scowled at Molly from behind the office desk. "We do not."

"Really?" She leaned a hip against the doorframe. "Then why are you always putting on lip balm? Your lips are chapped because you're always making out with your hot cop boyfriend. Not that I blame you. If he were mine, I'd kiss him all the time too."

Cole had just left the restaurant after coming here for lunch, and just like he always did when he visited, he'd given me a long kiss when he'd arrived and another before he'd left. And twice in between, just because.

Okay, maybe we were as bad as teenagers.

"My lips are chapped because of the weather," I lied. "It's dry this time of year." I looked down at the paperwork on my desk and rubbed my lips together. They were still puffy from Cole's kiss. "Though, he is a *great* kisser."

Cole and I had been together for two months now, and things between us were as hot as ever. We did kiss all the time. And the sex? We were going at it like rock stars. In fact, he'd fucked me right here in this office after I'd closed down the restaurant last night. Not that I'd be sharing that little detail with Molly.

"What are you working on?" Molly stepped farther into the office, taking the chair across the desk.

Our positions were switched from our normal office conversations. Usually she was the one sitting on this side of the desk, working on payroll or bookkeeping, while I was in the guest chair.

"I was just looking at those new income projections you put together."

She smiled. "Things are going so well. Better than I'd ever expected."

Sales at The Maysen Jar were just as high now as they'd been when we'd opened. In the five months I'd been in business, I'd learned a lot. I was better at ordering bulk supplies without getting too much or too little. I had refined the menu so it only included items that sold consistently. And much to Molly's delight, I'd learned to delegate and trust my small staff to run the place when I wasn't around. My days off weren't limited to once a month but once a week, and I'd figured out an evening schedule that let me spend quality time with Cole and Nazboo.

Molly pulled the draft schedule from the desk and glanced over the chart. "I think I'm going to ask Helen to come in and work on Saturday with me. She's looking for more hours to save up for the holidays."

"You're sure you don't mind working this weekend?" Molly normally took Saturday and Sunday off to spend time with the kids, but Cole and I had plans next weekend to do another list item, so she was covering the restaurant.

"Not at all. You haven't taken off a whole weekend since your Glacier trip. You deserve the break. Besides, since Finn has the kids this weekend, I'll be bored out of my mind at home. I'm glad I can come to work."

"Thank you."

She put down the schedule and leaned her elbows on the desk. "You're almost done with the list. How are you feeling about finishing it?"

How was I feeling? "I'm . . . okay. I guess I'm just at peace with it all."

"Good. Then you got what you wanted."

I smiled. "Yeah, I did."

Soon, I'd mark the last few check boxes from Jamie's journal and put it away. Jamie would always be a part of my heart, but going through his birthday list had given me an outlet to say good-bye.

"Have you decided who gets a free car?" Molly asked.

"No." I slumped onto the desk. Why Jamie had wanted to buy a stranger a car, I had no clue. "How do you pick a stranger and buy them a car? If I walk up to someone and say, 'Hey you! I want to buy you a car,' they'll think I'm crazy."

"I'll do it."

I sat up. "You will? Really?"

She shrugged. "Sure, I'll pick someone."

"That would be great. I'm too chicken."

"How do you want to pay for it? You're not going to just hand over a wad of cash, are you?"

I shook my head. "No, I want to make sure the person gets a car. I was planning on just financing with the dealership. Then once I sell the house, I can pay it back."

"Any progress on finding a rental?"

I sighed. "No. Honestly, I haven't even looked lately." I'd been spending so much time at Cole's house, moving had stalled. But I needed to resume my rental search again.

Jamie and I had been smart when we'd bought our house so the mortgage wasn't much, but I could use the money from the equity I'd built up over the years. I still needed to reimburse Cole for what he'd spent on Jamie's truck and soon I'd have a car payment for a car that I wouldn't be driving. Since my house sat empty most of the time, downsizing to a smaller apartment made sense.

Except what I really wanted to do was just live at Cole's.

These last two months, it had become *home*. Most of my clothes were already hanging in his closet, my kitchen appliances had all migrated to his cupboards instead of my own, and his bed was my bed. I doubted I'd even be able to sleep in my old room now.

"I don't know why you won't just move in with Cole," Molly muttered.

I sighed. "Because he hasn't asked." I wanted him to ask me, not feel pressured because I wanted to offload my house.

"Asked what?"

My eyes shot to the door as Cole walked into the office. "Nothing!" I shot Molly a *don't you dare* look.

She rolled her eyes and mouthed, *Fine.*

"What are you doing here?" I stood from the desk. "Did you forget something at lunch?"

He grinned. "I have a surprise for you. Grab your coat and come out front."

Molly and I both rushed to the coat hooks by the door, then followed Cole through the kitchen.

Helen was behind the counter this afternoon—studying, since we didn't have many customers. When she saw us come through the swinging door on Cole's heels, she slammed her textbook shut and jogged around the counter to catch up. Judging by the huge smile on her face, she must have been clued into Cole's surprise.

As we walked through the restaurant, Cole reached back and took my hand. His huge smile was infectious as he pulled me outside and around the corner of the building.

My free hand covered my gasp when I spotted the surprise.

Jamie's truck—gleaming, midnight blue and accented with polished chrome—was parked in the lot.

"It's done?"

Cole handed me a set of keys. "It's done. What do you think?"

"It's perfect." I was awestruck that he'd transformed an old yellow heap into this beautiful classic. I grabbed Cole's face with both hands and yanked it down for a hard, fast kiss. "Thank you."

He smiled against my mouth. "You're welcome. Go check it out."

A squeak escaped my lips as I jogged to the driver's side. I climbed in, filling my lungs with the clean, new smell. My hands stroked the buttery leather of the new cream bench seat before gripping the matching steering wheel. I ran my fingers across the dashboard and down to the new radio. The floor, the door panels, the ceiling—everything was new.

Cole had even replaced the old plastic visors.

I flipped one down, surprised when a photo fell onto my lap. It was the one Cole had found months ago. Cole had kept Jamie in his truck. I smiled at the picture and put it back into the visor just as the passenger door opened.

"Well?" Cole asked.

"It's incredible. Thank you."

"It was fun." He ran his hand over the seat, inspecting his work. "And it didn't take as much work as I'd thought. The engine was in good shape. My buddy at the body shop did a lot. Mostly I just put in new parts."

"You're not giving yourself enough credit. This truck has taken a lot of your evenings lately."

He shrugged. "I enjoyed it. It made me realize I need to find a hobby. Something to get my mind off work."

"Like what?"

"I don't know. Maybe I'll find another old car and fix it up."

"Can I pick the color?"

He grinned. "Of course."

I ran my hands over the steering wheel again. "I pick black." It was his favorite color.

Cole climbed into the truck and took out his phone, aiming the camera my way. "There. Now you've got your picture for the day." A picture of me in Jamie's truck was far better than the selfie I'd attempted this morning. "How about a quick drive?"

"Where to?"

He shrugged. "Anywhere."

I turned the key and smiled, then I drove us around the block and parked behind the restaurant.

When Cole gave me a funny look, I just shut off the truck and slid across the bench seat, showing him with my lips how much I appreciated his work on this project.

By the time we broke apart, I needed more lip balm.

———

NOT LONG AFTER Cole went back to work, Molly left the restaurant to run some errands before she had to pick up Kali and Max from daycare. It was just me and Helen for the rest of the afternoon and evening, so while she managed the counter, I was in the kitchen, chopping vegetables for my chicken noodle soup.

It was supposed to get cold tonight and I thought soup would be a hit with the dinner crowd. Plus, it was one of Cole's favorites. He was coming back here for dinner and I wanted to do something special for him, given all he'd done to fix up Jamie's truck—which was parked out back.

Cole had taken my car back to the station so I could drive Jamie's truck home tonight. As soon as we closed up The Maysen Jar, I was planning on driving around for a bit, listening to Jamie's favorite country station, then finding a spot to park and cross that item off his list.

"Hey, Poppy?" Helen poked her head into the kitchen.

"What's up?" I didn't look up from the carrots on my cutting board.

"That girl is back."

I dropped my knife and wiped my hands on my apron as I hurried to the door, peeking around Helen.

Sitting in the same seat she always did—tucked into the far back corner of the room—was a young girl who'd been coming into the restaurant regularly for the past few weeks. She always came at the same time, around three in the afternoon, and always wore the same clothes, faded black leggings and an olive-green coat that was two sizes too big and hung to her knees. On her feet were scuffed black ballet flats.

But even though her clothes were old and worn, she'd put effort into her appearance. Her face didn't need much makeup —her light brown skin was flawless—but she'd dusted her cheeks with a bit of pink to match the shadow she'd used to highlight her large caramel eyes. Her long hair hung nearly to her waist, and she'd added some product to tame the frizz from her ash-brown curls.

"Did she order anything?"

Helen shook her head. "No. She just took one of the free cookies and asked for a glass of water."

I frowned. The girl never ordered anything. Instead, she came and sat in that corner, attempting to blend into the wall as she read the same tattered book or worked on homework.

I didn't care that she wasn't a paying customer. I cared that she was young—probably only sixteen—and she seemed to be surviving on my free cookies alone. She'd gotten visibly thinner in just the time she'd been coming to The Maysen Jar.

But whenever any of us would approach and offer her something, she'd politely decline and leave the restaurant. So yesterday, Molly and I had told our staff to tell us immediately the next time the girl came in.

"Do me a favor," I told Helen. "Go put a chicken potpie and apple pie in the toaster oven, then make a vanilla latte. I'm going to get this soup on the stove and then I'll be out."

While Helen went to prepare the food, I hurried to finish my chopping and toss the veggies into my chicken stock. With the burner set to simmer, I washed my hands and untied my apron. When I came out front, Helen had everything on a tray.

"Thank you." I took the tray. "Wish me luck."

She crossed her fingers and smiled.

The girl noticed me when I hit the halfway point of the restaurant. She sat straighter, shoving a paper into her textbook before stuffing them both in a canvas backpack.

So I picked up my pace before she could escape. "Hi." I set down the tray just as she stood from her chair. "Please don't go. Please."

She eyed me warily but sat back down.

"Thank you." I took the chair across from her. "My name is Poppy. This is my restaurant."

The girl looked to the food, swallowing hard, then back up to my face, but she didn't speak.

"I was hoping you could do me a favor. I made a few changes to my piecrust recipe," I lied. "Maybe you could try these and give me your honest opinion. Tell me what you think."

"Oh, um, I don't—"

"I know it's after lunch and you might not be hungry, but even just a couple bites would help. And it's free, of course. Taste testers don't have to pay. What do you say? Lend me your taste buds?"

Her eyes dropped to the food again, and this time, she licked her lips. "Okay."

Victory! I held back my smile and stood. "I'll let you eat without me hovering. Just don't leave before you tell me what you think."

She nodded and waited for me to step back before she picked up her napkin and silverware.

I turned and walked right back to the kitchen, resisting the urge to look over my shoulder. Then I stood in the middle of the kitchen, counting to one hundred, before I came back out to the counter, pretending to take inventory of the display case.

"Is she eating?" I whispered to Helen.

"Yeah."

I sighed. "Good. I'm going to go make the noodles for the soup so they can dry for a while. When she's close to done, come and get me."

Helen nodded. "You got it."

I'd never made noodles so fast in my life. Nervous energy poured from my fingertips as I kneaded the dough, and by the time Helen came back to get me from the kitchen, I had the noodles all rolled and cut.

With a towel in my hand, I walked back to the girl's table and smiled. She'd finished everything except for the vanilla latte, which had gone untouched. "What did you think?"

"It was really good."

"Great!" I cheered and sat down. "I'll keep those changes then. Did you not like the coffee?"

She dropped her eyes to her lap. "I, um . . . can't have coffee."

"Are you allergic?"

It was a stupid question. The minute I asked, my eyes wandered to her stomach.

Her coat, which she'd always kept closed, was now unbuttoned. Underneath she was wearing a fitted black shirt that molded to her rounded belly.

"Oh!" I smiled wider, hoping to hide my shock that this young girl was pregnant. "I'm sorry. I didn't realize. How about a hot chocolate instead?"

"That's okay."

The girl spoke so quietly, I leaned my arms on the table to hear her better. "Are you sure? I make the cocoa mix from scratch. I'd be happy to make you one . . . I'm sorry. I didn't catch your name."

She pulled her coat tight around her shoulders without an answer or eye contact.

Was she afraid of me? Or was she worried she was in trouble? I didn't want to scare her away from coming back, but I also didn't want her to leave before I got some answers. This girl might not be asking for help, but she needed it.

"You're not in trouble." I gently placed my hand on the table. "You're welcome here anytime. If all you want are cookies and water, that's fine with me. Take as much as you'd like and stay as long as you'd like. I'll even mark this table reserved for you."

Her head was still ducked, but I caught a faint nod.

"And if you don't want to talk, that's fine. I'll leave you

alone, but I'd like to get to know you. I like to know all of my regular customers."

I waited. And waited. But she still didn't move. I was about to give up when her face lifted and she gave me a shy smile.

"Belle."

"Belle. That's a beautiful name." I held out my hand. "I'm Poppy Maysen."

She took my hand and looked around the room. "Maysen. Spelled like the restaurant?"

"Yep." I rubbed my hands over my arms, pretending to be cold. "It's kind of chilly in here. I think I'm going to make one of those hot chocolates for me. Sit tight, I'll whip one up for you too."

Before she could protest, I stood from my chair and grabbed her tray, taking it back to the kitchen. Then I went behind the counter and got out the whole milk. I didn't need the added fat, but Belle did.

Helen came to my side as I started the steamer. "How's it going?"

"Progress, I think. Did you notice she was pregnant?"

She shook her head.

"Would you pack up some stuff to go? I don't know if she'll take it, but I can try. Maybe do stuff that will last a couple of days or is easy to reheat, like stew and a mac 'n' cheese."

"Got it. I'll throw in a salad too for some vitamins."

While Helen made a to-go bag, I whipped up two hot chocolates in our largest mugs. Then I carried them back to Belle's table and sat. "Here you go. Cheers!"

I took a long sip of my cocoa, relieved as she did the same.

"So, Belle. How did you find this place? Do you live close by?"

She shook her head. "No, I heard some girls at school talking about it."

DEVNEY PERRY

"Do you go to Bozeman High?"

She nodded and took another sip of hot chocolate.

"Is this your senior year? Is that why you get out so early?"

"No, I'm a junior. But my last class is just study hall and the teacher doesn't make us stay if we have good grades."

A junior. Which meant she was probably only sixteen years old. Sixteen. Hungry. And pregnant. I hoped that she was at least getting meals at school.

"Do you have a favorite subject?"

"I like home ec."

"No way! That was my favorite class too. I loved the cooking, obviously. What's your favorite part?"

She smiled—the first genuine smile I'd seen—and it was stunning. "I love the cooking too."

"Have you ever made homemade egg noodles?"

She shook her head.

"Well, I'm making some today for chicken noodle soup. Want to help?"

She nearly dropped her mug at my offer. "Really?"

"Let me show you my favorite part of the restaurant." I winked. "Follow me to the kitchen."

An hour later, I had three times the egg noodles I needed for the soup and I was letting Belle mix a batch of triple berry pie filling. I'd done most of the talking in the past hour, telling her tidbits about myself and my cooking experiences, but as we'd started with the berries, she'd finally begun to open up.

I'd learned that she was sixteen, like I'd guessed, and lived with her dad. I also found out that she'd been walking here after school on the days when she needed a quiet place to do her homework.

And that she was definitely eating for two.

"How far along are you?"

"Six months, I think." Her shoulders folded inward as she whispered, "I'm not exactly sure."

"Have you been to the doctor yet?"

"I don't have insurance."

Most sixteen-year-old kids didn't. "What about your parents?"

She shook her head.

When she shied away even farther, I backed off the questions. I'd made a lot of progress with Belle today, and I hoped I'd earned her trust this afternoon. Maybe in time, she'd be more open to sharing about her life.

"Have you ever made corn bread before?"

She looked up and nodded. "Once in class."

"All right." I dug out my recipe card from the stack on the table and handed it over. "Show me what you've got."

By the time five o'clock rolled around, meal prep for the next two days was nearly complete. While I'd been distracted—trying to get tidbits of information from Belle—she'd focused completely on cooking, cranking out every recipe card I handed her with utter perfection.

"Thanks for all your help." I handed her a towel to dry her hands. "You're welcome here anytime. You're a natural in the kitchen." So much so that I was going to talk to Molly about hiring her part-time. At least that way, we could guarantee she was feeding herself and her baby.

"Thank you. I had so much fun." Belle beamed until she glanced at the clock above the sink. "But I'd better get home." The word "home" sounded like she was swallowing nails.

As she pulled on her coat and slung her backpack over her shoulders, I went to the kitchen door and surveyed the restaurant. Helen was helping a customer at the register and a couple of the tables were full, but we still had an hour before the dinner rush.

My eyes wandered to the windows up front. It was getting dark, the winter light not lasting long these days, and it would be cold for Belle to walk. The wind was picking up too.

"Belle, let me give you a ride so you don't freeze."

She shook her head, pulling on a pair of mittens that had seen better days. "I'll be okay."

"Please?" I begged. "I'll worry about you all night."

She walked by me and through the door, but stopped when her gaze hit the windows and she shivered. Her beautiful eyes came to mine. "Are you sure?"

"Yes." I smiled. "Come on, I'm parked out back."

I told Helen I was taking Belle home and left her in charge of the restaurant while I grabbed my coat from the office. When I opened the back door, the cold air hit me hard in the face and it only took seconds for my nose and ears to sting. I had no idea how far away Belle lived, but just a block in this weather and she would have turned into an icicle.

"I like your truck," Belle said as she climbed inside, running a hand along the leather seat.

"Thank you." I turned the key and fired up the heat. "So where to?"

Belle gave me directions as we drove, and as we got closer and closer to a sketchy part of town, the knot in my stomach tightened. Had she been walking home in the evenings all this way? Through this neighborhood? We were miles from the restaurant. We were miles from her school.

By the time I pulled into her trailer park, I'd made a decision. Molly didn't need to pick a stranger to receive a free car.

I was buying a vehicle for Belle.

"It's the last one on the right." She pointed down the dead-end road that led through the trailer park.

Belle's arms were wrapped around her belly as she huddled against the door. She did not want me seeing where she lived.

The only reason she was letting me drive her home was utter desperation.

Just as the last trailer down the road came into view, Belle's arms shot out. "Stop!"

I slammed on the brakes, jolting us both forward. "What?" I turned to her for an explanation.

"Can you just park here for a sec?"

"Um . . . sure." I pulled to the side of the road.

Her trailer was three down from where we were parked, close enough to see the siding was falling apart and two of the windows were covered with plywood. I was assessing the shiny black car out front—one that was much too expensive for the owner of that trailer—when a man stepped through Belle's front door.

The guy was tall, kind of lanky, and had perfectly styled dark hair. If not for the cigarette in his mouth, I'd consider him good-looking. Was that Belle's dad? If it was, why wouldn't she want to go home before he left? "Do you not want your dad to see that I drove you home?"

She shook her head. "That's not my dad. That's his friend Tommy."

The color drained from her face as Tommy got into the shiny black car. She didn't have to say anything for me to know she was terrified of him. The air in the truck turned cold with fear.

As Tommy pulled away from her house, Belle covered her belly and ducked down low below the dashboard. Only when Tommy had raced past us and his engine could no longer be heard in the trailer park did she finally sit back up.

"What's going on?"

She didn't answer as she stroked her baby bump.

Something was wrong. This entire situation screamed *wrong*. The hairs at the back of my neck were prickling, telling me that things were far worse for Belle than I could have ever imagined.

And I suspected Tommy was the cause.

I reached across the bench and put my hand on her shoulder. "Who is that Tommy guy?"

She stroked her belly without an answer.

"Um . . . do you have a boyfriend?"

She shook her head.

Damn it. That meant I couldn't skip my next question. "Belle, whose baby is that?"

She kept her eyes down and I was sure she wouldn't answer, but then she looked up and squared her shoulders. "Mine. This baby is mine."

That baby was Tommy's. She didn't have to say his name for me to guess the truth. And given her obvious fear, I was also guessing that her child hadn't been conceived with her consent.

"If something is happening with that guy, if he's hurting you, then we need to go to the police."

She shook her head. "No. It will only make things worse."

"Belle, you—"

"No!" She cut me off. "No."

I sighed. "What about your parents?" Did they even know she was pregnant?

"I just live with my dad and he's gone a lot. He's kind of out of it."

I ran a hand over my forehead. What was I going to do? I'd just met this girl, but I couldn't live with myself if I did nothing to help. If she was being abused by one of her dad's friends, she couldn't continue to live in that trailer. She certainly couldn't bring a baby into that trailer.

"Is there anyone else you could stay with?" Anyone with health insurance so she could see a damn doctor?

She shrugged. "My grandma lives in Oregon, and I could

probably live with her but I don't have any money. My dad, um . . . he usually needs it."

If money was all she needed, I'd gladly pay her way to Oregon. She could go by plane. Or by bus.

By car.

A plan rushed through my mind as I put the truck back in drive and steered us the rest of the way to her house.

When I parked and shut off the ignition, her hand shot out again. "You don't need to come inside!"

I took her hand in mine and squeezed. "It will go faster if we both pack your stuff."

"What?"

"Come on." I opened my door. "You're going to Oregon."

———

AN HOUR after I'd left the restaurant with Belle, we were back.

Belle's meager belongings were in Jamie's truck. She'd called her grandmother to announce her pregnancy and confirm she was still welcome in Oregon—which she was. And she'd left a note for her dad, something she didn't expect he'd see—or care about—until she was long gone.

So while Belle was inside the restaurant using the bathroom before her journey, I was sitting in the driver's seat of Jamie's truck, staring at the picture I'd pulled out of the visor.

"It's not exactly buying a stranger a car, but I think you'd be okay with it." I touched his face. "You've watched over me for long enough. Look out for her instead, okay?"

His frozen smile was all the answer I needed.

I pressed a kiss to my fingers, then to the photo, before tucking it back into the visor so it could be with Belle as she drove to Oregon. Leaving the truck running, I grabbed my purse and went inside. Then I walked straight to the office safe, where I pulled out all of the cash Molly had planned to take to the bank tomorrow.

"All set?" I asked Belle as she came back to the kitchen. She had the takeout bag Helen had made her looped over one wrist.

"Are you sure I can borrow your truck? I don't know how I'll get it back here."

I smiled. "You aren't borrowing that truck, Belle. It's yours."

"No, I can't—"

"Yes, you can. That was my husband's truck, and he'd want you to have it. No arguments. Just promise me to drive safe. Find somewhere to stay tonight before you get too tired." I handed over the wad of cash. "Here. For your trip."

She stared at it with wide eyes, probably never having seen that much money before.

"When you get settled, you'll need to send me your new address so I can transfer the title of the truck to your name. Okay?"

She was still staring at the money.

"Belle? I'll need your address, okay?"

Her eyes snapped to mine and she nodded wildly. "Okay."

"Good. Now you'd better get on the road if you want to make it to Missoula before it gets too late."

Tears flooded her eyes as she took the money and tucked it into her coat pocket. "Thank you."

I stepped up and wiped a tear from her face. A face so young, but so brave. "Keep in touch."

She fell into my arms, hugging me so tight with her thin arms I could barely breathe.

"Drive safe."

She nodded against my chest, then let me go, waving as she disappeared through the back door.

Keep her safe, Jamie. Get her to Oregon.

I wasn't sure if sending a sixteen-year-old on a twelve-hour road trip was smart, but it was better than the alternative. And I had faith that once Belle got to Oregon, her grandmother would see her through.

Until then, she had Jamie.

I ignored the burn in my throat and took a settling breath just as Helen came bursting through the kitchen door. I spun around to see her arms full of dirty dishes and stress written all over her face.

"I've got the counter. You take a quick break." I came unstuck, smiling as she sighed and went back to work.

Not long after the dinner rush subsided, Cole came into the restaurant with a manila folder under his arm. He came behind the counter for a kiss, then set the folder on the counter.

"What's this?" I flipped open the file. A school picture of Belle was the only thing inside.

"This is the cashier's daughter."

I stared with wide, unblinking eyes at the picture. At the bottom, written with a Sharpie, was her full name. Tuesday Belle Hastings.

Tuesday.

Belle had given me her middle name instead of her first. Had she told me Tuesday, I would have remembered her name from the newspaper articles about the murder. I'd memorized those articles—the ones printed alongside Jamie and Kennedy's obituaries.

"What are the chances?" I muttered. *Coincidences.* They really were our thing.

"What?" Cole asked.

I shut the folder. "You're never going to believe what I did this afternoon."

CHAPTER TWENTY

28TH BIRTHDAY: GO CROWD SURFING

COLE

"You're shitting me," Matt said, sitting on the edge of my desk.

"How fucking crazy is that?"

Matt shook his head, letting everything I told him sink in. "Holy fucking shit."

Holy fucking shit. Those had been my exact words to Poppy last night.

I was sick over what had happened to Tuesday Hastings. Her dad, Aaron Denison, was a meth junkie. His name was on the drug task force's watch list, but since he wasn't a major player, we hadn't brought him in. Instead, we'd been spending our time going after dealers like Aaron's friend, Tommy Bennett.

Tommy was one sick fucker. His specialty was getting young kids hooked so they'd help him sell drugs to their naïve friends, but unfortunately, we'd been having hell proving it. We hadn't even been able to bring him in for using—as far as we knew, he never touched the products he was selling. He got off on selling drugs to ruin the lives of others.

I cringed, thinking about the kind of pleasure he'd taken from Tuesday. And here Poppy had inadvertently gifted Jamie's truck to Tuesday. Kennedy Hastings's daughter. "We've got to get guys like Aaron and Tommy off the streets."

Matt nodded. "Too bad the daughter wouldn't tell Poppy if Tommy had assaulted her."

"I know," I sighed, "but it's given me a whole lot of motivation to bust his ass. We might not get him on sexual assault, but distribution to minors will set him up with a nice, long prison sentence."

And as soon as we put Tommy away, I was going after Aaron.

I hadn't kept tabs on Tuesday Hastings—or Poppy—these last five years. But when Poppy had asked me to check on her, I'd gotten curious too. Over the last month, I'd researched Tuesday, starting with her school. Things had looked promising at first. She was a straight-A student. She had perfect attendance and her teachers seemed to love her. Everything pointed to a smart, well-adjusted teenager.

Things had looked so good I hadn't rushed to investigate her home life.

Now, I regretted waiting so long.

Just yesterday, I'd learned that Tuesday had been placed with Aaron after Kennedy had been murdered. Kennedy had never married Aaron and had held sole custody of Tuesday— not even giving her daughter her father's last name. But after the murders, Aaron had been next in line for custody. At the time, he hadn't been a known drug abuser.

Either he'd hidden it well back then, or he'd gotten hooked on drugs while his daughter had shared his home.

"The timing of all this is the really crazy part," I told Matt.

"I called social services *yesterday* when I saw Aaron's name pop up as Tuesday's guardian. I told them that he was a known meth addict and it would be worth making a visit."

Matt chuckled. "But Poppy came to the rescue first."

"That she did."

Tuesday was Oregon-bound to live with Kennedy's mother, who would get the custody of her granddaughter she probably should have had all along. And I had come to the station this morning with a fire in my veins to put Tommy Bennett and Aaron Denison in jail so they could never hurt her again.

"Tommy is getting bumped up as target number one for the task force."

Matt nodded. "Agreed. He's got to go down."

"We'll make a plan when we meet with the rest of the team later." With a nod toward his desk, I changed subjects to the murder case. "The DMV just got back to me with registration info from that new set of plates we sent in. I put the list of names on your desk."

"Nice." Matt stood and went to his desk, opening up the folder I'd set there earlier. "God, I hope we find a lead here."

"Me too."

The months I'd spent working on the liquor store murder had worn me down. I hated that all we had to go on were old videos. I hated that, after all this time, we'd made so little progress. But mostly, I hated that I didn't have anything to give Poppy. I couldn't tell her we'd found Jamie's killer, but I also couldn't tell her that the case was cold.

The stagnancy—the helplessness—was gnawing at me.

But at least it wouldn't last forever. Matt and I were on our last-ditch effort to track down a lead.

"This list," Matt tapped the folder, "if it doesn't have anything, I don't know what else we'll do."

Nothing. If that list didn't turn up a lead, we were stuck. "I sure as fuck hope we find something, but I'm not holding my breath. If the women you questioned last month didn't give us a lead, I don't think we'll find anything here either."

"I don't want to admit defeat, but you're probably right."

Matt had spent last month interviewing potential suspects —six women in total. Each had been caught on camera leaving the grocery store complex the day of the murder. Each had dark hair and had worn jeans that day. Each had driven out of the parking lot alone. Six women, and all of them had been cleared.

Three of them had had alibis. Thanks to their phones, they'd been ruled out because of texts or phone calls made during the time of the murder. One woman's teenager had been with her at the grocery store, but since they'd arrived and left in separate vehicles, I hadn't paired them together on camera. And two other women had been at the register in the grocery store, checking out at the time shots had been fired. Their credit card statements had proved their innocence.

Confirming alibis—a miserably slow process—had been necessary for the investigation, but after the initial interviews, Matt and I had known that none of the six women we'd brought in were viable suspects. None of them had motive. Each of them were, and had been five years ago, plenty well-off financially. They'd had no reason to rob a liquor store for less than a couple hundred dollars.

Which meant going back to the video footage, spending our early mornings combing through it all over again. And this time, we'd pulled every woman on tape, period. We'd identified seventeen additional vehicles driven out of the complex with females inside. Next week, Matt would start bringing them in for questioning, and with any luck, we'd find a lead before Christmas.

Otherwise, the case was dead. Matt and I would have done everything we could.

"Have you told Poppy anything?"

I shook my head. "I don't want to tell her anything until I know for sure."

"Sorry."

"It's not your fault. We were grasping at straws to begin with. I think she knows the likelihood of us finding anything is small. I just . . . I don't want to let her down."

"I don't envy your position on this one."

I didn't either, but if all I had to tell her was bad news, I wanted it to come from me.

And I wasn't giving up yet.

———

"BIG DAY TODAY. How are you feeling?" Jimmy asked Poppy.

She leaned into my side as we stood behind the counter at the restaurant. "Good. I'm just hoping I don't freeze at the game."

Jimmy took a sip of his coffee, his eyes softening when he looked back at Poppy. "I'm proud of you for seeing this through."

"Thanks, Jimmy."

My arm around her shoulders pinned her close. "So am I."

Today, Poppy was doing the last thing on Jamie's birthday list.

I'd been prepared these last couple of weeks, watching her closely as I'd braced for a breakdown. But I should have known better. My Poppy was handling this with pure grace.

And I was simply glad that today was it. We were done. No more lists. No more looking backward. Poppy and I were free to look ahead, to whatever came our way.

"Let me get a few last things done in the kitchen and then we can go." She patted my stomach and I released my hold.

"Take your time. We don't need to leave for another hour."

"Do you guys want refills?" she asked Jimmy and Randall, getting two nods.

"I'll get it." I grabbed the coffee pot from behind me. "You head on back."

"Thanks." She smiled and disappeared into the kitchen.

I refilled Jimmy's and Randall's mugs before topping off my own. Then I made my way down the counter, chatting with customers as I offered refills. The restaurant was busy this morning. Both Molly and Helen were rushing around, clearing tables and delivering food. Poppy had been here since four a.m., making sure there was plenty of food for the weekend.

"It sure is crowded in here," Randall grumbled as I came back to visit with them.

"Good old Cat/Griz weekend. It's always a cluster."

The Montana State University Bobcats were taking on the University of Montana Grizzlies in the annual Cat/Griz football game. The rivalry—one that had become famous over the years—drew a huge crowd to Bozeman when the Cats hosted the game every other year.

Since the game was always the third weekend in November, more often than not it was cold as fuck. These past few years, I'd skipped the chaos of the stadium and just watched the game at my parents' house during their annual party, but this year, I was braving the cold with Poppy by my side so she could finish Jamie's list.

Today, she was going crowd surfing.

"Damn, I wish I had a ticket," Jimmy sighed. "I'd love to go up with her. Do you think she'll get on TV?"

The glint in his eyes made me laugh. "I'm taping the game at my house just in case."

Leaving Jimmy and Randall to bicker, I went to the register as a customer came up to pay. After ringing up the tab, I weaved around the tables, offering coffee refills.

I'd been pitching in at the restaurant lately. Whenever I was here, I did my best to help Poppy and Molly. I only tackled the little things, like filling coffee cups or waters. Cashing out tabs. Everything with the actual food I left for the actual employees. But helping with the minor tasks made me feel like a part of The Maysen Jar—something Poppy seemed to love just as much as I did.

When she came out of the kitchen and spotted me making a new pot of coffee, her smile made my heart skip.

Inside and out, Poppy was the most magnificent woman in the world. My life began the moment she'd walked into the dojo and captured my soul.

"Thanks." She stood on her tiptoes, tray in hand, to kiss my cheek.

"No problem."

She set down her tray and began unloading jars into the display case. "Would you do something for me?"

"In a heartbeat." That always made her smile.

"Would you try the banana bread I just made? It's in the kitchen. I added chocolate chips and I don't know if I like it or not."

"Why does he always get to try the new stuff?" Randall complained. "You should let some of us who will actually give you an honest opinion try it."

Poppy stood and planted a hand on her hip. "He gives me his honest opinions."

Randall rolled his eyes as Jimmy choked on his coffee.

Bastards. They were trying to get me in trouble.

Poppy's mouth fell open as she looked to me. "You've been lying?"

"No way." I held up my hands. "I always tell you the truth. I love your food."

She gave Randall a smug grin. "See?"

"Can I just get the damn banana bread or what?"

"Make that two," Jimmy ordered.

A young man next to Jimmy cleared his throat. "Sorry to interrupt." The kid was probably only twenty and his eyes were trained on me. "Officer Goodman, um . . . I don't suppose you remember me."

I set down my coffee and stepped up to the counter, offering my hand. His face I recognized immediately, even though he'd grown up, but it took me a moment to recall his name. What the fuck was his name? *Adam? Eric?* "Isaac?"

"Yeah." He grinned. "I didn't mean to intrude, but I saw you and just wanted to say hello before I left. And to say thanks. What you did for me back then? Giving me a once?" He held up one finger like I'd done the night I'd given him his once. "I've never forgotten about you."

I shrugged. "It was no big deal."

"It was to me." He held out his hand again. "Anyway, I'll let you get back to your conversation. Nice to see you again."

"Same to you."

He nodded once more, then turned and left. Poppy's, Jimmy's and Randall's eyes were on me, waiting for an explanation, but I stayed quiet and watched as Isaac left the restaurant.

When the door closed behind him, I picked up my coffee. "So, banana bread with chocolate chips? I'll go get them."

Before Jimmy and Randall could ask about Isaac, I ducked into the kitchen with Poppy right on my heels.

"What was that about?"

"Oh, nothing much. Just a kid who needed a break way back when."

"Is that what a 'once' is? A break?"

"Yeah." I nodded. "I had someone give me a once, and ever since, I've tried to pay it forward."

"Oh," she hummed. "Can you tell me about it?"

I didn't like talking about how I'd nearly fucked up my life, but Poppy deserved to know. So I pulled out a stool from the table in the kitchen and took a seat, confessing something only a handful of people even knew.

"I always knew I wanted to be a cop. Ever since I was a kid. After high school, I wanted to go straight to the academy, but my parents wanted me to go to college and get my degree. Dad said that if I had my bachelor's, it would help me move up the ranks on the force, so I agreed and enrolled at MSU. But I didn't take it seriously. At least, not at first. I skipped too many classes and went to too many parties."

Poppy took the stool next to mine. "Did you flunk out?"

I chuckled. "No, but I wasn't pulling As, that's for sure. But the partying got me in trouble. My freshman year, I went to a house party out of town. I had too much to drink but thought if I stayed on the back roads, I'd be fine. On my way back, I swerved to miss a deer, ran my truck into the ditch and got stuck in the snow."

My stomach rolled when I thought about that night. I was lucky things hadn't been worse. That I hadn't hurt someone. That I hadn't hurt myself. As it was, I hadn't even wrecked my truck.

"The officer who found me could have taken me right to jail. She could have given me a DUI, and my future career as a cop would have been over. But she didn't. She put her finger in my face and said, 'This is your once.' Then she drove me home, not to the dorms but to my parents' house, and kept my truck keys for a month."

"Were your parents pissed?"

"Worse," I sighed. "They were disappointed."

And from that night on, I'd tried to never disappoint them again. I'd gotten serious about school. I'd brought up my grades and kept myself out of trouble through graduation and into the academy. All because I'd been given a chance.

"So, you got a once and now you give them."

I nodded. "If the situation calls for it. I respect the law and we have rules for a reason, but not everything is black and white. Some people, like Isaac, deserve a second chance."

Poppy's hand came to my face. "How'd I get so lucky to find you?"

"It's the other way around, beautiful."

She leaned forward, pressing her soft lips to mine as the kitchen door swung open.

"Kissing again?" Molly snickered.

"Always." I wrapped my arms around Poppy's waist, pulling her off her stool and between my legs to take her mouth. This time, there wasn't a thing gentle or sweet about our kiss. This one was hot and deep—a kiss that left Poppy panting, Molly rolling her eyes and my dick hard behind my zipper.

"You'd better get me that banana bread," I whispered. "Otherwise I'll find something else to eat and we won't be going to the football game."

Poppy leaned in to my ear. "I'll make you a deal. You taste the banana bread, and later I'll do some tasting of my own."

I groaned against her lips. *I loved this woman.*

And since I still wasn't sure if I should say it, after the game, I'd show her just how much instead.

———

"WHAT IF THEY DROP ME?"

I kissed Poppy's worried forehead. "They're not going to

drop you. If you feel like you're starting to fall, just set your feet down."

We were standing in a sea of people. Seventeen thousand Bobcat and Grizzly fans all had their eyes aimed on the football field, but I couldn't look away from the beauty at my side.

After we'd left the restaurant, Poppy had pulled on a thick black beanie, and her hair was rolling over her shoulders in a loose cascade to her waist. Her nose was pink from the cold and she'd bundled up in her gray winter coat. Her jeans were tucked into a pair of black, knee-high snow boots.

She looked happy.

And I had the picture to prove it.

I'd taken a lot of pictures for Poppy these last few months— ones that she could count as her daily photo—but today's was a favorite. It ranked just as high as the picture I'd taken a month ago of her and Nazboo cuddling together, asleep on my couch.

A cheer from the crowd snagged my attention away from Poppy. It was just a first down, but the Bobcats were getting closer to the end zone.

"The next time we score, I'll hoist you up."

"Okay," she breathed.

We turned our attention back to the game and stood quietly as the kids around us cheered for the players and cursed at the refs. When we'd gotten to the game, I'd chosen to abandon our ticketed seats and squeeze into the jam-packed students' section. It was wild and crazy—noisy as fuck and I had to stand sideways—but it was the best place for Poppy to do her thing.

Just as I'd suspected, it didn't take long for the Bobcats to march down the remainder of the field and score a touchdown, sending the stadium into sheer pandemonium.

"Up you go!" I grabbed Poppy by the waist and hoisted her high.

The mass of fraternity guys in the rows behind us didn't let me down. They kept her high, sending her up the rows as she laid back flat.

Crowd surfing like a badass.

I laughed and held up my phone, taking a few pictures as she went higher and higher. When she finally reached a group of people that set her down, I pushed past the students in my row to the aisle. Then I took the stairs two at a time, meeting her on the steps.

I stopped one step below her so we were almost at eye level, giving me the perfect view of those cornflower blues.

"Fun?" I asked.

"Yeah. It actually was." She laughed and threw her arms around my shoulders.

I wrapped my arms around her tight, dragging in a few deep breaths of her hair. It smelled like vanilla and cinnamon mixed with the crisp air and everything Poppy.

"Thank you," she said into my ear. "For everything."

I let her go and leaned back.

The stadium was still deafening, but it was all just a dull buzz in the background when Poppy was in my arms. The cheers, the clapping, the whistles, it all just faded away.

There was only her.

I lifted a hand to her face. "Like I've told you, I'm glad to help you with the list."

"No, I'm not talking about the list. This is about everything else. Because of you, I wake up smiling. I look forward to each and every day. Because of you," she took my hand off her cheek and pressed it against her heart, "this only has happy beats."

She held my hand against her chest as her bright blue eyes sparkled.

I loved this woman. I loved this woman so damn much it consumed me.

What the hell was my problem? Why was I holding back

from telling her how I felt? Because I was scared that she was still in love with her husband? *News flash, Cole.* She would always have a special place in her heart for Jamie. That didn't mean she couldn't love me too.

He had her past.

I was taking her future.

I'd get to buy her another dog. I'd get to watch her have our babies. I'd get to dance with her at our golden anniversary. Because I was never letting her go.

As long as I lived, Poppy would be mine.

It had taken me a hell of a long time, but here in the deafening stadium, I finally got a clue. It was time to tell Poppy how much she meant to me—regardless of her response.

Behind us, the Bobcats kicker must have scored the extra point because the stadium erupted again. It was too loud for her to hear, so I mouthed my next three words. Three words that would only ever be hers.

I love you.

She smiled and mouthed, *I love you too.*

She loved me too.

Her lips had barely stopped moving when I crushed mine to hers. I thrust my tongue inside, devouring her mouth as she dueled right back. When I finally pulled away, her lips were wet and red and just how I liked them.

"Ma'am! Excuse me, sir!"

I tore my eyes away from Poppy's as a man scurried to our sides. He was wearing a neon-green vest with SECURITY written on the breast pocket. "I'm sorry, but I'm going to have to ask you to leave, ma'am," he told Poppy. "You can't crowd surf in the stadium."

"Sorry." She giggled, grinning at me before turning to walk up the stairs.

I laughed too, which just pissed the security guard off, and followed behind Poppy. By the time we reached an exit gate, the sounds from the stadium had dulled and I could hear again.

"I guess we'll be kind of early to your parents' after-game party."

I threw my arm around her shoulders, steering her toward the parking lot. "I've got an idea how we could kill a couple of hours."

Her eyebrows quirked. "Oh, yeah?"

"Oh, yeah."

CHAPTER TWENTY-ONE

25TH BIRTHDAY: WRITE A LETTER TO MYSELF IN TEN YEARS

POPPY

"Cole," I gasped, arching against his chest. I was on my side with him at my back. One of his arms was under my hip and his fingers were at my clit. The other hand was across my chest, rolling a nipple between his fingers. And while his lips were kissing my neck, his cock was thrusting inside.

"Come on, Poppy. Get there." He rammed his hips against my ass, sending his cock even deeper.

My legs trembled as he stroked harder, hitting the spot inside that would send me over the edge. The thunder of his heartbeat against my spine matched the rhythm of his hips. Every nerve in my body was alive—Cole had sparked them all to life with his burning touch.

"I'm—"

My orgasm hit hard before I could give Cole a warning. All of the muscles in my body convulsed as my hips bucked with every pulse of my sex. I forced my eyes open, blinking away the white spots and tears dancing in my vision.

"Oh my god," I panted as Cole slid out and rolled me to my back. When he slammed back inside, I nearly came undone again.

He pressed his hips hard against mine. "You feel so fucking good."

I hummed my agreement, closing my eyes to savor the feel of Cole on top of me. He found a new pace in this position. One that never failed to work me back up to another blinding release.

"I'm there, beautiful."

Speaking was impossible since I could barely breathe, so I just nodded and let go. Wave after wave rushed over my body. Incoherent whimpers escaped my lips at the same time Cole's roar echoed through the bedroom. His hot release slickened between us as his strokes slowed.

As we both came down, Cole slid out and collapsed by my side. The comforter had long since fallen onto the floor and the sheets were balled up by the footboard.

"I fucking love vacation."

I giggled and rolled into Cole's side, tossing a leg over his. "Me too."

He kissed my hair. "It was nice to see your parents, but I'd be lying if I said I wasn't a little glad they're gone. I missed you."

"I missed you too."

It was the week between Christmas and New Year's and Cole and I were finally back together in his bed. My parents had come to Bozeman for a week, and rather than stay in a hotel, they'd stayed at my house. I hadn't wanted to leave them alone since I rarely saw them, so I'd stayed there too while Cole had stayed at his place.

The unspoken boundary around my house had kept us apart for seven nights, but we'd dropped my parents off at the airport this morning and immediately come back to his house. With a trail of clothes leading from the door to the bedroom, we'd wasted no time making up for a week of nights apart.

And now we were having a mini-vacation.

We'd both taken two extra days off of work to spend together. Our plan was to barricade ourselves in Cole's bedroom, other than going to dinner at Brad and Mia's house. Since Cole had spent actual Christmas Day with me and my family, we were celebrating with his family tonight. Cole's sister, Evie, and her husband, Zack, would be there so we could all have a nice dinner and exchange gifts.

Then it was back to bed.

"What time do we need to leave?"

Cole looked at his alarm clock. "An hour."

"Then I'd better get in the shower."

His hand traveled down my hip to squeeze my bare ass. "Want some company?"

I smiled, loving Cole's ambition. We'd already had sex three times today, but far be it from me to deny my man a shower.

"Yes, please."

———

"SO WHAT DID Cole get you for Christmas?" Evie asked.

"A whole new set of Williams Sonoma pots and pans for his kitchen."

"Pots and pans? Oh, brother, no. You don't buy your girl-friend cookware for your first Christmas together."

I laughed. "Probably not most girlfriends, but for me, it was the perfect gift. His pots and pans were atrocious and all my good stuff is at the restaurant. Since I've laid claim to his kitchen for my recipe experiments, they were just what I wanted."

She looked at me like I was crazy for not wanting jewelry. "What did you get him?"

"A tool chest for his garage. Your dad actually helped me pick it out."

Cole had started searching for an old car to restore and I wanted him to be able to work in his own garage this time. That way, when I was in the kitchen with my new gear, he could be in the garage with his.

"Tools." Evie shook her head. "You guys are the least romantic new couple on the planet."

I smiled. "Maybe." *Or maybe not.* If she had any idea what we'd been doing all day, she'd probably think differently.

But I kept that to myself and took a sip of beer.

Evie and I were sitting at the island in Brad and Mia's kitchen. Mia had refused to let me help cook, so while Evie and I chatted, Mia was at the sink peeling potatoes. Cole, Brad and Zack had all gone to the basement—with Nazboo at their heels —to get more drinks from Brad's wet bar.

"How are you feeling?" I asked Evie. At nearly six months pregnant with triplets, she had a beautiful pregnant glow, but she looked ready to topple over when standing.

"Enormous." She rubbed her belly. "I'm just grateful for every day the doctor doesn't put me on bed rest."

"Bed rest won't be so bad," Mia said from the sink. "Think of how much fun you'll have ordering Zack around while you watch TV."

She laughed. "Good point, Mom. Maybe I should buy a little bell so I can ring for him."

"What's this?" Zack appeared at Evie's side, kissing her temple before splaying his hand on her stomach.

"Oh, nothing." She grinned into her water glass.

Zack's hand stayed on her belly as it rubbed slow circles.

The image of Cole's hand on my pregnant belly popped into my head, and I jerked, surprised for a moment, until a sense of longing chased it away. I wanted his hand on my growing belly. On our baby. I wanted his hand to have a band like Zack's, something that showed the world he was mine.

"Poppy?"

My head whipped up to Cole. "Yeah?"

"I asked if you wanted another beer."

"Oh." My cheeks flushed as I came back to reality. "Sorry."

His forehead creased. "Are you okay?"

I nodded and smiled. "I'm great. And yes, please. I'll take one more."

"I'll get it." Brad grabbed me a bottle from the fridge before turning to Cole. "So I talked to the city manager again this morning. He'd like you to start sitting in on meetings."

Cole tensed at my side. "Dad. No."

"It's just a few meetings. It won't interfere with your caseload. But if you want to be chief, you need to get to know him."

"Dad, I never said—"

"Hold that thought." Brad held up a finger as he emptied the bottle of wine into Mia's glass. "Let me get another bottle of wine." He smiled at me, then walked out of the kitchen, heading back downstairs to their wine cooler.

"What's going on?" I whispered to Cole when Brad was out of sight.

Cole pushed out a loud breath and nodded toward the living room.

I followed him out of the kitchen, waiting to speak until we were alone. "I thought you didn't want to be chief of police."

"I don't. But I'm having a hard time getting through to Dad. I just . . . he's got these plans for me and I hate letting him down."

I gave him a sad smile. "I think the only way you could let him down would be by taking a job you don't want just to make him happy. Don't you think it would be better if you were honest with him about how you feel?"

Cole ran his hand over his face as he considered my advice. "You're right," he breathed. "I need to make him hear me. I'll tell him when he comes back upstairs."

I stepped into his space, wrapping my arms around his waist. "Want me to stay?"

He hugged me back and kissed my hair. "No. Thanks, beautiful. But I'll handle it."

"Okay." I let him go and went back to the kitchen just as Brad was coming back upstairs. When Cole called him into the living room, Mia shut off the water in the sink and came to the island.

"Is Cole finally going to make Brad listen to him? It's about time."

"What?" My chin dropped. "You knew?" *I* hadn't even known.

Mia shrugged and took a sip of wine as Evie laughed. "Oh, Poppy. Mom knows everything."

"Just wait until we do presents later," Zack said. "We make her tell us what's in every one of her boxes before she opens them. In all the Christmases and birthdays I've seen, Mia has never gotten one wrong."

"It's true." Evie nodded. "She's been like that forever. None of us can pull off a surprise. Maybe you'll be the one family member who can stump her."

Family member. Those two words sent a surge of warmth through my heart as I realized just how true they were. I was a part of Cole's family, just like he'd become a part of mine. Brad and Mia. Evie and Zack. They'd let me into their lives, their family, taking the love that Jamie's parents no longer wanted.

I smiled at Evie, glad I could be part of this tradition. "Maybe I will get to surprise her. I doubt she'll guess what we bought for her."

"Please," Mia huffed. "I've known for weeks what you and Cole got me."

"What? Did he tell you?"

She shook her head. "No. I just figured it out."

"No way." There was no chance she'd ever guess our gift.

"No way, what?"

Cole and Brad walked back into the kitchen. Brad looked sullen but he was trying to hide it, while Cole's relief radiated through the room.

No one brought up their conversation in the living room. Instead, Evie brought them both into ours. "Mom said she knows what Poppy and Cole got her for Christmas, but Poppy doesn't think there's any way she could have guessed."

Brad chuckled. "Take my advice, Poppy. Just accept that there is no such thing as surprising Ms. Crane. The harder you try, the faster she figures it out. Save yourself the stress."

"But, how could she possibly—"

"You got me a puppy like Nazboo."

My chin fell open as I gaped at Mia. *Impossible.* Cole and I had just ordered the dog yesterday. The puppy wasn't even weaned yet, so we'd had to wrap up a collar and leash along with a picture.

"How— I don't—" I blinked and closed my speechless mouth.

"See what I mean?" Zack muttered.

I took a long gulp of my beer and looked up at Cole. "So much for our big surprise."

Cole chuckled. "Sorry. I should have told you about Mom's superpower. Honestly, I thought we might have had her on this one, but I guess not."

"Are there any other family secrets I should know about?"

"Don't tell her!" Brad shouted as both Mia and Evie opened their mouths. "If I'm lucky, it will take her a few years to figure out mine."

The kitchen erupted in laughter as Mia kissed Brad's cheek and went back to making dinner and Zack and Evie started debating baby names. And I just smiled and leaned into Cole's side, happy to be part of it all.

Hours later, after too much food and drink and gifts, Cole and I loaded up a sleepy Nazboo and drove home.

"How did it go with your dad?"

"Better than I expected. He didn't want to hear me at first, but when I told him that I'd make a shit chief of police because my heart wasn't in it, he started to come around. I still think he was disappointed though."

I knew Cole hated disappointing people, but in this case, he'd done the right thing. Reaching across the console, I took his hand. "He'll come around."

"Yeah." He kissed my knuckles. "Did you have fun?"

"Yes, so much. I love your family."

"They're yours too. You're stuck with me, so you're stuck with them."

I smiled out the dark windshield. "I like stuck."

"Good." He laced our fingers together. "How would you feel about being stuck at my house? Maybe make it our house?"

My head whirled toward him. Cole was grinning into the night. "Really? You want me to move in?"

He looked over and nodded. "Pretty much since the first night you stayed over but I thought that might be too soon."

"Finally!" My shout startled Nazboo in the backseat. "Sheesh. I've been stalling my realtor for months."

He chuckled. "So that's a yes?"

"That's a yes, Detective."

———

"GOODMAN."

I frowned as Cole answered his phone. It was the morning after our dinner at Brad and Mia's and we were supposed to have the Friday alone together.

I'd gotten up early and made us both breakfast—we were eating in the dining room for the first time in ages. We'd been talking about taking Nazboo for a walk when his phone had rung, and since it was the station on the other line, it couldn't be ignored.

"Yeah, I'll be there in twenty."

Damn it. So much for our day off.

"Sorry." Cole gave me a sad smile as he hung up the phone. "If I could stay, I would, but I really need to head into the station."

"Okay." I couldn't fault him for putting the chance to make an arrest ahead of couch time with me. "Be safe."

"I will." He stood and kissed my forehead, taking his plate to the sink.

I stood and followed him with my own. "I'll take care of the dishes. You go ahead."

"I'll make it up to you." He took the plate from my hand, set it down, then hoisted me onto the counter.

I brushed his dark hair off his forehead as he stepped between my legs. "What did you have in mind?"

"How about I pick up Chinese takeout on my way home and we have a late lunch and watch a movie?"

"Do I get to pick what we watch?"

He nodded. "Yes, but I get two vetoes."

"One."

"One." He leaned in and brushed his soft lips to mine. "I'll hurry."

"Text me when you leave the station. I might take Nazboo over to my place to start packing."

"Don't wear yourself out. Save some energy for me." He grinned and kissed me again before rushing out of the kitchen. His sweatpants hinted at the perfect ass beneath the gray cotton.

I'd hoped to spend a lot of time squeezing that ass today. Instead, I'd get a head start on packing so I could officially move in.

I sighed and hopped off the counter, rinsing the dishes and putting them in the dishwasher. I was just about to go upstairs when Cole came back down, dressed in jeans and a thick green sweater. The cable knit made the green in his eyes pop more than his usual black polo.

"I love you." I wrapped my arms around him, taking a deep breath of his fresh smell.

"I love you too." He leaned me back so his lips could mold to mine. His tongue slipped between my teeth, tickling, before he pulled away. "See you soon." One more kiss to my forehead and he was gone, striding toward the garage.

I held Nazboo back as we went to the front door to wave good-bye from the porch.

Nazboo let out a whimper as he backed out of the garage and onto the street, leaving her behind with her second-favorite owner.

"Sorry," I rubbed her ears, "but he'll be back soon. Come on. Let's get some packing done before he gets back."

I hurried through my own shower—not bothering to wash my hair but rather leaving it up—then pulled on some skinny jeans, an oversized gray turtleneck and my favorite black TOMS. Nazboo rode shotgun as we crossed town, and when we got to my house, I decided to start packing up the small office.

Two hours later, I was sitting on the floor, sorting books and papers into three stacks: keep, throw and Jamie. The keep pile had been growing the fastest, with the throw pile a close second. The Jamie pile was the smallest with a few of his old books I was going to give to Jimmy.

"Nazboo!" I called, taking a break from sorting.

She'd disappeared about fifteen minutes ago and I couldn't hear her paws clicking on the hardwood floors, which meant she'd either fallen asleep or she was causing trouble.

I waited and listened, but nothing. "Nazboo!"

This time I heard a scurry from the living room before she came trotting down the hallway and into the office with a book in her mouth.

"No!" I jumped up from the floor. "Bad girl." I yanked the book from her mouth and pointed my finger in her face. "Bad girl, Nazboo. No. No. No. We don't chew books."

Damn it. She wasn't entirely to blame. In my hurry this morning, I'd forgotten her rawhide sticks.

I walked out of the office and to the kitchen, grabbing a paper towel to wipe off the book. Once it was dry, I recognized it as one from the Jamie pile.

"Jimmy isn't going to want this one now." The cover was destroyed with teeth marks and slobber, though the inside wasn't too bad. I thumbed through the pages, surprised when a letter tucked into the middle popped out.

Folded in thirds, the top flap had been inscribed *To Jamie on his 35th birthday.*

"Oh my god." I gasped and covered my mouth.

This was it. The letter I'd thought was lost. The letter Jamie had written to himself in ten years.

The letter Jamie had written the day he'd died.

This letter was one of only two things on the birthday list Jamie had done himself. I'd searched for this letter. I'd torn the house apart the year after his death searching for it but I'd never been able to find it. But here it was all along, tucked into a book that Nazboo had used as her chew toy.

And now I could finally read the last words Jamie had ever written.

Tears threatened, but I swallowed the burn in my throat and took two long breaths. Then I went to my small dining room table and took a seat. Carefully, I opened the letter, smiling at Jamie's sloppy handwriting. It only filled the top half of the page. Of course his letter wasn't long—that hadn't been his style.

I inhaled, filling my lungs completely, before reading his words.

OLD ME,

YOU'RE GETTING UP THERE, *dude, so before you hit forty, I wanted to give you some advice. Don't have a midlife crisis. Don't be that guy. It's sad and pathetic and would really piss me off. Look around. I'm sure you're still cool since you're me. Your wife is smoking hot. Life is good. So stay cool, and be good to Poppy. She's the best thing that ever happened to you.*

DON'T FUCK IT UP,
   Young Me

I LAUGHED as tears filled my eyes. This was just . . . so Jamie. This letter was all the wonderful, ridiculous, sweet things that my husband had been.

And I was just so glad that I'd found it. Now I could put it with his birthday list, where it belonged.

Thank you, Jamie. Thank you for helping me find this.

Whether it was Jamie or not, I didn't know. I was just grateful that another coincidence had led me to his letter.

These incredible coincidences.

And maybe it was silly, but I was thanking serendipity for bringing me Cole.

I sniffled, smiling again through blurry eyes as I reread the letter. Then I folded it back up and took it to my purse, tucking it into Jamie's journal. Tomorrow, I'd let Jimmy read it too. He'd like that.

After the journal was safely stowed, I bent low to scratch Nazboo's ears. "I guess you're not in trouble. But no more chewing books, got it?"

She licked my face.

"I'm taking that as a yes." I stood and nodded to the garage. "Come on. Let's see if we can find some boxes."

Another hour later, I'd boxed the keep pile and loaded it into my car. I'd finished trashing the throw pile and was checking my phone to see if Cole had texted. He hadn't, so I decided to start packing the kitchen.

An hour later, when all the drawers had been emptied and cleaned, I checked my phone again, still seeing nothing from Cole.

"He's probably just busy," I told Nazboo.

Her brown eyes opened, but otherwise, she didn't move from where she'd fallen asleep next to the fridge.

"I'll send him a text."

I fired off a quick note, asking if he had any idea when he'd be done at the station, and then I went back to packing.

The minutes ticked on, and my phone stayed silent on the counter. My eyes darted to the screen so often, I lost focus on packing. But no matter how hard I tried to concentrate on sorting dishes and random kitchen appliances, I couldn't stop myself from constantly checking my phone. And every time it turned up blank, my panic grew.

There was something eerily familiar about this. Something entirely unwelcome. Memories plagued my mind from the last time I'd been in this kitchen, desperate for my phone to chime.

He's okay. He's just at work. I reminded myself over and over that Cole was fine. That the anxious prickling on the back of my neck was just because I was here. That finding Jamie's letter had freshened old memories. *This is just déjà vu.*

Despite my best efforts not to compare the past to the present, when the doorbell rang, a lance of terror cut through my racing heart. I held my breath as my unsteady feet rounded the corner of the kitchen.

My eyes searched the window of the door, and for a moment, I was taken back five years. It took me a second to separate the memory from reality, but when I did, the wave of relief that crashed over me nearly knocked me over.

Cole's handsome face was on the other side of the glass.

I hurried down the hall—Nazboo rushing to catch up—and turned the lock.

"Hi," I breathed, pressing a hand to my still pounding heart. "That was the most intense déjà—"

I stopped talking at the look in Cole's eyes. They were full of pain. Of dread. I'd seen that combination in his eyes before. It was the same look he'd had the night he'd stood on this very porch and told me that my husband had been murdered.

"Cole?"

My voice seemed to make the pain worse and his entire face twisted in agony.

"You're scaring me. What is it? Tell me." I waited three heartbeats. "Please."

He swallowed hard. "We found the person who killed Jamie."

My hand clamped over my mouth but a sob still escaped. No amount of calming breaths could keep my tears away, and they flooded my eyes, trickling down my cheeks. "You did? It's over?" An unbelievable sense of finality settled in my chest. I was still crying, but the drops were no longer filled with fear. They were full of relief. *It was over.*

Cole nodded but didn't seem at all relieved. Wasn't this good news? A killer was off the streets. He'd found the bad guy. Why did he still look like he wanted to be anywhere but on my porch?

"There's more." His voice cracked.

Tension came rushing back, filling my muscles as I stood silently, waiting for Cole to continue.

When he looked to his feet and then back up again, the tears in his eyes pounded a hammer to my chest.

"What?" I begged. "What don't you want to tell me?"

A tear rolled down his cheek. "It's my fault. It's my fault Jamie was killed."

CHAPTER TWENTY-TWO

COLE

F *ive hours earlier ...*
"Hey." I stepped into the observation area attached to
the interrogation room. Matt was standing by the two-way
mirror, staring at the woman he'd called in for questioning.

"Hey. Sorry to call you in, but I think you're going to want
to be here."

"Okay." I stepped up to the glass.

The woman at the table was young, probably in her early
twenties. Her hair was trimmed short, like a man's, except for
the mass of bangs that covered her forehead and fell completely
over one eye and covered part of the other. The roots were
black but the bangs had been bleached to near white. Her
shoulders were hunched forward as her elbows rested on the
table, but even with her slouched position, you could tell she
had a broad frame. Much bigger than most women.

And she was familiar. Her head was tipped down so I
couldn't get a good look at her face—that damn hair was in the

way—but she was familiar. I searched my memory but when nothing came up, I shrugged it off. I probably just found her familiar because I'd seen her on video surveillance.

"Who's this?"

Matt handed me a manila file. "Nina Veras. She's number eleven on our list of potential subjects, and I brought her in this morning to ask her some questions about the murder. When I got two different answers to the same question, I stepped out and called you. I've got a feeling we're onto something here."

I nodded and flipped open the file.

Nina Veras was twenty-two. She worked as a barista at one of the downtown coffee shops. She had no criminal record. No speeding tickets. No parking tickets.

"I trust your gut, so if you've got a feeling, I'll go with it. But, Matt, this girl is squeaky clean."

"You're right. *She* is. But take a look at this." He handed me another file. "That's her boyfriend. I pulled it right before you got here. Look familiar?"

The mug shot paper-clipped inside raised the hairs on my arms. With dark eyes and a red bandana tied over his black hair, the man in the photo was wearing a white, threadbare tank top as he glared at the camera and held his identification board. A dog paw print was tattooed on one shoulder. Across the base of his neck were the letters *MOB*—Member of Blood.

I had no trouble putting his face to a name.

"Samuel Long is her boyfriend?"

Matt nodded.

"Shit."

Samuel was a known gang member with the Bloods. Him and a couple of his cohorts were currently under surveillance by the gang task force. I scanned Samuel's file, stopping after the first three pages because I'd seen enough. Vandalism. Theft. Drug trafficking.

All gang related.

Montana had seen an increase in gang activity over the last ten years. Gang transplants from California had come to Montana to stake their claim. Our department had been diligent in making it clear that Bozeman was no place for them, but as the town grew and our resources stretched thin, keeping a handle on their influx had become more difficult.

Nina Veras didn't look like a murder suspect, but I'd learned over the years to never rule out the influence of a gang. They were masters of brainwashing, trapping kids into their circle so tight not even parents could pull them out.

And if Samuel Long had his hooks into Nina Veras, there was no telling what he'd asked her to do.

"So what's your plan?"

Matt set the files down on a chair behind us. "I know you aren't going to like this, but I'd like Simmons to come in and help with the questioning."

"No."

"Hear me out." He stopped me before I could object again. "Simmons is shit at fieldwork, we both know that, but he's got more documented confessions than any other officer in the BPD. If we're going to get anything out of her before she clams up, he's our best bet."

I blew out an angry breath, rubbing my jaw as I considered Matt's point. Simmons had a knack in the interrogation room, I'd give him that much. He was able to build trust with his subjects faster than anyone else I knew. Maybe it was his pudgy nature—he was far from intimidating—but Matt was probably right. Bringing Simmons in to help was smart.

"Fine."

Matt clapped me on the shoulder and walked out of observation without another word. Fifteen minutes later, I stood at the mirror as he entered with Simmons on his heels.

"Nina, this is Detective Simmons." Matt took the chair across from her. "He's going to be listening as we talk, okay?"

She nodded, her eyes darting to Simmons, before returning to her fingers. She was picking so nervously at her cuticles, one had started to bleed.

I took a seat in one of the chairs and watched as Matt asked some basic questions. *Do you remember the liquor store murder five years ago? Can you recall where you were at that time?* Every question was answered with a shake of her head. The minutes passed and my hopes of getting Nina to give us any clue as to her whereabouts that day shrank further and further. Her answers were as short as possible and she refused to make eye contact with Matt—who was getting just as frustrated as I was, based on the fists he was making under the table.

Matt circled back to the beginning, repeating a question he'd already asked, when Simmons held out a hand, stepping in.

Simmons began asking Nina questions that had nothing to do with the case. He did it for an hour. Then another. And by the time I'd been watching her in that room for nearly three hours, her shell was finally beginning to crack. They talked about her job at the coffee shop. What she'd done for Christmas last week. How she was enjoying the fresh snow.

As Simmons and Nina chatted about a movie they'd both seen recently, Matt excused himself from the interrogation room and joined me in observation.

We watched as Simmons got up and brought her a paper cup of water from the cooler in the corner. "I appreciate you coming in to visit with us today. I'm sorry it's taking so long."

"Can I go?"

"Soon." Simmons sat back down. "But first I need to ask you some questions about your boyfriend."

Nina's face paled. "Okay."

I raked a hand through my hair. "Where's he going with this, Matt?"

"Fuck if I know, but he's gotten farther with her than I did so I'm sure he's got a plan."

I sure as hell hoped so. The longer I watched, the tighter the ball in my gut twisted. Matt was right. There was something here. Just like him, I had a feeling about this woman, and we couldn't afford to have Simmons fuck it up.

"Nina, I know Detective Hernandez explained that you were here because we had some questions about a murder five years ago."

She nodded to Simmons.

"Do you remember that day at all?"

Her eyes darted to the mirror. "No."

Lie. Her body language was all over the place. She sure as fuck remembered that day. I'd bet my life on it.

"Hmm." Simmons hummed. "It was in May. The murder happened at a liquor store. It's closed now, but it used to be next to the grocery store on Twenty-Third Street. Do you know which one I'm talking about?"

"Yeah. I guess."

"Well, it was a long time ago. I can see how you'd forget something after five years. You would have been what, seventeen?"

She nodded.

"And your boyfriend, he would have been twenty-three. Is that right?"

"Um, twenty-two. He's five years older than me."

"You're right." Simmons chuckled. "I never have been good at math. Good thing one of us has some brains in here."

Nina gave him a small smile but kept her eyes pinned on the table.

"Listen, I'll be straight with you. We have reason to believe that your boyfriend committed the murders at the liquor store."

Her head flew up, her eyes like saucers as she gasped.

"What the fuck?" I muttered, shifting to the edge of my seat. What was Simmons doing?

"You seem like a nice girl, Nina. But your boyfriend is mixed up in some bad stuff. We're bringing him in later today and charging him with two counts of first-degree murder. I don't want you to get mixed up in all of that, so I need you to think. Think hard. Where were you at the time of the murder?"

She shook her head, her eyes filling with tears. "No. No, he didn't kill anyone."

"This is really important, Nina." Simmons pressed harder. "The district attorney wants to ask for the death penalty. You could be brought in as an accomplice if we can't verify your alibi. So think. Where were you?"

A tear rolled down her cheek as she shook her head. "He didn't kill anyone."

"Nina, he did. He's going to jail for the rest of his life. If he's lucky, they'll give him two life sentences. He'll spend the rest of his life in prison and that's if he's lucky enough to find a judge that won't order lethal injection. Samuel is gone. He's dead. Don't end up in jail too. Tell me, where were you the day of the murder?"

She cried harder, burying her face in her hands as her shoulders shook.

I almost felt bad for the girl. Almost. Simmons was using the love for her boyfriend and some well-strung lies to break down her walls. He was capitalizing on her youth and the emotional stress of being trapped in a colorless room for hours. Simmons was using it all to push her over the edge.

"Nina," he said gently. "Just tell me what happened. I'll do whatever I can to help you. Just . . . let it out. Tell me what happened."

She sobbed again, then dropped her hands. Her eyes were begging Simmons to understand. "Samuel didn't kill them. Please, it wasn't him."

Simmons waited, stretching the silence out until it was nearly unbearable, until finally, Nina whispered, "It was me."

The words came out of her mouth and rang in the air as guilt and relief and sorrow washed over Nina's face.

Maybe she'd been wanting to confess. Maybe she had been tired of keeping it in. Whatever the reason, there was no doubting the truth in her voice.

Nina Veras had killed Jamie Maysen and Kennedy Hastings.

I fell back into my chair, shocked to my core.

Simmons had done it. He'd been the key to breaking this case all along.

I'd been holding out hope, praying that we'd be granted a miracle. I'd wished that this day would come. But I'd never actually thought it would happen. I'd never thought about how I'd feel in this moment.

I was relieved. I was grateful. But it was painful too.

I hurt. For Jamie. For Kennedy. For Poppy. My heart hurt now that we'd learned the truth.

That a seventeen-year-old girl had killed two people.

"He did it," Matt whispered. "Holy fucking shit, he did it."

Simmons reached across the table and took Nina's hand as she cried. "Okay, Nina. Tell me what happened."

Over the next thirty minutes, Matt and I sat and watched as Nina Veras gave a complete confession to the liquor store murder.

As Matt had suspected, her involvement with Samuel had been the motive. The couple had just moved to Montana from

Los Angeles, where Samuel had been a long-standing member of the Bloods. He'd been sent here to branch out, to make money and start a new crew for the gang.

And part of his crew was a girlfriend willing to do whatever he'd asked, no questions.

So Samuel had sent Nina into the liquor store with a gun and clear orders. Get the money from the register. If anyone refuses or puts up a fight, kill 'em.

It had been her test.

Nina swore up and down that the first shot had been an accident. That she hadn't wanted to kill anyone, but the gun had gone off in her shaking hands. Maybe that was true for the first shot. But twice? I wasn't buying it. I think she'd panicked and killed Kennedy to save herself—not that my opinion mattered.

A judge and jury would decide her fate.

"I can't believe all this." Matt shook his head. "We should have found her in the bathroom."

"Yeah." I scoffed. "We should have."

After she'd run out of the liquor store, Nina had disappeared behind the shopping complex. She'd stripped out of her sweatshirt and baseball hat and, just as I'd suspected, snuck into the loading dock at the grocery store.

She'd hidden in a cabinet under the sink in the women's bathroom—a place very few men would fit, which is likely why no one had checked. She'd stayed hidden for two hours, only to come out when Samuel had texted her that the police had finished sweeping the grocery store.

Samuel—that fucker—had been sitting in the parking lot the whole time.

He'd come inside the grocery store, snatched a couple of plastic bags, then snuck into the bathroom. Then the pair had carried Nina's disguise and gun through the front doors like they'd just bought steaks for dinner.

Being so young, I had dismissed Nina when I'd seen her on the video footage. Just like all of the cops had done that day as they'd watched the young couple walk to their black car and drive away.

Leaving ruined lives in their wake.

"How am I going to tell Poppy all of this?"

"I don't know." Matt stood from his chair. "But it's good that you can be the one to break the news."

I followed Matt out of observation to the hallway but stopped as the door to interrogation opened. With Simmons gesturing her through the door, Nina stepped into the hallway. Her eyes were aimed at her feet, but when she saw Matt and me, she looked up. Then with one hand, she brushed her hair back, holding it out of her eyes.

For the first time, I got a full view of her face. A face I recognized after all. A face I knew from years ago.

My feet faltered and my shoulder crashed into the wall.

Time slowed as Nina stared at me, recognition dawning on her face at the same time it did on mine. She held my eyes, unblinking, until Simmons shuffled her along, down the hallway to process her arrest.

No. No, it couldn't be her. Nina Veras couldn't be the young girl I'd caught six years ago one night on patrol. It couldn't be her.

Except it was.

"PLEASE. PLEASE, OFFICER, PLEASE." *The girl clung to my arm.* "Please don't arrest me. I promise, I'll never do something like this again."

"Look, kid. I'm sorry. But you and your friends were vandal-

izing private property. Graffiti is illegal, even if that building is condemned. I can't let you go." Especially because she was the only one of her gang that I'd managed to snatch.

"No." Her eyes begged me as she spoke. "I swear. I wasn't even painting. Look." She held up her fingers, all of which were clean.

"Then you won't get in much trouble. Let's go." I took her elbow and started walking her back to my car.

"Please." She was tall, probably five ten or eleven, so she kept up with my steps as she kept pleading. "I'm only sixteen. If you take me in, they'll send me back to California. But I can't go back. I can't. My mom's boyfriend . . ." She stopped her feet, tugging my arms so I stopped too. "Please. I can't go back to live with him." With her free hand, she lifted the long, dark hair off the nape of her neck, revealing a cluster of six cigarette burns shining under the streetlamp.

Fuck. This girl might be playing me, but the tears in her eyes and the torment on her face looked like the truth.

"You're sixteen?"

She nodded.

"How did you get to Montana?"

"I came with my boyfriend. He's twenty-one and we moved here together. But my dad lives here, he just doesn't have official custody."

"And was this boyfriend one of the punks who was vandalizing that wall?"

She shook her head. "No."

My eyes narrowed at her lie. "Really?"

"I won't do it again," she whispered. "Please."

I let her arm go and took a deep breath. Without a trace on her hands, I couldn't prove she'd been spray-painting. All I could show was that she was with the crowd, which meant she'd probably get a slap on the wrist and a one-way ticket to Cali-

fornia from social services. So instead of dragging her to my cruiser, I put one finger in her face. "This is your once. Your one chance. If I catch you again, I'll drive your ass to California myself."

"Thank you." She threw her arms around my middle. "Thank you." The second she let me go, she turned and ran in the opposite direction.

"Be good!" I called to her back.

"I will!" She waved and disappeared around the corner.

"COLE." Matt put his hand on my shoulder. "Cole, are you okay?"

I watched as Simmons steered Nina Veras down the hallway. When they were out of sight, I shook my head, sinking to the floor as the world tipped upside down.

If not for me, Nina Veras would have gone back to California.

She would have been in the system. She would have been a thousand miles away from the liquor store and Samuel Long.

And Poppy's husband would be alive.

CHAPTER TWENTY-THREE

50TH BIRTHDAY: CHANGE SOMEONE'S LIFE

COLE

Three days later . . .

The shrill ring of my alarm sent blinding pain through my skull. I buried my face in the pillow as I hammered my fist on the nightstand, missing the alarm the first time but smashing it silent with the second. Then I covered my head with another pillow—Poppy's pillow—and willed the pounding in my temples to stop.

"Fuck," I groaned as it just got worse.

I couldn't gripe. I'd earned this hangover. For everything that I'd done, this was just a fraction of the punishment I deserved.

It had been three days since I'd gone to Poppy's house and told her the news. Three days since I'd sat by her side on that single porch step and explained it all. How Nina Veras had killed Jamie. How she'd eluded the police and escaped. How the only reason she'd even been in Montana was because I'd been too much of a pushover to send her ass back to California.

How the loss of Poppy's husband had been my fault.

She had stayed silent as I made the confession. She'd sat like stone, staring blankly at her front yard. The only movement came from her shallow breaths and the tears streaming down her face as I broke her heart. Only after I'd been done, after we'd sat in excruciating silence for an hour, had she finally asked me to leave.

Driving home that night, I knew I'd lost her.

I'd texted her the next day, just to check in, but hadn't gotten much of a response. *I'm fine. Just busy. I'll call soon.*

Busy.

I'm sure she'd been busy. Busy telling her family and Jamie's the news of the investigation. Busy blocking me from her mind.

So I'd spent the last three days locked in my house, waiting for the phone to ring, mourning the best thing I'd ever had and lost.

The bourbon I'd guzzled last night hadn't helped. My heart was still in pieces—the ache in my chest just another fucking bonus to go along with my splitting headache.

"Cole!" Dad's shout carried up the stairs.

Goddamn it. I never should have given him my house key. The last thing I wanted was to see Dad. To see the disappointment etched on his face too. I didn't need a fucking audience as my life spiraled out of control. Couldn't I just be left to suffer alone?

"Cole!"

I guess not.

Whipping the sheet off my legs, I pushed myself to sitting. The room was spinning as fast as my stomach, but I swallowed down my urge to hurl and stood. On unsteady feet, I shuffled my way out of my bedroom and down the hall.

"Cole! Get your ass down here!"

"I'm coming," I yelled as loud as my head and raspy voice would allow. "Just give me a fucking second."

Every step throbbed behind my eyes—the light from the windows only making it worse. By the time I made it downstairs, I walked straight to the couch and collapsed so I wouldn't puke or pass out. "What are you doing here?"

Dad sighed and sat on the coffee table. "Matt Hernandez called me this morning. He's been trying to get ahold of you since last night but kept getting voicemail."

Shit. Where was my phone? It must have died sometime in the evening and I'd been too drunk to notice. Had Poppy tried to call?

"What did Matt want?"

"Just to check in."

"Did he . . ."

"Tell me you found Jamie Maysen's killer on Friday? Yeah."

I grunted. I didn't have the energy to rehash the story again and I was sure Matt had told him all about Nina Veras. "So?"

"So, I got the story from Matt." He paused. "And then I went to her house and got the rest from Poppy."

My eyes flew open as I sat up straight. "You saw her? Is she okay?"

It was New Year's Day—Jamie's birthday—and I couldn't imagine today would be easier on her. I hated that I wasn't by her side, but the last thing I wanted was my presence making things worse.

"She's okay. Sad, as to be expected."

I slumped back into the couch and stared at the ceiling. All that time I'd been working so hard to make Poppy happy. If only I had known that the best thing I could have done for her was to stay away.

"Cole, look at me." Dad's eyes softened with his voice.

"There's only one person to blame for that murder. It's not you."

I shook my head. "No. No, it *is* my fault."

"Bullshit." His bark made me wince. "We all give warnings. Every single cop in America has given a warning. Whether it be a speeding ticket to a soccer mom. A college kid that's had too much to drink. Or a girl who was spray-painting an old wall that has since been torn down. If you're to blame, then you might as well condemn the rest of us too."

I sighed and hung my head. "Poppy lost her husband. I could have prevented that."

"I just don't believe that's true, and if you would stop to think about it for a minute, you probably wouldn't either. There's no guarantee that girl ever would have been sent away. And even if she had been shipped back to California, all it would have taken was a bus ticket to get her back. The only person to blame for that murder is her. Are you hearing me? Her. Not you."

My throat started to close. "It doesn't matter. All that matters is Poppy, and I lost her."

"Then go find her."

Without another word, Dad stood and let himself out. He left through the front door, but his words stayed, echoing in my living room.

Then go find her.

She'd asked me to leave. She hadn't called. She wouldn't want me around. Would she? As the question went unanswered, I pushed myself off the couch and shuffled into the kitchen. Dad's words were still ringing in my ears.

Then go find her.

I filled a glass of water, chugging it down along with three pain pills.

I wanted to see her, but the truth was, I was scared. I hadn't stayed away because of some text. I'd stayed away because of my own insecurities—my own jealousy. I'd assumed she was still so in love with Jamie that she'd never see past this horrible coincidence. That she'd never forgive me.

When in reality, I hadn't given her enough faith.

Poppy had enough love for us both.

Then go find her.

Maybe things really were that simple.

I put my glass in the sink, ignoring the pain in my temples, and jogged to the stairs. Heading straight for the bathroom, I didn't wait for the water to warm up before I stepped inside the shower. Then I washed away the booze and self-loathing, stepping out clean and ready to find Poppy.

There was no guarantee that she'd forgive me. No guarantee that we'd make it through this together. But I was going to find her and find out. I wasn't going to let my own issues keep me away for another moment.

I drove to the restaurant first, but since her car wasn't there, I flipped my truck around and went the opposite direction toward her house. A new *For Sale* sign was in the yard with a *Sold* placard already slanted across its front.

What the fuck? She'd sold her house already? I'd been here three days ago and it hadn't even been listed.

I parked in front of her garage and went to her door, knocking but not expecting an answer. Every window was dark, and inside, I could only see empty rooms. Where was she? Where were her things?

My hand dove into my pocket for my phone. "Shit," I muttered when it came out empty.

I didn't have my phone. It was dead somewhere in my house.

Cursing myself for getting so drunk last night, I raced back toward my house, mentally drafting my apology speech once I got my phone charged.

I pulled up to my house, hitting the remote for the garage, but did a double take when I noticed the porch.

Two white rocking chairs—chairs Poppy had sworn she was going to buy after moving in—were placed perfectly in front of the railing.

She'd been here? I scanned the street, looking for her car, but it wasn't here. Which meant we'd crossed paths. While I'd been searching for her, she'd been here. But why had she left?

Not wasting time by parking in the garage, I left my truck in the driveway and hustled across the snow-covered yard, taking the porch steps two at a time. But the moment my foot landed at the top, I froze.

Leaned against the front door were two books. One I'd never seen before. One I had. It was Jamie Maysen's journal for his birthday list. And on top of both books was a letter with my name curled in Poppy's fancy handwriting.

I picked up both books and the letter, not bothering to go inside and get out of the cold, then sat in one of the rocking chairs and started with the letter.

COLE,

EXACTLY ONE YEAR AGO, *I decided to finish Jamie's birthday list. I was standing in the kitchen at my house and taking a selfie. That's how this all started. One selfie of me crying in front of a chocolate birthday cake.*

. . .

I WISH *I could go back to that day, not to erase this last year, but to tell myself to hold on. To tell myself to keep breathing, because pretty soon, someone special would come into my life and make it easier. I'd tell myself not to cry, because he'd be there to help me finish the birthday list. He'd hold my hand when I needed to borrow some strength. He'd let me cry into his shirt when I couldn't hold back the tears. He'd make it easy to fall in love again.*

BECAUSE I DO. *I love you, Cole. I can prove it too. Do me a favor. Put this letter down and look at the big book. And don't just flip through it. Really stop and look.*

I SET down the letter and opened the large book. Except it wasn't a book—it was a photo album. Poppy had printed out all of her daily pictures and made me this book.

My heart twisted as I stared at the first page. Seeing her first picture hurt. Just as she'd described in the letter, there was Poppy—beautiful, but miserable—standing next to a cake filled with burning candles.

The pages that followed weren't a lot better. Her blue eyes were dull and her smiles were forced. She looked like a ghost of my Poppy.

I kept flipping, hating every one of these pictures, until I got about halfway through the book and the pain in my chest started to ease. The halfway point was when the photos started to include the restaurant. Poppy's smiles actually reached her eyes, and a handful of pages later, I found the photo I'd taken of her the day we'd walked in the park. The day she'd joked about having a big nose.

From there, the photos were all ones I recognized, since I'd taken most of them. I thumbed through the rest of the book quickly, wanting to get back to Poppy's letter, but I stopped on the last page.

Unlike the middle of the book, this page wasn't a collage, but just one photo. It was a simple picture, entirely of Poppy's face. Her eyes were bright, like they were whenever I made her laugh. Her smile was wide, like it was whenever I told her that I loved her.

Her happiness radiated off the page, and I soaked it up for a few moments before going back to the letter.

DID YOU SEE IT?

I NODDED.

YOU DID THAT, Cole. You. You and all of these crazy coincidences that brought us together. Now do one more thing for me. Flip through Jamie's birthday list.

I SET down the letter again and opened the leather journal. I went through it quickly since not much had changed from the first time Poppy had shown me this list. The only difference was that she'd added marks to the items she'd completed.

All of them were marked, except one.

50th Birthday: Change someone's life

Why hadn't she marked that one done? She'd changed many lives. Tuesday Hastings's. Jimmy's. Randall's. Molly's. Finn's.

Mine.

So why would she leave that box empty?
Confused, I went back to the letter.

I'M NOT CHECKING *the last box, because I don't have to.
Jamie finished that one himself. He changed my life. And he
changed yours. His birthday list changed us both. I started his
list, hoping I'd find closure. Hoping I'd be able to let go of the
past and start to live for the future. But I was wrong. Finishing
the list didn't give me a future.*

YOU DID.

READ *these words until you believe them. Nothing you did
caused Jamie's death. Nothing you did could have prevented it. I
know it to the very bottom of my soul. Just like I know now that
I'm not to blame either. And just like I know that life is too short
to waste.*

LOVE,
Poppy

THE MINUTE I read the last line, a car door slammed shut,
bringing me back to reality. Poppy's car was parked on the
street and she was opening up the trunk.

The dull throb in my head vanished and the ache in my
chest disappeared with just one look at her beautiful face. If I
was her future, then she was mine.

She ducked into the trunk, lifted out a box, then shoved the trunk closed with her elbow before coming up the sidewalk. Her nose and cheeks were pink from the cold and her breath trailed behind her in tiny, white clouds as she stepped up to the porch.

I set aside the letter and the books, then stood from the rocking chair to take the box from her hands, putting them down by my feet. "Hi."

"Hi. Did you get my letter? I probably should have left it inside, but you weren't here and I thought you'd see it with the chairs."

I nodded. "I did."

"Good. I wanted you to have some time to read it alone." She stepped past me, walking the length of the porch and inspecting her rocking chairs before coming back to lean on a post and look out into the yard. "I'm sorry it took me so long to come over. I tried to call you last night, but I got your voicemail."

"My phone died."

"I figured. I also figured you wouldn't turn me away if I just showed up." She grinned over her shoulder. "I'd actually planned to be here earlier this morning, but I wanted to have the photo album done first and putting it together took longer than I'd thought with everything else going on. Then your dad came by. It's been a hectic three days."

I didn't doubt that. If her house had sold, she'd been packing on top of everything else.

"It's okay." I crossed the space between us, standing by the post but facing her instead of the street. My hands were itching to touch her, to pull her into my arms and hold her tight, but I didn't want to press, so I stuffed them into my jeans. The second she gave me any kind of opening, they'd be ready.

"I'm sorry, Cole. I'm sorry that I asked you to leave the other night. I just needed some time to process everything.

Maybe some time to finally forgive myself and realize you were right. I'm not to blame for Jamie's death and neither are you. Can you understand that?"

I leaned into the post, breathing easy for the first time in days. "I get it, and there's no need to apologize. I'm just glad you're here."

She smiled. "Me too."

"How are you doing today?" Jamie's birthday had to be taking its toll.

She pushed away from the post and stepped in front of me, then wrapped her arms around my waist as she shuffled close. "I'm better now."

My hands abandoned my pockets and tucked her into my chest. The second she was in my arms, three awful days just disappeared. *This.* This is what I'd been needing for the past three days. Not bourbon or time alone or even words of wisdom from my dad. What I needed would always be Poppy.

I considered myself a strong man, but this tiny woman in my arms had me beat every time. Three days after I'd rocked her world, and here she was, bringing peace and love back into my life.

"I love you, Poppy."

She gave me more of her weight. "I love you, Cole."

We stood on the porch, holding each other and letting the silence say the rest. I don't know how much time passed with Poppy's cheek pressed against my heart. But I did know that we were going to be fine. That we would have our future.

"Do you know what I like best about New Year's Day?" she whispered.

"What?"

"Everyone gets a new beginning."

I smiled and pressed a kiss to her hair. Behind me, a set of brakes squeaked to a slow stop on the street. Finn was parking a U-Haul behind Poppy's car with Nazboo at his side.

"New beginnings?"

She nodded. "I think we deserve a new beginning, don't you? Only this time, let's start from a different porch."

EPILOGUE

F*ive years later . . .*
"What the hell is this?" Randall glared at the plate in front of him.

"That would be a birthday cake. You know, for birthday parties. You're at a birthday party. We just sang 'Happy Birthday' to my son."

"Smart-ass." He sneered. "Why's it on a plate?"

"Because eating off the floor is unsanitary."

At his side, Jimmy laughed as Randall's face turned a darker shade of red. "But we're at the restaurant."

"Yes, I'm aware. I've been here all afternoon to decorate the room and make *the birthday cake.*"

Molly and I had closed The Maysen Jar tonight for a private family function. All of my family and friends were here, enjoying pizza and beer and cake as we celebrated my son's first birthday.

Everyone I loved was here for the party. Adults were smiling. Kids were laughing. Everyone was having fun.

Everyone, except Randall.

"I come here," Randall stabbed his finger on the counter, "to sit on this stool and eat food from your *jars*. It's been that way for almost six years. I could stay at The Rainbow if I wanted to eat from a plate."

I blinked at him, dumbfounded. "So you're mad because I didn't make Brady's birthday cake in jars? You know that's ridiculous, right?"

He grumbled something and stabbed his fork into the cake. "For every one of MacKenna's birthdays, you made desserts in jars. How was I supposed to know you'd change for Brady? I don't like surprises."

Jimmy had been trying to hold back his laughter, but as Randall shoved a huge bite of cake in his mouth, he burst out howling at his best friend. "You old grump. You don't like anything. Shut up and eat your damn cake." He winked at me before diving into his own cake and ice cream.

"Are you going to join the party?" I tilted my head toward the tables I'd pushed together for the party. "Or are you going to stay at the counter and be antisocial?"

"Antisocial," Randall muttered before taking another enormous bite.

Jimmy just shrugged. "This is my seat."

"Fine." I got them each a glass of water before leaving them alone to join the party.

It didn't surprise me that they were in their stools. Jimmy and Randall, sitting in the same spots as they had nearly every day since I'd opened The Maysen Jar, had become fixtures in the restaurant. They were as much a part of this place as the brick walls or wood floors.

Last year, when I'd won an award for Bozeman's best restaurant, the newspaper reporter had spent more time interviewing those two than he had me or Molly. They'd practically become famous after that. There wasn't a day that went by anymore where the counter wasn't full of their friends from The Rainbow.

But no one ever dared sit in their stools.

There had only been one incident when a poor, unsuspecting fool had tried to take Randall's seat. He'd chased away the "stool thief" with a tongue-lashing and some wild swinging of his cane. Thankfully, no one had gotten hurt, but ever since, Molly and I had marked those stools as reserved to avoid the risk of assault.

And if they wanted to sit in their seats, far be it from me to insist they move.

I crossed the restaurant with my eyes locked on a little girl bouncing off her seat to race my way.

"Mommy!" MacKenna's chin and cheeks were covered in blue frosting. Her green eyes, the ones she'd inherited from Cole, were darting back and forth between me and the present table. "Time for pwesents?"

I smiled and stroked her brown curls. "Not quite yet. Let's give everyone a chance to finish eating their cake."

Her three-year-old face formed a scowl. "But I eat mine alweady."

"MacKenna Lou," Mia called from the table. "Come sit by me and you can have more cake."

The scowl disappeared from my beautiful daughter's face as she raced to her grandmother's side.

Mia was MacKenna's favorite person on the planet other than her baby brother. Cole came in a close third with me trailing a distant fourth. But I loved that my daughter had such a close relationship with her nana.

Really, she was close with all her grandparents.

Just as he'd planned, Brad had retired as chief of police a few years ago. He and Mia spent some time traveling, but for the most part, they were wholly dedicated to their grandchildren. Evie and Zack's triplets—three rambunctious boys—had just turned five. MacKenna was three.

And today, Brady James Goodman was one.

Just like his sister, Brady loved his grandparents, but while Mia and MacKenna had a special connection, Brady was more attached to my mom.

I walked around the table and took the free chair between my parents. Brady, who'd been sitting on my mom's lap and sharing her cake, lunged for me the moment I sat down.

"Hi, baby." I kissed his cheek. "Did you like the cake?"

His answer was to stick his fingers in his mouth and suck off the frosting.

Like MacKenna's, Brady's hair was brown like Cole's, but while MacKenna had gotten Cole's green eyes, Brady's were completely unique. They were blue, like mine, but a brighter shade with small green flecks around the middle.

"How is it?" I asked Mom as I picked up my own fork.

She swallowed her bite of cake. "So. Good. I love the almond flavor you added. You've inspired me to do some experimenting."

"Like what?" I took a bite of my own piece of cake. With a mental pat on the back for one hell of a good cake, I kept eating as Mom and I chatted about new recipe ideas. Something we did a lot these days.

My parents had moved to Bozeman from Alaska last fall. Sadly, all of my grandparents had passed within the last four years, and since my parents no longer had family in Anchorage, they'd retired and moved here to be closer to their grandchildren. Dad had gotten a part-time job at the private airfield—

mostly so he had an excuse to leave the house—and Mom came into the restaurant most days to help me cook.

I loved that they were closer. Everyone did. Kali and Max had been overjoyed when they'd moved here, and my kids wouldn't remember a time when they didn't have four grandparents at their beck and call.

Like Finn and I when we'd been kids.

"Where did your brother disappear to?" Dad stood to clear his plate.

"He and Cole went to buy more beer. When they get back, we'll open presents."

Dad smiled and patted my shoulder. "Everything was delicious. Don't tell your mother," he leaned down but didn't even try to whisper as he grinned at Mom, "but I think you've surpassed her."

Mom just laughed. "I know she has."

"I ate too much." Molly slid past Dad and into his empty seat, collapsing and rubbing her stomach. "But it was so good. We need to add that cake to the menu."

"Or maybe we should make a cake every week, just for the staff to share."

"Yes!" Molly cheered. "They'll love that."

Mom, Molly and I visited for a while until the cake was demolished and the kids were chasing each other around the tables. So while everyone was enjoying the conversation, I left Brady under the watchful eye of his grandparents and snuck away to my office.

I flicked on the light and pulled out my phone, swiping to find the right picture. Then, using the special printer that Cole had gotten me last year for Christmas, I hit *print*.

A few moments later, I was smiling at the picture in my hands.

Brady was sitting on Cole's lap. MacKenna was on mine. In

front of us was the birthday cake I'd made with a single lit candle in the middle. Brady was staring at the flame with wide eyes while MacKenna leaned over the table, her mouth in a perfect O as she prepared to blow it out for her brother.

I stared at the picture for another second, then went to the desk, getting out a pushpin for my wall.

My wall of memories.

After I'd finished Jamie's birthday list, I'd contemplated starting one of my own. But plotting the future had been Jamie's thing, not mine. So I dismissed the idea and settled on something else.

I'd covered one entire office wall with corkboard to pin up special pictures.

I didn't have a list of things I wanted to do in my life. I had a wall of memories of the things I'd already done.

I had pictures of Nazboo chasing my kids in our yard. Of Cole as he fixed up cars in our garage. Of board game nights with Finn and his girlfriend. Of Molly and her kids carving pumpkins for my porch.

My wall was full of memories I wanted to keep close, and tonight, I'd add one from Brady's first birthday.

I stepped up to the wall, searching for just the right spot.

There was a small space open next to the picture from the day Cole had proposed. He'd taken me to Glacier and gotten down on one knee in front of Lake McDonald. After I'd said yes and we'd kissed, he'd taken a selfie for my wall, making sure to capture the solitaire diamond shining brightly on my hand.

Next to that photo was my favorite photo from our wedding day. After I'd moved into his house, we'd gotten married in the spring in a small ceremony at a local church. The reception had been catered at The Maysen Jar. It had been such a hectic day that Cole and I had hardly spent time together, so we'd snuck away for a few quiet moments to share a piece of cake at the kitchen table. Just like our first date. Molly had poked her head through the swinging door and caught it on camera.

Most of the others were pictures of the kids. I'd pinned photos from the day each was born. One of Cole kissing MacKenna's forehead after the nurse had handed her over. One of Jimmy whispering a secret to a swaddled Brady.

I had a couple old pictures from college of me, Jamie, Finn and Molly. I had pictures of our niece and nephews. I even had a picture of Tuesday Hastings and her daughter, Kennedy, standing by Jamie's old truck.

Tuesday had flourished in Oregon. She'd taken a job working with her grandmother at a bed-and-breakfast on the coast. I didn't hear from her often, but every once in a while, she'd send me a picture with a recipe on the back.

Not once since the night she'd left had she ever come back to Montana. Not even after Cole had put Tommy Bennett in prison for twenty years. Not even after a judge had sentenced Nina Veras with two life sentences in prison for first-degree murder.

Nina wasn't the only one in prison either. Her boyfriend, Samuel Long, had been sentenced to sixty years without parole for conspiracy to commit murder. He'd denied his involvement, of course, but when the police had found the murder weapon in his house, he'd had a harder time peddling his lies.

And the day of the sentencing hearing had been the day I'd put it all in the past. So had Cole. It had taken some time, but he'd stopped blaming himself for the murders. The hearings had given us both some overdue closure.

Jamie's parents had attended the sentencing hearings too. They'd sat behind me and Cole in the courtroom as the judge had handed down sentences, but that was the last time I'd seen Kyle and Debbie. I wasn't sure if they'd ever move on from their son's death. Now that I had children of my own, I didn't know if I would have been able to either. But I hoped, for their sake, they'd find some peace.

"There you are." Cole stepped into the office. "What are you doing?"

I held up the picture. "I was just deciding where to put this."

He stepped closer, looking down at the photo. The smile that spread across my husband's face made my heart flutter just as strong as it had five years ago.

"Where are you going to put it?"

I turned back to the wall, assessing my options. The eye-level strip was full, but I still had plenty of space to fill up to the ceiling or down toward the floor. I had plenty of room for more memories.

"How about here?" I stood on my tiptoes and pointed to a free spot toward the ceiling. "Would you hang it for me?"

"In a heartbeat."

He took the picture and I stepped back, watching as he pinned the photo.

"I like it." Cole stepped back from the wall and pulled me into his arms, kissing me softly, before looking back to the pictures. "We have a good life, beautiful."

I hugged him tighter. "We do."

One I'd never take for granted. One I'd always cherish.

Minute by minute.

Read Molly and Finn's story in *Letters to Molly*.

PREVIEW TO INDIGO RIDGE

Please enjoy this preview to Indigo Ridge.

WINSLOW

"Could I get another . . ."

The bartender didn't slow as he passed by.

"Drink," I muttered, slumping forward.

Pops had told me that this bar was where the locals hung out. Not only was it within walking distance of my new house in case I decided not to drive, but I was a local now. As of today, I lived in Quincy, Montana.

I'd told the bartender as much when I'd asked for his wine list. He'd raised one bushy white eyebrow above his narrowed gaze, and I'd abandoned my thirst for a glass of cabernet, ordering a vodka tonic instead. It had zapped every ounce of my willpower not to request a lemon twist.

The ice cubes in my glass clinked together as I swirled around my pink plastic straw. The bartender ignored that sound too.

Main Street had two bars—tourist traps this time of year, according to Pops. But I regretted not choosing one of those to celebrate my first night in Quincy. Given his attitude, the bartender, who must have thought I was a lost tourist, regretted my decision too.

Willie's was a dive bar and not exactly my scene.

The bartenders downtown probably acknowledged their customers, and the prices were listed on a menu, not delivered using three fingers on one wrinkled hand.

He looked about as old as this dark, dingy building. Like most small-town Montana bars, the walls were teeming with beer signs and neon lights. Shelves stacked with liquor bottles lined the mirrored wall across from my seat. The room was cluttered with tables, every chair empty.

Willie's was all but deserted this Sunday night at nine o'clock.

The locals must know of a better place to unwind.

The only other patron was a man sitting at the farthest end of the bar, in the last stool down the line. He'd come in ten minutes after I'd arrived and chosen the seat as far from me as possible. He and the bartender were nearly carbon copies of one another, with the same white hair and scraggly beards.

Twins? They looked old enough to have established this bar. Maybe one of them was Willie himself.

The bartender caught me staring.

I smiled and rattled the ice in my glass.

His mouth pursed in a thin line but he made me another drink. And like with the first, he delivered it without a word, holding up the same three fingers.

I twisted to reach into my purse, fishing out another five because clearly starting a tab was out of the question. But before I could pull the bill from my wallet, a deep, rugged voice caressed the room.

"Hey, Willie."

"Griffin." The bartender nodded.

So he was Willie. And he could speak.

"Usual?" Willie asked.

"Yep." The man with the incredible voice, Griffin, pulled out the stool two down from mine.

As his tall, broad body eased into the seat, a whiff of his scent carried my way. Leather and wind and spice filled my nose, chasing away the musty air from the bar. It was heady and alluring.

He was the type of man who turned a woman's head.

One glimpse at his profile and the cocktail in front of me was unnecessary. Instead, I drank this man in head to toe.

The sleeves of his black T-shirt stretched around his honed biceps and molded to the planes of his shoulders as he leaned his elbows on the bar. His brown hair was finger-combed and curled at the nape of his neck. His tan forearms were dusted with the same dark hair and a vein ran over the corded muscle beneath.

Even seated, I could tell his legs were long, his thighs thick like the evergreen tree trunks from the forests outside of town. Frayed hems of his faded jeans brushed against his black cowboy boots. And as he shifted in his seat, I caught the glimmer of a silver and gold belt buckle at his waist.

If his voice, his scent and that chiseled jaw hadn't been enough to make my mouth go dry, that buckle would have done it.

One of my mom's favorite movies had been *Legends of the Fall*. She'd let me watch it at sixteen and we'd cried together. Whenever I missed her, I'd put it on. The DVD was scratched and the clasp on the case was broken because I'd watched that movie countless times simply because it had been hers.

She'd always swooned over Brad Pitt as a sexy cowboy.

If she could see Griffin, she'd be drooling too. Though he was missing the hat and the horse, this guy was every cowboy fantasy come to life.

Lifting my glass to my mouth, I sipped the cold drink and tore my gaze from the handsome stranger. The vodka burned my throat and the alcohol rushed to my head. Ol' Willie mixed his cocktails strong.

I was unabashedly staring. It was rude and obvious. Yet when I set the glass down, my gaze immediately returned to Griffin.

His piercing blue eyes were waiting.

My breath hitched.

Willie set down a tumbler full of ice and caramel liquid in front of Griffin, then, without giving him the fingers to pay, walked away.

Griffin took a single swallow of his drink, his Adam's apple bobbing. Then his attention was on me once more.

The intensity of his gaze was as intoxicating as my cocktail.

He stared without hesitation. He stared with bold desire. His gaze raked down my black tank top to the ripped jeans I'd put on this morning before checking out of my hotel in Bozeman.

I'd spent four and a half hours driving to Quincy with a U-Haul trailer hitched to my Dodge Durango. When I'd arrived, I'd immediately jumped into unloading, only breaking to meet Pops for dinner.

I was a mess after a day of hauling boxes. My hair was in a ponytail and whatever makeup I'd put on this morning had likely worn off. Yet the appreciation in Griffin's gaze sent a wave of desire rushing to my core.

"Hi," I blurted. *Smooth, Winn.*

His eyes twinkled like two perfect sapphires set behind long, sooty lashes. "Hi."

"I'm Winn." I held out a hand over the space between us.

"Griffin." The moment his warm, calloused palm grazed mine, tingles cascaded across my skin like fireworks. A shiver rolled down my spine.

Holy hell. There was enough electricity between us to power the jukebox in the corner.

I focused on my drink, gulping more than sipping. The ice did nothing to cool me down. When was the last time I'd been this attracted to a man? Years. It had been years. Even then, it paled in comparison to five minutes beside Griffin.

"Where are you from?" he asked. Like Willie, he must have assumed I was a tourist too.

"Bozeman."

He nodded. "I went to college at Montana State."

"Go Bobcats." I lifted my drink in a salute.

Griffin returned the gesture, then put the rim of his glass to his full lower lip.

I was staring again, unashamed. Maybe it was the angular cheekbones that set his face apart. Maybe it was the straight nose with a slight bump at the bridge. Or his dark, bold browbone. He was no ordinary, handsome man. Griffin was drop-dead gorgeous.

And if he was at Willie's . . . a local.

Local meant off-limits. *Damn.*

I swallowed my disappointment with another gulp of vodka.

The scrape of stool legs rang through the room as he moved to take the seat beside mine. His arms returned to the bar, his drink between them as he leaned forward. He sat so close, his body so large, that the heat from his skin seeped into mine.

"Winn. I like that name."

"Thanks." My full name was Winslow but very few people ever called me anything other than Winn or Winnie.

Willie walked by and narrowed his eyes at the sliver of space between Griffin and me. Then he joined his doppelganger.

"Are they related?" I asked, dropping my voice.

"Willie Senior is on our side of the bar. His son is mixing drinks."

"Father and son. Huh. I thought twins. Does Willie Senior have the same glowing personality as Willie Junior?"

"It's worse." Griffin chuckled. "Every time I come through town, he gets crankier."

Wait. Did that mean . . . "You don't live in town?"

"No." He shook his head, picking up his drink.

I did the same, hiding my smile in the glass. So he wasn't a local. Which meant flirting was harmless. *Bless you, Quincy.*

A hundred personal questions raced through my mind, but I dismissed them all. Skyler used to criticize me for going into interrogation mode within ten minutes of meeting someone new. One of many critiques. He'd used his profession as a life coach as an excuse to tell me anything and everything I'd been doing wrong in our relationship. In life.

Meanwhile, he'd betrayed me, so I wasn't listening to Skyler's voice anymore.

But I still wasn't going to bombard this man with questions. He didn't live here, and I'd save my questions for the people who did: my constituents.

Griffin looked to the far end of the room and the empty shuffleboard table. "Want to play a game?"

"Um . . . sure? I've never played before."

"It's easy." He slid off his stool, moving with a grace that men his size didn't normally possess.

I followed, eyes glued to the best ass I had ever seen. And he didn't live here. An imaginary choir perched in the bar's dusty rafters gave a collective *yeehaw*.

Griffin went to one end of the table while I walked to the other. "Okay, Winn. Loser buys the next round of drinks."

Good thing I had cash. "Okay."

Griffin spent the next ten minutes explaining the rules and demonstrating how to slide the pucks down the sand-dusted surface toward the point lines. Then we played, game after game. After one more round, we both stopped drinking, but neither of us made a move to leave.

I won some games. I lost most. And when Willie finally announced that he was closing at one, the two of us walked outside to the darkened parking lot.

A dusty black truck was parked beside my Durango.

"That was fun."

"It was." I smiled up at Griffin, my cheeks pinching. I hadn't had this much fun openly flirting with a man in, well . . . ever. I slowed my steps because the last place I wanted to go was home alone.

He must have had the same idea because his boots stopped on the pavement. He inched closer.

Winslow Covington didn't have one-night stands. I'd been too busy wasting years on the wrong man. Griffin wasn't the right man either, but I'd learned in my time as a cop that sometimes it wasn't about choosing right from wrong. It was choosing the *right* wrongs.

Griffin. Tonight, I chose Griffin.

So I closed the distance between us and stood on my toes, letting my hands snake up his hard, flat stomach.

He was tall, standing two or three inches over six feet. At five nine, it was refreshing to be around a man who towered over me. I lifted a hand to his neck, pulling him down until his mouth hovered over mine.

"Is that your truck?"

369

———

"Shit." I cursed at the clock, then flew into action, flinging the covers off my naked body and racing for the bathroom.

Late was not how I wanted to start the first day of my new job.

I flipped on the shower, my head pounding as I stepped under the cold spray and let out a yelp. There was no time to wait for hot water, so I shampooed my hair and put in some conditioner while I scrubbed Griffin's scent off my skin. I'd mourn the loss of it later.

There was an ache between my legs that I'd think about later too. Last night had been . . .

Mind blowing. Toe curling. The best night I'd ever had with a man. Griffin knew exactly how to use that powerful body of his and I'd been the lucky recipient of three—or had it been four?—orgasms.

I shuddered and realized the water was hot. "Damn it."

Shoving thoughts of Griffin out of my head, I hurried out of the shower, frantically swiping on makeup and willing the blow dryer to work faster. Without time to curl or straighten my hair, I twisted it into a tight bun at the nape of my neck, then dashed to the bedroom to get dressed.

The mattress rested on the floor, the sheets and blankets rumpled and strewn everywhere. Thankfully, before I'd headed to the bar last night, I'd searched for bedding in the boxes and laid it out. When I'd finally gotten home after hours spent in the back of Griffin's truck, I'd practically face-planted into my pillows and forgotten to set my alarm.

I refused to regret Griffin. Kicking off my new life in Quincy with a hot and wild night seemed a little bit like fate.

Serendipity.

Maybe on his next trip through town, we'd bump into each

other. But if not, well . . . I didn't have time for the distraction of a man.

Especially not today.

"Oh, God. Please don't let me be late." I rifled through a suitcase, finding a pair of dark-wash jeans.

Pops had told me specifically not to show up at the station looking fancy.

The jeans were slightly wrinkled but there was no time to find whatever box had stolen my iron. Besides, an iron meant fancy. The simple white tee I found next was also wrinkled, so I dug for my favorite black blazer to hide the worst offenders. Then I hopped into my favorite black boots with the chunky heels before jogging for the door, swiping up my purse from where I'd dumped it on the living room floor.

The sun was shining. The air was clean. The sky was blue. And I had no time to appreciate a minute of my first Quincy, Montana, morning as I ran to the Durango parked in my driveway.

I slid behind the wheel, started the engine and cursed again at the clock on the dash. *Eight-oh-two.* "I'm late."

Thankfully, Quincy wasn't Bozeman and the drive from one side of town to the police station on the other took exactly six minutes. I pulled into the lot and parked next to a familiar blue Bronco and let myself take a single deep breath.

I can do this job.

Then I got out of my car and walked to the station's front door, hoping with every step I looked okay.

One disdaining look from the officer stationed behind a glass partition at the front desk and I knew I'd gotten it wrong. *Shit.*

His gray hair was cut short, high and tight in a military style. He looked me up and down, the wrinkles on his face deepening with a scowl. That glare likely had nothing to do with my outfit.

And everything to do with my last name.

"Good morning." I plastered on a bright smile, crossing the small lobby to his workspace. "I'm Winslow Covington."

"The new chief. I know," he muttered.

My smile didn't falter.

I'd win them over. Eventually. That's what I'd told Pops last night when he'd had me over for dinner after I'd returned the U-Haul. I'd win them all over, one by one.

Most people were bound to think that the only reason I'd gotten the job as the Quincy chief of police was because my grandfather was the mayor. Yes, he would be my boss. But there wasn't a nepotism clause for city employees. Probably because in a town this size, everyone was likely related in some manner. If you added too many restrictions, no one would be able to get a job.

Besides, Pops hadn't hired me. He could have, but instead, he'd put together a search committee so that there'd be more than one voice in the decision. Walter Covington was the fairest, most honorable man I'd ever known.

And granddaughter or not, what mattered was my performance. He'd take the cues from the community, and though my grandfather loved me completely, he wouldn't hesitate to fire me if I screwed this up.

He'd told me as much the day he'd hired me. He'd reminded me again last night.

"The mayor is waiting in your office," the officer said, pushing the button to buzz me into the door beside his cubicle.

"It was nice to meet you"—I glanced at the silver nameplate on his black uniform—"Officer Smith."

His response was to ignore me completely, turning his

attention to his computer screen. I'd have to win him over another day. Or maybe he'd be open to an early retirement.

I pushed through the door that led into the heart of the station. I'd been here twice, both times during the interview process. But it was different now as I walked through the bullpen no longer a guest. This was my bullpen. The officers looking up from their desks were under my charge.

My stomach clenched.

Staying up all night having sex with a stranger probably hadn't been the smartest way to prepare for my first day.

"Winnie." Pops came out of what would be my office, his hand extended. He seemed taller today, probably because he was dressed in nice jeans and a starched shirt instead of the ratty T-shirt, baggy jeans and suspenders I'd seen him in yesterday.

Pops was fit for his seventy-one years and though his hair was a thick silver, his six-three frame was as strong as an ox. He was in better shape than most men my age, let alone his.

I shook his hand, glad that he hadn't tried to hug me. "Morning. Sorry I'm late."

"I just got here myself." He leaned in closer and dropped his voice. "You doing okay?"

"Nervous," I whispered.

He gave me a small smile. "You'll do great."

I could do this job.

I was thirty years old. Two decades below the median age of a person in this position. Four decades younger than my predecessor had been when he'd retired.

The former chief of police had worked in Quincy for his entire career, moving up the ranks and acting as chief for as long as I'd been alive. But that was why Pops had wanted me in this position. He said Quincy needed fresh eyes and younger blood. The town was growing, and with it, their problems. The old ways weren't cutting it.

The department needed to embrace technology and new processes. When the former chief had announced his retirement, Pops had encouraged me to toss my name into the hat. By some miracle, the hiring committee had chosen me.

Yes, I was young, but I met the minimum qualifications. I'd worked for ten years with the Bozeman Police Department. During that time, I'd earned my bachelor's degree and a position as detective within their department. My record was impeccable, and I'd never left a case unclosed.

Maybe my welcome would have been warmer if I were a man, but that had never scared me and it certainly wasn't going to today.

I can do this job.

I would do this job.

"Let me introduce you to Janice." He nodded for me to follow him into my office, where we spent the morning with Janice, my new assistant.

She'd worked for the former chief for fifteen years, and the longer she spoke, the more I fell in love with her. Janice had spiky gray hair and the cutest pair of red-framed glasses I'd ever seen. She knew the ins and outs of the station, the schedules and the shortcomings.

As we ended our initial meeting, I made a mental note to bring her flowers because without Janice, I'd likely fall flat on my face. We toured the station, meeting the officers not out on patrol.

Officer Smith, who was rarely sent into the field because he preferred the desk, had been one of the candidates for chief, and Janice told me that he'd been a grumpy asshole since the day he'd been rejected.

Every officer besides him had been polite and professional,

though reserved. No doubt they weren't sure what to make of me, but today I'd won Janice over—or maybe she'd won me. I was calling it a victory.

"You'll meet most of the department this afternoon at shift change," she told me when we retreated back to the safety of my office.

"I was planning on staying late one evening this week to meet the night shift too."

This wasn't a large station, because Quincy wasn't a large town, but in total, I had fifteen officers, four dispatchers, two administrators and a Janice.

"Tomorrow, the county sheriff is coming in to meet you," Janice said, reading from the notebook she'd had with her all morning. "Ten o'clock. His staff is twice the size of ours but he has more ground to cover. For the most part, their team stays out of our way, but he's always willing to step in if you need help."

"Good to know." I wouldn't mind having a resource to bounce ideas off of either.

"How's your head?" Pops asked.

I put my hands by my ears and made the sound of an exploding bomb.

He laughed. "You'll catch on."

"Yes, you will," Janice said.

"Thank you for everything," I told her. "I'm really looking forward to working with you."

She sat a little straighter. "Likewise."

"Okay, Winnie." Pops slapped his hands on his knees. "Let's go grab some lunch. Then I've got to get to my own office, and I'll let you come back here and settle in."

"I'll be here when you get back." Janice squeezed my arm as we shuffled out of my office.

Pops simply nodded, maintaining his distance. Tonight,

when I wasn't Chief Covington and he wasn't Mayor Covington, I'd head to his house and get one of his bear hugs.

"How about we eat at The Eloise?" he suggested as we made our way outside.

"The hotel?"

He nodded. "It would be good for you to spend some time there. Get to know the Edens."

The Edens. Quincy's founding family.

Pops had promised that the fastest way to earn favor with the community was to win over the Edens. One of their relatives from generations past had founded the town and the family had been the community's cornerstone ever since.

"They own the hotel, remember?" he asked.

"I remember. I just didn't realize there was a restaurant in the hotel these days." Probably because I hadn't spent much time in Quincy lately.

The six trips I'd taken here to participate in the interview process had been my first trips to Quincy in years. Five, to be exact.

But when Skyler and I had fallen to pieces and Pops had pitched the job as chief, I'd decided it was time for a change. And Quincy, well . . . Quincy had always held a special place in my heart.

"The Edens started the hotel's restaurant about four years ago," Pops said. "It's the best place in town, in my opinion."

"Then let's eat." I unlocked my car. "Meet you there."

I followed his Bronco from the station to Main Street, taking in the plethora of out-of-state cars parked downtown. Tourist season was in full swing and nearly every space was full.

Pops parked two blocks away from Main on a side street, and side by side, we strolled to The Eloise Inn.

The town's iconic hotel was the tallest building in Quincy,

standing proudly against the mountain backdrop in the distance. I'd always wanted to spend a night at The Eloise. Maybe one day I'd book myself a room, just for fun.

The lobby smelled of lemons and rosemary. The front desk was an island in the grand, open space, and a young woman with a sweet face stood behind the counter, checking in a guest. When she spotted Pops, she tossed him a wink.

"Who's that?" I asked.

"Eloise Eden. She took over as manager this past winter."

Pops waved at her, then walked past the front desk toward an open doorway. The clatter of forks on plates and the dull murmur of conversation greeted me as we entered the hotel's restaurant.

The dining room was spacious and the ceilings as tall as those in the lobby. It was the perfect place for entertaining. Almost a ballroom but filled with tables of varying sizes, it also worked well as a restaurant.

"They just put in those windows." Pops pointed at the far wall where black-paned windows cut into a red-brick wall. "Last time I talked to Harrison, he said this fall they'll be remodeling this whole space."

Harrison Eden. The family's patriarch. He'd been on the hiring committee, and I liked to believe I'd made a good impression. According to Pops, if I hadn't, there was no way I'd have gotten my job.

A hostess greeted us with a wide smile and led us to a square table in the center of the room.

"Which of the Edens runs the restaurant?" I asked as we browsed the menu card.

"Knox. He's Harrison and Anne's second oldest son. Eloise is their youngest daughter."

Harrison and Anne, the parents. Knox, a son. Eloise, a daughter. There were likely many more Edens to meet.

Down Main, the Eden name was splashed on numerous storefronts, including the coffee shop I wished I'd had time to stop by this morning. Last night's antics were catching up to me, and I hid a yawn with my menu.

"They're good people," Pops said. "You've met Harrison. Anne's a sweetheart. Their opinion carries a lot of weight around here. So does Griffin's."

Griffin. *Did he say Griffin?*

My stomach dropped.

No. This couldn't be happening. It had to be a mistake. There had to be another Griffin, one who didn't live in Quincy. I'd specifically asked him last night if he lived in town and he'd said no. Hadn't he?

"Hey, Covie."

So busy having my mental freak-out that I'd slept with not only a local man, but one I needed to see me as a professional and not a backseat hookup, I didn't notice the two men standing beside our table until it was too late.

Harrison Eden smiled.

Griffin, who was just as handsome as he had been last night, did not.

Had he known who I was last night? Had that been some sort of test or trick? Doubtful. He looked as surprised to see me as I was to see him.

"Hey, Harrison." Pops stood to shake his hand, then waved at me. "You remember my granddaughter, Winslow."

"Of course." Harrison took my hand as I stood, shaking it with a firm grip. "Welcome. We're glad to have you as our new chief of police."

"Thank you." My voice was surprisingly steady considering my heart was attempting to dive out of my chest and hide under the table. "I'm glad to be here."

"Would you like to join us?" Pops offered, nodding to the empty chairs at our table.

"No," Griffin said at the same time his father said, "We'd love to."

Neither Pops nor Harrison seemed to notice the tension rolling off Griffin's body as they took their chairs, leaving Griffin and me to introduce ourselves.

I swallowed hard, then extended a hand. "Hello."

That sharp jaw I'd traced with my tongue last night clenched so tight that I heard the crack of his molars. He glared at my hand before capturing it in his large palm. "Griffin."

Griffin Eden.

My one-night stand.

So much for serendipity.

ACKNOWLEDGMENTS

I am so grateful for the incredible team who supports me through every book. Thanks to my editor, Elizabeth Nover, for teaching me with every project and pushing me to get better. To my proofreader, Julie Deaton. Thanks to Jenn, for the hours spent reading this at the last minute and giving me such helpful input. To Kaitlyn, for always being there to help, no matter what I need. Thanks to my cover designer, Sarah Hansen, for creating my beautiful cover.

To all of the bloggers and my fellow authors who have helped spread the word about this book, thank you for your incredible support. To my ARC team, thank you for the excitement you bring to each release. And to Jenn, Ana, Karen and all the members of Perry Street, thank you for being my cheerleading squad.

To my family and friends, thank you for all your love and encouragement. For believing in me when, at times, I don't believe in myself.

And lastly, to my readers. There are a lot of books in this world. I am honored and so very grateful that you chose to pick up one of mine. Thank you.

ABOUT THE AUTHOR

Devney is a *USA Today* bestselling author who lives in Washington with her husband and two sons. Born and raised in Montana, she loves writing books set in her treasured home state. After working in the technology industry for nearly a decade, she abandoned conference calls and project schedules to enjoy a slower pace at home with her family. Writing one book, let alone many, was not something she ever expected to do. But now that she's discovered her true passion for writing romance, she has no plans to ever stop.

Don't miss out on Devney's latest book news.
Subscribe to her newsletter!
www.devneyperry.com

Made in the USA
Columbia, SC
26 July 2022

64070463R00233